LIFE AFTER

Katie Ganshert

CENTER POINT LARGE PRINT
THORNDIKE, MAINE

The text of this Large Print edition is unabridged.
In other aspects, this book may vary from the original edition.
Printed in the United States of America on permanent paper.
Set in 16-point Times New Roman type.

ISBN: 978-1-68324-406-6

Library of Congress Cataloging-in-Publication Data

Names: Ganshert, Katie, author.
Title: Life after / Katie Ganshert.
Description: Center Point Large Print edition. | Thorndike, Maine :
Center Point Large Print, 2017.
Identifiers: LCCN 2017008788 | ISBN 9781683244066
    (hardcover : alk. paper)
Subjects: LCSH: Survival—Psychological aspects—Fiction. | Man-
woman relationships—Fiction. | Life change events—Fiction. |
Guilt—Fiction. | Large type books. | BISAC: FICTION / Christian /
Romance. | FICTION / Contemporary Women. | FICTION / Romance
/ Contemporary. | GSAFD: Christian fiction. | Love stories.
Classification: LCC PS3607.A56 L54 2017b | DDC 813/.6—dc23
LC record available at https://lccn.loc.gov/2017008788

To Mom, Dad, and Peggy.
For everything.

Who has known the mind of the Lord?
Or who has been his counselor?

ROMANS 11:34

LIFE
AFTER

Prologue

We rarely know when death will come.

Some are warned in sickness—like the track of dirt that runs around the edge of a baseball field, cautioning outfielders that they are running out of room. The end is near. But others—many others—meet death without any warning at all, in an unforeseen moment that wrenches consciousness in two, separating the living from the dead.

That's how it would come on this particular evening for twenty-two individuals.

A darkened sky released sheets of overzealous, unwelcome flakes into the air. The wind caught them up and blew them sideways. The same wind tore strands of hair from the woman's ponytail and whipped them about like flickering candle flames. She clutched a box tightly to her chest, the contents rattling, as she hurried up the cement steps.

With her chin burrowed deep into her scarf and eyes lowered, the woman didn't see the man as she reached the platform. She didn't see him stare at the train. She didn't see him as he exhaled a cloudy breath. And she didn't see him when he spun around.

The two collided, as lives sometimes do.

The woman tottered and fell, the box upending.

She landed hard on the snow-covered cement, auburn hair spilling about her face.

The man moved to her, pulled her up. "Are you okay?"

"I-I think so."

He scrambled to collect the scattered contents— a handful of business cards, a spiral-bound notebook, a balled-up T-shirt, an opened bag of Tootsie Pops, and a picture frame.

"I'm sorry," he said.

"No, it was my fault. I wasn't looking. I didn't want to . . ." Her words swirled off into the wind. She tucked her hair behind her ear, her attention moving to the broken picture frame he held in his hand.

He shook pieces of glass into the snow, then returned the framed photo to the box and handed it over. "Are you sure you're all right?"

"I'm fine." And yet she was unable to hide the wince that came with her words.

The railcar waited behind him, its doors open.

She hugged the box to her chest and stepped forward, before they closed. Before she had to wait for the next train to come along.

Dry air washed over her face and neck. The doors slid shut. The railcar released its brakes. A voice distorted with static sounded over the intercom as the train lurched forward. She steadied herself against a nearby pole and stared out the window. The man stood beneath the awning, watching the train slide past as snow and wind swirled in a frantic dance across the sky.

Circles of pain radiated from her backside. She brushed a patch of white clinging to her coat and glanced down the railcar. Her attention caught on a lady with hair like her own, sitting close by, clutching an expensive-looking handbag while she dabbed her cheeks with a crumpled pink tissue.

As if sensing the attention, the lady's watery eyes rose up to meet the woman's.

Flushing, she turned away. The car wasn't too full, so she slid onto an empty seat a couple rows ahead, setting the box beside her.

Cold stuck to her skin. Her teeth chattered. She yearned for a hot cup of tea. A long soak in a warm bath. Something that might chase away the coldness that had seeped inside her bones long before she stepped outside.

She removed the five-by-seven picture frame from the box and flicked a sliver of glass from the photograph when someone tapped her shoulder.

It was a man.

He sat behind her wearing a green-mesh John Deere hat with a straight bill, like he'd never bothered to break it in. His back was hunched with age. "Crazy weather this evening."

She nodded.

"Last time we got this much snow this late in the year, I had more hair up here." He took off his cap and with a chuckle, rubbed the top of his shiny brown head. "They say when all's said and done, we could get up to a foot."

The woman's lips pinched in the corners—a polite but discouraging smile.

Maybe if she had known that this would be the old man's last conversation, she would have done a better job. Maybe if she had known, she would have been more attentive. At the very least, she could have shown a glimmer of kindness.

But she didn't know. None of them did.

Not the girl with the pixie haircut and the pair of tattooed butterflies rising on the nape of her neck. Not the Latino boy slumped down in his seat, earbuds jammed inside his ears. Not the harassed-looking mother trying to corral a wild young child. Not the businessman tapping the keys on his opened laptop. Not the crying wisp of a lady with the crumpled pink tissue. Not the old man who smelled of analgesic cream and bacon and prattled on about snowstorms in March.

Not the woman with the box, whose phone began buzzing. She gave the gentleman an apologetic look and pulled the phone out of her pocket. A text message lit the screen:

R u alive?

A short huff.

She slipped off her mother's ring and stared at the familiar design. If she hadn't done that—if she would have just given it a twist instead of removing it altogether—maybe some things would have turned out differently. But she did take it off. She turned it over in her hand, clasped it inside her palm. And then she tapped out a text with trembling thumbs. It was a message that would never be sent. One that would be lost with all the other things that were lost on that day. Halfway through her typed reply, a second ticked from one to zero.

Fate detonated.

An explosion of heat blasted through the air.

Windows shattered.

Metal twisted.

Stars burst like kaleidoscopes behind the woman's eyes, and life as she knew it disappeared completely.

One

Sirens wailed.

A woman screamed.

Impossible heat reached out heavy fingers and dug into her flesh, pulling her into darkness. Charred gloves circled her wrists and dragged her from the wreckage as flames swallowed the world.

Autumn Manning jolted awake.

Sweat dripped down her back as she shoved away the sounds, kicking them off like an unwanted blanket. She pushed at the sheets covering her legs and tore at her face, clawing at tubes that were no longer there. Tubes that had been removed months and months ago.

Panic swelled.

It scratched up her chest, heaving her upright in bed.

It was just a nightmare. Fiery wreckage didn't engulf her. There was no hospital or beeping monitors. She was in her apartment bedroom, where all was quiet and still and safe.

The clock on her nightstand read 3:36 a.m.— an hour most people didn't care to know. But 3:00 a.m. and Autumn had become well acquainted. At 3:00, sleep turned into a will-o'-the-wisp— teasing her as it danced forever out of reach.

It was better not to chase it at all.

She swung her legs around and shoved her feet into a pair of slippers, slid her arms into the robe hanging on one of her bedposts and shuffled past the closet that made her family worry.

Ten minutes later, Autumn was curled up in an armchair with a hot cup of tea, flipping through options on Netflix, trying to ignore the ghosts that called to her from down the hall. She had promised her sister that she would stop, that she would find a way to let all of this go.

But the dead were loudest at night.

Ribbons of steam curled up toward her chin. Autumn selected an episode of *Gilmore Girls* and turned her attention to the jigsaw puzzle scattered across the coffee table. The more things she could distract herself with, the better.

Television, tea, puzzle.

This one was called "Forest Gnome" and was extra difficult, given that most of the pieces were the same shade of barky brown. Mindlessly, she picked at a cuticle as she searched for a piece of the gnome's hat.

Pick, pick, pick until her skin stung.

She stuck her thumb in her mouth and sucked, then pulled it free and watched as red beaded up into a droplet of blood. If she didn't cover it, she would continue picking—an unflattering habit she developed as a girl.

"Stop picking, my love," her mother would say, peeking at her in the rearview mirror of their Buick LeSabre. *"Your nails look dreadful."*

Autumn headed to the bathroom, where she wrapped her thumb in a lime-green Band-Aid and stared at her reflection in the mirror. A straight scar slashed across her temple. A feathery one peppered her right jawline like white stubble—so vague now a person had to squint to see it. There was another on her shoulder where she'd had surgery—this scar more serious looking than the others. But that was it. The only outward sign that she'd survived anything at all.

Three faint scars, where skin had been savagely torn but stretched and bound together again.

Gilmore Girls banter filtered down the hallway.

Autumn knew she should return to her chair and her tea and work on the puzzle while Taylor Doose tried bringing the citizens of Stars Hollow to order. When the episode ended, she could clean out her refrigerator—scrub it with baking soda and vinegar until she found a way to remove the mysterious sour smell that came and went in whiffs without any rhyme or reason. When that was through, she could lace up her shoes and go on an early-morning run.

But temptation was hard to resist at three in the morning.

She was impossibly drawn to the things she promised to throw away.

With resignation, she grabbed a pair of scissors, the copy of the *Tribune* featuring the articles she read before bed, and the binder from the top shelf of the hall closet. She pressed her back against the wall and slid to the floor, where she cut out the newest headline.

Tragedy on the Tracks: One Year Later

The alliteration grated. It had always grated, causing a grimace whenever she saw or read it.

The commission board in charge of erecting a memorial had worked with a local artist to design a fountain. They'd settled on a large steel phoenix, taking flight from the water. A symbol of hope.

Beauty from ashes. A symbol Autumn had yet to see unfold in real life. Even the beauty of justice eluded her.

The bomber, Benjamin Havel, was still on the loose.

The ground surrounding the fountain was embedded with twenty-two red bricks, each one inscribed with a name. Nearby a plaque explained all that it represented. It was a plaque that would remain largely unread, and eventually, the fountain would be nothing more than a wet trash can for unwanted pennies and stale gum.

Autumn sighed.

Was Chad right? Had she turned cynical?

She finished cutting out the article, trying not to think about the voice mail from the chairman of the board, inviting her to cut the ribbon at the opening ceremony. Or her sister Claire's disbelief when Autumn told her she wouldn't be going.

"You're really not going?" she'd asked.

"Trust me," Autumn had said. "Those families don't want me there."

Why would they? To them, she was salt in a wound. A bitter reminder. A cruel question mark. *Why did that woman survive when my husband (wife, dad, mom, son, daughter, friend) didn't? What's so special about her?*

Autumn didn't want to see the questions that haunted her reflected in wet eyes. And she refused to be a mascot. If she went, she would be a distraction. A spectacle. The focal point. The memorial wasn't about her. It was about them—the ones who hadn't survived.

She didn't need to cut a ribbon to pay her respects.

She did that every day.

Every night.

While the city slept, she paid them over and over again.

Her attention wandered to the binder in her lap. She paged past the stack of obituaries—all of which had been written and published while she was still unconscious. By the time she opened her eyes, the dead were already buried. Autumn had to Google their names to read their stories, and gather old newspapers from libraries for physical, tangible records. To her family's dismay, she turned into a morbid kid collecting a set of tragic baseball cards, determined to gather her favorite players. Only instead of a bonus stick of bubblegum with each find, she got a knife to the gut.

She turned past each one of them until she reached the letters—all from one address. They began arriving a few days after she woke up and the media descended.

At first, the letters just confused her.

Eventually it became clear. Autumn understood what it was like when your mind fixated on something. When it gnawed and gnawed like a dog with a bone. That must be it. For reasons she thought she understood, she had become that bone.

She got up from her spot in the hallway. She didn't think as she powered up her Mac, and she didn't think as she logged onto a fake Facebook account, and she didn't think as she typed names and hashtags into the search bar. Always the same ones. It had become a tick. A compulsion. Like picking at her cuticles. She had to do it, even though it never made her feel any better. Not when her searches produced something new and not when she discovered accounts had finally been deleted. No matter what Autumn found, all of it ended the same way—her, sitting there, nursing the wounds all the picking left behind, not a Band-Aid in sight.

Three hundred and sixty-five days.

One whole year since the people inside the binder had ceased living.

Twelve months with the same question as her constant, vigilant companion. The same question her two-year old niece had begun asking repeatedly a couple of weeks ago.

Why? Why? Why?

With a deep breath, Autumn picked up a nearby pencil and snagged a piece of paper and tried— for the hundredth time—to write a letter back.

Two

All day the sun had shone brightly—almost obnoxiously. A burst of intense gold dawdled across the blue expanse—not a wisp of cloud in sight. At its height the temperature had stretched into the midseventies, causing people to shrug off cardigans and remove sports jackets. Now it had curled into a comfortable high sixties as the sun sank toward the horizon. It was as if the weather were a small child doing its very best to win back a parent's favor.

I know I was horrendous on this day last year, it said. *But I promise to be better. Look at how good I can be.*

As though the weather should be the focal point of this day.

Maybe, in another lifetime, it would have been.

Maybe people would comment, as they hustled about the city—"Can you believe it was snowing this time last year?"

"Not just snow. A complete whiteout!"

But nobody mentioned the weather. The city of Chicago had turned solemn. Inside coffee shops, patrons and baristas nodded knowingly at one another. In the Loop, businesspeople and taxi drivers did the same. Even Michigan Avenue, populated mostly by outsiders with money to spend, had adopted a deferential air. CTA workers and police officers moved about with an extra degree of vigilance. And whenever anybody did speak, the weather wasn't part of the conversation at all.

"Hard to believe it's been a whole year."

"I remember exactly where I was when I heard the news."

"Can't believe they haven't caught him yet."

The more everyone ignored the weather, the more the weather showed off. And now, a whole throng of people had gathered together on the grass in Lincoln Park, in the waning daylight, completely unappreciative of nature as the mayor called for a moment of silence.

The weather had had enough. Spots of dark clouds began to gather over the horizon, and a gust of wind pushed against the crowd.

Paul Elliott clamped his hands on his children's shoulders. Seven-year-old Tate, to keep him from asking some sort of loud question in the midst of the reverent hush. Twelve-year-old Reese, to remind her that he was there and always would be. A stronger gust came, right on the heels of the other, and Paul tightened his grip.

Two more hours.

He'd run a marathon once, four years ago with his friend and pastor, Mitchell Wyatt, who now stood a little ahead of him and off to the right. At mile twenty-four, Paul hit a wall. If not for

Mitch reminding him that they only had 2.2 miles left to go—and what was 2.2 miles in light of 24?—he might have stopped altogether.

This was no different.

The past twelve months had been a long, grueling marathon. And in two more hours, he could put his kids, this day—the whole exhausting year—to bed.

His mother looped her arm through his and squeezed. Her eyes were a little damp, her shoulders broad and sturdy, as if designed for the very purpose of carrying heavy loads. To her left was Paul's grandfather, frowning down at his walker.

Regina Bell stood on Paul's other side.

This was his mother-in-law, all sharp lines and bony angles, her high cheekbones long since narrowing from regal to severe. Grief, for Regina, manifested itself in a diminishing frame. It was an alarming transformation, because, outside of the rare Skype session, he hadn't seen her since his wife Vivian's funeral. She carried herself the same way now as she had then—like they were standing in front of a casket instead of a fountain, her mouth pursed tightly. She would be staying one more night with them. So maybe this whole two-hour pep talk Paul was currently giving himself wasn't true. Maybe he thought he was on mile twenty-four, when really he was only on mile twenty, and six miles were a whole lot more than two.

Especially when it came to unabashedly critical Regina.

Thankfully, Vivian's father hadn't come. He'd called last week to let Paul know that he was terribly sorry, but he couldn't get away from work. Regina acted as though the man had stabbed her in the chest, which meant that a substantial portion of her disapproval had been relegated to her ex-husband.

A small mercy, Paul supposed.

The moment of silence came to an end.

The mayor said some words into the microphone, none of which Paul heard. His attention wandered, catching on several news stations poised and ready to squeeze one final story from the tragedy that had clogged the media for weeks afterward.

A child around Tate's age stepped forward to cut the ribbon.

Cameras clicked.

People clapped.

And slowly, the crowd began to disperse.

Paul let out his breath.

He didn't plan on lingering. He had no desire to stand around reminiscing. All he wanted to do was forget. To steer his children away from the cloying sadness, toward home, but Reese hadn't moved.

She stood up on tiptoe, searching the crowd. "Where is she?"

"Where is who?" Paul asked.

Everyone that belonged to them was milling nearby. Mom, Pop. Regina. Mitch and his wife, Lisa. Paul's long-suffering assistant, Margo, who kept his life organized. Their neighbor, Delilah Green, who was as helpful as she was irritating. Mrs. Ryan and her daughter Mia, who had been Reese's best friend since kindergarten. Along with several casual friends and acquaintances from church and school and work.

All of them had come to show their support.

"The woman who survived."

Everyone looked at Paul. Some more covertly than others.

Paul studied the concrete.

"She has to be here." Reese craned her neck. "Right?"

"It's a big crowd, sweetheart," Mom said. "I'm sure she's here somewhere."

Paul wasn't as confident. As far as he understood, the woman had gone out of her way to avoid the media, and this park was currently crawling with reporters. One was interviewing the mayor. Not too far away, another spoke with a group of women who were wiping fresh tears from their cheeks.

A year later, and their grief was still palpable.

Paul scratched beneath his collar.

It was time to go.

Three

Sunday, April 2, 2017

A pen coupled with paper
can serve as a powerful life tool.
—Maud Purcell

I don't know who Maud Purcell is, other than a woman who wrote an article on Psych Central titled "The Health Benefits of Journaling." I stumbled across it on Facebook, and the title did its job and snagged my attention.

According to Maud, journaling can result in reduced stress, clarity of thought, and often leads to unexpected solutions to seemingly unsolvable problems. Keeping a journal allows a person to track patterns, trends, improvement, and growth over time. Maud says this journal will become an all-accepting, non-judgmental friend, as well as the cheapest therapy I will ever find.

I wonder if journaling will suffice for my meddlesome sister-in-law, Jane, who staged an intervention. An actual, real-life intervention.

Two days ago, I walked into her house, a

little annoyed that she needed my help to move around boxes in the basement, only to discover my entire family sitting there in the living room looking terribly uncomfortable. My father, worst of all. None of them said a word as Jane sat me down and asked, with insulting slowness—like she does with her children when they are on the cusp of a temper tantrum—if I've ever wanted to hurt myself.

That's when I saw the pamphlets they were holding.

Jane handed me one.

It was about survivor's guilt, and inside, she had kindly highlighted the more morbid manifestations, the worst of which was suicide.

I sat there dumbly as Jane laid out all their concerns and explained how seeing a therapist was nothing to be ashamed about. If it were a matter of financial feasibility—since being a virtual assistant didn't exactly lend itself to great health care coverage—everyone would be more than happy to pitch in. She'd even gone to the trouble of writing the names of several reputable therapists on a notecard, along with their phone numbers.

Last night, when my sister came over with Chinese food, I expected an apology. I thought we might laugh about it together. But Claire arrived all fired up about her job. She's a teacher, so she has lots to get fired up about. I listened patiently as she vented and vented, and then, out of the complete blue, she said, "I think it's a good idea."

"What's a good idea?" I'd asked. "Common Core?"

She waved her chopsticks at me. "No. Therapy."

This is what Claire does.

She picks up conversations that happened hours, days, weeks earlier as though no time has transpired at all and everyone should know what she's talking about.

My sister thinks therapy is a good idea. My sister has taken Jane's side.

The word *suicide* drove her there, I'm sure.

Anyway, here you are. My brand-new, all-accepting, nonjudgmental, therapeutic friend, courtesy of Walgreens.

Maybe I should call you Maud.

The small, outdated bungalow that housed Autumn's childhood squatted before her, its windows yellow with light. She held a pan of strawberry pretzel salad, her regular contribution when it came to Sunday night dinner, and tried to prepare herself for people and conversation—something that took concerted effort on any given Sunday over the last year—but extra this time, in light of Jane's pamphlets. Would they talk about the intervention, or would they pretend the whole thing never happened?

She knocked on the front door.

It swung open almost immediately, and there was Leanne, wrapping her skinny arm around Autumn's shoulder in a tight squeeze, like it had been years instead of days since they last saw each other.

Autumn patted her stepmother's elbow. The two of them could never seem to find a natural rhythm. By the time she let go, Claire had come out from the kitchen.

Autumn's eyes widened. Her sister's hair was brown.

Not subtle brown either, but a rich chocolate brown. Yesterday, her sister's hair had been ginger. Her sister's hair had always been ginger. Like Autumn's. Like their brother Chad's. Like their mother's.

"When did you do that?" Autumn asked.

"Two hours ago." She gave her hair a wiggle and a pat. "Do you love it?"

Autumn blinked, looking from Claire to Claire's boyfriend, Trent, who was slowly extricating himself from the couch, his and Dad's eyes glued to the baseball game unfolding on the television screen. It was opening night, a moment her father eagerly anticipated every year from the final out of the World Series onward.

"I think it brings out her eyes," Leanne said,

wrapping her arm around Claire's waist. This was how it was between them. Effortless.

Claire had even adopted some of Leanne's mannerisms over the years, and right then, as they stood there arm in arm with their matching brunette heads, they looked every inch the mother-daughter duo.

Autumn's heart squeezed. The kind of squeeze that felt a little bit like choking. The kind that made her want to retreat, draw back across town and into her apartment—just her and twenty-two ghosts. She no longer fit in with this land of the living.

A burst of conflicting noise came from Dad and Trent. One whooped. The other groaned. Followed by some good-natured ribbing. Anthony Rizzo had just hit a home run, right over the center field wall.

The beloved Cubbies seemed to be picking up right where they'd left off.

Grinning victoriously, as though he'd been the one at bat, Trent planted a kiss on Claire's temple. "You could shave your head bald and still be beautiful." Then he gave Autumn a hug, which always felt like being engulfed, as Trent was a giant teddy bear of a man with arms like tree trunks and a soft middle.

Dad was next. He wasn't nearly as large as Trent, or as comfortable with the hugging, but it was something they all did now. They were huggers. It started when Leanne entered the picture, because Leanne loved to hug.

Autumn stepped away from Dad's awkward back pat.

"Chad texted a little bit ago saying they were running late." Leanne took the pan of strawberry pretzel salad with a smile. "Impossible to be on time with two little ones. We all know how that goes."

Except no, they didn't.

Dad, maybe. But not Leanne.

She became a mother by marriage, when Autumn was eleven, Chad fourteen, and Claire six. Six was the closest Leanne got to knowing what life was like with a little one underfoot, and at six, Claire had been fully capable of tying her shoes and zipping her own coat, which had to be two of the biggest perpetuators when it came to young families and tardiness.

After five or ten minutes of small talk, wherein nobody said a word about their meeting from two days ago, the door flew open. Four-year-old Cal and two-year-old Lulu burst into the living room like a pair of Tasmanian devils.

The girls' actual names were Calliope and Talulah.

Chad and Jane were expecting their third child in May. The coveted boy. Claire and Trent were already making bets on what his name would be. Probably something like Axel or Hugo or Jagger, only everyone would call him Ax or Hu or Jag. Jane was like most women these days when it came to naming babies. The more unique, the better.

Lulu wrapped her small body around Leanne's knees and demanded a Mentos. Leanne always carried a pack in her purse for the girls. Not the minty kind that made them wrinkle their noses but the fruity kind that filled the room with the scent of strawberries the second anybody bit into one.

"No candy before dinner." The very pregnant Jane walked inside with Chad, setting off another round of hugs.

In the midst of her family's embracing and Lulu's whining, Autumn was positive that Chad shot Trent a questioning look. She was equally positive that Trent gave his head an almost imperceptible shake. Whatever Chad's question meant, Trent's answer was no.

Or more likely, *Not yet.*

Autumn's heart squeezed again.

She was pretty sure that Trent was ready to propose. She was happy for them. She really was. Trent and Claire were great together, and they'd been dating for sixteen months now. Oddly, it was Seth who had set them up. Autumn's ex. At the time, she'd been shoving her way up the ranks at Fishburn & Crandal, a prestigious PR firm downtown, and Seth had just taken a job at the

31

Creative Group, where Trent worked. Autumn no longer worked at Fishburn & Crandal, and Seth no longer worked at TCG. He was now free-lancing full-time, but he and Trent still played racquetball and grabbed the occasional burger.

Autumn wondered if Trent had told Seth he was going to propose. She wondered what went through Seth's head and if he'd be in the wedding and if Claire would arrange it so that Autumn would have to walk down the aisle with him. She wondered how bizarre it would be, knowing that it should have been them, had life not thrown them such a gigantic curveball.

These were the thoughts filling her mind as they gathered around the dinner table. She assumed their conversation would resort to the usual—baby names and baseball. She assumed Dad and Chad would talk about the White Sox lineup while Trent muttered good-natured insults under his breath, because Trent was a die-hard Cubs fan. Something else he and Seth had in common.

But before the dinner rolls had made one full pass around the table or Cal had a chance to refuse Leanne's meatloaf, Jane sat down with bright, eager eyes and made an announcement.

"Autumn, I found you a job."

Four

Pale moonlight spilled in from a nearby window, outlining his wife's lithe figure as she beckoned him from the top of the staircase. "I'm waiting for you."

Desire awakened.

"Come up here," she crooned. "Be with me."

He placed his hand on the smooth railing and climbed the stairs.

She stood at the end of the hall, inside the doorway of their bedroom, crooking her long, slender finger before disappearing inside.

Paul went after her, but when he rounded the corner, there was nothing but another stairwell. He caught a flash of white nightgown through the dark.

"Come find me," she called.

He reached the top and stepped into the cold dark. "Vivian?"

Laughter—teasing and flirtatious—echoed all around him.

"Vivian, where are you?" Desire turned to desperation. He turned around, and there she was, standing so close he could feel her breath on his cheek.

"I'm dead, Paul."

He jolted awake, his eyes wide in the dark, the side of his face pressed against his pillow, staring at the empty side of the bed. Reaching out, he placed his hand over the comforter. Then he kicked off his covers and went into the bathroom, where he splashed water on his face and set his hands on either side of the sink and stared down into the drain, droplets of water dripping off the end of his nose onto the porcelain.

With a shuddering breath, he looked up at the man in the mirror—a man who didn't sleep—and ran his hand over the stubble on his cheek. "Get it together."

"Dad?"

Paul jumped.

Reese stood in the doorway, looking ghost-like, frizzy hair framing a thin, pale face as she clutched her ragged stuffed animal—a once-white-now-gray puppy named Gipper—as though she were two instead of twelve.

Paul exhaled. "Are you okay?"

"Tate keeps snoring."

It was nearly two in the morning. And Tate didn't snore. He breathed loudly when he slept but not loud enough to keep Reese awake. Something else was bothering his daughter. Over the past few days, she'd been moodier—more withdrawn than usual. The therapist in him said this was normal for her age, but he still worried.

"I have my presentation at school tomorrow."

34

Her voice escaped in an anxious whine. "But I can't fall asleep."

Sleeplessness beget more sleeplessness. Paul knew this to be true. The longer a person tossed and turned in bed, the more the frustration and anxiety grew, and the more the frustration and anxiety grew, the more slippery sleep became. He'd helped enough clients through the years to understand how the cycle worked. He just never thought the condition would get ahold of his daughter. Unfortunately, this wasn't the first *I never thought* that had weaseled its way into his reality.

All it took was a slight nod of his head. The smallest of invitations.

Reese climbed into his bed and nestled under the comforter.

He climbed in beside her and rubbed circles into her back and hummed the song he wrote just for her. A song he used to croon in her ear when she was a baby and colic was the thing that kept her awake at night. A song he sang whenever he bandaged a scraped knee or a stubbed toe, back when a simple kiss could chase the bad things away. He prayed for relief. He prayed for her nerves to settle. He prayed that in this simple act of rubbing her back and humming this song, he would be able to help his daughter.

Slowly, Reese's breathing turned soft and rhythmic.

A gust of wind whistled against the windows,

dredging up memories he didn't want to remember. The ribbon cutting for the memorial fountain had come and gone. Regina was back in North Carolina with her latest husband. This nightmare of a year was over.

With grit and determination, Paul had pulled his children away from the wreckage of all that awfulness as unscarred as possible. The sun had started to shine again. Breathing wasn't quite so laborious.

But at night? The wind continued to howl.

Forty-nine-year-old Brenda Vance sat inside Paul's office, her frustrated tears from their first session now replaced by a hopeful smile. "He said my hair looked pretty."

Late-afternoon sunlight streamed through his windows as she relayed the entirety of the story. Paul listened attentively, his optimism expanding like a water-filled sponge. One that had been sitting in the cabinet for too long—shrunken and brittle and hard. His work life had been particularly satisfying these days. Brenda wasn't his only client making positive strides. Coupled with Tate's progress report from yesterday, and the sponge of optimism grew big enough to shadow Reese's sleeplessness.

She was going to be okay.

They were going to be okay.

"This morning at breakfast, he asked me about

our sessions." Brenda's face took on a bridal-like glow. "He wanted to know if we talk about him."

"What did you say?"

"I told him that I've tried, but you have this annoying way of bringing the conversation back around to me."

"How frustrating."

She laughed.

Brenda first showed up two months ago, a mother of four whose youngest had left the nest, leaving her and her husband alone and undistracted—the tattered state of their marriage thrust into glaring fluorescents. She wanted to fix it. Her husband didn't think there was anything to fix. "He seemed more open to the possibility of coming."

A knock sounded at the door.

Paul swiveled around in his chair.

Margo poked her head inside his office looking wholly apologetic. She knew not to interrupt unless there was an emergency. "I'm so sorry, Dr. Elliott, but Mrs. Ryan is on the line for you."

His concern came instantaneously.

Mrs. Ryan was the mother of Mia, and Mia had invited Reese to hang out after school today. He was too jarred by the interruption to feel embarrassed. "I'm sorry, Brenda, but I have to take this."

She held up her hands, as if to say, *Please don't worry about me.* He was very clear with his clients from the start that his children had to come first. Not everyone was quite so understanding as Brenda.

He rolled himself to his desk and picked up the phone. "This is Paul."

"Hi, Paul, it's Allison. I'm so sorry to bother you at work."

"Is everything all right?"

"Well . . ."

His grip on the phone tightened. If anybody knew how quickly life could change—how fast tragedy could pounce—it was he.

"Reese was caught shoplifting."

"What was that?"

"I thought it would be fun to take the girls to Aaron's Apothecary. The clerk caught her putting some lip gloss in her bag."

Paul swiveled his chair away from a watching Brenda and pulled at the back of his neck, where heat was rising.

"The clerk didn't call the police or anything. I was going to wait until you came to pick Reese up after dinner, but then I thought, if it were Mia, I'd want to know right away."

"Of course."

"She is more than welcome to stay as planned."

"No, no. I'll come get her right now." He couldn't let his daughter do something as serious as shoplift, only to go on having fun eating pizza at a friend's house. What was Reese thinking?

He thanked Mrs. Ryan for calling, hung up, then turned around to face his client. "I am terribly sorry, Brenda, but—"

"Duty calls."

"Yes, it does."

Compassion clouded her eyes. She knew Paul was a single father. The entire world seemed to know. And despite the degrees and certificates on his walls, she looked at him now like so many well-intentioned women tended to look at him. Like he was flailing in the waves of single-fatherhood and she wanted to be the one to toss him a life ring.

He strode to the office door and held it open for Brenda.

Out in the lobby, Margo sat behind the simple welcome desk.

"Hey, Margo, could we get Mrs. Vance rescheduled as soon as possible? We'll have to reschedule my last appointment too." And by *we,* he meant her. She deserved an award for the world's best assistant. "I can come in early tomorrow, or any day next week if necessary."

"Sure thing. Is everything okay with Reese?"

"I'm sure everything will be. I just have to sort some things out." Paul snagged his jacket off the rack by the entrance and slid his arms inside the sleeves. "Any messages for me before I go?"

Margo held up a Post-it note. "Mitch called. So did your agent."

Something snarly scratched up his spine.

Brenda, however, perked at the news. "Are you going to write another book?"

Doubtful, considering he'd been so wishy-washy about the first. Also doubtful, considering his daughter's latest shenanigans. He zipped up his jacket. "I'm not sure I'd have the time."

Brenda gave him that look again. Like he was helpless. Paul hated helplessness. It was—hands down—one of the worst feelings in the world.

Especially when it came to his family.

Five

Shock and concern gave way to anger and embarrassment. First, his daughter shoplifted. Then she went on to treat Mrs. Ryan with animosity—as though it were Mrs. Ryan's fault she wouldn't be staying for dinner. What was worse, Mrs. Ryan acted like Reese's behavior was to be expected. Like she had an excuse. Well, his daughter didn't get to use her mother's death as an excuse for poor behavior. Not anymore.

And Paul needed a shirt that said "We're Fine," because Mrs. Ryan had looked at him the same way Brenda Vance had looked at him back at his office.

Paul glanced in the rearview mirror. Reese sat

in the backseat, silent and stone faced. A one-eighty from the girl who had climbed into his bed last night. That girl had resembled his baby—the one who used to whisper into his ear that someday she was going to marry him. That girl was gone now, replaced by a preteen filled with so much anger it was startling. He wrapped his fingers tighter around the wheel and told himself this was normal. Reese wasn't going to adore him forever. She was searching for some autonomy.

But shoplifting? Flat-out rudeness?

He didn't raise her to act that way.

He pulled into the alley behind their home.

The second he shifted into park, Reese jumped out and slammed the door.

He went after her, the grass still wet from a hard, early-morning rain. "We're going to talk about this."

She stalked inside and kicked off her Converse All Stars, tossed her backpack on the floor by the door, and marched through the kitchen. "I don't want to talk."

"Too bad, kid. Stealing warrants a discussion."

"It was just some lip gloss."

He caught up in two easy strides and stepped in front of her. "It doesn't matter what it was, Reese. Shoplifting is wrong. It's stealing."

Reese crossed her arms tightly in front of her chest. Closed off from him. Closed off from the world.

He ran his hand down his face and prayed for patience, for wisdom. Was this behavior a cry for help, or just a natural by-product of her age—a grand entrance into adolescence? He really hoped it wasn't the former, but man, if it was the latter, this was not a good indication of the next few years. "Reese, what's going on?"

"Nothing."

"Shoplifting isn't nothing. Treating Mrs. Ryan horribly isn't nothing."

"Can I please go to my room?"

"Not before we discuss this."

"I don't want to discuss anything!" The heated words rang through the house, leaving an unsettled silence in their wake. An abandoned bowl of Rice Krispies sat on the counter, soggy and half-eaten from this morning—when his daughter hadn't yet turned into the unrecognizable, red-faced creature in front of him.

Paul forced himself to take a breath.

Emotions were running high. For him, and most certainly for her. Whatever "conversation" they had now would not be a productive one. Better to let her calm down, let himself calm down. After dinner he would try again.

He stepped to the side. "Okay."

Pulling her arms tighter, she stomped past him and up the stairs. A few seconds later, her bedroom door slammed shut, rattling the walls of the house.

• • •

After a long run on the treadmill in the basement and a quick shower, Paul stood at the counter in the kitchen, flipping through a stack of mail. Bill, junk, junk, insurance statement, bill, and then a piece addressed to Reese Elliott.

Paul squinted at the return address. There was no name. Just an apartment number in Lakeview. As far as he knew, Reese didn't have any friends who lived there. And he did a pretty good job of keeping tabs on her friends.

Paul turned the envelope over in his hand, curiosity rising. It was the size and shape of a birthday card. Odd, considering Reese's birthday had been two months ago. Perhaps this was a birthday party invitation. One she definitely wouldn't be going to. Not if she kept up this fun and fabulous new attitude of hers.

The front door opened.

Tate came running into the kitchen, sneakers squeaking across the hardwood—a flash of blond hair and energy. He hugged Paul's waist, his face splitting with an uneven smile, thanks to two front teeth growing in at different speeds. "Grandma got our favorite pizza!"

Love swelled—an all-consuming, protective love. And gratitude. For at least one kid nowhere near the angsty throes of puberty and a mother who turned the impossible task of single-fatherhood into something not so impossible. "Pizza, huh?"

43

Mom walked in carrying a box from Bricks, an invisible cloud of pepperoni and sausage and oregano following her into the kitchen.

"Hey, Ma."

She smiled and gave the box a lift. "I promised Tate a special reward."

"For?"

She set it on the counter and shot him a wink. "He got another eighty percent on his spelling test today."

That made three in a row.

Paul raised his eyebrows, then looked down at his boy. While Reese could get perfect scores in her sleep, his son had to work for every one of those percentage points. He ran his hand over Tate's curls. "That's awesome, buddy."

"Mrs. Cranswick put a Jedi sticker on the top of my paper. Wanna see?"

"Of course."

Tate slid his backpack off his shoulders and began digging through the mess of crumpled papers he'd shoved inside his bag. By December, he'd already lost three take-home folders. By February, Paul had given up on replacing them. So far, Mrs. Cranswick hadn't said anything.

There were some battles you just had to surrender.

Paul set the stack of mail on the counter and gave his mom a kiss on the cheek. "How's Pop?"

A couple of weeks ago, his grandfather had taken a nasty spill. Thankfully, he hadn't broken any bones, although he had sustained a thorough lecture from his doctor.

Mom sighed. "Using his walker now, at least."

"Have you thought anymore about—?"

She raised her hand and gave him the same look she used to give him when he was a boy standing on the cusp of mischief. Like the time she caught him up on the roof looking down at the newly raked pile of leaves while his big brother, Brandon, called encouragement from the ground. "I don't want to hear it, Paulie. You know what I think about the matter."

He did.

And while a big part of him agreed, because he couldn't imagine his grandfather in an assisted living home either, no matter how much Pop insisted he'd be fine, Paul also knew his mother was constantly taking on too much. She did it for him and the kids. She did it for her father. And now that the doctor didn't want Pop using the stairs on his own anymore, taking care of him would be all the more challenging.

"I'm just saying," he said. "It's a lot."

"It's not a lot. It's life. And exactly what you would do for me."

"You wouldn't let me, and we both know it."

Before she could answer, Tate popped up from his squat and waved the spelling test in the air.

"Eighty percent. And that's a sticker of Plo Koon. He's from Dorin."

"That's pretty awesome, Taters. Why don't you go hang it on the fridge, then get your sister before the pizza gets cold? She's up in her room."

Tate hung the test at a skewed angle using the "I Will Write for Food" magnet Margo got Paul the day he signed his book contract, then raced out of the kitchen and up the stairs.

"Reese is here? I thought she was eating dinner over at Mia's tonight."

Paul inhaled a deep breath, then let it rush away in a loud sigh.

"What happened?"

Oh, nothing much. His twelve-year old daughter had just been unaccountably rude to an adult and had committed a crime. That was all.

The whole thing dug into his shoulders—concerning, yes. But also incredibly frustrating. He should be able to help Reese with whatever emotions were brewing. It was his job to help people.

Mom placed her broad palm on his cheek. Her eyes—the same earthy green as his own—filled with concern. "What is it?"

Tate raced down the stairs and around the corner, rattling the moment away. The kid was as loud as a herd of stampeding elephants.

"Reese isn't up in her room," he announced.

"What?"

"Reese isn't here."

"Of course she is."

Tate shook his head. "I checked her room and my room and your room *and* the bathroom. They were all empty."

A deep divot furrowed Paul's brow. He waited a beat, and then he called his daughter's name. Loudly.

There was no answer.

Exchanging a worried glance with his mom, he skirted around her and up the stairs, climbing them two at a time. "Reese?"

By the time he checked the basement and circled back into the kitchen, she hadn't responded to any of his or his mother's calls. And there, by the back door, was a small puddle of water where her shoes had been.

Six

He ran from the empty bus stop toward Belmont, an awful sense of déjà vu turning his panic unreasonable. He held his transit card against the reader, pushed through the turnstile, and sprinted up the stairs to a semicrowded platform, his attention darting one way, then the other.

People milled about, staring down at their phones as daylight darkened into dusk.

There was no sign of Reese.

Downstairs, he grabbed the attention of the CTA employee sitting inside the booth. "Excuse me, sir. Have you seen a girl, about this tall?" He held his hand up to his sternum. "Skinny. Dark hair. Blue eyes."

The man shook his head apologetically.

His panic grew, choking out reason.

The CTA employee started to say something, offer assistance in some way, but Paul had already turned and started running for home, positive that Reese had turned up in his absence. Positive she'd be there, waiting inside the house. He would crush her against him in a hug, and then, once his heart rate returned to normal, he would never let her out of his sight. He would confiscate her transit card. He would put a tracking device on her ankle. That phone she wanted so badly? Not a chance. He would ground her until she was eighteen.

Maybe longer.

When Paul crashed into the house—panicked and breathless—there was no sign of Reese anywhere. Just Mom, hanging up the phone in the kitchen entryway. The second they realized Reese was gone, his mother had begun making phone calls to all her friends.

"No luck?"

She shook her head.

He pushed his hand through his hair.

"Let's not panic," Mom said. "You said you checked on her after your run, which means she hasn't been gone for very long. And Reese is a responsible girl."

Who ran away from home after having shoplifted. Paul wasn't sure *responsible* fit his daughter anymore. And even if it did, there was no controlling others. Chicago was no place for a girl to wander alone at night.

His stomach turned over.

She had taken her transit card, which meant she could be anywhere. And it was getting dark. He grabbed the phone off the wall. "I'm calling the police."

"The police?" The whimpered question belonged to Tate. He sat at the dining table with his bottom lip quivering—a picture so painfully reminiscent of one already branded in Paul's memory, when he'd had to tell Tate that his mother wasn't coming home. "Is Reesie okay?"

"She's fine, buddy. Reese left without permission, that's all. We'll find her." Paul gave his son an encouraging smile, refusing to believe any other option might exist.

Walking among the dead at night wasn't normal.

But ever since the world flipped upside down, that was what Autumn did. This ritual she saved for the dark, when nobody could see.

The air was damp, the wind sharp, the contents of Jane's pamphlet fresh in her mind as she made the familiar trek to the tombstone. She'd finally read the brochure this evening. A mistake, apparently, as it only served to rile her up. She didn't need her sister-in-law to tell her what she was going through. Autumn knew perfectly well what she was going through.

She could actually think quite logically about it.

She could see herself doing these things, and she knew, with absolute certainty, that they weren't healthy. But all the knowing—all the pamphlets in the world—didn't keep the crazy away. And habits were sneaky things. They weren't something a person just decided to do one day. At least, not the bad ones. Those crept up on a person, slowly, until the "one time" thing became a "just one more time" thing and then one day an "I can't stop" thing.

The first time, her physical therapist had just cleared her to drive, and she was desperate to catch up with the rest of the world. When she woke from the coma, disoriented and confused and panicked with no idea where she was or what had happened, the funerals were already over. The terrible, awful mix-up wherein first responders had incorrectly identified her had already been corrected. The city had done its mourning and had zeroed in on her.

When Autumn woke up, the city celebrated.

All of it had been so *jarring*.

Autumn had needed something to help her wrap her mind around everything. So she made her rounds. The first time, the graves had been covered with flowers. Some had cards and notes. The following month, she went again. Not in an attempt to catch up, but in an attempt to move on. A grasp at closure. But some of the notes had blown away, and the flowers weren't as fresh, and suddenly, her visits became a matter of obligation. Of duty. These people would not be neglected. They would not be abandoned. Not on her watch.

She became their self-imposed keeper. A living person haunting twenty-two graves.

She stopped at one of the tombstones, picturing the girl with the art portfolio and the butterfly tattoo—two monarchs, emerging from the collar of her shirt. Black-inked wings rippling over the bumps of the girl's spine.

Chloe Collins was the one victim Autumn remembered, and only because she'd seen her on the transit system before, not because she could remember anything about that day, or any of the days leading up to it. The blast of the explosion had wiped all those memories away. When Autumn awoke, the last thing she could remember was Seth, crawling around on all fours in her apartment, whinnying as little Cal rode on his back. She had been babysitting for Chad and Jane. According to her family, that had been two weeks before the explosion.

Autumn set a bouquet of fresh daisies by the smooth granite tombstone when her phone buzzed inside her pocket. She pulled it out and looked at the screen.

Where r u?

The text message belonged to Claire, and it put her on the defensive.

Where are YOU? she shot back. It was an evasive maneuver, answering a question with a question.

At your apartment.

Why?

To make sure you've interacted with at least one human for the day.

Irritation tangled inside her chest. Claire was not Autumn's babysitter.

"I'm fine," she texted. But the second she hit Send, she experienced one of those disconcerting jolts. Reality grabbed her by the shoulders and gave her a sharp, violent shake. Suddenly, she could see herself with astounding clarity, sitting in the middle of a graveyard—at night. Claire had every right to check on her. Her worry and Jane's worry and Chad's worry and Leanne's worry—all of it was well founded.

As typically happened at the tail end of such jolts, Autumn was struck with a sudden, desperate determination to stop. To prove to the world and herself that she could function like a sane person.

Lunch tomorrow? she typed.

A long pause followed, wherein Claire's disapproval oozed through the silence. A gust of wind howled through the trees, which were just beginning to bud. The tissue paper holding the bouquet together crinkled and flapped. Finally the phone buzzed again.

K

Funny how a single letter could communicate so much judgment.

Autumn didn't continue her rounds after that. She got into her car and grabbed some Chinese takeout from Yen's and checked her mailbox in the lobby, where she found a carefully folded application tucked inside.

It was for the job her sister-in-law had found.

She'd included a note that read: *This is right up your alley!!*

Autumn rode the elevator up to the fourth floor, glaring at the exclamation points as the spicy-sweet scent of General Tso's filled the lift. Was it really necessary to add two of them? Why was Jane even giving her applications when Autumn already had a job?

"Not one that pays the bills," she muttered to herself.

The elevator doors slid open.

"You can't be in here." The voice belonged to Roland, who stood in the hall. He was Autumn's neighbor—a chain-smoker who never wore a shirt. He had leathery skin and caveman hair and a tattoo of a bar code on his chest. She was always tempted to ask how much he cost. "This apartment building is for residents only. No trespassers allowed."

It took a step or two for Autumn to see that Roland wasn't muttering to himself, like she was. He was talking to a person.

A girl sat in the hallway with her back against the wall, skinny arms wrapped around her knees, thick hair pulled back into a messy ponytail. She looked up at Roland, tears swimming in a pair of crystal-blue eyes. "I'm not trespassing. I'm waiting for a friend."

Autumn stopped midstep.

It was Reese Elliott—the girl who had been writing the letters.

Seven

The phone in Paul's hand let out a loud ring. He shoved it against his ear. "Hello?"

There was a brief pause, and then, "Is this Paul Elliott?"

"Yes. Yes it is."

"Um. Your daughter is here, at my apartment."

"Is she okay?"

"Yes, she's fine. A little shaken up, but perfectly intact."

Relief. Blessed, sweet relief. It poured over him like buckets and buckets of water. Reese was alive. He could call the police and tell them he wouldn't have to file a report after all. Paul nodded at his mother, who pressed her hand against her chest and practically melted into a puddle right there on the floor.

So much for not panicking.

"Would you like my address so you can pick her up?" the woman asked.

"Yes, please." He grabbed a notepad and pen from the junk drawer in the kitchen and told her he was ready. The address she recited had him stopping midscrawl. He set the pen down and picked up the card that arrived in today's mail. The one addressed to Reese Elliott. The address this woman read to him now was the same one scrawled in the upper left-hand corner.

"I'm sorry, who is this?" he asked.

There was another pause—longer this time. "My name is Autumn. Autumn Manning."

"Is he coming?"

Unable to find her voice, Autumn nodded. She set her phone on the countertop with jittery fingers, her heart knocking a fast-paced staccato against her chest. Reese Elliott was standing inside her home, and Reese's father was on his way.

Somehow Autumn's real everyday life had intersected with the alternate reality in her mind, one occupied by the dead and the people they left behind, one rooted in obsession and probably fiction too. The two worlds collided the moment she realized who Roland was heckling. And now, Reese stood inside her door. In the flesh. A real, living person. One who walked and talked and breathed independently of Autumn's preoccupation.

The whole thing made her dizzy.

The real Reese was smaller than the one in Autumn's mind. Her hair frizzier. Her eyes more striking in their blueness. She wore Converse All Stars, pink-and-black zebra-print leggings, and a puffy black coat unzipped over an oversized T-shirt with the word "Whatever" scrawled across the front. She was a normal-looking twelve-year-old, slight and pale and thanks to Roland, visibly rattled.

"Would you like anything to drink?" Autumn asked.

Reese shrugged.

Desperate for something to do with her hands, Autumn took the gesture as an affirmation and poured milk into a coffee mug. The sour smell had returned, subtle but there, wafting into the air as soon as she opened the refrigerator. She quickly shut the door and placed the mug in the microwave. It was something her mother used to do for her and Chad and Claire when they were young and frightened.

"Warm milk and cinnamon chases the bad dreams away," she would say.

She swallowed. "You can sit down if you want."

Reese shuffled to the sofa and sat near the arm.

Autumn peeked at her as the microwave hummed and the mug spun a slow circle inside. Was she here because of the letter Autumn had finally written? Had she already received the second one—the one that induced panic the second Autumn dropped it into the mailbox on the corner? So much that if a mail carrier had happened nearby, she would have grabbed him or her by the lapels and begged for it back. But a mail carrier hadn't come, and beneath her frenzied second-guessing, she knew that ignoring the occasion would have been cruel.

A shiver worked its way into her jaw. Her body was filled with nerves and cortisol. For as long as she could remember, this was the way the two manifested themselves—in shivers and shakes and chattering teeth.

The microwave dinged.

She sprinkled the milk with cinnamon and brought it into the living room.

When Reese took the mug, she looked down into its contents, then back up again.

"Warm milk and cinnamon. It helps when I'm upset."

"Thank you." Reese took a tentative sip.

"I'm sorry about Roland."

"Who?"

"The guy in the hallway. His bark is a lot worse than his bite."

"He wasn't wearing a shirt."

"He doesn't usually."

She wrinkled her nose.

Autumn smiled, one or two knots in her muscles unwinding, and motioned to the coffee table. "Do you like jigsaw puzzles?"

Another shrug. Another sip.

"This is my twenty-seventh one." As soon as she said it, she wasn't sure why. Nor was she sure whether it should be impressive or pathetic. Pathetic, probably, given that it was her twenty-seventh one this *year.*

"They seem a little boring."

"It's something to do when I watch TV." Autumn sat at the opposite side of the couch, fingers twisting. She wanted something to do to avoid the two of them sitting there just staring at each other. And so she picked up a piece and set it in place. "It's nice when you find one that fits."

"Did he sound mad?"

"What was that?"

"My dad. Did he sound angry?"

"I don't think so."

The knots that had unwound themselves tied tight again. Autumn didn't want to imagine it. But it came like it always did—a contraction, this horrible thing that clamped down on her mind no matter how hard she resisted. A vision of Paul Elliott racing into the hospital room. Did he notice immediately? Or was the swelling and bruising so bad that he took her hand first? Did he hold it to his face before realizing that the woman it belonged to wasn't his wife? Autumn tried not to think about the fact that this very same man was on his way.

"Are you cold?" Reese asked.

"What's that?"

"You're shivering."

"Oh." Autumn rubbed her arms. "I guess I'm a little chilly."

A knock sounded on the door.

No warning buzzer. No time to catch her breath. Roland was probably already filing a complaint with the landlord about the front lock.

Reese pressed herself against the couch and muttered, "He's going to kill me."

Hyperbole, of course. And yet, as Autumn made her way to the sound, she felt very much like a woman marching to a firing squad with no way to escape. Paul Elliott was knocking, and she had to answer.

She wiped her sweaty palms on her jeans and pulled the door open.

He stood out in the hallway, in the flesh—this man who haunted the darkest corners of her mind—his hair disheveled, blinking at her like an elephant had answered the door.

Or maybe a roach.

That was how she felt anyway. Offensive and unpleasant, standing there healthy and whole, with nothing but two incriminating scars a person had to squint to see. She wanted to shrink. She wanted to disappear. She wanted to scuttle away into a dark corner and hide forever. Instead, she reminded herself to breathe and opened the door a little wider, motioning to Reese on the couch.

Paul swooped inside, filling up all the space like a thundercloud.

Autumn braced herself for an explosion. She waited for him to yell, release a few choice words like her father had whenever he lost his temper. But the explosion didn't come. Paul's shoulders lifted and fell with a deep breath, as if he were using the oxygen to weigh his words. Then, suddenly, he turned to Autumn, his eyebrows fixed in a frown. "Can we talk out in the hall?"

He didn't wait for an answer. Before she could even open her mouth, he stepped outside. She followed, glancing once at Reese, who was looking at her apologetically. He shut the door behind them, and then he pulled a familiar-looking envelope from his back pocket, the seal untouched. "Can you please explain to me what this is?"

"It's a card."

"Why are you sending a card to my daughter?"

Autumn hugged her arms to her chest. If she let them, her teeth would start chattering like the hall was Antarctica. "She mentioned something about a birthday. I thought it might be a hard day for her."

The confession hovered between them like Vivian's ghost.

A birthday.

It sounded so innocuous.

Never mind whose.

"She mentioned it?" He articulated each word. Enunciated each syllable.

Autumn nodded.

"When did she mention it?"

"She brought it up in her last letter."

That was when it became obvious. Paul Elliott had no idea his daughter had been writing to her. He dragged his palm down the length of his face. "Reese sends you letters?"

"Yes."

"And you write back?"

"Only once. And then yesterday, I sent that card." She nodded lamely at the envelope he held in his hand, her emotions going from nauseous to horrified to surreal. Like a broken traffic light, she couldn't seem to land on one. She couldn't seem to process the fact that she was out in the hallway, having a conversation with this particular man. "I didn't want her to think I was ignoring her. I wanted her to know I was listening."

"Listening to *what?*"

"I don't know. *Her.*" Her grief. Her questions. Her memories and her musings. Sometimes, Autumn suspected that Reese had made Autumn into her own personal journal. Autumn was Reese's Maud.

"How long has this been going on?" Paul asked.

"A while."

"I need something a little more specific."

"The first letter came two days after I woke up in the hospital."

He pushed his fingers through his hair, then wrapped his palm around the back of his neck, shaking his head.

Autumn stood there, twisting her ring around her finger. But that made her sad, so she stopped. The ring she wore now was a consolation. A gift from her dad as soon as he realized that the original ring—her mother's beloved Claddagh ring—was gone. The explosion on the train must have blasted it off her finger. It disappeared. Vanished amid the rubble, like so many other things.

"I'd appreciate it if you wouldn't write to her anymore."

The request made her sad too, only she wasn't sure why. It wasn't like she had planned on keeping up the correspondence. She was only ever going to send that one letter, and that one letter alone.

"I'm sorry if I'm being rude," he said. "I just think it's best for Reese to . . . move on."

Right.

Move on.

Oh, how Autumn hated those words.

"I understand."

Paul stared for a beat, his eyes bracketed with tension. He looked like he had other things he wanted to say. But instead of saying them, he went back inside. He collected his daughter, who thanked Autumn again for the milk. And just like that, the real-life Paul and Reese were gone.

By the time Autumn turned the lock, her entire body was trembling.

Wednesday, April 6, 2016

Dear Miss Manning,

My name is Reese Rosamund Elliott. My mother's name was Vivian Rosamund Elliott. We shared the same middle name, after my great-grandmother Rosa. Whenever I got into trouble as a little girl, my mom would say, "Reese Rosa Elliott, you get over here right now." Because that's what moms do when they get angry. They call their children by their middle names.

She was on the train that day. She was killed in Tragedy on the Tracks.

For a little while, we all thought she was the survivor.

I told my best friend Mia that I was going to write to you. She thinks it's weird. It probably is. But today you woke up and everyone is calling it a miracle. I looked the word up online. I already knew what it meant, but I like to look up definitions.

Miracle: an unusual or wonderful event that is believed to be caused by the power of God.

Do you believe in miracles?

At first, I didn't think it was a miracle. Because it definitely wasn't wonderful, and if God was involved, wouldn't He save everyone? But then I saw a picture of the train after the explosion. My dad didn't want me to see it. He's trying to keep me and my brother, Tate, away from the television. But it's all anybody can talk about. Mia and I Googled it on her laptop. As soon as I saw the picture, I changed my mind. I think it was a miracle. I think only God could have saved you.

I tried to talk to my dad about it, but he gets weird whenever I mention Mom or Tragedy on the Tracks. He's a therapist, but I honestly think he has no idea what to say. That bothers him. I can tell.

Yesterday, he cleaned out their bedroom closet.

He put all of Mom's clothes into garbage bags and donated them to the homeless ministry at our church. I wonder why a homeless woman would want a fancy business suit. The homeless people I see always look cold. I think they'd rather have a coat than a blouse.

After he finished, I went into the closet and sat down.

It was really empty.

Mom had a lot of clothes. She loved to go shopping. Especially for shoes. It was something we did together. She would always say, "Reese, a girl can never have too many pairs of shoes."

There was a tan one on the floor when I walked in. I think it fell out of a bag when Dad was dragging them downstairs. It had a really high heel. Mom liked to wear high heels. She wore them every day to work and every Sunday to church. She said they were a must-have accessory for the vertically challenged. I remember the way they clicked against the floor whenever I got ready for school in the morning.

I put the shoe in the bottom drawer of

my dresser. I don't think any of the homeless women will mind.

From,
Reese Rosamund Elliott

P.S. Is it okay if I write to you again?

Eight

Urgency pressed a firm hand against Autumn's back, shoving her forward. But someone grabbed her arm and yanked her to a stop.

It was Roland, his eyebrows pulled tight in an angry, accusatory furrow as he held up a hair bow—red and blue and white, like the American flag. "Why did you give this to me?"

She tried to apologize, but the words wouldn't come. The tautness in her throat kept them trapped inside.

Roland's grip tightened. "Tell me *why.*"

Autumn owed him an explanation.

He deserved one.

But she twisted free and kept running through swirling fog, her feet becoming harder and harder to lift. Gum. Everywhere she stepped, it stuck to the soles of her shoes as a crowd of nameless, faceless people pushed in on all sides.

"Why?" they demanded. *"Why?"*

The question turned into a woodpecker's incessant tapping.

She clamped her hands over her ears. Then she tripped and fell.

The gum turned into shards of glass that scraped and scratched her palms. Jagged pieces of broken glass glinting like sharp incisors. They were everywhere, surrounding her on all sides. And she had to get on the train. It was right there. In front of her, the doors sliding open. But the crowd would not let her pass. They demanded she pick up the mess, as if the glass belonged to her.

The doors slid shut.

Panic ripped up her throat in a desperate scream. She had to get on. She had to make the train stop. She had to make everyone get off before it was too late. But it already was too late.

The train pulled away.

All that remained was the snow and the roar of wind and a woman's face through the fogged-up window. It was her. It was Autumn. She watched herself banging on the glass, her face twisted in horror, her eyes wild as she screamed.

She tore out of sleep with a loud gasp. She swiped at her face, her heart pounding into the silence.

Get them off. Get the tubes off!

But there weren't any tubes. There weren't any machines. Just sweat dripping down her back, and lungs that heaved, and a digital clock that read 3:17 a.m.

Two hours later, she had completed her twenty-seventh puzzle.

Autumn looked down at the fidgeting hands in her lap. They didn't feel like her hands. They didn't even look like her hands, not with the imposter-of-a-ring circling her finger. She wasn't even sure why she bothered wearing it. It gave her something to do, she supposed. Something to twist when her thoughts turned tumultuous.

She was sitting in her therapist's office.

She had one now. Autumn had finally called one of the numbers on Jane's list, and here she was, at her first appointment, self-conscious and sleep-deprived.

Her name was Jeannie True and she was very, very tall. The kind of tall that probably had strangers asking if she played volleyball or basketball. Her office smelled like grape jelly. She had framed certificates on her walls and cactus plants in her window and a bright-red betta fish on her desk that kept darting about, circling the plastic green plant in the center of the bowl as though there had to be more.

"You think it was a mistake?" Jeannie asked.

"I think it was a big one."

"Why?"

"Because, if I hadn't written her a letter, she wouldn't have come to my apartment. And if she hadn't come to my apartment, I wouldn't have had to call her dad to come get her." But she had written the letter. Reese had been inside her home. Paul too. The whole thing felt like a dream. If not for Roland grumbling the next day about loiterers in the hallway, Autumn might have believed it to be.

"That must have been very difficult," Jeannie said. "Facing them."

No. Finding a parking spot downtown was difficult. Getting Lulu to sit still during a movie was difficult. Facing Paul Elliott and his daughter was something else altogether. She'd never be able to scrub the strange encounter from her mind. It would be stuck there for all eternity, like a grease stain that had been dried into a shirt on high heat.

Autumn rubbed her knuckles, then found a dry piece of skin near the cuticle of her left pinkie and began picking. By the time this appointment was through, she'd need Band-Aids for all ten of her fingers. Autumn sighed. She didn't want this to be her life any longer. She didn't want to worry her family or visit cemeteries at night or wake up at three in the morning in a cold sweat.

Hence, her appointment with Jeannie True.

She stared hard at the frantic, going-nowhere fish. "I know that I need to quit doing these things. I know none of it's healthy. The logical part of my brain is telling me to stop. Stop obsessing. Stop reading the obituaries. Stop searching for dead people on the Internet. Stop—"

"Why don't we change tracks?"

"What do you mean?"

"Instead of focusing on all the things you want to stop, let's focus on something you can do. Something productive. Something healthy."

"Like?"

Leather squeaked as Jeannie shifted her weight. "You tell me."

Autumn's mind wandered to the application Jane had stuffed inside her mailbox. "My sister-in-law thinks I should apply as a corporate relations specialist for Exelon."

"A job."

"Yep."

"That sounds productive."

"Sure."

"You don't sound sincere."

"Exelon is located downtown." Autumn's car was on its last leg and even if it wasn't, driving downtown every day would be incredibly impractical. And since using the transit system like every other Chicagoan was out of the question, the job didn't seem to be up her alley at all, no matter how many exclamation points Jane added to the statement.

"And?"

"And I don't take the train."

"Ah."

Yes. *Ah.*

Autumn didn't get on trains. Not anymore. The

70

very thought filled her with terror. Even the thought of getting on a bus gave her heart palpitations.

Jeannie drummed her fingers against the arm of her chair. "Well, applying for the job doesn't require getting on a train, does it? Why don't you apply, and we can deal with the next step when it comes."

And so Autumn had her first assignment.

Before her next session with Jeannie True, she was supposed to fill out the application for the position at Exelon and submit it online.

On her drive home, she ignored a phone call from Chad. Just as she'd ignored several from Claire. Her sister would come knocking soon. She would not accept—nor understand—Autumn's latest regression. Over the past several weeks, Autumn had gotten much better at answering her phone and returning phone calls—not that she received very many anymore. Ever since Reese showed up in her hallway on Monday?

Not so much.

She let herself into the lobby of her apartment building and unlocked her mailbox. There was an electricity bill inside. And also, a small package. One with a familiar name in the return address.

As soon as Autumn saw it, her hands grew clammy. The muscles in her jaw tightened like they did whenever her teeth were about to start chattering. She tore the package open and pulled out a folded slip of paper:

Thank you for the sympathy card you sent about my mom on her birthday. It meant a lot. I want you to have these. They are the earrings my dad got for my mom on their last anniversary.

A small velvet box slid onto Autumn's palm. She opened it and gasped.

A pair of diamond earrings glinted up at her.

Autumn stared, dumbfounded. Why would Reese send these to her? And how could she possibly think that Autumn would keep them?

Nine

There was a chill in the air that had Autumn hunching her shoulders up around her ears. She stood on the corner of Magnolia and Diversey, a comfortable distance away from the house that once belonged to Vivian Elliott, her heart creeping further and further up her throat.

On her walk over, the disappearing sun had painted the western sky a gorgeous dark pink. Since she'd become immobile—all stalker-like in the shadows—the pink had given way to deep navy, casting the small lawn and the two-story brick home into darkness.

Several cement stairs led up to the front stoop, protected by a portico with off-white columns that matched the front door. She knew it was the right house, thanks to the four gold numbers on the black mailbox, which was attached to an equally black iron gate that was part of a black iron fence that ran along the edge of every property on the quiet, tree-lined street.

Coveted real estate in a city like Chicago.

Autumn jammed her hands deeper into her pockets and wrapped her fingers around the small jewelry box. The way she saw it, she had two options: stick the box inside the mailbox and hope Reese didn't try sending it back. Or, buzz the intercom located beside the mailbox and hand deliver the expensive jewelry. This was probably the brave thing to do. Paul should know that his daughter was now sending her jewelry.

But Autumn wasn't feeling particularly brave.

And she still wasn't over their first encounter.

So she pulled a piece of paper from her purse, along with a pen, and decided on option three: go against Mr. Elliott's wishes and write one last, very quick note, explaining why she couldn't keep the earrings and why she would no longer be writing.

Hopefully, Reese would get the mail before her father. Hopefully, Reese would understand. Hopefully, nobody would be looking out the window when she worked up the courage to quickly stick the earrings and the note inside the mailbox.

Silly conversation from one of the *Madagascar* movies wove its way into the kitchen as Paul opened the oven. A wave of heat washed over his face. He stuck the pan of lasagna inside and set the timer, then moseyed into the living room, where Tate bounced on the edge of the sofa cushion, his eyes glued to the television screen. The *Madagascar* movies were part of a select few that could actually hold his attention.

Reese sat in her favorite spot—the bench tucked inside the bay window—where he was guaranteed to find her reading a book or filling up notepads with penciled stories. His daughter was a good writer. Granted, her stories had developed a dark edge these days, and she wasn't as eager to share them as she'd once been. But she had undeniable talent. This evening, she sat with her legs curled up to her chest, her pointed chin resting on pointed knees as she read a well-worn copy of *A Wrinkle in Time.*

This was day number three of her grounding.

Three days into her sentence and she was still furious with him. It wasn't the kind of fury that left her yelling or screaming or stomping about, either. It was the kind that left her tight-lipped and glowering. She'd barely spoken more than five words to him these past three days, even though *she* had been the one to shoplift. *She* had been the one to treat Mrs. Ryan rudely. *She* had been the one to run away.

To Autumn Manning's apartment, no less.

Paul rattled his head, unsure how to process the

fact that his daughter had been writing to her. *Her,* of all people. His daughter had been looking for answers to questions he didn't even know she had, a truth that made him shift uncomfortably. He was her father. It was his job to know these things. And yet he had been completely oblivious.

What else didn't he know?

He leaned against the wall by the doorway, studying his little girl. She wore the same outfit she wore to school, except she'd exchanged the Converse All Stars she'd bought with her allowance money last fall for a pair of electric-pink fuzzy socks.

For some reason, the sight had Paul's chest pulling tight. He wanted to go to her and wrap her in a hug. He wanted to cradle her to his chest like he did when she was a curious toddler and managed to touch everything hot and sharp. He wanted to understand what was going through her head, but his daughter had turned into a question mark. One without an answer. He moved to the armchair near Reese's spot in the window and sat down.

She bristled like a cat.

His very presence annoyed her, which in turn, annoyed him.

"Are you working up an appetite?" he asked.

She turned a page and kept reading.

"I'm making your favorite."

Nothing.

"Liver and onions."

Nada.

"With a side of tripe."

"I don't even know what that is," she mumbled, shifting to show him more of her back.

"How long are you gonna keep up the silent treatment, kid?"

She turned another page and continued right on. There was no way she could actually read that fast.

Paul scraped his hand over his face, hating this growing sense of impotence. "Listen. I understand that you're upset. Trust me, I hear that loud and clear. What I don't understand is *why* you're upset."

Her attention snapped up from her book, her eyes narrowing. In accusation, it seemed. Like he had no right not to know. Like mind reading was the easiest thing in the world.

He raised his eyebrows at her. "Are you going to enlighten me?"

"You told her not to write to me."

"Reese."

She looked away.

"I don't understand why you *want* her to write to you."

But it was hopeless. Reese had already returned to her book, her lips tight and small. It made him want to yell. Or punch something. She should be bringing her thoughts to him, not some stranger.

Not Autumn Manning.

The second he'd faced her, the second she opened the door of her apartment building, the memory that haunted him, the memory he tried hardest to bury resurrected itself like it had thousands of times before. Following a nurse in blue scrubs down a corridor. Walking into a sterile white room. Beeping monitors. The *swish-whoosh, swish-whoosh* of the ventilator. His chair creaking as he sat by her bed. The slow and confusing realization that something wasn't right . . .

Tate's laughter brought him back into the present. He cackled at something on the movie, completely oblivious to the terse, mostly one-sided conversation unfolding off to his right. It was a good sound. A great sound. One he wanted to bottle up and keep in his pocket. When was the last time Reese had laughed like that?

Paul rubbed his jaw. "I'm changing my mind."

"About what?"

"Your grounding."

"You're shortening it?"

"That's up to you."

Her eyes narrowed.

"Once you decide to talk to me—and I mean *really* talk to me—you'll no longer be grounded."

"That's blackmail."

"That's parenting."

Reese scowled.

Paul knew his daughter. She'd been stubborn since infancy. Thankfully, she'd inherited that from him, and he had more practice. He'd give her a couple more days, and if nothing changed? Well, he wasn't above taking away her books and her notepads, even if every English teacher across America would disapprove.

He clapped his hands over his knees and pushed himself to a stand, then returned to the kitchen to take out the trash. He pulled it out, tied it up, and walked through the yard to dump it in the bin by the garage out back. When he finished, he rubbed his hands together to ward off the early April chill, wondering what to do with himself.

There was the *Tribune* on the front stoop, rolled up in the plastic bag it came delivered in every morning. He had no idea why he kept up the subscription. Despite Reese and Tate being fully capable of dressing and feeding themselves, getting them out the door in the morning was like herding cats. It left no time for sitting down at the table with a coffee and the paper. On the rare occasion he did have the time, he wasn't inclined to take it. He'd acquired a distinct distaste for the news approximately one year ago.

Right now, though? He wouldn't mind catching up on the rest of the world. Maybe the headlines would put his own problems into perspective.

Paul shoved his hands deep inside his pockets,

cut through the house, stepped out the front door, and stopped short.

Someone was standing outside, sticking something inside his mailbox.

"What are you doing?"

Her attention jerked up from the other side of the gate. It was Autumn, looking very much as if she'd been caught with a proverbial hand in the cookie jar.

He hurried down the stairs. "What did you just put in my mailbox?"

"Nothing. I'm sorry. I should . . ." She took a small step back, her attention flitting down the street as though she might turn and run.

He reached inside and pulled out a small package, the dull thud of his heart picking up speed. He asked her not to write. Three days ago, he'd looked into her face and explained that it would be best for his daughter if they discontinued the correspondence. And Autumn had agreed. She'd looked right back at him and said she understood.

"It's not what you think," she said.

At that particular moment, Paul didn't care much about privacy. He didn't care that his name wasn't the one on the package. He only cared that this woman was subversively undermining his parenting. And Reese was refusing to talk to him. So he tore open the envelope and pulled out . . . a small jewelry box? He flipped it open. A pair of diamond earrings glinted in the moonlight.

His mounting exasperation crumbled into confusion. Pure, absolute confusion. "You're sending my daughter jewelry?"

"I'm not sending. I'm returning."

He pulled out a slip of paper and unfolded it.

Dear Reese,

These belonged to your mother. They are a piece of her, one you will cherish forever. I hope you understand why I can't keep them. Also, your father asked me not to write anymore. I hope you also understand why I have to respect his wishes.

Take care,

Autumn

He turned his attention to the earrings in his palm. A picture of Vivian flashed in his mind—smiling as she turned her head in front of their bedroom mirror, admiring the new gift. "Reese sent these to you?"

How? When?

Besides school, his daughter had been at home. At least, she was supposed to be. There was that ninety-minute window of time between the end of her school day and the end of his workday, when she was supposed to be at home watching Tate. Had she left her seven-year-old brother alone to stop by the post office?

Paul looked up, completely bowled over by his

daughter's defiance. "Why would she send these to you?"

"I don't know." Autumn took a step away.

Paul stepped with her, angry, but unsure with whom. "She had to have written something."

The front door flew open.

Reese rushed outside, no longer tight-lipped or glowering, but flushed and almost . . . almost triumphant. Her attention slipped from Autumn to the small velvet box and the note Paul held in his hand.

"I'm sorry," Autumn said. "I can't keep the earrings."

"I understand," his daughter blurted, without a trace of hurt feelings.

It was almost as if she hadn't expected Autumn to keep them at all.

It was almost as if . . .

"You told her not to write me."

Reese was angry because Paul cut off communication. And so, it seemed, she'd taken matters into her own hands. She sent something to Autumn that couldn't be ignored. If he wasn't so disturbed, he'd probably be impressed.

"I should get going." Autumn cast him an apologetic glance and pointed lamely over her shoulder.

"Wait!" Reese stepped up to the gate. "Do you want to stay for dinner?"

"Reese." His voice came out low.

"My dad makes the best lasagna," she continued.

"It's from a box," he said.

"But it's really, really good. And we can never eat it all on our own. Right, Dad?" She stared at him with eager desperation. Like this was the best gift he could possibly give her.

Autumn, on the other hand, didn't look eager at all. She did, however, look desperate. To escape. To grow a pair of wings so she could fly fast and far away. It was obvious that she was every bit as uncomfortable with him as he was with her. How couldn't she be? The tie that bound them was bizarre and confusing and terribly distressing.

He put the jewelry box back in the package. "Reese, could you give us a minute?"

"But—"

"A minute, please."

Her shoulders slumped. She looked for a long second at Autumn before climbing the stairs and slipping inside.

Paul dragged his hand down his face, unsure what to do. He was stuck. At a loss. Confident that this—whatever this was—could not be a healthy path for his daughter. And yet this was the first time in weeks he'd seen a spark of life in Reese's eyes. All due to this woman standing on the other side of his fence. Her presence resurrected every horrible emotion he felt in that hospital room. She was irrevocably wrapped up in a day he wanted to forget.

This woman who had access to his daughter. Access he wanted.

He didn't have to look at the bay window to know that Reese would be sitting there, staring out at them. He pictured her watching as they went their separate ways. He pictured her mood darkening. Her stubbornness morphing into an impossibly thick wall of animosity. Weeks of silent treatment turning into months, turning into years. He pictured her dressing provocatively or cutting her arms. Behavior that would lead to teen pregnancy or self-loathing. All of which could be traced back to this day, this moment. When he turned Autumn Manning away.

A breeze whispered down the street, winding its way through budding branches. They swayed and creaked in reply.

Paul shifted uncomfortably and swallowed his better judgment. "Do you want to join us for dinner?"

"What?"

"I'm sorry. I know this is awkward." At the moment, she looked a lot more than awkward. She looked horrified. Like he really was going to serve tripe for dinner and then force her to eat it.

"I thought you wanted her to . . . move on."

"I do. But for some reason, she really wants you to join us." He unlocked the gate and held it open while a world of tumult swam in Autumn's eyes. "Please?"

Ten

When Paul opened the gate and said please, the sane part of her brain said no. Turn around, go back home. She couldn't eat with these people. But every night, every moment her mind wasn't distracted with some other noise, she imagined life right here, at the Elliotts'. Or the Montgomerys'. Or the Huetts'. She had visions of twenty-two families, going through the motions with ghosts in the rooms—their dead father or sister or son— and Autumn. *This is how we survive,* they whisper.

She felt beckoned. Impossibly enticed. Like an alcoholic staring down a snifter filled with the finest cognac. She nodded slightly and walked through the gate.

Reese was waiting as they stepped inside. "You're staying?"

"I guess so." Autumn's voice didn't sound like her voice. Her body didn't feel like her body. She'd gone blank inside, strangely numb, as though the part of her brain responsible for emotions had short-circuited.

Her obsession had invited her in, and instead of saying no, as Claire and Jane and Jeannie and the pamphlet would have recommended, she entered. And now she was standing in the foyer of Vivian's home, taking in the vaulted ceilings and the open floor plan, a large bay window, a fireplace and mantle with a television mounted on the wall above. And also, a blond-haired boy sitting on the couch. He pointed a remote at the television, muting the sound that had been playing from the speakers. Seven-year-old Tate—Vivian's son—looking at her with his head cocked. "Who are you?"

"This is Autumn," Reese said.

"Miss Manning," Paul corrected.

"Miss Manning," Reese parroted, the eye roll in her voice an audible thing. "She's going to eat dinner with us."

Her name didn't seem to carry any weight or significance to Tate. No shadow crossed his face at the mention of it. His expression was open and friendly as he set the remote on the cushion beside him. "Have you ever watched *Madagascar*?"

Autumn shook her head.

"It's my favorite movie. I got to watch it because I scored another eighty percent on a spelling test. That makes three in a row. My grandma calls that a turkey."

"Congratulations."

"I hate spelling more than anything. Except for reading. Reese reads all the time. Even more than she watches TV." As if to prove his point, Tate pointed to the worn paperback in Reese's hand.

A Wrinkle in Time.

"That's one of my favorites," Autumn said.

"It is?"

"I must have read it a dozen times as a kid."

"This is my third."

"It gets better with every read." Autumn smiled. And then quickly remembered herself—who she was, *where* she was, who she was *with*. Her attention slid to Paul, his expression unfathomable as he stood there watching the interaction, and the strange numbness lost some of its footing.

"Do you want a tour of our house?" Tate asked. "Grandpa gave it to us for a wedding present."

"He didn't give it to *us*," Reese said. "He gave it to our parents."

"He lives on a yacht in the ocean because he's filthy rich."

"Tate!" Paul barked.

"What?"

"It's not polite to talk about money."

"Reese talks about money."

"With *you,* doofus."

"Reese."

His kids fell silent.

Paul scratched the side of his neck. The package that had gotten them to this moment in time was still in his hand. "I should go put this away."

"We're going to give Autumn a tour," Reese said.

Paul nodded absentmindedly.

Tate grabbed Autumn's hand and tugged her along.

They started in the basement, which included a family room with an impressive entertainment center and a folded-up treadmill pushed off into the corner that was currently acting as a clothes-line. Did Vivian use to run on it? Was this where she'd done her thirty minutes of exercising each day? When she was done, did she pop her head into Paul's downstairs office to see how his book was coming along?

A guitar case was propped in the corner behind his desk. Had Paul used it to serenade his wife? Before Autumn could park too long on the image, he called down the stairs, requesting Tate's help with the salad.

Reese led Autumn through the main level, up to the second floor, where she gave a halfhearted point toward the master bedroom and Tate's bedroom before inviting her inside her own bedroom. This, Autumn suspected, was the pièce de résistance. The whole reason Reese brought her on the tour to begin with. To get to here, her bedroom.

While Autumn had always had to share hers with Claire, Reese had a room all to herself, with pale-pink walls, a four-poster bed with a white lace duvet, and a tattered stuffed animal on top of her pillow. A library's worth of books lined a whitewashed bookcase, a matching desk show-cased a rhinestone-studded cup full of different colored gel pens, and hanging on the wall above it was a black-and-white photograph, the kind that looked like it came from a fashion magazine—except the girl in the photo was Reese.

Autumn ran her fingers along the edge of the frame. "Did your mom take this?" she asked, turning around.

Reese nodded, pink spots blossoming on each of her cheeks.

Vivian was a photographer. Not by trade. Not for a living. But a photographer nonetheless. Autumn knew from the obituary she'd memorized. "My mother was a painter," she said.

"Was?"

It was an astute observation. Most people wouldn't have noticed the past tense. Or if they had, they wouldn't have asked about it. "She died when I was eleven."

The significance settled between them.

They were the same age when they lost their mothers.

"Was she good?" Reese asked.

"Very."

"Were you two close?"

"Very," Autumn said again.

Reese sat down on her bed and took the stuffed dog in her lap, a small V etched between her eyebrows. "My mom and I were close too."

Deep inside Autumn's chest, she felt the faintest of twists.

Reese rubbed the dog's ears between her thumb

and finger. The spot was extra worn, as though this was something Reese did often. Maybe even in her sleep. "Can I show you something?" she asked.

"Of course."

"I have to use your phone."

Autumn slid it from her pocket and sat on the edge of the bed. Reese made quick work of pulling something up on the Internet before handing the phone back. "Have you heard of her?"

A pretty girl with caramel skin and thick, kinky hair filled the screen in a frozen YouTube frame.

Autumn squinted at the username. "Kay-C Sparks?"

"She's fourteen, only two years older than me. Everybody in my class follows her. She lives in Los Angeles now, but she used to live here in Chicago, and she makes these really funny videos about all the famous people she runs into.

"Last month, her brother was killed in a drunk-driving accident. He was just starting to break into the rap industry. She made him this tribute and look." Reese pointed to the number below the freeze-frame.

It had surpassed one million views.

Reese hit Play.

What followed was a four-minute, thirty-three-second conglomeration of pictures and video, some of Kay-C's brother, some of people talking about her brother, all to the backdrop of a song he'd written and performed.

It was beautifully done.

When it ended, Reese went to her desk and pulled out a small stack of pictures from the top drawer. She set them on the bed between them. "I want to do the same thing for my mom, but these are the only pictures I can find."

Autumn gently touched a few, spreading them out on Reese's duvet, her body temperature rising. These weren't photographs she could find online. They weren't on Facebook or Twitter or Google. Looking at them felt like looking at a handful of rare and precious jewels. Vivian Elliott, standing with her arms spread wide, a breathtaking view of the Grand Canyon behind her. Vivian Elliott, dressed in a hospital gown, a squalling, pink-faced newborn cradled in her arms. Vivian Elliott, holding a little girl's hand, squinting at the camera while sunlight sparkled like diamonds over the surface of Lake Michigan. Each one, a puzzle piece, making the picture more complete.

"I can't find any videos." Reese gathered the photographs into a thin stack, straightening them over her knees. "Nobody would probably watch it anyway."

"I would."

"You would?"

Autumn nodded. "I think a lot of people would.

I think making a tribute in honor of your mother is a beautiful idea."

"Really?" Reese stared at her in this hopeful, almost hungry way.

Something dormant stirred to life. A flutter of wings on a creature thought dead. Autumn wanted to help this girl. She wanted to help her desperately, and right then Reese needed some affirma-tion. She reached out and placed her hand on her shoulder. "Really."

A throat cleared.

Autumn jerked her hand away.

Paul was standing in the doorway, his eyebrows pulled together in a troubled furrow. "Dinner's ready."

Eleven

"I can turn up the heat."

"What's that?"

Paul set the lasagna in the center of the table. He wore an oven mitt, and the sleeves of his dress shirt had been rolled halfway up his forearms. "You seem cold."

"Oh." She forced herself to stop hugging her arms. "I'm fine."

This, of course, was a big, fat lie.

The thing that fluttered to life inside her up in Reese's room had rattled her awake. Autumn

91

experienced another one of those disconcerting jolts, only this time she wasn't standing in the cemetery. She was sitting at the Elliott dinner table, almost certainly in Vivian's chair, which meant she was as far from fine as a person could be.

But it was too late to leave now.

"Tate, could you go turn the heat up a few degrees?"

With an enthusiastic "Aye, aye, captain," Tate set the bowl of salad next to the lasagna and trotted off to the thermostat on the wall next to the main-level bathroom. When he was done, he snagged the chair on Autumn's right and reached for her hand. She startled like she'd never been touched before, her skin flushing with embarrassment.

"We hold hands when we pray," Tate said.

"Do you want to bless the food?" Paul asked.

For one scatterbrained second, she thought Paul was speaking to her. But then Tate bobbed his head, and Reese slipped her hand inside Autumn's free one, and everyone closed their eyes.

"Dear Jesus," Tate began, "thank You for our guest. I like having another girl at the table, so thank You for Miss Manning and thank You for my spelling turkey and thank You for the food even though Grandma's lasagna is a lot better. Amen."

Reese and Tate let go.

The furnace kicked on.

Paul got to work serving his son a portion while Tate used the moment to stuff as much garlic bread into his mouth as humanly possible. Reese passed Autumn the bowl of salad, and although her appetite would most definitely not be making an appearance, she politely scooped some onto her plate.

Silence and clinking silverware battled for attention.

Autumn prodded some lettuce with her fork, trying to keep her shoulders from shivering and her attention away from the canvas photograph hanging on the wall behind Paul. Brother and sister stood arm in arm, a backdrop of blurred green grass behind them. Except for the same wiry frame, the two didn't look anything alike. Reese had dark hair; Tate had blond. Reese had frosty blue eyes; Tate's were a warm hazel. Even their smiles were different—with one resembling Mona Lisa, and the other, a grin that split his entire face. Only instead of permanent teeth growing in at crooked angles, Tate had a mouthful of baby ones, which meant that photo had been taken *before.*

Probably by Vivian.

Autumn pictured her, posing them, with their arms positioned just so while Reese and Tate complained over the forced affection. Or maybe, back then, posing hadn't been necessary. Maybe she'd simply pointed the camera at them and sang, "Say cheese!" and this was what they did naturally.

She imagined Paul standing beside his wife when she took it. Had they given each other one of those awestruck looks that Chad and Jane gave each other whenever Cal or Lulu did something especially adorable? Had they sucked up every ounce of joy from the moment? Or had they taken it for granted, unaware that life was short and fragile and about to upend itself?

A sudden and intense fury came with the tumult of questions. Wasn't it enough that death could snatch away life so quickly? Did it really have to do so without warning? Without any rhyme or reason? A thoughtless, avaricious grab at whoever happened to be standing in the way?

"Autumn?"

She flinched, startled at the sound of her name.

Paul and Reese and Tate were all staring.

"Sorry, what was that?"

"I asked if you've always lived here in Chicago," Paul said.

"Oh. Yes. I grew up in Beverly."

"Do your parents still live there?"

"Her mom is dead."

"Reese." Paul closed his eyes.

But it was true. Her mother was dead. And Reese's mother was dead. And Autumn shouldn't be here. What in the world was she doing?

94

Intruding on this family. Intruding on Vivian's memory. The problem was, she had walked in. She said yes to Paul's invitation, and now here she was, tensing her muscles to keep them from trembling. "My dad still lives there," Autumn said. "He's a police officer."

Tate's third piece of bread dropped to his place. "Your dad is a police officer?"

"Yes, he is."

"That's what I'm going to be when I grow up." He set his elbows on the table. "A cop came to our school this fall. His name was Officer Mike. He got shot in the shoulder when he was thirty-six. Is your dad named Officer Mike?"

Autumn shook her head. "His name is Officer Tom."

"Did he ever get shot?"

"Thankfully, no."

"Does he have a dog?"

"No. No dog."

"I'm gonna be a policeman when I grow up, *and* I'm going to have a police dog that will be able to sniff out the bad guys. You don't have to be good at spelling to be a police officer."

"Maybe I should start calling you Officer Tate." The kid laughed.

He had a funny laugh. One that sounded like the kookaburras at the Lincoln Park Zoo. One that would have made her smile if she weren't working so hard to keep her teeth from chattering.

Autumn forced herself to loosen her grip on the fork. "The lasagna's really good."

"Not as good as Grandma's," Tate said. "Her lasagna is the only lasagna I like. She makes it a lot in the winter because it's her comfortable food."

"*Comfort* food," Reese snapped. "Lasagna is Grandma's *comfort* food."

Tate's eyes narrowed. He seemed to be searching for something equally scathing to say, and for reasons she didn't quite understand, the impending squabble made Autumn anxious.

"My comfort food is Tootsie Pops," she offered quickly.

It worked.

"Comfort food can be candy?" Tate asked.

"It can be any kind of food, as long as it brings you comfort. When I was your age and had to get shots at the doctor's office, I'd always get a Tootsie Pop afterward. As soon as I pulled off the wrapper, it made everything instantaneously better."

"I don't like Tootsie Pops." Tate wrinkled his nose. "Pastor Mitch always has the same two in the candy bowl he keeps on his desk because nobody wants to eat them."

This time, Autumn couldn't help herself. She smiled.

"What if we made one together?" Reese asked.

The question came so out of left field, they all stopped and stared.

"Made what together?" Paul asked.

"A tribute." Reese looked from him to Autumn, her eyes taking on an excited glow. "What if we made a tribute for all of them?"

Autumn set her glass down. Very carefully. Very delicately.

"Made a tribute for all of who?" Paul asked, his voice slow and cautious.

"The victims of Tragedy on the Tracks."

"Reese."

"Autumn said it's important."

Every last drop of attention swiveled in her direction. Autumn became a deer in the headlights, only instead of headlights, she was facing the full brunt of Paul's stare. She had said it was a beautiful idea, not an important one. And that had been regarding a tribute for Reese's mother, not everyone on the train.

"You said it in that interview," Reese said.

"What interview?" Paul asked.

Autumn knew. She knew exactly what interview. It was the only one she'd done, despite requests from *Good Morning America* and *People* magazine. One small interview for the *Chicago Sun-Times*, because Claire had convinced her that if she didn't do something, the media would hound her for all eternity.

"In the paper," Reese said. "You said it's important that we never forget the victims. That's what you said, but you didn't go to the memorial."

"I didn't want to be a distraction." Autumn looked at Paul, hoping for some kind of rescue. A rope to grab onto. Something that would pull her—pull *them*—up to safety. But he just sat there, a muscle ticking in his jaw. This string of tension that throbbed like a heartbeat.

Reese didn't seem to notice. Or maybe she just didn't care. She leaned forward, her eyes as bright as they'd been when she ran outside earlier this evening. "We could make a tribute together and put it up on YouTube, just like Kay-C Sparks. I bet we could even put it on that website—the one the memorial commission put together."

"Reese."

"All they have up right now are grainy pictures and a lame video of the fountain being constructed. We could contact the families and—"

"That's enough."

"But, Dad, you don't—"

Paul's eyes flashed. "I said, *That's enough.*"

Twelve

Thursday, April 6, 2017

Every day, people make thousands of small,
forgettable decisions. But for a handful
of people on September 11, 2001, those
seemingly inconsequential decisions made
the difference between living and dying.
—Madison Park

Smoking saved Greer Epstein's life.

Smoking.

Had she not gone on a cigarette break that
fateful Tuesday morning, she would have been
sitting in one of the offices that got run
through with an airplane. Had she not gone
on a cigarette break that fateful Tuesday
morning, Greer Epstein would be dead.

I learned this while reading an article titled
"Small Choices, Saved Lives: Near Misses
of 9/11."

There are stories like this that surround
every great tragedy, not just 9/11. The Virginia
Tech shooting. The attacks in Paris. Plane
crashes. Even the awfulness that was Sandy
Hook. Who lived and who died depended
upon the seemingly innocuous chain of events
that led to a person's survival or demise.

What I can't figure out is whether it's random or orchestrated.

When the car battery dies and the person misses their flight and that flight ends up crashing, was it God who killed the battery, or random dumb luck? What about when the commuter takes the seat on the left instead of the seat on the right and the seat on the left happens to be the only survivable seat on the train?

Random? Or orchestrated?

These are the thoughts I can't escape.

After I woke up and had to wrap my mind around all that had happened, I spent an inordinate amount of time trying to remember. Trying to piece together the events of that day, as if all the little decisions and choices would fit together like the jigsaw puzzle on my coffee table. And maybe, if I could get it all to fit, everything might finally make sense.

But every memory of that day is lost.

All I have are the pieces others have given me.

According to Seth, we talked once during his lunch break and again in the afternoon. Brief, inconsequential things, like what he should get Cal for her fourth birthday. According to coworkers, I left work at 5:00 p.m. Odd, since I almost always worked late on Mondays. According to my assistant, Charlene, I hadn't been myself. When she asked if I was okay, I told her I had a head-ache, which could have explained my early departure. But then we enter the missing hours. The phantom hours. The ones I can't remember and nobody else can fill in. I left my work at five, but I didn't board that train until seven, and nobody has any idea what I was doing in the interim.

This is the information I have to work with.

When I asked Claire if she had any pieces to add, she said she sent me several text messages that day, but I never replied to any of them. Not that unusual on a Monday. Then she went on to explain how the night had unfolded for her.

The whole dreadful account.

Finding out the news while she was watching a movie with Trent. The chaos, the confusion, the panic that followed when it was discovered that I'd been on the train. Rushing to Dad's house, where the family huddled together until the phone call came. According to Claire, it was the worst moment of her life. It was also the moment she realized that she would probably marry Trent. According to Claire, he'd folded her up in his arms, as solid as a rock and as comforting as a baby blanket. According to Claire, Seth sat on the couch as white as a sheet with his head in his hands, not saying a word. According to Claire, Dad cried.

I've never seen my father cry.

Not even when Mom died.

And then, hours and hours later, while they were still firmly planted in stage one of the grieving process, another phone call came.

Vivian Elliott was not the survivor.

Autumn Manning was.

Turned out, I wasn't dead after all, but in critical condition at the hospital.

Claire said she'd never felt anything like it—this wave of emotion that washed over her. The shock. The relief. The celebration. According to Claire, it was the first time she really, truly believed in God.

The whole time she talked—the whole time she spilled her guts—a voice in my head had screamed for her to shut up, to close her mouth, to stop speaking words. I didn't want to hear them. The whole time she talked, I imagined the Elliott family.

The chaos. The confusion. The panic. Receiving the news that Vivian was alive. She was the survivor pulled out from the aftermath. The relief. The celebration. And then the cruel twist of fate. The utter despair.

A lot of different nurses cared for me after I came out of my coma. One was a pudgy middle-aged woman named Kelly who said quite casually, while changing my catheter: God must have big plans for you.

Tonight, as I walked home from the most surreal meal of my life, I passed in front of a mulching truck. It was idling in an alleyway, facing the street, and as I walked in front of it, I stopped. I just stood there, imagining the brakes giving out. The truck lurching forward, flattening me against the pavement. I imagined the headlines:

One Year Later: Miracle Survivor Killed in Freak Accident

What would Nurse Kelly have to say about that?

What would a man like Paul Elliott think about her comment to begin with? Didn't God have big plans for Vivian's life? What about the twenty-one others who died that day? Didn't God have plans for them?

It's all so overwhelmingly confusing that I don't want to think about it anymore. I need a distraction. I need a job. I need to complete my assignment for Jeannie True like the good little nonprocrastinator I've always been.

Relations Specialist for Exelon!!

A position that is so up my alley, it deserved two exclamation points.

Except, nothing inside me comes to life at the thought of it.

It's one of the reasons I never returned to my old job at Fishburn & Crandal. After I woke up, it all seemed so pointless. Like a hamster in a spinning wheel. Putting out fires. Covering up scandals. Spinning a story in just the right way. Elvis Costello had it right. What does reputation matter, really, when yesterday's news will always become tomorrow's fish-and-chip paper?

The human attention span only lasts so long.

People forget.

People move on.

Except for me.

And Reese Rosamund Elliott.

I can't stop thinking about the YouTube video she showed me. The photographs in her desk drawer. The way her eyes came to life when she started talking about a tribute. The way they died when her father silenced her. As soon as he did, that thing that had stirred inside me in her bedroom stretched and opened its eyes.

A tribute for the victims.

These people I can't escape. These people who will haunt me forever unless I do this. I will be ninety, hunched over with arthritis, flipping through my binder. Because no matter how hard I try, I can't let them go.

Maybe the only way I will ever lay them to rest is by remembering.

Maybe Reese Rosamund Elliott is onto something.

Thirteen

"Where's your sister?"

Tate had just emerged from the upstairs, and Reese was nowhere in sight. Before answering, he jumped from the fifth step, fell into a roll on the floor, and popped up onto his knees. Paul should have known better than to let him watch *American Ninja Warrior* on Friday. All weekend, he'd been diving and rolling from one place to the other. "I don't know." He crouched low, like he was going to try to pounce onto the armchair a good six feet away.

"Buddy, I'm gonna need you to stop jumping on the furniture. And your shirt is on backward."

"No, it's not."

Paul flipped Tate's collar out and showed him the tag.

Tate gave his forehead an exaggerated smack, then pulled his arms in through the sleeves and started twisting it around.

Paul headed upstairs, where he poked his head inside Reese's room. It was dark and empty—a sight that had his blood pressure climbing. Her runaway stunt from last Monday was still all too fresh in his mind.

"Reese?" he called.

Nothing but the swirl of Tate's ceiling fan across the hall.

Paul quickly checked the bathroom, then his room, just in case. A soft glow came from his walk-in closet. He found Reese sitting inside, cross-legged on the floor with an open box of jewelry in front of her.

Vivian's.

The floor creaked beneath his feet.

If Reese heard him, she gave no indication. She didn't turn or twist around. She didn't even twitch. She just sat there, shoulders slumped, elbow on her knee, cheek resting on her fist as she ran her fingers through a long strand of pearls in the same absentminded way she rubbed Gipper's ear.

She hadn't spoken to him all weekend long.

In fact, she hadn't said a word to him since the nightmare that was dinner on Thursday. He had hoped that inviting Autumn in would somehow help. That hope had completely backfired. As soon as she left, Reese had gone mute. At least, whenever she was in front of him she was mute. He knew her voice still worked, since he'd over-heard her talking with Tate.

Paul checked his watch.

Church would start in twenty minutes. His children hadn't eaten breakfast. Reese was still wearing pajama pants. If they didn't get going right now, they would be impossibly late. But Paul joined her on the floor.

In the early days, right after Vivian died—when his brain was stuffed with fog and every ounce of his energy consumed with the well-being of his children—he hadn't wanted to keep the jewelry. It encompassed too many memories, and they'd all felt sharp and jagged. If it had been only him, he would have packed all of it up and donated it to the nearest Goodwill. But it wasn't only him. There was Reese to consider. He figured that someday she might want some of her mother's jewelry. He never figured that someday she might randomly mail some of that jewelry to a stranger.

The earrings? Her odd suggestion regarding a tribute? Maybe it was all reactionary. Maybe the one-year anniversary had everything rising up to the surface and this was her attempt to grasp at the things that were fading. Maybe if he could find a way to talk about Vivian without losing so much of his breath, Reese would let the other stuff go. Paul picked up a diamond tennis bracelet and turned it over in his palm. "Your mom sure loved this stuff."

She didn't look up, but her ears seemed to perk.

"I got this one for her at a charity auction before you were born." When the house was this brand-new, over-the-top gift that had him working furiously to finish his doctorate so he could start pulling in some income. He hated feeling like a mooch. "The company your mom worked for at the time was one of the corporate sponsors."

His fingers itched with memory. The feel of smooth fabric as he zipped the back of her little black dress. The warmth of her skin and the tickle of her hair as he clasped a choker at the nape of her neck. Right here, in this closet. While she tied his tie, he'd complained a little about the event. *"You know I'm not comfortable with those rich, stuffy types."*

"You just described my father," she'd replied, laughing.

The sound of it echoed through space and time, so crystal and clear he was positive Reese should hear it too.

His daughter, already twelve.

How had that happened? How was the little girl—with messy pigtails and sticky fingers and opinions as high as the sky—already on the cusp of being a teenager? He watched her pour the pearls from one palm to the other, letting them slide and spill over. Back and forth, back and forth. Hypnotizing them both.

"Mia was always obsessed with Mom's jewelry," she said.

Paul sat up a little straighter, hope stirring.

His daughter had just spoken a complete sentence.

"Mrs. Ryan never wears anything but her wedding ring." The pearls went still in her hands. "You took yours off."

He flexed his fingers, suddenly self-conscious.

He didn't remember how long ago it had been. He just knew that he took it off for something, and when it was time to slide it back in place, he couldn't do it.

"Where did you put it?" she whispered.

A loud thud rattled the walls.

There was a hiccup of silence, and then a frantic scream pierced the air. One that had Reese dropping the pearls. Father and daughter tore from the closet, the opened jewelry box abandoned on the closet floor.

When Paul reached Lou Malnati's in Lincoln Square, he was five minutes early for lunch and strung out on caffeine. Margo had gotten one good look at him when he arrived at the office and kept him supplied with coffee throughout all his morning appointments—which had gone well. But Paul was having a hard time appreciating any of it.

He grabbed a booth by the window and placed his and Mitch's order with the waiter—the Malnati Chicago Classic with mushrooms. He probably should have used the wait to call his agent, who had left a second message with his assistant. Instead, he spent the time gazing out the window, watching as people walked back and forth. Some slowly. Most quickly. Some smiling. Most frowning. Some in pairs, but most on their own, looking down at their phones. Each person had a life and goals and relationships and stress and almost certainly, hardship.

It made him feel alone and less alone all at the same time.

At ten past noon, Mitch arrived.

He slid into the booth across from Paul, his eyes pinched in the corners, his mouth tighter than usual. "I'm so sorry I'm late, man. It's been a day."

"It's all right. I went ahead and ordered for us."

Nodding, Mitch grabbed the saltshaker and began volleying it back and forth. This was what Mitch did. He was the kind of guy who needed to keep his hands busy. He squeezed stress balls. He juggled oranges and apples. He twirled writing utensils around his thumb. Today, though, there was an anxious edge to his activity.

"How's the elder situation?" Paul asked.

Mitch shook his head.

Bill Meadows had been an elder at Redeemer for going on ten years, and apparently, trouble was brewing. A couple of weeks ago, his wife, Nancy, resigned from the position as Redeemer's communications consultant with little-to-no warning, sending a rampage of rumors through the congregation. Paul didn't take much stock in gossip, and Mitch was being tactfully vague in order to respect Bill and Nancy's privacy. But he had asked Paul to pray.

"We had to dismiss Bill."

Paul raised his eyebrows. "It was that serious?"

"Unfortunately. I tell you what. Nothing good comes from hiding the ugly."

The waiter dropped off a water for Mitch.

Mitch peeled open his straw and took a long drink, like the whole unpleasant ordeal had left him dehydrated. When he finished, half of his water was gone. "I don't want to think about it anymore, man. It's too depressing. Let's talk about you."

"I spent yesterday in the ER with Tate."

"What?"

"He jumped off the back of the couch and busted his head open."

"Oh no."

"Nine stitches. Thankfully, no concussion." And the emergency had completely obliterated the moment he'd been sharing with Reese in the closet. Tate's immediate physical pain had taken precedence. When they finally got home, Paul tried to get the moment back, but it was hopeless. Reese had retreated into her cave. Late last night, while she was sleeping, he placed Vivian's jewelry box on her desk. She hadn't said anything about it this morning.

"In completely unrelated news, Reese has been writing letters to Autumn Manning."

Mitch stopped spinning the saltshaker. "*The* Autumn Manning?"

Paul nodded. "She ate dinner with us on Thursday."

"What?"

"Apparently, my daughter sent her a pair of Vivian's earrings. Autumn came over to return them, and Reese invited her to join us for lasagna."

"She accepted?"

"I might have put some pressure on her." Paul scrubbed his hands up and down the length of his face. "Reese has been ignoring me. Completely shutting me out. I thought if I invited Autumn in, she might open up."

"Did it work?"

"Nope."

"Wow." Mitch shook his head. "I can't believe Reese has been writing her letters."

"It's like she's developed some sort of fascination."

"Do you think it's because of the mix-up?"

"Probably. I don't know what else it would be." Paul scratched his chin. "Do you think it's crazy if I ask to read them?"

"If it were my daughter, I wouldn't hesitate."

The waiter brought their pizza. He served a slice to Mitch and a slice to Paul—cheese stretching, steam rising—and left them to their meal. Paul's stomach let loose an appreciative grumble. As soon as Mitch finished saying grace, Paul took a bite with his fork and closed his eyes in order to fully enjoy the rich flavor. Lou Malnati's pizza took the edge off most things.

"So," he said as soon as he swallowed, "what

did you want to talk to me about?" They didn't typically meet on Mondays for lunch.

"The marriage campaign," Mitch said.

Paul had expected as much.

It was something that had been in the works for months—a collaboration among several churches in the Chicago area. The idea had been Mitch's brainchild, of course. It was one of the things Paul loved about the guy. He was more passionate about building the church universal than he was about increasing attendance at his particular church in Lakeview.

As part of this passion, Mitch had formed a fellowship of pastors, and every single one in the fellowship was concerned about the escalating divorce rate within their church walls. The idea of a citywide marriage campaign came into being. One that would culminate in a conference led by Paul Elliott.

All of that was *before.*

Before Tragedy on the Tracks.

Before twenty-two Chicagoans lost their lives.

Before the churches in Chicago shifted into crisis intervention mode and the marriage campaign fell by the wayside.

"We're starting to talk about it again. The other pastors wanted to know if . . ." Mitch seemed embarrassed. Uncertain. Like he was Peter step-ping out of the boat, only instead of waves, there was an ocean full of eggshells.

"If I'd do it?"

"I don't want you to feel any pressure. I wasn't even going to ask at all, but every morning for the past two weeks, when I sit down to pray, I get this nudge. Like I'm supposed to check in with you about it."

Paul shoved another bite into his mouth.

"I didn't want to go looking for someone else without talking to you about it first. Just in case God was nudging you too."

"I don't know, Mitch. I'm pretty sure my ministry has run its course."

"Permanently?"

"I'm not married anymore."

Mitch furrowed his brow as though he were chewing over the statement. "I'm a pastor."

"A really good one."

"It's a gift—a passion—that God's planted in my heart."

Paul waited, positive that a moral was right around the corner.

"If something happened, and God forbid, I lost every person in my flock, I'd still be a pastor. All the experience I've been blessed with and the particular wisdom God's given me along with it. It wouldn't just go away because Redeemer did."

Mitch served himself another piece of pizza. "Look, I won't pretend to understand what it would be like if I lost Lisa. All I know is that I've watched you walk this road with courage and integrity. And I've witnessed what a gift you have in speaking truth to husbands and wives. Losing Vivian doesn't mean you have to lose your ministry too."

Paul set his fork on the table. One slice in and he'd lost his appetite.

Fourteen

As soon as Autumn closed her journal, the intercom in her apartment buzzed. Thanks to Roland's complaints, the landlord had fixed it.

It was Claire, most likely.

She was always stopping by unannounced. Even before Autumn woke up in the hospital, she would swing by without calling or texting, a reality that used to drive Seth crazy. *"Hasn't she ever heard of something called advance notice?"*

Autumn would laugh, because back then, Claire wasn't stopping by to check up on her, so it wasn't nearly as irritating. Back then, Autumn had found her impromptu visits as endearing as they were inconvenient. Back then, Claire had been the one seeking advice and Autumn had been the one doling it out.

She uncurled herself from the armchair in her living room to go push the button on the intercom. "Hello?"

"Hey." The deep voice that came through the speaker did not belong to Claire. "It's Paul."

Paul Elliott? What in the world was he doing here?

"Do you mind if I come up?"

Come up? Paul Elliott wanted to *come up?*

Autumn glanced around her home like she might find Reese hiding beneath the end table. Only Reese was nowhere to be found. It was just the notebook on the armchair and the new jigsaw puzzle on the coffee table, along with a cup of lukewarm cinnamon spice tea, and her, wearing pajama bottoms and slippers. At five o'clock at night, which might not be the worst thing if she hadn't been wearing them all day—one of the many benefits of being a virtual assistant. It might not pay the bills as well as a corporate position at Exelon, but she could look like a bum and her boss would be none the wiser.

The intercom crackled. "Hello?"

"Oh, sorry. Come on up."

She pushed the button to let him in and immediately regretted it. She ran her fingers through her hair, throwing it up in a messy bun, then rushed into her room where she kicked off her pajama bottoms and hurriedly stepped into a pair of jeans, trying to figure out why in the world he'd come here. Could it be the tribute? Had he changed his mind?

A knock sounded on her door.

It was him.

When she answered, he looked slightly uncomfortable, but not nearly as disheveled as last time. His hair was wind-tossed but obviously washed and combed at some point earlier in the day. He wore pressed slacks and a nice jacket unzipped over a button-down shirt. Here was a man who lived out in the world and worked out in the world and interacted with actual people out in the world.

"I'm sorry for dropping by unannounced like this," he said. "I would've called, but I don't have your number."

"It's okay."

He removed his hand from his pocket and scratched the back of his neck. "I was wondering if I could read the letters."

The request came so unexpectedly that Autumn had to replay it. He wanted to read the letters? *Reese's* letters? "But they were written to me," she said, more to herself than to him.

"I know."

"So . . . ?"

"I'm her father."

Anger pounced, as swiftly and unexpectedly as Paul's visit. It grabbed her by the throat and squeezed. He was right. He was her father, which meant he should care. He should care that Reese wanted to remember her mother. He should care enough to listen to her idea about a tribute. Instead, his fatherhood gave him license to silence her at the dinner table and intrude upon her privacy.

"Normally I wouldn't ask. I understand confidentiality. It's a big part of my job. But Reese's behavior has been concerning lately. I'd really like to know what's going on inside her head."

The words seemed to cause him physical pain.

And just like that, Autumn's anger washed away. It released her as quickly as it had grabbed on, leaving her limp and slightly cold. This was the man who had raced to the hospital expecting to find his wife, and got her instead. The man who had to sit his children down and tell them that their mother wouldn't be coming home. The whole reason he was concerned right now was steeped in Autumn's survival.

"I'll go get them."

His shoulders sagged with relief. She hadn't noticed how stiff they'd been until all the tension melted away. "Thank you."

Smiling weakly, she walked down the short hallway, opened the door to the closet, pulled down the binder from the top shelf. With a noticeable tremble in her fingers, she removed the letters. Slowly. Painfully. It felt like a betrayal. Reese had meant these for her, and now, she was handing them over to him. She had to remind herself that Reese was a minor and Paul was a concerned father.

She was doing the right thing.

But then he folded the stack in half and tucked it

inside his coat pocket, and Autumn started to panic. He wasn't just going to read them; he was going to take them.

"Thank you," he said once more. "I really appreciate it."

And with that, Paul Elliott started walking away.

Autumn lurched forward in the way someone would when something very precious, very valuable, was being carted away with little-to-no notice. "Are you going to give them back?"

He stopped. Turned.

Her cheeks flooded with warmth. She shouldn't care this deeply about a stack of letters written by a kid. And yet those letters were as valuable to her as the obituaries. Those letters kept her company at night, while the ghosts stood sentry.

Fifteen

Autumn watched a documentary once about an obsessive-compulsive patient who shot himself in the head with a .22 rifle. He survived the shot, but damaged his brain in a way that eliminated his obsessive symptoms. This was an actual, real-life story.

As she sat in Jeannie True's office, watching the betta fish dart around its bowl all over again, it seemed reasonable to conclude that the inverse could occur. When she was blasted from the train, she must have suffered permanent damage to her basal ganglia or her caudate nuclei or whatever structure was responsible for obsession and now she was incapable of being a normal person who could think about something for a bit and move on.

Once her brain grabbed hold of a certain thing, it could not—would not—let it go. Her brain had grabbed hold of Reese's suggestion at the Elliott dinner table, and Paul's impromptu visit on Monday had her brain tightening its grip. Now, when she woke up at three in the morning, instead of distracting herself with Reese's letters, Autumn's mind circled around Kay-C Sparks' YouTube video and the twenty-two people who didn't have one.

"How did you do with our assignment from last week?" Jeannie asked.

"I have an interview tomorrow afternoon."

"An interview." Jeannie smiled. "That's great."

"Do you think I'm wearing an iron mask?"

Her smile melted away. "What do you mean?"

"Last night I read this article by a doctor named Alex Lickerman. He said that at its worst, obsession is an iron mask that permits us to gaze in only one direction at one thing. Or it's like a giant tidal wave that crashes through our minds and washes all other concerns away."

As evidence, take the precarious state of Autumn's financial situation.

Her savings were gone. A person could only sustain herself on a virtual assistant's salary for so long while living in a city like Chicago. As much as she didn't want to get in her car tomorrow and drive downtown for that interview, she didn't have a choice. "If I don't get that job, I won't be able to afford next month's rent."

There it was. Out loud, for all the world to hear.

Or at least, Jeannie True and her betta fish.

"It's a serious situation. I should be really worried. I should be focusing all my mental energy on tomorrow's interview so I get the job and don't get evicted, but instead, I keep thinking about Reese."

"The girl who writes you letters."

Autumn nodded, then went on to tell Jeannie about her increasingly bizarre encounters with the Elliott family. Receiving the earrings when she got home from last week's appointment. Her failed attempt at returning them unnoticed. Reese's odd invitation. Paul's even odder one. Watching the Kay-C Sparks video on YouTube. Reese's idea at the dinner table and Paul's harsh reaction to it. Was it this reaction that left her obsessing the way that she was? If he would have been more supportive of Reese's desire to remember and honor the victims, would she have just eaten the lasagna on her plate and wished them well?

Jeannie listened, completely poker faced, while

Autumn filled the empty space with more words than she knew she had.

"Shouldn't he care that this is important to her? Reese is looking for a way to honor her mother. She wants to do something meaningful. But her dad completely shut her down. I understand why it would make him uncomfortable." Her dad was the same way. He never talked about Mom—not her life, and certainly not her death. Tears burned behind Autumn's eyes. She quickly blinked them away. "But shouldn't he care more about his daughter's well-being than his own discomfort?"

Jeannie lifted her eyebrows.

Autumn wasn't going to let her get away with it. She honestly wanted an answer. So she raised hers right back. "Well? Shouldn't he?"

"I think what's important here is that *you* care."

She did.

She cared deeply.

"Autumn," Jeannie said, "is this tribute important to you?"

Yes.

The tribute *was* important to her. Maybe it always had been—this need she didn't know how to properly express. It wasn't enough to walk with the dead at night. She wanted to walk with them in the day too. She wanted to know them. *Really* know them. More than what could be known from a few blocks of text in an obituary. She needed to bring them back to life. But until Reese had given that need some legs at Vivian Elliott's dinner table, Autumn hadn't known how.

"I think doing the tribute will help me let go."

She braced herself for *the look*. The cloudy-eyed one that always came with a frown whenever a person was worried about someone or disagreed with them, only instead of saying so, they hemmed and hawed and mumbled things like "Are you sure?" and "I don't know." Always under their breath, in a drawn-out, lilting way that screamed disapproval. Leanne did that. Claire too. She probably got it from Leanne, which might be one of the reasons it drove Autumn so crazy.

"If that's what you think, it sounds like a great idea."

Autumn blinked. "Seriously?"

"Seriously."

"You don't think I'm grasping for an excuse to hang on?"

"I thought you just said that it will help you let go."

That was the moment Autumn decided. She really liked Jeannie True. And it was time to take off the iron mask.

Saturday, May 7, 2016

Dear Autumn,
  Do you believe things happen for a reason?

I've heard people say it at least ten times since my mom's funeral. At first, I thought it was from the Bible, but I looked it up on Google and it's actually a quote from Aristotle.

I don't know if people believe it or if they just need something comforting to say and so that's the thing they pick. But if you think about it, it's not really comforting. The reason the Holocaust happened is because Hitler was crazy and hated Jewish people. If I were Jewish, that wouldn't be very comforting.

The reason Benjamin Havel put a bomb on the train is because he got fired from his job and he had a chemical imbalance in his brain. I don't think that's very comforting either.

Maybe Aristotle meant that there's a reason you survived and my mom didn't. Maybe one day you're going to find the cure for cancer, so God saved you instead of her. Or maybe one day you and Seth Ryker will have a baby who will grow up and cure cancer. That's a little bit comforting. I read the article about your engagement.

My mom didn't want any more kids.

She said she had one of each—a girl and a boy. What more could she ask for?

I would have liked a sister. My friend, Mia, has two. An older sister named Skye and a younger sister named Lily. They are all eighteen months apart, and they fight A LOT, but they also get to share clothes and nail polish and do fun things together. Tate's not only a boy, he's in first grade. First-grade boys aren't that much fun to hang out with.

From,

Reese Rosamund Elliott

P.S. Is it okay if I call you Autumn? My dad doesn't like when I call adults by their first name without permission. If you don't want me to call you Autumn, speak now or forever hold your peace.

Sixteen

The throbbing started at the base of her skull. By the time Autumn pulled into a parking space and turned off her car, it had slowly and methodically wrapped itself around her entire head. She sank back against her seat as the engine whirled and ticked, settling into rest. She needed a moment to breathe. But her phone rang. The standard sound almost every iPhone made anytime a call came.

She considered shuffling it to voice mail, but it was Chad, and all she'd done lately was shuffle him to voice mail. Maybe if she answered her phone more often, she wouldn't have run into the problem she had earlier. She scrunched her eyes shut and said hello.

"Hey." His greeting was friendly on the other end. He never gave her a guilt trip for falling off the face of the planet. "Claire told me you had an interview today."

"Did she also tell you that she called me in the middle of it?"

"She left that part out."

Autumn grabbed her purse and climbed out of the car. "Genius that I am, I forgot to turn off my phone, and halfway through, it started blaring 'Pocket Full of Sunshine.' "

"What is 'Pocket Full of Sunshine'?"

"That really obnoxious song from that movie Claire loves—*Easy A*? She programmed it into my phone as her own personal ringtone, and since I couldn't find my phone, it just kept playing on repeat while I dug around inside my bag." Autumn clicked the lock and headed toward her apartment building, the sky above a taciturn gray that perfectly reflected her mood. "I was so flustered after the phone call that I . . . well, the interviewer had this very distinct birthmark on his face and I'm sure you've heard of Freudian slips."

Chad laughed.

"It's not funny." She considered telling him about her financial situation, but if she told Chad, he would tell Jane, and then there'd be more pamphlets. Maybe another intervention. Her financial crisis would just have to stay between her and Jeannie and the betta fish. At least until she got evicted. Then she would have to move into meddlesome Jane's basement.

"Well, if this one doesn't pan out, there will always be the next one."

Autumn said something vague in return. And Chad got to the point of his call, which had to do with Easter this coming Sunday. Jane usually hosted dinner at their house, where the girls searched for plastic, coin-filled eggs out in the yard, but since Jane was so uncomfortably pregnant, they were moving the festivities to Dad and Leanne's.

They said good-bye, and Autumn stuck her apartment key into the front-door lock.

"Hi."

She yelped, her phone clattering to the ground.

It was Reese.

Reese!

She had stepped out from the shadow of a nearby lilac bush.

"I'm sorry," she said. "I didn't mean to scare you."

"It's okay; I just didn't see you." Autumn scooped up her phone and tried to get a handle on the erratic thudding of her heart. "Wh-what are you doing here?"

"I wanted to give you this."

The words had her stomach flip-flopping.

But Reese didn't hand her any more jewelry. With bright eyes, she handed her a sheet of paper —a spreadsheet of e-mail addresses and names. Many of them familiar. Autumn looked up. "Where did you get this?"

"I e-mailed the lady in charge of the memorial commission board. I told her about the Kay-C Sparks video and the tribute."

Autumn's heart responded.

The iron mask.

Bringing the victims back to life.

"She thinks it's a really good idea," Reese said.

Autumn smiled at her.

But then the front door opened, and Roland stepped outside, his hair wild and his chest bare, a cigarette tucked behind his ear and a full trash bag slung over his shoulder. He pushed between them, snapping the invisible cord that had reached out from Reese's soul and wrapped itself around Autumn's. Reese didn't belong to her. She belonged to Paul and Vivian, and one-half of that pair would not approve of this list.

"Does your dad know you're here?"

Reese hooked her thumbs beneath the straps of her backpack and nudged some landscaping pebbles with the toe of her Converse All Stars.

As much as Autumn hated to do it, she handed the paper back.

Reese's cheeks turned as pink as the lilacs behind her.

"I think you should talk about this with your dad first," Autumn said.

"My dad doesn't understand."

"Maybe he would if you talked to him about it."

"He won't. He doesn't listen to me." She kicked a rock and sent it scuttling toward the door, then peeked up at Autumn. "He would listen to you though."

"What?"

"You could talk to him."

"Reese."

"My mom died. I have to do something. I have to remember her." The glow in her eyes turned bright. Feverish. "Can you please help me?"

Frozen rain clung to the branches of budding trees, weighing them down along the length of Belmont Harbor. The surface of Lake Michigan rolled and tumbled with the wind. Last night the weather had been manic. Flip-flopping from rain to sleet to snow, from rain to sleet to snow—every bit of which whipped against Autumn's apartment windows while she lay awake and frustrated. At one point, she gave up on sleep and started searching for jobs online. Until she found one so laughably ironic, she almost threw her laptop into the storm.

Now the weather had mostly settled.

Now she was the manic one, lying in wait for a man who might not come. She knew from one of Reese's letters that Paul went running every Saturday morning along the lake. He used to go with his wife. They would run together while their neighbor, Delilah Green, watched Reese and Tate. Now Reese and Tate were old enough to watch themselves for an hour while Paul ran alone.

Autumn yanked on her shoelace to the blast of Adele's "Rolling in the Deep." She lunged to the left, sinking into a stretch. Her head pounded. Her gut churned. The utter lack of sleep made her jittery, as though she'd guzzled an entire pot of coffee. Her thoughts chased one another, around and around and around. Like a psychotic dog determined to catch its tail.

Reese, standing in front of the lilac bushes.

Reese, handing her the list of names and begging for help, like she was wearing an iron mask too.

And so, after a night of tossing and turning and fitful, anxiety-ridden dreams, Autumn shoved her feet into a pair of running shoes and came here, eyes glued to every single person who passed by.

The clouds began to drizzle—a light, misty rain that slowly soaked through her clothes. Autumn shifted her weight to stretch her opposite leg when a person materialized through the fog.

A man. With brown hair and confident shoulders.

Paul Elliott, running alone. He jogged past, his stride long and sure as he focused on the path, unaware that someone was watching.

Autumn pulled out her earbuds. "Hey!"

He glanced over his shoulder and did a giant double take, confusion flashing across his face as he slowed to an uneasy stop. He grabbed onto the sides of his shirt, fisting the material as he caught his breath and looked around, like maybe this was a practical joke and somebody was secretly filming him from behind a bench.

Autumn closed the gap between them before panic, or sanity, could chase her away. "Hi," she said, trying to sound lighthearted and casual. But it was no good. Whenever she was this nervous—this deliriously sleep-deprived—her tone rarely matched her intention.

Concern scrolled across his face, like she looked as crazy as she felt. "Is everything okay?"

"Yeah. I, um . . . I just saw you running by."

"Sorry I haven't returned the letters. I haven't had a chance to bring them over."

"It's fine. That's not why I'm here."

Paul's brow furrowed.

Autumn's heart skipped a few beats, because those words didn't make sense. Not if she'd just seen him running by. "I mean, that's not what I wanted to talk to you about."

His furrow deepened.

"Reese came to my apartment again."

"What?" Paul wiped sweat—or maybe rain—from his forehead. "When?"

"She stopped by yesterday, after school."

"Was Tate with her?"

"No. I don't think so." Was he supposed to have been? Was Reese supposed to be watching her little brother? Autumn wanted to help, not get her into trouble. She shifted, trying to focus on the task at hand. But she was distracted. How could he go running like this? How could he do this thing he used to do *before* like doing it now was no different? Her head pounded over thoughts that were increasingly disjointed. "She really wants to do a tribute."

A biker whizzed by and the drizzle thickened.

"I was actually talking to my therapist about it, and she thinks it's a good idea."

Raindrops fell on the tips of Paul's eyelashes. His expression had gone from disbelieving to outraged. "No offense," he said, "but I don't care what your therapist says."

"If you just—"

"I'm not going to let my daughter fixate on death."

But she already was. She *was* fixated on death, because her mother had died. Along with twenty-one others who had done nothing but get on a train. Maybe, if she and Reese saw this obsession to its end, they could finally do what Paul and

Claire and everybody else was so eager for them to do—move on.

"It's not healthy for anyone, especially not a twelve-year-old."

"But—"

"No." Paul brought his fingers to his temples and laughed a humorless laugh. "My answer is no." His voice was overly patient. Exaggeratedly calm as he slowly started to back away. "She's not going to do a tribute."

"Well, I am."

He stopped.

"I sent everyone an e-mail last night." In the midst of her insomnia. Reese had insisted she keep the list of names and e-mails, and in a moment of weakness, much like this one now, Autumn had composed an e-mail about a tribute and hit Send. "To the families of the victims. You should find one in your inbox. I think their stories deserve to be told. I think they deserve more than a brick in Lincoln Park."

His face had gone white. Pained. Her words were hot coals, dragging across the surface of his skin. He closed his eyes, probably because he couldn't stand to look at her—a horrible reminder that it should have been Vivian. She should have survived. Then he would be running with his wife, and Reese wouldn't be writing anyone letters. She wouldn't care about remembering her mother, because her mother would be here. Alive, on this bike path. And Autumn would be six feet under, with all the people she spent her nights with.

Something rent loose.

It rose up from the depths of her soul.

A need that burned in her lungs.

"I'm sorry," she blurted.

"Then don't do it. Don't do the tribute."

"No. That's not what I'm sorry about." Locks of hair stuck to the sides of her face. The mist left her lips wet with rain. "I'm sorry it was me. I'm sorry you had to find me in that hospital room. I can't imagine what that was like. I can't imagine how horrible it must have been."

Pain raged in the green of Paul's eyes.

She was rubbing it in. She was making it worse.

But she needed him to say it was okay.

She needed absolution.

"I'm so terribly sorry."

He shook his head, and held up his hands like a man being arrested. "I have to go."

He left her standing there, all alone, as drizzle turned into cold, fat teardrops falling from the sky.

Seventeen

Her throat grew tighter and tighter. It was almost impossible to breathe as her running shoes pounded the pavement, splashing and slurping up rainwater. Autumn ran fast. She was desperate for safety and comfort and solitude. She was desperate not to cry until she reached her apartment. She bit the inside of her cheek and lengthened her stride, ignoring the stitch that had formed beneath her ribs.

Pushing her fist against the pain, she turned up the walkway and found her sister huddled beneath the awning. Autumn swallowed a groan. What was Claire doing here at 8:15 on a Saturday morning? Claire never woke up before 8:15 on a Saturday. She was one of those obnoxious adults who could sleep until twelve if the day gave her permission. And yet here she was, bright eyed and well rested, a stack of magazines tucked under her arm.

"What are you doing here?" Autumn asked, breathing heavily as she stepped out from the rain and retrieved the key from her shoe.

"I was too excited to sleep, and I knew you'd be awake."

Autumn glanced at the magazines in Claire's arm. They weren't just any magazines. They were wedding magazines. Bridal magazines. Her attention slid to Claire's left hand. The bangles on her wrist. Fingernails painted an almost-black purple. And there, in all its sparkling glory, was a beautiful antique ring.

It was like Candy Land all over again, when they played with Grandma Ally. Autumn always managed to get stuck in Molasses Swamp, and she could never seem to draw the right card to get herself going again. Even though she always started out ahead, Claire inevitably passed her by.

The world kept spinning. By nature, people moved forward. Except for her. She was the anomaly, stuck forever in Molasses Swamp. Autumn unlocked the door and let them both in.

"Trent proposed?"

"Last night!"

"Congratulations." Autumn wiped rain and sweat from her brow. Her heart was still pounding. Her throat was still tight. She stopped in front of the elevator and swallowed in an attempt to loosen it.

"You look like you're going to throw up."

Autumn cupped her forehead. She didn't feel well. In fact, she felt like she might faint. Maybe it was the lack of sleep, or the lack of food. Maybe it was both. "I think I need to lie down."

By herself.

But Claire stepped onto the lift with her. Autumn was too zapped to argue. She ignored Claire's prodding stare as the elevator deposited them on the fourth floor. Autumn moved as quickly as possible toward her apartment, her knees shaking. As soon as she got inside, she grabbed a carton of lemonade from the refrigerator and took a long drink, bracing herself against the counter.

Claire flopped the magazines onto the table. "What's wrong with you?"

"Nothing."

"Did you sleep?"

"Does lying in bed with my eyes closed count?"

"Autumn."

"Let's talk about your wedding."

"Autumn, seriously. What's going on?"

She didn't want to talk about it. She didn't want to talk about any of it. Ever. Not to Maud. Not to Jeannie. Certainly not to Claire.

"I don't understand. You seemed to be doing a little better. You were answering your phone more. You were returning my text messages. But all of a sudden, you've gone comatose again."

Autumn took a long drink, directly from the container. It was tart and cold, but not refreshing enough to loosen the muscles in her throat.

"Was it the intervention?"

"Claire."

"I don't know why I let Jane talk me into it. She was just so darn convincing."

"Claire."

"She started showing me that pamphlet and talking about suicide and I don't know. I just freaked out, I guess."

"Claire!"

Claire closed her mouth.

"It wasn't the intervention."

"What was it, then?"

"Paul Elliott!"

There was a moment of stunned silence. Her

sister knew that name. Of course she knew it. Thanks to the whole Lifetime movie mix-up fiasco, the man had made headlines almost as much as Autumn had. The media had treated his horrendous loss like tragic entertainment.

A bubble of hysteria rose in her throat, and with a shuddering breath, words began to tumble forth. "His daughter has been sending me letters. I finally wrote her back a couple of weeks ago, which was the biggest mistake of my life, because she showed up. Here! At my apartment. I had to call Paul, and then he came here, and then she sent me her mother's earrings, and when I returned them, I ended up eating lasagna at their dinner table. I sat in Vivian's chair. Reese wants to do this tribute, and I think it's a good idea, but Paul acts like I'm trying to stab him. And then this morning I hunted him down on the bike path like a psycho."

Autumn set the carton of lemonade on the counter and sank down onto the linoleum. She gulped in a large breath and gave in to the tears that had threatened ever since Paul cut off her apology. "I haven't slept in days, and whenever I do, I dream about Seth or Paul or Benjamin Havel. I'm all out of money, and there's this job opening at that big church a couple of blocks away that really is *right up my alley*, but I can't apply for it because Paul goes there and I can't keep stalking him."

Claire didn't speak. She stood there, processing Autumn's frantic monologue. Then she grabbed a Kleenex box by the toaster and eased onto the floor beside her sister, offering Autumn a tissue.

Autumn used it to mop her eyes.

"You have dreams about Seth?" Claire asked.

"Of everything I just said, *that's* what you're focusing on?"

"I'm sorry. It's just, Trent mentioned the other day that Seth still asks about you. If you're having dreams about him, then—"

"Claire!"

She held up her hands.

More silence.

"Okay," Claire said. "Let's back up. Who is Reese?"

"Paul's daughter."

"She's been writing you letters?"

Autumn nodded, plucking another tissue from the box and blowing her nose. The crying jag had turned the pounding in her head to jackhammers.

"Since when?"

"Since I woke up from the coma."

Claire raised her eyebrows.

Autumn mopped her tears and told her sister everything—every last detail, from the letters, the diamond earrings, and everything else that followed. When she was finished, Claire let out a whistle. "You think making a tribute for the people who died is a good idea?"

"My therapist does."

"Really?"

"She thinks it'll give me closure." Actually, that was a lie. Autumn said it would help her let go, and Jeannie agreed that letting go would be a good thing. Whether or not a tribute would actually accomplish that remained to be seen. "The problem is, I don't know anything about creating a video montage."

"We know somebody who does."

"No."

"Why not?"

"Because I have no right to ask him for anything."

Claire pursed her lips, then flicked a nearby crumb. It tumbled and slid beneath the refrigerator.

"I'm not going to bother Seth," Autumn said.

"I don't think it would bother him."

Autumn shook her head. The last time she had seen Seth, she'd handed him back his engagement ring—the one he slid on her finger a couple of days after she woke up. Another story the media grabbed hold of and wrung out for all it was worth.

Miracle Survivor Gets Happy Ending

Seth had called her ridiculous.

He said she was breaking up with him because

she didn't think she deserved a happy ending. *"But you do,"* he'd said, grabbing her hands. *"You do deserve one."*

And then he cried.

Autumn closed her eyes against the memory, guilt piling itself on top of guilt. Brick by heavy brick. Burying her alive. She wondered if she would ever get out from under it.

Paul sat in his basement office, staring down at the letters Reese had written. He opened the top drawer of his desk and found a small pouch stuffed in the back, behind pencils and pens and staples and Post-it notes.

Inside were two rings.

One titanium, size 11. The other, a princess-cut engagement ring, soldered to a diamond-encrusted band, size 5. The coroner had presumed Vivian wore a wedding ring. He told Paul that the blast of the explosion was so intense, it must have blown the ring off her finger.

But Paul knew the truth.

"Nothing good comes from hiding the ugly."

He pushed a path through his hair and rubbed the back of his neck, his prayer unintelligible—a groaning from the deepest part of his soul. A groaning that matched the wind outside.

Mitch didn't understand. Sometimes people didn't set out to hide anything. Sometimes the walls came up so slowly that they weren't noticed until it was too late. Until the ugly was so wretched and foul that the walls had to stay put.

He pressed the heels of his palms against his eyes, but the events from that horrible weekend came back like rancid bits of memory.

Finding the inappropriate text messages. The sense of betrayal. Whispered, heated arguments behind closed doors. The hurt and the anger. And then numbness. This feeling of being emotionally done. Praying—no, *begging*—for all of it to just go away, but knowing it couldn't. All the while, working hard to hide everything from his children.

On Monday, he went to work.

That evening, he found the note. It was propped on the counter, pitching a tent over something shiny and round. Warmth had drained from his face and pooled in his fingers. He stood there, frozen in place, afraid to move any closer. As though the note might rear back and scream. Alerting his children. Alerting the media. Alerting his fear.

Dear Paul, I love him.
   —V

After everything, she left. She was willing to inflict their children with the same scars he'd grown up with. Only this time, Paul could do something about it. This time, there was too much at stake. Crumpling the note into his fist, he raced out into the storm after her.

An hour later, a train would explode.

First responders would pull one female survivor from the wreckage.

A female thought to be Vivian Elliott.

Paul leaned back in his chair and slid the diamond ring onto his pinky, picturing Autumn's face as she apologized in the rain. The torment. The guilt. He couldn't handle hers. Not when he had his own to bear.

He shut his eyes and for a moment relived the memory that haunted him most. Following a nurse in blue scrubs down a corridor. Walking into a sterile white room. Beeping monitors. The *swish-whoosh, swish-whoosh* of the ventilator. His chair creaking as he sat by her bed. The slow and confusing realization that something wasn't right.

It wasn't Vivian.

For one sliver of a second, he felt the full brunt of the discovery all over again. He felt it as sharply, as keenly, as he had back then. The shock. The confusion. The loss. And also, the relief.

Crushing, debilitating, horrendous relief.

Vivian could no longer ruin anything.

Paul hated himself for even thinking it.

Now Autumn wanted to remember.

She wanted to tell their stories.

But some stories were best left forgotten.

Eighteen

Paul moved his queen three spaces forward.

Pop rubbed his chin and examined the board—a gesture that sounded like peeling Velcro, thanks to his gray whiskers. In all of Paul's years of playing his grandfather in chess, he had yet to win. He'd gotten close a few times but had never uttered the word *checkmate*. That was fine. He didn't play Pop in order to win; he played Pop in order to talk.

That's the way it had always been.

Whenever Paul had something he needed to get off his chest, Pop would set up the game and somehow, through the course of moving pawns and knights around the board, all the stuff bottled inside would find its way out.

Well, Paul had a lot on his chest right now.

Mom must have noticed, because as soon as they arrived for Easter brunch, she ushered Reese and Tate into the kitchen to help her cook and told Paul to relax and get out the chess set. Pop had been wanting to play all weekend.

He wondered if he was really that transparent. If the circles beneath his eyes were really that dark.

If Reese had suffered from sleeplessness last night, she hadn't come into his room looking for

144

help in the midst of it. He'd told her before bed, in no uncertain terms, that she was not to go to Autumn's apartment ever again. That she was supposed to be watching her brother. She'd gone to bed, furious with him.

He, on the other hand, had hardly slept at all.

His mind raced in too many directions. Reese's letters. His run-in with Autumn Manning. This blasted tribute. His desperate hope that it would fizzle and die—that her sudden and unexpected presence in their lives would go away as quickly as it came. And circling over all of it like an opportunistic vulture, the marriage campaign.

He told Mitch his ministry was over. Paul had set it down. Marked it with a big red sign that said Do Not Touch.

But like a little kid who couldn't seem to help himself, Paul kept picking it back up, turning it over in his curious hands. What did it mean, that Mitch felt nudged to speak with Paul every time he prayed about the campaign?

"Losing Vivian doesn't mean you have to lose your ministry too."

Would Mitch still say that if he knew the truth?

A loud cough came out of nowhere, wracking his grandfather's body. He was dressed in a pressed pair of khaki slacks and a carefully ironed short-sleeved white button-down with his standard bow tie. According to Paul's mother, she'd wanted to keep Pop home this morning, but Pop refused to miss church, especially on Easter Sunday. They went to a small Baptist church in Evanston. The same one Mom had taken him and Brandon to when they were wild boys with skinned elbows and grass-stained knees, before Dad left and Pop stepped in to fill the void.

"You okay?" Paul asked.

"The doctor put me on an antibiotic to combat the bronchitis. And your mother put me on a probiotic to combat the antibiotic." Pop wiped his mouth with a tissue and shook his head, like the whole thing was utter nonsense, then moved a pawn one space forward.

Paul had no clue why, but surely his grandfather had his reasons. When it came to chess, Pop saw things Paul never could.

"What do you think about that one on top?" Pop asked, motioning to the stack of brochures beside the chessboard. Each one advertised a different assisted living home. Much to Mom's chagrin, Pop had called several in the area and asked if they wouldn't mind mailing him some information. "I think it looks nice."

"I think it does too. But Mom will never agree to it."

"She's as stubborn as a mule."

"You're not exactly pliable yourself, you know."

Pop chuckled, then doubled over with another coughing fit.

It was hard, watching a man as strong as his grandfather turn old and frail. Growing up, Pop's strong, sure hands could fix anything. A sink. A car. A person. As Paul castled with his right-side rook, he thought about his brother. When their dad took off, leaving behind a couple of hurting boys, Paul turned his brokenness to over-achievement. Brandon turned his to drugs and alcohol. If not for Pop single-handedly pulling Brandon from the black vortex he was spinning into, Paul's brother would be dead in a gutter instead of an ER doctor in Birmingham.

"So, are you going to tell me what's got your brow so furrowed? Something tells me it's not the game, as awful as it's going for you." Pop moved his knight. "Check."

"Mitch asked if I'd consider doing a marriage conference this summer." Paul moved his king one space to the left, out of harm's way. "I told him no."

"Won't even consider it, huh?"

Paul shifted uncomfortably. When he buried his wife, he swore to himself he would bury her secret too. Deep down in the ground where it couldn't hurt anyone, especially his children. There was no point in airing it now. Except he really could use some advice and Pop couldn't give it if he didn't know the context of the situation. He glanced over his shoulder to make sure Reese and Tate and his mother were nowhere in sight, then turned back around and lowered his voice, thankful his grandfather wasn't hard of hearing. "The truth is, my marriage wasn't in a good place when Vivian died."

Wasn't in a good place was hardly the full scope.

Still. He'd said it. The Marriage Doctor was having marital problems.

Now Pop could properly advise him.

"Did you pray about it?"

"What?"

"This marriage conference doodad. Did you pray about it before you gave Mitch an answer?"

Paul clasped his hands between his knees. No, he hadn't.

"Seems like the kind of thing you ought to do before giving answers, doesn't it?"

Paul chuckled a little, then took one of his grandfather's pawns with one of his own. "I don't know, Pop. It sort of seems like I lost the right to speak on the subject. Who am I to stand up in front of a large audience and dole out marital advice when I was having problems of my own?"

Pop moved his bishop. "Checkmate."

And there it was.

His king was officially trapped.

"You know what I think?" Pop said, scratching the whiskers on his chin again. "I think that the second we find ourselves asking 'Who am I?' is the second we become the perfect person for the job."

> The best way to make a decision
> is with a pro/con list.
> —Jane

Pro/Con List: Communications Consultant Position at Redeemer

Pros:

I will be able to avoid public transportation.

I'm well qualified for the job. It's in my field of training.

I'll be able to afford rent, which means I won't have to move into anyone's basement.

Functioning daily in society would be a healthy step in the right direction.

Redeemer is so big that I'll probably never run into Paul or his children.

Con:

It's Vivian's church.

The sand in my hourglass has been slowly running out. Claire thinks I should apply for the position at Redeemer. She thinks the decision is a no-brainer. On paper, it might seem that way. The pros vastly outweigh the cons. But sometimes a con is so big it blows every other pro to dust.

The mix-up at the hospital divided people into two distinct camps: those who celebrated, and those who mourned.

The small number of attendees at Christ the King Presbyterian celebrated.

The gigantic number of attendees at Redeemer mourned.

What sane person applies for a job at a place where they will be nothing but a constant, tangible reminder that sometimes God doesn't answer prayers? And besides, should I really be working at a church as big and loud and on fire for Jesus as Redeemer when the state of my own faith has become so anemic?

Nineteen

The second Cal greeted Autumn with an enthusiastic, "Auntie A, Auntie A, look who's here!" she knew. Cal had always loved Seth—illogically, in that weird way kids sometimes attach themselves to certain people for no conceivable reason. Autumn and Seth had broken up seven months ago, and it was only last month that Cal stopped asking about him. Six months was a long time for a kid her age to hold on to anything.

Claire had been two years older than Cal when Mom died, and she never held on at all.

Sure enough, there he was—in the corner of the

small living room along with Chad and Jane and little Lulu—who was spinning circles in a frothy pink tutu.

Cal wrapped her arms around Seth's legs like he was her favorite uncle. In a different life, he would have been. "He gave me an Easter bunny made out of chocolate!"

Their eyes caught and held.

Autumn's stomach dipped.

"Happy Easter," he said.

"You too," she said back, her mind reeling. What was he doing here? She understood that Easter dinner had turned into a celebratory event, thanks to Claire and Trent's new engagement, but were Trent and Seth really that close?

She gave her sister a questioning look. Claire ignored it as she came in for an excited hug, setting off the usual rounds. Seth was inevitably dragged in, and after seven months apart, the two were out of sync. When he leaned left, Autumn did too. Their noses bumped. She let loose a very high-pitched, unnatural laugh—one that sounded nothing like her. He attempted to kiss her cheek, but she moved in too fast, so he accidentally brushed her earlobe with his lips.

By the time they fell apart, her heart was racing.

"Your hair's longer," he said.

"Yours is shorter."

"I figured it was time to own the receding hairline." He rubbed the top of his head. "Didn't want to turn into one of those old guys with an embarrassing comb-over."

This was Seth, to a T.

He had mastered the art of confident self-deprecation. It was one of the things that had charmed Autumn, back when they were dating.

Claire grabbed Seth's arm, her eyes glowing in the same way Reese's had outside Autumn's apartment when she handed over the list of names and e-mail addresses. "Doesn't he look great?"

Autumn was going to strangle her later.

For now, she forced a smile and nodded lamely, her mouth Sahara Desert dry. He did look great. In fact, the shorter hair suited him. He'd also lost weight. During their two-year courtship, his middle had gone a bit soft—a little pudgy. He must have cut back on the chili fries. Or maybe it was all the racquetball he was playing with Trent.

Seeing him standing there brought every doubt, every second-guess, rising to the surface.

Dad emerged from the kitchen holding a large platter of carved ham.

Cal and Lulu cheered. They loved ham. It was one of the few things they ate without complaining.

At the table, Autumn and Seth were shoved up next to one another. And while everyone shuffled and situated, he leaned in and spoke in a voice only for her. "I take it your sister didn't tell you I was coming."

"No, she didn't."

"I'm sorry."

"It's okay."

"Claire and Trent invited me last night. I said no, but then Claire mentioned something about you wanting to call me and feeling like you couldn't, so I thought . . ." Seth shook his head. "I'm sorry, Autumn. I didn't mean to catch you off guard."

"Really, it's not a big deal." He needed to stop apologizing. She was the one who'd given him the ring back. She was the one who couldn't give him a logical reason as to why. She unfolded her napkin and placed it on her lap, wishing she could block out the sounds of Jane and Leanne gushing over Claire's diamond. From her ears and from Seth's.

She reached for the dish of corn at the same time he did. Their hands grazed. She jerked back so suddenly, she let out another one of those atrocious laughs and her cheeks caught fire.

Seth apologized again.

Her dad caught her eye and shot her a comforting wink as conversation turned from rings to wedding dress shopping.

Leanne wanted to go next weekend. Jane too. When Claire asked Cal and Lulu to be flower girls, Lulu started clapping her pudgy hands so enthusiastically that she spilled her milk. Chad grabbed it lightning quick—the reflexes of a father who was used to things tipping—and

Leanne blotted up the small puddle with her and Dad's napkins.

Autumn kept her feet as tucked beneath her chair as possible so she wouldn't accidentally play footsie with her neighbor—and tried not to think about Mom.

She would have loved to plan a wedding for her youngest daughter.

She also would have realized that doing so in front of Autumn's ex-fiancé wouldn't be the most comfortable thing in the world.

Her throat tied into a knot.

Grief was a funny thing.

People liked to say that time healed all wounds, but it had been twenty years. Twenty years since Autumn had heard her mother's laugh or caught a whiff of her lavender-scented shampoo or felt the gentle stroke of her hand. And yet twenty years later, she had only to catch a scent of lavender and the wound that Mom's death left behind showed itself every bit as open and raw and bleeding as the day they lowered her into the ground.

As she pushed food around her plate, she found herself apologizing all over again. Only this time, she wasn't apologizing to a man on a bike path with tortured eyes. She was apologizing to a ghost—the very first one that haunted her. Her mother should be here for this.

"Autumn?"

She looked up.

Everyone was staring.

Jane had asked her a question.

"Sorry. What was that?"

"Chad was telling me that you had an interview at Exelon."

"Oh, right." She swirled some corn into her potatoes. "It didn't go so well."

"That's okay," Claire said. "She's going to apply for a job at Redeemer."

"That is still undecided," Autumn said, glaring at her sister.

"Redeemer is that big church in Lakeview, right?" Jane sat up a little straighter. "We've been trying to find a good one for the girls. We keep hearing wonderful things about their Awana program."

"I have a buddy from narcotics who goes to Redeemer," Dad said.

Officers in narcotics usually had dogs, which made Autumn think about Tate.

"So, Seth," Claire said, serving herself another piece of ham, "what have you been up to?"

It was a question Claire already knew the answer to.

"Nothing too exciting. Work, mostly. I'm free-lancing full time now."

"And doing really well, from what Trent says." Claire looked more at Autumn than Seth when she said this, as if the news about his successful freelancing career should make her want to jump him at the dinner table. "You know, Autumn was talking to me about this video tribute she wanted to put together."

Once, when Claire was eight, she drew all over Autumn's favorite shirt with permanent marker. Autumn had been so furious that she'd been in tears. Grandma Ally told her that one day she would love having a sister. Grandma Ally, may she rest in peace, couldn't have been more wrong.

"A tribute for what?" Chad asked.

"The victims of Tragedy on the Tracks." Claire must have noticed the worried looks that immediately began volleying across the table because she rushed on to clarify. "Her therapist thinks it's a good idea. Something about bringing her closure."

"You're seeing a therapist?" The question belonged to Seth; it was soaked in hope.

"She's going to need help putting the video together," Claire said.

Autumn let her fork drop to her plate.

It clattered loudly.

"I can help," Seth said.

"No, really. I don't want to inconvenience you."

"It wouldn't be an inconvenience. Not if this is something that could help you." His eyes were every bit as infused with hope as his voice. She could tell what he was thinking. Looking for a job. Seeing a therapist. Maybe she was finally getting better. Maybe this meant she was emerging from whatever existential fog she'd been living in for the past year and he could give her back the ring.

Everybody was staring. Waiting for Autumn to respond.

She couldn't say no. She couldn't reject him again, not in front of her family. And if she was honest, she needed help. Four people had already responded to her sleep-deprived e-mail, and all four were in favor of the tribute. She couldn't do this on her own, and Seth was superbly talented. "Are you sure you don't mind?"

"Not at all."

Leanne beamed at them both. "I think it's great you're getting some closure. Speaking of which, Tom has an announcement."

All eyes turned to Autumn's father.

He looked pale.

Autumn shared an uneasy look with Chad. Was their father sick?

Dad cleared his throat. "I'm retiring."

The announcement was so shocking, Autumn forgot about her anger. She and Claire and Chad all exchanged unspoken concern—unsure what they should offer. Congratulations or condolences?

She tried to picture her dad without his badge, but it was impossible. His badge was as much a part of him as his callused hands and his deep and abiding love of the White Sox. He never took time off, not even after Mom died. Apparently the city had needed him more than his grieving children.

His solution for that had been Leanne. Fill the empty space their mother left behind as quickly as possible, then pretend nothing bad had happened.

"This is a very good thing," Leanne said, placing her hand over Dad's. "It was time."

Dad nodded and for a second seemed to lose himself in her eyes.

Autumn wondered if he'd ever looked at Mom that way. If he had, she couldn't remember it.

Twenty

Sunglasses swallowed Autumn's face as she sat on a bench, her back to the bridal boutique's front glass window—arms crossed, legs crossed—like she was trying to hold herself together. As discreetly as possible, she people-watched the window shoppers—smiling, laughing, twirling bags and talking.

Nobody stared at her.

Nobody even noticed her.

Proof that she was paranoid.

The sun peeked out from behind a wall of clouds and reflected off a puddle that had formed, thanks to a brief rain an hour or two earlier. Seth had called, wanting more information about the tribute. Autumn still couldn't believe she was (1) actually doing it and (2) letting Seth help her. She'd spent the week responding to e-mails from family members of the victims, her stomach tied in knots with every typed word. So far, nobody had told her where she could go.

"Autumn!"

Claire waved from the middle of a nearby crosswalk, an oversized purse slung over her forearm, the sun outlining the unnatural mahogany shade of her hair. She and Leanne approached arm in arm, looking very much alike.

Autumn stood.

Black dots danced in the periphery of her vision. She closed her eyes and waited for the dizziness to pass.

"Are you okay?" Leanne asked, taking her elbow.

"I'm fine. I just stood up too fast."

"Are you eating? You hardly ate anything at dinner last Sunday."

"That's because I didn't have much of an appetite." Autumn glared at her sister. Maybe she would have forgiven her by now had Claire bothered to apologize.

Claire rolled her eyes. "I know, I know. It was *awful* of me to invite Seth."

"Girls," Leanne warned, like they were little kids bickering over a Barbie doll.

Claire didn't listen. "You're the one who said you needed help with the tribute."

"I'm also the one who said I wasn't going to ask Seth for help."

"Well, I asked him for you. Now you can make your video and get the closure you need."

She said it so flippantly. Like getting closure was as simple as following a few steps. Like a traumatic event as huge in scope as the one she'd lived through was something a person could ever get closure from. There was no point in getting into this with Claire when she didn't understand. There was no point trying to explain her anger when her sister honestly didn't think she'd done anything wrong. "Where's Jane?"

"She said she had an upset stomach," Leanne said.

"She's gonna have that baby early," Claire added.

"A grandson." Leanne folded her hands beneath her chin, a dreamy-eyed expression taking over her face.

"One they will name Mustafa. And call him Musty."

Autumn snorted.

Leanne tsked. "You two are incorrigible."

With that, they filed inside the boutique, where hundreds of white gowns glittered back at them. Leanne gave her hands an excited clap and flitted off to a nearby rack, as though she'd already zeroed in on the perfect dress. Autumn had to swallow a moan. This was the last thing she felt like doing.

"C'mon," Claire said, grabbing her elbow. "As my maid of honor, you're obligated to get into this."

"I'm your maid of honor?"

"Obviously."

Autumn didn't find it so obvious. Claire had a wide array of friends. Unlike Autumn, Claire was a social butterfly.

"You're my sister." She said it in a way that implied she wasn't just her sister, but her *dumb* sister.

"You haven't asked me."

"I didn't think I had to."

Autumn narrowed her eyes. "Who's the best man?"

"Don't worry. It's Trent's brother, not Seth. But he is going to be in the wedding. Is that okay with you?" Sarcasm dripped from every word.

She wasn't really asking, so Autumn didn't feel the need to answer.

Claire brushed her fingers along the dress on display in the window. She tapped her bottom lip with her fingernail and moved her hand along the hem of the skirt. After a moment, she turned away. "Do you think we should throw him a party?"

"Seth?"

"No, not Seth. Dad."

Claire was doing that thing she did. Where she expected whomever she was talking with to follow along, even though whatever she'd just said had nothing to do with the conversation at hand and everything to do with whatever rabbit trail her mind had hopped down.

"For his retirement," she said.

"Oh, that."

Claire's phone let out a ring from inside her purse. She dug it out and looked at the screen. "Ugh, I have to get this. Roommate drama." She hit Talk and pressed the phone against her ear. "Hello?"

Autumn stood there, surrounded by white tulle, watching her sister.

"Are you serious?" Claire turned away sharply, pivoting decidedly on her heels. "I thought you said you were going to break up with him?"

Leanne caught Autumn's eye over a rack as Claire pushed her way outside. She paced in front of the window, using her hands as she talked. Claire was a hand talker, especially when she got worked up about something. Whatever was going on, it wasn't good.

"What's wrong?" Leanne asked when Claire had stalked back inside.

"Rachel's boyfriend is moving in. He's moving in!" Claire covered her face and shook her head. "I cannot live there with them. He's such a bully. You should hear the way he talks to her. You should see the way he treats her. And he doesn't *do* anything. He doesn't have a job. He just sits around all day like a bum."

Autumn's face went warm. She sort of did the same thing.

"He is the laziest, meanest . . ." Claire released

a frustrated growl. "This is the worst possible timing. Why couldn't she just have waited six months? Six months and I'd be married and moving in with Trent. Where am I going to find a place to live for six months?"

As soon as the question popped out, Autumn could see the lightbulb going off in her sister's head. It was like a literal light sparked to life as she turned puppy-dog eyes in her direction.

Autumn held up her hands. "I only have one bedroom."

"We grew up sharing a room. It will be like old times."

"But . . ." But what? She needed her own space so she could obsess in privacy, without Claire's constant judgment? Autumn could hardly say that out loud.

"If you think about it, it's kind of perfect. I can help with rent. This will give you time to get a job, sort out your finances. Come on, Autumn. It's only for six months."

Six months.

She looked at her kid sister. The one who drove her crazy half the time. As much as she wanted to say no, that Claire would just have to tough it out with Rachel and her lazy boyfriend, she couldn't. Just like she could never tell Claire to go away when she would drop by on her and Seth unexpectedly. Apparently, her old self was still alive and kicking.

Tuesday, April 25, 2017

Claire moved in today. Heaven help me.

Monday, May 1, 2017

> It happens because our beliefs
> influence our actions.
> —Jeannie True, after I asked her about
> the self-fulfilling prophecy

I believed that the e-mail I sent about the tribute would go ignored.

Almost everyone has responded.

I believed Claire and I would be at each other's throats two days into our new living arrangement.

So far, it's been strangely okay.

I believed some sort of blaring siren would sound the second I submitted my online application for the position at Redeemer. I waited for a scathing reply—something like, "How dare you, of all people, submit an application to this church when we are still mourning the death of Vivian Elliott."

Instead, I was called in for an interview.

I believed it would go as badly as the one at Exelon.

It went surprisingly well.

I sat across a table from Mitch—the head

pastor—and a white-haired grandfatherly man named Ferguson. They started things off with a prayer, entirely different from my experience at Exelon. Entirely different from my experience with any job. While I was definitely nervous, my phone didn't ring once. And there were no embarrassing Freudian slips.

I don't think I believed in the self-fulfilling prophecy.

As soon as I walked out into the afternoon sunlight, that strange feeling of peace dogging my steps, Dad called. Jane had the baby. Two weeks early, as Claire predicted. A perfectly healthy seven-pound, seven-ounce, nineteen-inch-long little boy. They weren't sharing the name until we got there.

All of us went to the hospital to meet our newest family member.

He had a head full of thick, dark hair and a squished red face that reminded me of Elmer Fudd—exactly the same as Cal and Lulu had looked as newborns.

"So . . ." Claire said, taking the tiny infant from Chad. "What's his name?"

I waited for something as strange-sounding as Calliope and Talulah had sounded the first time I heard them.

Jane beamed, the quintessential love-struck mother. "Isaac."

I won't lie, Maud. It felt a little anticlimactic.

Twenty-One

Paul pulled two pieces of whole-wheat bread from the bag, scattering a host of crumbs on the counter, and unwrapped a piece of cheese to make Tate's lunch, since he didn't want hot and he was definitely not old enough to pack his own. A lesson Paul had learned on Monday, when Tate threw two packages of Pop-Tarts in a sack and called it a day. Paul had no idea until later, when he was going through Tate's school bag and found the wrappers, along with a crushed carton of chocolate milk and an abysmal spelling test. Mrs. Cranswick had not put any stickers—Star Wars or otherwise—on the top of the sheet. But she had jotted a note, asking Paul to call at his earliest convenience.

Tate had a particularly rough afternoon.

Maybe the timing was coincidental. Or maybe Tate's behavior was directly related to his consumption of nothing but sugar and processed flour for lunch.

Either way, Paul wasn't going to let it happen again.

He pulled the turkey meat from its container and gave the mustard bottle a good, hard shake. "Tate, turn off the TV and go brush your teeth," he called into the living room.

"I'm watching my favorite show!"

"I don't care. We're running late!" He waited, ears perked, until the cartoon went silent.

Reese sat at the dining table, eating a bowl of Rice Krispies with a cut-up banana on top, reading the newspaper. This was a new thing she did, thanks to a current events assignment at school. His subscription for the *Tribune* was finally being utilized.

"Hey," she said.

Paul stopped his mustard squirting and looked into the dining area, where his daughter held the newspaper aloft in the air.

"What's up?" he asked.

"She's doing it."

"Who's doing what?"

Reese poked her finger at the page. Not at a headline story, but a smaller article in the local section, one most people would skip right over. "Autumn Manning is doing the tribute."

The muscles in his stomach went tight and cold.

The same way they had when Mitch told him they were calling Autumn in for an interview for the position at Redeemer. It had come like a giant wallop. He wanted her out of his life, and now she was applying for a job at his church? Mitch apologized and admitted that it was strange, but he was desperate to fill the role Bill's wife left behind, and Autumn was the first promising applicant.

All last week the kids had been on spring break, and Paul had braced himself, positive she would pop back into their lives again. He was sure Reese would find a way to pull Autumn back in, as his daughter had plenty of free time to plot. But Mom had planned all sorts of fun things for the kids, and Reese was very absorbed in this new story she was writing, and then school resumed and she'd gotten equally absorbed in the current events project.

Paul naively assumed he'd dodged a bullet.

They had hit a rough patch with the one-year anniversary, which was somewhat expected. But they were finally moving forward.

Now this.

Reese stuck her thumbnail between her teeth and read with an intensity that left his chest every bit as tight as his stomach.

He glanced at the clock. If they didn't get out the door in the next five minutes, he would be late for his first appointment. "Hey, Reese, why don't you grab your backpack, then check on Tate. Make sure he's brushing his teeth."

"I'm reading the paper."

"It'll have to wait until after school, kid."

He waited for Reese to argue. Complain.

She did a lot of both lately.

Instead, she let out an exaggerated sigh, then pushed away from the table and marched upstairs.

Paul stared for a beat at the abandoned paper.

And then, without overthinking, he tore out the local section, crumpled it into a ball, and stuffed it inside the trash compactor. Out of sight, out of mind. It probably wouldn't work, but on the off chance it might, he had to try. He didn't want Reese stewing over this tribute or the woman in charge of it. Aside from the Pop-Tarts fiasco and the disconcerting news about Autumn's interview, the last two weeks had been blessedly uneventful.

Except, of course, the sleeplessness that visited at night.

Reese.

And himself.

Usually, he found himself lying in bed, thinking about Mitch's proposition, Pop's advice, and whether or not they'd found anyone to take over the marriage conference. So far, Paul hadn't asked. He secretly hoped his friend would broach the topic again, explain that the God-nudges hadn't stopped. Paul wanted a clear, undeniable sign to point him in the right direction. Instead, all he had was a confusing, guilt-riddled sense of longing that was impossible to tease apart. He missed teaching at conferences. He missed standing behind the podium. But was that a sign?

He quickly finished Tate's sandwich, threw in a low-sugar juice box, some pretzels, and some carrots.

Reese poked her head into the kitchen. "I need a binder clip."

"Is Tate brushing his teeth?"

"Yes. Do we have one?"

"They should be in a bowl on top of my desk."

She hurried down the stairs as Tate walked into the kitchen, his shoes unlaced on his feet, his curly blond hair sticking up in every single direction. Paul should probably wet it. At the very least, attempt to tame it. But they didn't have time. And while Tate had gotten his stitches out and was more than on the mend, he was still very sensitive whenever Paul touched his head.

"Tie your shoes, bud."

"I don't know how."

"Tate, you know how to tie your shoes."

"No I don't." To prove his point, he crouched over and made a pathetic attempt with the laces, his entire body tensing with visible frustration. He hated shoe-tying almost as much as he hated school.

"Reese!" Paul called down the stairs, bending over to tie his seven-year-old son's shoes. It wasn't good parenting. He should teach Tate to fish instead of handing him fish. But right now, he didn't have time for fishing. It seemed like he never had time for anything. "Reese, let's go!"

Nothing.

He pulled tight on the double-knots, then patted Tate's leg. "Go grab your jacket. It's chilly out this morning. Reese, come on!"

"Maybe she ran away again," Tate said.

Paul waited a second, then two.

No response from his daughter.

With a mounting sense of frustration, because the five minutes had passed and he loathed being late for his clients, Paul hurried down the steps. "What's going on down here? We're running late."

He stopped short in the doorway of his office.

Reese was sitting at his desk. And she was holding a stack of letters.

Her letters.

The letters she'd sent to Autumn. The ones that tied his stomach into a thousand concerning knots. He'd stuffed them in his bottom drawer. The binder clips weren't in his bottom drawer. "What are you doing?"

She looked up at him, her face white. Not sick-white, but furious-white. She held the stack in the air, her eyes wild with fury. "Why do you have these?"

Paul didn't know what to say.

"I didn't write them to you," she said.

"I know."

"Then why are they here?"

He took a step into the room, holding his hands up in that way a person would if they were facing a deranged person with a gun. "I went to her apartment and asked if I could have them."

Reese's fury bulged. "When?"

"I don't know. A few weeks ago."

"Why would you do that?"

Paul took another step, holding his hands up higher.

"These aren't any of your business! I wrote these to her!" She tore them in half, then in fourths. When her destruction was complete, she whipped the pieces into the air like mad confetti and tried to run out of the room.

Paul stepped in front of her.

She pushed at him.

He took her wrist gently. "Reese."

"You had no right to read them!" She tugged away from his hold, then pushed him again, her eyes pooling with tears.

Paul pulled his daughter close.

She squirmed and she flailed, but he wrapped her in a hug.

"Let me go!" she screamed.

He didn't. He held on tight while Reese beat at his arms. He held on tight until his daughter stopped yelling. Until she went limp like a rag doll, her shoulders shaking with defeated tears.

His own throat clogged with emotion.

Paul swallowed it down. "You have every right to be mad. But I love you. And I'm worried about you. You're barely speaking to me. You refuse to tell me what's going on. I'm your father." He pressed his hand to his chest, where her tears had soaked through his shirt. "It's my job to know. I'm not going to let you shut me out."

"If you loved me," she said, in a broken whisper,

"if you cared about me, then you'd let me do the tribute with Autumn."

"Reese."

"It was *my* idea. I'm the one who came up with it." She sniffed, then wiped her hand across her face. "*Please,* Dad, I want to help her."

As soon as Autumn saw her name in newsprint, her hands started shaking. She skimmed the words, not processing anything but a few select phrases.

Tragedy on the Tracks . . . Miracle survivor . . . Commemorating the death.

She picked up her phone and dialed Seth.

He answered halfway through the second ring.

"You promised you weren't going to say anything to the media."

"Well, good morning to you too," he said.

Autumn pressed her lips together. Thanks to Seth's previous jobs, he was friends with a handful of reporters around the Chicago area. "Have you seen the paper this morning?"

"Yes. I'm reading it now, in fact."

"Have you seen the article about the tribute?" Autumn snatched up Claire's bowl of milk and a few uneaten Cheerios from the table.

"Yes, I have."

She dropped the bowl into the sink. "Seth, I specifically asked you not to say anything."

"And I specifically listened. A lot of people know about the tribute. It was probably a family member, excited about the project." There was a long sigh on the other end. "Autumn, did you read the article?"

"Yes!"

"Thoroughly?"

She twisted her lips to the side.

"It's a well-written piece."

She picked at the cuticle on her thumb and began skimming the article again. At second glance, she could see Seth's point. It wasn't so much a media circus as it was a respectable exposé about a project that not only meant something to her, but was starting to mean something to others as well.

"We want people to know about this, right?" Seth's voice was patient and kind. It was more than she deserved. "We want people to watch the video. Otherwise, why are we doing this?"

Her shoulders deflated. "I'm sorry," she said.

"It's okay."

No, it wasn't.

Seth was going out of his way to help her without any compensation. And here she was, unleashing her crazy. Seeing her name in the newspaper was apparently some sort of trauma trigger. She'd read an article about them once, a few months ago.

The second she saw her name, her heart started

to race. It went from zero to sixty in no time at all. Before she'd given the article a coherent read, before the reasoning part of her brain had a chance to see that while the article *mentioned* her, it was by no means *focused* on her, she called her ex-fiancé and started tossing around accusations.

"Maybe I should start popping valium before I read the news."

Seth chuckled.

She wasn't joking.

"I'll see you tomorrow," he said.

For their first interview. With Ina May Huett.

And then, on Monday morning, she would have a second interview at Redeemer, this time, with the entire elder board.

She couldn't decide which interview made her more anxious.

Twenty-Two

Ina May Huett was an elderly black woman with a hunched back and white hair and hands that smelled of cocoa butter. She lived in a squat little duplex with peeling paint and weeds that had overrun the flower beds, giving it the same run-down appearance as every other duplex on this particular block.

Inside, Autumn Manning sat straight-backed on a sagging tartan armchair while Ina May fixed tea in the kitchen. The small living room had worn carpet and flower-patterned wallpaper and a curio cabinet that displayed a diverse assortment of cat decor. The air smelled musty, like the windows hadn't been opened in years, and on a chipped end table stood a framed photograph of her husband who had died. Autumn recognized him from his obituary picture. Lazarus Huett, bouncing a drooling baby on his knee. Wearing a mesh green John Deere hat. The sight of which—for one split, unreasonable second—made Autumn want to flee.

A bird popped out of the cuckoo clock on the wall.

She jumped as its mechanical head pivoted about. Seth should have been here by now with his camera equipment, filling up the space with small talk. Seth was the king of small talk. He could talk to a person for hours without really talking about anything at all. It was an impressive skill. One Autumn didn't have.

Especially not with her thoughts so distracted.

When she sat in Jeannie True's office, talking about doing this, she hadn't thought through the actuality of it. Sitting inside a home that belonged to one of the victims, feeling his presence like a ghost behind her. She said it would bring her closure, when at the moment, it was just making her dizzy.

Ina May pushed through the swinging door holding a silver tray, complete with a porcelain teapot, three teacups sitting atop saucers, and a matching creamer and sugar bowl. The saucers rattled as the old woman took slow, deliberate steps toward the coffee table. Autumn came out of her seat and took the tray, then set it carefully on the glass-topped table.

"Do you take cream and sugar?"

"Neither, thanks," Autumn said.

The old woman eased onto a matching tartan sofa—equally saggy—and got to work spreading apart the three saucers and pouring the steaming tea into each of the cups, every movement creaking with age and time.

Autumn sat back down in her chair, her underarms clammy. She scratched her shoulder. Then her cheek. Then her neck. Not only was the living room musty, it smelled like cats. Autumn was allergic to cats—something Claire had held against her ever since Leanne married Dad and had to give her Persian fur ball to the neighbors. Was it the cat allergy making her breathing more difficult?

"I think this tribute is a lovely idea," Ina May said.

"Thank you. I'm sorry that my . . . the camera guy isn't here yet."

"Oh, I don't mind. It's nice having company."

A floorboard creaked behind her.

Autumn looked over her shoulder, her heart beating too fast for the occasion.

"Will we be able to watch it?" Ina May asked.

"Sorry?"

"When it's done. I assume you'll be showing the video somewhere."

"Oh." Autumn wiped her hands on the armrests. "I'm planning to upload it to YouTube."

"You-What?"

"YouTube. It's an online video site."

Ina May's already-wrinkled brow furrowed with a troubled V.

"It'll also be on the memorial website."

"Don't you think it'd be nice if we could all watch it together? We could have a reception, with coffee and tea and cake."

"That would be nice."

The old woman nodded matter-of-factly, then handed Autumn a cup and saucer.

Autumn took it, disoriented. She wasn't planning on organizing a reception. That wasn't currently on the horizon. Her attention returned to the framed photograph. The old man's twinkling eyes. And that hat. Why did a shiver race up her spine at the sight of it?

"Laz loved himself some babies."

"Is that your grandchild?"

"Heavens, no. The Lord didn't give us any children of our own." Ina dropped a lump of sugar into her cup using a pair of small metal tongs. "That there is Cora Brown's granddaughter. Cora and I used to sing in the church choir together."

"Oh."

Ina May stirred her tea while ribbons of steam curled into the air. "My husband sure loved his tea. After he retired, we shared a cup every single morning. It was one of my favorite parts of the day."

Autumn pressed the saucer against her knees. "You were married for sixty-five years."

The old woman's eyes brightened. "He started courting me two months after my fifteenth birthday. Three days after the United States dropped an atomic bomb on Nagasaki. Seems foolish to be falling in love in the middle of so much ugly. But that's love for ya. It rarely comes at the right time."

Autumn nodded, like she understood.

"My daddy was a serious man. He sat Lazarus down that first date and said, 'Young man, what are your intentions with my daughter?' And Laz looked my father straight in the eye and said, 'I plan on marrying her, sir.' Hoo boy, we were babies. Of course, we didn't think we were babies." Her face split with another grin. And then she plucked a tissue from a nearby box and dabbed her eyes. "You never realize how young you are until you get old."

Autumn shifted uncomfortably.

"If Laz were here, he'd wag his finger at me and say, 'Ina Girl, I'm livin' it up with my King. Quit that blubbering and be happy for me, will ya?' " She crumpled the tissue and pressed her hands together in her lap. "Even after all this time, I still feel like I'm missing half my thoughts."

"I'm sorry."

Ina May waved the tissue at her, like Autumn didn't need to apologize. But she did. She needed to apologize because she was sitting there in that saggy armchair when Lazarus Huett was dead in the ground.

"Dying is just part of living, honey," Ina said.

"The way he died shouldn't be."

She conceded Autumn's point with a nod, then took a sip of tea. "For now we see in a mirror dimly."

"What's that?"

"It's a verse. From First Corinthians. Life is hard, and almost always confusing. But one day we'll see clearly. One day it'll all make sense."

Autumn wanted to believe Ina May's words. She so desperately wanted to believe them. But what if they weren't true? What if Ina May's words were nothing more than the hope of an old, lonely woman trying to make sense out of all the pain? What if in the end the pieces just didn't fit?

Ina May set her teacup on the table. "Do you remember him?"

The question came like an unexpected slap to her face.

"Did you see him that day, on the train?"

"I'm sorry," she said. "I don't remember anything from that day."

It wasn't fair.

Not only had Autumn survived, she couldn't even give the people left behind a final moment. She couldn't offer any consoling words like "He was laughing with someone." Or "He was smiling at the snow." Autumn wouldn't know, because Autumn couldn't remember.

Maybe it was for the best.

In reality, it was unlikely that anybody was laughing. In reality, most people were probably grumbling about a March blizzard or staring mindlessly down at their phones, because who had time to converse with a fellow human being when there was a newsfeed to scroll through?

It's how Autumn rode the train—when she used to ride it.

"I didn't figure you would." Ina May shooed her hand in the air again. "Enough about me. Tell me, what do you do?"

"Nothing."

The answer popped out in all its incriminating truth.

Autumn Manning—miracle survivor—did absolutely nothing.

Her attention slid again to the picture of Lazarus and the hat, a deep and abiding shame rising in her cheeks.

Twenty-Three

At some point over the weekend, the job at Redeemer had become immensely important. If she got it, the next time Autumn sat down with a spouse or a child or a parent or a friend of a victim from Tragedy on the Tracks and they asked what she did, she would have a better answer.

And so, when Autumn walked into the room where Pastor Mitch and the entire elder board waited for her, she swallowed every one of her nerves, gave each man a firm handshake, and put on the performance of her life.

When it was over and she was walking down the hallway toward the front exit, she felt something she hadn't felt in a long time—a thrill of accomplishment.

A girlish laugh greeted her as soon as she stepped into the office lobby. It belonged to the same woman who had welcomed Autumn on her way in—a blond, bright-eyed, perky girl who barely looked old enough for high school but was in college. Autumn knew because of a Moody Bible Institute coffee mug. It had been sitting on the welcome desk, by the girl's hand, and when Autumn asked if that's where she wanted to go, the girl had laughed and said she just finished her third year.

Currently, a man was leaning his elbow against that same desk, one leg crossed in front of the other, and judging by the starry-eyed way the young woman looked up at the man, he was probably cute.

Autumn lifted her hand in a polite, nonintrusive wave and was just about to let herself out when the change of angle had her pausing. There was something recognizable about the man's shoulders. For she had set her sights on them three weeks ago on Lakefront Trail.

The young, enamored receptionist was chatting with Paul Elliott.

Autumn's breath caught in her throat. She couldn't let him see her. He would think she was stalking him again. She ducked toward the door, but before she could slip away unnoticed, the receptionist returned Autumn's wave, and Paul turned around.

She cringed, expecting his eyes to widen. His countenance to darken.

But Paul didn't look surprised at all.

Brooding? Yes.

Shocked? No.

"Hi," he said.

"What are you doing here?" she replied, cringing all over again at the note of accusation weaving around her words. This was Paul's church. *She* was the intruder.

"I needed to talk to Mitch. He mentioned

something about you coming here for a second interview." Paul pulled a plastic bag off the top of the desk and held it in his hand. "Do you mind if we talk for a second?"

Autumn's confusion multiplied. "Um, sure."

He said good-bye to the young woman and led the way out of the office lobby into the bigger church lobby—the one everybody congregated in before and after weekend services.

Paul glanced over his shoulder, as if to make sure they weren't being watched or followed. His eyes were strained. The muscles around his mouth —tight. For one illogical second, she imagined him pulling out a gun. For one illogical second, she envisioned the headlines.

Tragedy on the Tracks Widower Snaps: Miracle Survivor Shot Dead

"I'm sorry," she said. "I saw the job opening, and it's so close to my apartment. I wasn't going to apply because, well . . . My sister convinced me that I needed to try. I'm really sorry." Her face was officially on fire. She needed to stop apologizing to this man. He obviously didn't want to hear it. He made that clear on the bike path.

"Autumn, it's fine. I didn't come here to give you a hard time." He pulled a package of Tootsie Pops from his bag and handed it to her. "For your recovery."

Autumn took them. "From what?"

"The interview. They can be pretty nerve-racking."

She turned the package over in her hand, disproportionately touched by the gesture. He had remembered her passing, forgettable comment about candy.

"Reese found your letters."

"What?"

"I was going to return them, but she tore them up."

Autumn blanched, imagining the scene. Reese Rosamund Elliott stumbling upon the familiar lined paper, recognizing her own handwriting. The confusion she must have felt as she riffled through them, the sense of rising betrayal.

"You did the right thing," he said, as though reading her mind. "I needed to know what she wrote."

"She must hate me."

"She doesn't hate you." He rubbed his jaw as though he were trying to loosen it. It was a nice jaw. Strong and symmetrical. "She read the article in the paper—about the tribute."

Autumn held her breath. Surely now he would rip into her.

"She really wants to help you."

"Oh."

"It's not good for kids her age to fixate on death."

"But we're not fixating on their deaths." That

was the whole point. These people were more than victims of some meaningless tragedy. They'd lived real lives before it happened, and those lives had been cut short. Those lives deserved to be known. "We're focusing on their lives."

"Right." Paul didn't look very comforted. In fact, he looked pained. Like someone was forcing him to swallow a mouthful of tacks. He scrubbed his face, then dragged his hand through his hair. That was nice too. Paul Elliott was a handsome man. Vivian Elliott had been a handsome woman. Together, they looked like the kind of couple that deserved space in a celebrity magazine. "Is there a way for Reese to be a part of it?"

She blinked, momentarily stunned. Did he just say what she thought he said?

He raised his eyebrows.

"Of course. I'd love for Reese to be a part of it." The first interview had been a bust. Not only had Autumn frozen after Ina May asked her the most basic of questions, but Seth had gotten held up with a client. By the time he made it through traffic, Autumn's allergic reaction to the invisible cats was in full throttle and Ina May had to leave for an appointment at the hair salon. She wasn't frazzled or annoyed or inconvenienced at all with the prospect of rescheduling. She actually seemed quite happy about it. "I'll get out the photo albums," she'd said, patting Autumn's arm.

"We have an interview lined up for tomorrow

evening. The woman's name is Anna Montgomery. She has two small kids, and she hasn't been able to find anyone to watch them. It'd be great if Reese could keep them entertained."

"Like babysitting?"

"If she'd rather help with something else, that's fine. I just thought—"

"No, that's great. That's perfect, actually."

"Good." Autumn's thrill of accomplishment expanded. He was going to let Autumn help his daughter. When all this was said and done, maybe she and Reese would finally find some understanding where there didn't seem to be any. "I should probably get your number."

"Right."

She pulled out her phone and entered his contact information, hiccupping for a second over his name. Paul Elliott. She was putting Paul Elliott's number into her phone in the lobby of Vivian's church. She shook her head. This was way too bizarre.

"Are you okay?"

"Y-yes. I'm fine." Autumn forced her thumbs to move.

"We could have a reception, with coffee and tea and cake."

Autumn found herself surveying the large space. Perhaps Ina May's idea was worth looking into. Maybe Pastor Mitch would consider opening the doors of Redeemer for such an event.

●●●

Paul was falling with nowhere to land. Even worse? His daughter was falling alongside him. He walked down the office hallway, stewing over his decision as he approached Penny—Mitch's long-time assistant—sitting at her desk.

She was straightening a stack of church bulletins, a big yellow feathered pen tucked behind her ear. The first time Tate met her, he mistook her for Big Bird. Quite loudly, in fact. He'd been three years old and Penny had been wearing a canary-yellow dress. Paul had closed his eyes in embarrassed horror, but Penny just laughed, then proceeded with a very impressive Big Bird impersonation.

"Hello, you," she said, the feather on her pen fluttering like giant eyelashes. "What brings you in on a Monday morning?"

"I was hoping to catch Mitch before he left." His friend didn't typically work on Mondays. Most pastors didn't. Unless, of course, there was an elder crisis to deal with or a job position to fill. "Did I make it in time?"

"The last I checked, he was still in there."

"Thanks, Pen."

She gave him a wink.

Paul knocked on the half-opened door of Mitch's office and poked his head inside. He was on the phone, squeezing a stress ball. Before Paul could duck away, Mitch waved him inside and mouthed the words *It'll just be a second.*

He slid onto one of the chairs and propped his elbows on the armrests, replaying the look on his daughter's face as she tore up the letters. He couldn't scrub it away.

Ten years counseling others, but what did it mean when it came to your own child? He knew depression, anxiety, and other mental health issues could be in her genes. What if this was just the beginning for Reese—the top of a slow downward spiral, like his brother? He wondered, with all his training, if he had the same abilities that Pop did—to bring someone back from the edge. But Reese wasn't just a person, she was *his* person. His baby. It scared him to his core, knowing that despair could swallow her, knowing that he might be powerless to stop it.

Just as he'd been powerless to stop Vivian.

Mitch hung up the phone and tossed the stress ball from one hand to the other. "Hey, man."

"Hey."

Mitch gave the stress ball another toss. "What are you doing here?"

Paul scratched the fabric of the armrest. Despite Pop's advice, he was as conflicted as ever about the marriage campaign. He had a demon on one shoulder and an angel on the other. One kept insisting that he follow through on his commitments. He promised to do the conference a long time ago. He should be a man of his word.

The other wouldn't stop screaming the word *hypocrite*. For the life of him, he couldn't figure out which one was which, no matter how hard he prayed. "I've been thinking about the marriage campaign."

"You and me both."

"How are things going?"

Mitch's mood lost some of its buoyancy, as if Paul had just reminded him that he should be squeezing the stress ball, not tossing it back and forth. "We've reached out to a few speakers, but the fees are pretty steep."

And there was Paul's answer.

He was so sick of the confusion, so tired of waiting for Mitch to broach the topic again, that he decided to come in today and kill two birds with one stone. Talk to Autumn about the tribute, and talk to Mitch about the campaign. If he'd already found someone to take over, great. That would be his answer. If not, that would be his answer too. "I'm willing to do it."

"Seriously?"

"I thought about what you said, and I've been praying about it, and I think I feel that same nudge."

He did, right?

That's why he couldn't stop thinking about this, wasn't it?

"Are you sure?"

"Yes."

Paul expected Mitch to look relieved. Instead, he looked hesitant.

"Unless you don't want me . . ."

"No, it's not that." He exchanged the stress ball for a pen, which he waggled between two of his fingers. "We're going to offer the communication position to Autumn. If she accepts, she'll be a part of the campaign. And if you're in charge of the conference, that would mean the two of you would be doing some work together."

Paul leaned back in his seat.

"Look, man. If that's too hard, I totally understand."

"It should be fine."

Mitch didn't look convinced. It was obvious that if the roles were reversed, Mitch wouldn't have been *fine* working so closely with the woman he saw lying in a hospital bed where his wife should have been. But then, Paul's marriage to Vivian had been nothing like Mitch's marriage to Lisa.

Not even close.

Twenty-Four

The Elliott household looked different in the sunshine. Friendlier, somehow. With a small tree growing up in an equally small front lawn. Autumn hadn't noticed the tree the first time around. Probably because she was too preoccupied with stuffing diamond earrings into a mailbox before she was caught.

The sun that shone on the house poured from the sky like a warm drink on her skin. She rested her arm on the edge of her open car window, wishing the extra dose of vitamin D would chase away her anxiety.

In a couple of minutes, Paul Elliott would most likely escort his daughter outside. Reese would climb in, and together they would drive to Anna Montgomery's home in Wilmette. They would talk about Anna's late husband, Daniel Montgomery III, the fourth obituary in Autumn's binder. The only young, successful CEO on the train.

Autumn stepped out into the late afternoon air, buzzed the intercom on the gate, and hurried around the front of her car to get back inside. She had no idea why, but she wanted to be sitting behind the wheel when Paul came out with Reese. She didn't want to be standing there, out in the open, with nothing to do with her hands.

The front door swung open.

Reese appeared, wearing pink Converse shoes laced over skinny jeans with a plaid buttoned top, her thick hair pulled into a loose side ponytail. She was holding a book. Maybe she would read on the drive.

Three steps later, Paul followed.

Autumn gripped the steering wheel. He had

sought *her* out yesterday. It had been weeks since she'd stalked him on the bike path. She had respected his wishes. In all her planning for the tribute, she hadn't called him or his daughter. He'd been the one to ask if Reese could help.

Reese opened the passenger door of the Honda Civic and took a seat.

Paul shut her in and rested his elbows on the ledge of the passenger-side window. "Seat belt," he said.

Reese pulled the belt across her chest and clicked it into place while Paul turned his eyes on Autumn. "Hi."

"Hi," she said back.

The greeting was followed by a short, uncomfortable lull, like a misplaced comma in the middle of a sentence.

Autumn scrambled to fill it with something casual.

Tootsie Pops!

All that came to mind were Tootsie Pops.

"I heard they offered you the job," he said.

"Oh. Yes, they did."

"Congratulations."

"Thank you."

"I guess we'll be working together."

"What?"

"On the marriage campaign. I'm sure Mitch mentioned it."

The marriage campaign, yes. They'd mentioned

it quite a bit. It would be her first big undertaking as communications consultant for Redeemer. The fact that Paul would be a part of the campaign, no. In fact, she distinctly remembered Mitch mentioning the possibility of Mr. What's-His-Face, that popular Christian speaker from Oklahoma. She remembered it so distinctly because as soon as he started talking about a marriage campaign, Autumn's mind had immediately gone to Paul. She'd been both surprised and relieved when his name wasn't mentioned. And then ashamed at her surprise, because of course Paul wasn't going to be leading a marriage campaign so shortly after his wife's death, if ever again at all.

"I didn't realize you were going to be a part of it," she said.

"I committed to it a long time ago."

Before.

When his wife was alive.

Autumn cleared her throat. "Anna Montgomery lives in Wilmette. We should probably get going."

"You have my number in case anything comes up."

"Dad." Reese dragged out the word.

Paul was undeterred. "Make sure you're on your best behavior."

She gave him a look, like *Did you really need to say that?* And he gave her a look back, like *Of course I did. I'm your father.* He told her he loved her, a declaration that came without a response; then he stepped away from the car and tucked his hands into the pockets of his jeans.

Paul Elliott was a good father.

Autumn wondered if Reese realized that.

She shifted into first gear and gave him a wave as she pulled away from the curb, watching as he grew smaller and smaller in her rearview mirror.

Autumn's grip tightened on the steering wheel. She'd never been alone in a car with a twelve-year-old before, at least not in her adult life. She peeked at her from the corner of her eye. Warm air breezed through the open windows, fluttering Reese's bangs. Paul said his daughter didn't hate her, but so far, Reese hadn't smiled or addressed Autumn at all. "Your dad told me that you found the letters."

Reese fiddled with the worn corner of her paperback.

"I'm sorry for giving them to him."

"I'm sorry for ripping them up."

"They were your letters."

Her attention rose from the book. "No, they weren't. They were yours."

Autumn pressed the brake as they approached a stoplight.

"Did my dad say anything about them?"

"The letters?"

Reese nodded.

"Just that he wanted to read them."

"I mean, after."

"Oh." Autumn merged onto Lake Shore Drive. "No. He didn't."

The answer seemed to release some sort of pressure valve in the girl. She relaxed against the seat.

"I'm happy he's letting you help. It didn't feel right, doing this without you."

"I still can't believe he changed his mind. My dad *never* changes his mind."

"Never?"

"He's always telling me and Tate that his yes means yes and his no means no." She deepened her voice over that last part in an impressive impersonation of her father. "I think this is the first time ever that his no turned into a yes."

"Wow."

Reese was folding the corner of her paperback again. Over and back, over and back until it lost its shape.

Autumn read the title. *Freak the Mighty.*

"What's the book about?" she asked.

"These two boys. Max and Freak. His real name is Kevin, but he calls himself Freak because he's super small and has this birth defect. But he's also a genius. Max is the opposite—really big and strong and not very smart. It's about their friendship."

"Sounds interesting."

"It's one of my favorites." Reese opened up to a

page that had been earmarked and smoothed her fingers over the crease. Then she refolded the corner and closed the book. "Do you think a person can alter their memories?"

"What do you mean?"

"Freak says remembering is a great invention of the mind. He says a person can basically remember anything they want to remember. Whether it happened or not. Do you think that's possible?"

"I'm not sure."

Reese gazed out the window, working the same muscle her father worked in his jaw whenever he seemed to be thinking intensely about something. Autumn wondered what she was thinking. What memories would Reese want to alter?

Twenty-Five

When Autumn pulled up to Anna Montgomery's very large home in Wilmette, Seth's car was already there. He stepped out as soon as Autumn turned off the ignition.

"Who's that?" Reese asked.

The sun shone behind him so brightly that if not for the familiarity of his vehicle, Autumn might not have known.

"Oh. That's . . . His name is Seth."

"Seth Ryker?"

It was disconcerting, hearing Reese say his last name. But of course she knew it. Thanks to the media circus that ensued after Seth's proposal and Reese's odd obsession with Autumn, Reese knew all about Seth Ryker.

"Aren't you getting married?"

"No. Not anymore." Her attention darted to the man in question, who was removing camera equipment from his trunk. Not only had she broken his heart, she'd sentenced him to humiliation, one that would strike every time someone slapped him on the shoulder and asked him about the big day. "He's going to be our camera guy. Take care ofthe video and the production."

"He used to work for WMAQ."

Autumn tilted her head. "How did you know that?"

"I read it in that article."

Ah, yes.

That article.

Since reporters couldn't get to her, they'd started hounding him. And Seth had responded. He provided the news with enough kindle to keep their fire fed. She'd been very upset with him at the time—probably overly so.

"Can I meet him?" Reese asked.

"Of course."

She set her book on the console and got out of the car.

Seth was closing his trunk.

"Those look heavy," Reese said.

He twisted around to look over his shoulder and quickly straightened. Autumn had failed to mention that anybody would be joining them. Maybe she needed to improve her communications skills.

Ironic, considering her new position at Redeemer.

"This is my friend, Reese." Her full name got stuck in Autumn's throat. She couldn't say it. She didn't want to see the look on Seth's face when she did. Inevitably he would find out. Reese wasn't just Reese, but Reese Elliott, daughter of Vivian, the woman who sat on the throne of Autumn's obsessions. Right now, though, on the cusp of meeting Anna Montgomery, with Seth standing there all ready to help, she would just remain Reese. "She's going to help with the little ones while we do the interview."

Seth shook Reese's hand.

"A reporter came to our school last week for a current events project we're doing. She was from WMAQ."

He rocked back on his heels and shot Autumn a questioning look. *How does this Reese know about my connection to WMAQ?* She could tell that the news article which had provided Reese with the information was nowhere on Seth's radar. She could see the conclusion forming in his eyes. He thought Autumn had been talking about him on the ride over.

"She gave me her business card," Reese said. "Her name's Mandy Prescott."

"I worked with Mandy on several stories. Autumn's worked with her too."

"You did?"

Autumn nodded. Back when her life had involved press conferences, she had worked with Mandy on several occasions. She was an absolute bulldog when it came to going after a story. Autumn knew firsthand, as Mandy had gone after her the second she woke up from the coma.

"I want to be a news anchor for *Good Morning America* when I grow up."

"I thought you wanted to be a writer."

"I can be a writer *and* a news anchor." Reese turned her attention to Seth. "Do you think they would show the tribute on the news?"

"We could try. If Mandy gave you her business card, she should have included her e-mail. She's always on the hunt for a good story to tell."

Reese seemed to tuck the information into her pocket as the three of them headed for the house.

"You doing okay?" Seth asked Autumn.

"Yeah. Why?"

"You're shivering."

Autumn rubbed her arms.

Halfway up the walk, the front door opened.

Anna Montgomery stepped onto the front porch, looking smaller than her Facebook pictures let on. In real life, she was a frail slip of a woman with dark circles bagging beneath chocolate eyes and a rosy-cheeked baby on her hip. The baby was named Lilian Grace, and she would grow up without a single memory of her father. Anna had been pregnant when Daniel lost his life. It was an injustice that left Autumn doubled over and breathless the first time she read it.

An injustice that had Autumn obsessing over Anna's pregnancy, counting down the days. As the due date approached, she spent each night in an imagined delivery room. She placed herself there, right beside Daniel, two phantoms in the corner as Anna brought forth a healthy baby with nobody beside her.

"Thank you for coming," Anna said, shaking hands with Autumn first, Seth second. Her eyes softened when she got to Reese. Did the two know each other like Autumn knew them? Was Anna aware that Reese was a fellow sojourner on this painful journey, or was the softening simply due to Reese's young age? "This is Lily, and this is Sam."

Peeking through his mother's legs was a little boy with glasses and wispy white hair. His name was Samuel John, and Anna was desperate to break his thumb-sucking habit. Autumn knew because Anna had solicited advice in a Facebook post three months ago. Apparently, nothing had worked, because Samuel looked up at Autumn with eyes magnified by smudged lenses, his thumb securely tucked inside his mouth.

Autumn tried her best to smile down at him. She tried her best to grab hold of the purpose that swelled inside her over the weekend. But purpose refused to be grabbed. She couldn't see the purpose in any of it—not in Daniel Montgomery's untimely death, not in Anna's widowhood, not in these tiny children growing up without a father.

Inside, the house smelled as lovely as it looked —fresh linen with a hint of lemon.

Anna led them through the large, open foyer into the great room while her baby gummed her necklace and her son toddled close behind, peeking suspicious glances at Autumn and Seth over his little-boy shoulder.

"I thought we'd do the interview in here, since there's a lot of natural light."

"It's perfect," Seth said, looking up at the skylights.

Anna lay the baby on her stomach in the middle of the floor. The little girl pushed up to her hands and knees and rocked back and forth, like she was warming up for a crawl that wasn't quite ready to come. The boy squatted in front of his sister, cocked his head, and made a noise like a loud monkey.

The baby erupted into giggles.

Autumn couldn't look away. This was disturbingly different than her time with Ina May, a woman bent over with age, at the tail end of her life. Anna was smack dab in the middle of hers, with two little ones who'd barely crossed the starting line. Autumn stole a glance at Reese.

"Can I get you anything to drink?" Anna asked. "Water or juice? Soda?"

Autumn and Seth politely declined.

And then, without any prompting at all, Reese sat cross-legged on the floor and started playing patty-cake with the baby.

Autumn released a breath she hadn't realized she'd been holding and took a seat on one end of the couch, her feet decidedly cold.

"I've never been on camera before." Anna fidgeted with the hem of her shirt. "I'm a little nervous."

"You'll do great," Seth said, offering her his kindest, most encouraging smile. "You're just going to talk to Autumn. Don't pay any attention to the cameras at all. If you get tongue-tied, we can start over again."

"That doesn't sound so intimidating."

Seth gave Autumn's shoulder a comforting squeeze and set up another camera to capture a different angle while Reese took the kids into an open play area—far enough away from the microphone, but close enough for Sam to see his mother.

Reese pulled the baby into her lap and patted the spot next to her on the floor. The boy crawled closer, holding a large board book, his glasses sliding down his nose. He pushed them up as Reese opened to the first page.

Seth mouthed the words *We're rolling* over Anna's head.

Autumn mashed her clammy hands together between her knees. "Why don't you tell me a little bit about yourself?"

"My name is Anna Montgomery. I'm thirty-eight years old." She looked at her children and a smile spread across her face—a smile that would probably forever hold a twinge of sadness. "I have two children. Sammy is two and a half, and Lilian turned eight months last week."

"They're adorable," Autumn said.

"Sam looks exactly like his dad."

Autumn swallowed. "Do you want to tell me a little bit about your husband?"

"Where do I start?"

"You could start with his name. How the two of you met."

"His name was Daniel. We met in college. I was a freshman. He was in grad school." Her voice cracked. "I'm sorry. I'm feeling emotional today. I think it's because I'm nervous."

"It's okay."

Anna had every right to be emotional.

Sam crawled into Reese's lap next to his sister, enraptured by whatever she was pointing to on the page.

"We got married the summer after he graduated.

We waited a long time to have children. Originally, we didn't even want children. But then we did all our traveling, and Daniel was settled in his job, and we both adored his sister's kids, so we thought, why not give it a try? But it didn't work. And the more we couldn't get pregnant, the more determined we were to get pregnant. After two rounds of IVF, Sammy was born and Daniel was hooked. He wanted at least four more. Lilian was a frozen embryo. We have one more in storage."

Autumn blinked, trying to maintain a poker face, like Jeannie True.

But this was something she never learned on Facebook. This was something too strange to include in Daniel's obituary.

"He was the CEO of Montgomery Enterprise. I'm not sure if you've heard of it. It's a pretty big company his grandfather started. His dad never wanted the job, so it was Daniel who got to fill the role. My husband was very business savvy. He has several awards hanging in his office, if you'd like to see them."

Autumn glanced at Seth, who gave her a nod and moved one of the cameras to his shoulder. They followed Anna down the hallway, into Mr. Montgomery's office.

Framed certificates and plaques hung on one of the walls. Another was covered in photographs. Daniel and Anna pretending to hold up the

Leaning Tower of Pisa. Daniel and Anna in front of this very home, his arm wrapped around her waist. Daniel and Anna holding a pink-faced baby wrapped in a blue receiving blanket. Daniel at a Cubs game with a little boy on his shoulders. And then Anna with Samuel and his new baby sister in a hospital bed.

Daniel wasn't in that picture.

Autumn was impossibly drawn. She stood in front of it, unable to look away. "How did you do it?" The words came out in a whisper. They floated in the room.

How did this woman give birth to new life in the wake of so much death? How did she leave the hospital and feed her children? How did she put one foot in front of the other each and every day? Autumn turned around, desperate for an answer. "How did you keep going?"

Seth shifted uncomfortably.

Anna fiddled with her necklace.

"I couldn't for a while," she finally said. "My parents had to take care of the children. Every day felt dark. And then one day . . . Sammy crawled into my bed and he said something funny and I laughed. I don't know. I guess some light showed up again."

It was quiet.

All that could be heard was Reese, reading to the kids from down the hall. Her voice came back to them, the only noise in the room.

"When we got married, we hardly had any money. Daniel's family was quite rich, but they didn't believe in handouts. The two of us lived in the teeniest, tiniest efficiency apartment." Anna let out a soft laugh. "On our very first date, he found two of those gaudy brass candle holders from a consignment store, packed up some peanut butter and jelly sandwiches, and took me out for a picnic in the park. But he hadn't checked the weather. So we ended up eating under a bridge by candlelight in the middle of a downpour."

It was a beautiful memory.

One that made Autumn's heart pinch. Seth had been her only serious boyfriend, and he had always been a meticulous planner. They'd never once got caught in the rain because Seth had a radar app on his phone. A hint of showers and he'd make sure to carry an umbrella.

"I was trying to think about which memories I'd share. Like the day he proposed, or the day Samuel was born. But the moments I find myself thinking about the most are the little ones. Like the way he used to blow raspberries on Sam's belly.

"This one time, on the tail end of Sam's very first ear infection, Daniel had been working late almost every night that week, and oh, we'd been at each other's throats. By the time Saturday morning came, we were tangled up in the worst argument. I don't even know about what; I just know it was the kind that went around and around with no end in sight. Finally, Daniel took our son from my arms, lifted up his shirt, and started with the raspberry blowing. Oh my goodness, he got Sam laughing so hard, all three of us were in tears on the kitchen floor."

Anna placed her fist over her lips, like the memory and the smile it induced were something private. Something too intimate and cherished to share with others.

"I guess that's what life is, though, isn't it? A whole bunch of little moments that don't seem significant or life-altering at the time, but when you look back . . ." She shook her head. "I don't know. They become the most profoundly beautiful things."

Twenty-Six

It is not so much the finding of the "reason"
that misfortune has befallen a person that is
essential. The "why" that needs to be
answered is about finding a reason to keep
living and keep growing, even though
a crisis has occurred.
—Suzanne Degges-White,
from an online article
about survivor's guilt

For Anna Montgomery, that reason was her children.

The baby inside her kept growing. Until one day—ready or not—Lilian Grace needed out. Life birthed in grief. Life that needed feeding and clothing and rocking and caring for, just like big brother Sam.

Once upon a time, I used to thrive on busyness. I used to interact with multiple people throughout the day and then go on to enjoy business dinners at night. I used to manage a large list of impressive clients, and I made myself available to those clients whenever they needed help. I was the queen of stomping out fires. I practically wore a cape that said Captain Damage Control.

"It's like you have a motor strapped to your back," my assistant would say.

And I'd puff up with pride, like Charlene was paying me a compliment.

I think it made Seth proud too.

Then the train exploded and my motor stopped.

I turned into Anna's frozen embryo.

I turned into the neon billboard I passed while driving Reese home tonight. Instead of advertising cheap insurance or discounted tires it said: No Schedule Found!

No Schedule Found!

Complete with an exclamation point.

Whoever was in charge of the billboard hadn't programmed whatever needed to be advertised, and so the bright, flashy neon sign had gone this boring whitish yellow with boring black words that said: No Schedule Found!

That's me. I'm that billboard.

Except now, I do have a schedule.

Tomorrow morning, I have to get up early with my sister, shower, dress in something other than sweatpants, and walk to Redeemer for my first day of gainful employment. When I dropped Reese off at her house, Paul wished me good luck. I asked him when we could schedule his interview.

"What interview?" he'd asked.

"For the tribute," I'd said. "For Vivian."

There was a brief moment wherein he looked truly horrified. For a fraction of a second I was terrified that if I looked down, I wouldn't be wearing a shirt. That's how horrified he looked.

The whole thing left me stammering about how I assumed he was doing an interview, since he'd agreed to let Reese help with the tribute and how sorry I was if I'd made an unfair assumption. I swear, my face was so hot, it could have melted wax. He finally interrupted with a very brisk, very cold, "I'm free on Saturday."

Maud? I think I'm getting an ulcer.

Fifty-four minutes. According to Paul's watch, that was the amount of time he had to pick out a new pair of soccer cleats for Tate, grab a few groceries and a Mother's Day card at Treasure Island, and get home before the interview—one he'd been agonizing over since Tuesday. At least a hundred times, he'd pulled up Autumn's contact information on his phone to cancel. But he never did it. Because why would he?

What excuse did he have not to participate in a tribute honoring his late wife, especially now that Reese was helping? If he called Autumn to cancel, she'd ask when they could reschedule, and if he said never, surely that would raise some red flags. It was better to just get it over with and move on.

Move on.

Something he wanted so acutely. But every time they seemed to step forward—every time a ray of sunlight pierced through clouds—something happened to yank them back. The clouds would thicken, and the sun would disappear, and he'd be left tossing and turning at night, dreaming about his wife.

"I like these!" Tate declared.

Paul blinked away his darkening thoughts. "Is there room to grow?"

Tate made a face, like he was wiggling his toes. "Yep."

"Good. Get your shoe back on, and let's go."

Halfway to the front of the store, Tate said he had to go the bathroom. When he was littler, he used to do the potty dance—hopping from one foot to the other, holding himself without any shame. Now he was too old for a potty dance, but when he had to go, he had to go.

They hurried toward the checkout while Tate whined about the fullness of his bladder. The cleats were ridiculously expensive, but Paul didn't have the luxury of searching for a bargain, so he paid the cashier and steered his son toward the restrooms.

They now had thirty-nine minutes to grab the milk and the peanut butter and the Mother's Day card at Treasure Island and make it home in time to meet Autumn.

He hurried Tate forward.

Just as they reached the men's restroom, the door swung open. A man stepped out so quickly that Tate knocked right into him.

"Whoa, watch out . . ." The man's voice fell away.

And for one millisecond, Paul's heart stopped.

Judging by the look on the man's face, he recognized Paul the second Paul recognized him. They stared at each other, momentarily stunned, as if they'd both forgotten the other was real—that they had continued to exist after Vivian's death.

Paul hadn't seen him since the funeral.

A year later and the shock of it still pulsed through him—hot and strong. Seeing him there amid the grieving crowd, blending in like he belonged, looking completely wrecked. It had ripped a hole straight through Paul's composure. He wanted, more than anything, to drag the man out from Redeemer's lobby and threaten him, make him swear to stay away from Paul's family. But he couldn't. Not with Tate yanking uncomfortably at his tie and Reese standing there—silent and pale—and a never-ending line of nameless, faceless people offering their condolences.

Now here he was again. That same man, with the same animosity slowly seeping into his eyes.

As if Paul had been the one to kill Vivian instead of Benjamin Havel's bomb.

"Do you know each other or something?"

Tate's voice snapped Paul back into reality.

His son's head had turned into a swivel as he looked back and forth, from Paul to the man.

He set his hand on the back of his son's neck. "No, we don't."

"Oh, come on. Don't lie to your kid."

The beating of his heart turned violent. He looked down at his son and nodded toward the bathroom. "Go on, bud."

Thankfully, the fullness of Tate's bladder outweighed his curiosity.

He pushed through the door and disappeared inside.

The two men stood there for a few beats, facing each other. A silent challenge, it seemed. One Paul wasn't going to take. He moved to step around him.

"Cute kid," the man said. "Are you sure he's yours?"

Paul Elliott saw red.

Until that moment in time, it had been a saying. A clever idiom to describe a person's anger. But now, it was literal. Paul literally saw red.

He became the bull, driven by instinct.

Before he could think, before he could stop himself, he drew back his fist and punched the man in the face.

• • •

Autumn twisted her Claddagh ring around her finger, trying not to panic at the sight of Seth pulling up behind her. The ensuing introduction had cold sweat slicking her palms.

Seth, meet Paul, Vivian Elliott's husband.

Paul, meet Seth. My happily-ever-after ending.

No, we're not married.

No, we're not getting married.

Funny how life works, isn't it?

With a deep, rattling breath, she shook out her hands and stepped out of the car. Seth was already outside, staring at the house—thinking what, she couldn't tell. He knew whose house it was. He knew who they were interviewing. She just hadn't explained yet that Reese was Reese Elliott, daughter of Paul and Vivian Elliott, and would be waiting for them inside.

"Hey," he said.

"Hey," she said back.

They stood there, uncertain. It seemed impossible that at one point in time, being with Seth had been the most natural thing in the world. Their silences hadn't been filled with her uncomfortable fidgeting. Seth's eyes hadn't held such strained concern.

"How's the job going?" he asked.

"A little overwhelming."

Seth chuckled. "New jobs tend to be that way."

Except this was more than a little. Her office

had turned into a revolving door. One introduction after the next, and she was horribly out of practice. The second she tried to familiarize herself with the church's website or social media accounts or figure out a good e-mail password, someone new would pop inside.

A big-boned lady wearing a canary-yellow blouse who gave her a small pot of daffodils. A high-spirited middle-aged woman who oversaw women's ministry. A local outreach pastor who wore Birkenstocks and had hairy toes. A junior high director who spoke in fluent sarcasm and cackled when he laughed. A never-ending stream of assistants and interns.

"I can't seem to remember anybody's name."

"You'll catch on." Seth smiled. "You always do."

Autumn rubbed her hands together, unsure what to do with the compliment.

He pulled on his earlobe. "So, this is gonna be a weird one, huh?"

"Yeah." She turned to face him, her heart skipping a few beats. "Look, I should probably tell you—"

The front door opened before she could tell him anything.

Reese stepped outside, her hair in the same low ponytail it had been in on Tuesday. "My dad's not home yet," she said, opening the gate.

"Your dad?" Seth asked.

Autumn swallowed, pressing her hands together harder. "Reese is Paul's daughter."

She watched as the news sank in. Reese Elliott. Autumn had a relationship with Reese Elliott. She could practically see his questions formulating. How? How had she become so well acquainted with Vivian's daughter?

"He went on some errands with Tate a while ago." A worried frown etched itself between Reese's eyebrows, and Autumn noticed that she was wearing eye shadow. A bold smoky gray that wasn't applied very subtly or deftly but somehow worked. Reese had the most striking eyes. "I tried calling him, but he's not answering his phone."

Claire told Autumn once, several months ago, that anytime Dad's number came up on her phone, a flash of panic would shoot through her veins. This was Claire's trauma trigger. A girl like Reese was bound to have a few of her own.

"I'm sure he'll be back soon," Autumn said, a lame attempt at assurance. "Why don't we go inside and get ready while we wait?"

Seth didn't say anything while he set up the equipment in the living room.

He'd gone silent, introspective.

Autumn tried not to pay attention to his brooding. Instead, she asked Reese about school and her friends and the book she was reading and the story she was writing, an attempt to distract them both.

Finally, at quarter past eleven, the back door flew open and Tate came racing inside, his eyes frantic with excitement.

"Dad punched someone in the face!" he proclaimed.

"What?"

Reese and Autumn spoke the word at the same time.

"Right outside the bathroom!" Tate reenacted the punch like a small, blond Rocky Balboa just as Paul shuffled into the living room, his hair a mess. His face white and strained.

If ever a man epitomized grimness, this was it.

Reese stared, wide-eyed, at her father.

Autumn stared, wide-eyed, at his red, swollen knuckles.

Tate wasn't joking.

Paul had actually punched a man.

And a long-buried instinct kicked into effect— the once-familiar urge to make herself useful. Autumn breezed into the kitchen like she owned the place, opened up the freezer, and pulled out a bag of corn.

"Here," she said. "You should ice that."

But Paul didn't take it.

He had yet to acknowledge Seth at all.

"Dad." Reese's voice was small and unsure. "Did you really hit someone?"

"He really did!" Tate exclaimed, unaware that nobody else found this news quite so thrilling.

Paul seemed levelheaded. To have punched a man, something horrible must have happened. Someone had accosted a woman or tried to kidnap Tate. Or a psychopathic terrorist like Benjamin Havel had pulled a gun. Autumn stood there, holding the bag of frozen corn, running all the different scenarios through her mind when Paul cleared his throat.

He looked from the camera equipment to his children, his jaw impossibly tight. "We're going to Grandma's."

"What?" Reese cried.

"I thought we were doing the interview," Autumn said.

"I can't right now." His voice was sharp. His words, clipped. "I'm sorry, but we'll have to reschedule."

Twenty-Seven

"Bad things always happen on the thirteenth."

"Nu-uh." Tate was trying hard not to be gullible, something for which Reese teased him mercilessly. "I was born on the thirteenth. That's not bad."

"Depends who you ask," Reese said.

Paul shot her an ominous look, one filled with warning.

She twisted around in the front seat to address

her brother. "Do you remember when Edward died?"

"His name was *Luigi*."

Luigi was Tate's first pet. A tan-and-white hamster. A week after they picked him up from the pet store, Luigi bit Tate on the thumb and Reese started calling him Edward, after everyone's favorite vampire. Every single time, Tate rose to the critter's defense, despite the fact that the bite had drawn blood.

"Fine. *Luigi*. Do you remember when he died?"

Paul glanced in the rearview mirror and watched Tate shake his head slowly, suspiciously, in the backseat.

"The thirteenth of December. Do you remember when our principal had a heart attack?"

Minor heart attack. The principal had a minor heart attack.

"The thirteenth of October. And guess what today is?"

"The thirteenth?" Tate offered.

Reese nodded emphatically. "And Dad bit Autumn's head off."

"I did not bite her head off."

"Yes, you did." Reese turned back around to face forward, her arms crossed, eyebrows raised. "If I treated someone that way, you would ground me."

"If I punched someone in the face," Tate quipped from the back, "would you ground me?"

"If he did, that would be hypocritical."

"Reese, that's enough."

She shrugged, like she didn't need to say anything more—her point had been made—and then spent the rest of the drive shooting him furtive glances from the corner of her eye. He wanted to hand her a tissue and tell her to wipe that gray stuff off her eyelids. Where had she even gotten it from?

Shoplifting, probably.

Paul's knuckles throbbed.

He had no idea what had come over him. How could he haul off and hit someone like that? Not lightly either, but so sudden and hard and out of the blue, it had knocked the man to the floor.

Worry and regret twisted inside his stomach as he thought about the way the guy had run his hand across his jaw and looked up at Paul with equal parts shock and loathing. This man, with the power to destroy Paul's career, the power to hurt his children. Before he had a chance to stand up and hit back, Paul grabbed his son—who was standing there with half his shirt tucked into his shorts, his mouth hanging open like a fish—and pulled him out of the store, not caring that Tate had left his new, expensive cleats in the bathroom.

What if the guy called the cops?

What if Paul was arrested for assault?

What if, after everything, the truth he'd worked so hard to keep hidden came flooding out into the light, along with a newspaper picture of his mug shot? Did they release those to the media? It seemed like they did.

The whole thing left him in need of a Xanax.

Paul pulled into his mom's driveway and shifted into park. He wanted to set his forehead on the steering wheel and disappear. He wanted this entire morning to be one horrible nightmare. But Tate hopped outside and ran to the front door, and Reese let out a loud sigh, as if to say *Here we go,* then climbed outside too. He had no choice. He forced himself to go after them, dragging like a man with no energy. He'd zapped his adrenal glands at the sporting goods store.

Tate pounded once, then flung the door open.

"Tate, wait! Your grandmother isn't expecting us."

But it was too late.

Tate had already let himself in, and Reese went after him.

Paul hurried up the walk.

Inside, Pop sat on the recliner, his walker set off to the side, massaging the tops of his knees with age-spotted hands. As a kid, Paul thought those hands were big enough to hold the entire world together. Now, they were gnarled and arthritic.

Mom stepped out of the kitchen holding a plate of food, her eyes widening with delight at the sight of them standing in the small entryway. "What a fun surprise! Is this my Mother's Day gift a day early?"

"Dad punched a guy in the face!"

Paul closed his eyes.

Why had he come here? At the time, his priority had been to get away. Away from the cameras in his living room. Away from the woman with the frozen corn and the guy who was watching curiously from behind the couch. But coming here probably wasn't the wisest move.

"Paul?"

He opened his eyes.

Mom stood close, her head tilted slightly to the side.

"It was nothing," he said.

But it was. It was a big thing. *Walk away.* Why hadn't he just walked away? Isn't that what Pop taught him as a boy? *"If someone provokes you, be a man and walk away. You don't hit anyone unless they throw the first punch."*

Why hadn't Paul taken Pop's advice?

Reese slipped off her shoes and sat down on the couch. "We were supposed to do the interview for the tribute. We had the camera equipment set up and everything. But Dad bit Autumn's head off."

"I did not bite anybody's head off."

Mom set the plate of food on a nearby TV tray and moved it in front of Pop's recliner, her worried eyes never leaving Paul's face.

"Go on outside, Linda," Pop said, batting her away. "Have a word with my grandson while I catch up with these two ruffians."

"Really, Pop. I'm all right."

"You think I'm doing this for you?" he growled.

Paul glanced at his mother, whose face had gone white.

"It's a nice day out. Enjoy the weather, son. Leave us to our baseball game." The White Sox were playing the Astros on the television. Pop pulled the TV tray closer and offered a potato chip to Tate, leaving Paul with little choice.

He opened the door, waited for his mother to step through, then sat on the front stoop with his elbows on his knees.

Mom gently took his injured hand in her own. "You need ice."

No, he didn't.

He needed his own therapist. He needed God to wipe the memories of Vivian—the good and the bad—away. If only the guy had punched him back. Right in the head. Paul would gladly take some amnesia.

"I don't understand," Mom said. "You've never laid a hand on anyone. Not even a fly."

"You're forgetting the daddy-longlegs incident." Wherein big brother Brandon dared him to pull the legs off a spider. When Paul said no, Brandon teased him for being a wuss. He managed to yank off one leg before he ran upstairs and slammed his bedroom door.

"Guilt tormented you for weeks," Mom said.

Paul dug the fingers of his uninjured hand into his hair.

"Are you going to tell me what happened?"

"I'd rather not."

"Paulie."

"I don't know, Ma. The guy was . . ." Sleeping with his wife before she died. How could he ever say those words? He pressed the heels of his palms against his eyes. "He was heckling Tate."

The white lie slid off his tongue so effortlessly it was disturbing.

"Heckling Tate? Why in the world would a stranger be heckling Tate?"

"Trust me, I didn't like it either."

"If a full-grown man was heckling a little boy, I think you should call the police."

"And what—turn myself in for assault?"

"You tell them what happened. They'll be on your side."

"It's fine. We don't need to call the police."

Unless, of course, the police had already been called. What would he do if he drove home and a cop car was parked out front, waiting for him? What would his kids do if the police officer started reading him his rights? Knowing his life, it would probably be Autumn's dad, and Tate would probably pummel him with questions about what it was like to be an officer in the city.

"I don't know what's wrong with me. I don't know why I got so angry." It was as if it had always been there, idling beneath the surface, waiting for the smallest opportunity to burst through. "I think I'm losing my mind."

"Honey, anger is part of the grieving process."

Her words crawled under his skin and scratched with craggy nails. This was so much more complicated than grief.

"On top of that, you're a single working father, with a daughter on the cusp of adolescence and a son with a lot of energy. No wonder you're losing your mind. You work so hard. You want to be there for everyone. Fix every hurt. But there's only so much of you to go around."

"Are we talking about me right now, or you?"

Mom gave him a motherly smile. "You've always been so intense. Even as a boy, you were that way. You need a break. You need to unwind. You need to relax and have some fun."

He laughed. Relax and have some fun? He didn't even know what that looked like anymore.

"Why don't you let me take the kids tonight?"

"No way."

"Why not?"

"It's Mother's Day tomorrow."

"All the more reason. What better way to celebrate than waking up to my two beautiful grandchildren?"

"I'm not dumping my kids on you on Mother's Day Eve. Especially not when you already have your hands full with Pop."

"Paulie, my grandkids are not a burden. Stop

making them sound that way. They keep me young. They keep Pop young. We'd be happy to take them. We'll pop some popcorn and watch a movie. I'll make cinnamon rolls in the morning. And then you'll come over after church, just like you were planning anyway—well rested and ready to spoil me rotten. It'll be a win for all of us."

He sucked a deep breath into his lungs, then pushed it out into the air. "I don't know. Maybe you're right."

"Of course I'm right." Mom wrapped her arm around his elbow and rested her head on his shoulder. "I'm your mother."

Twenty-Eight

In the dark silence Paul rested his elbows on the tops of his knees and buried his face in his hands. There had been no police cruiser waiting for him when he drove home to grab an overnight bag for Reese and Tate. But that didn't mean he was free to exhale. It didn't mean the guy wouldn't go to the media, or post something about their encounter on Twitter.

His mother had exhorted him to unwind, have some fun.

Instead, Paul had gone into work—hoping to utilize the rare free time to catch up on e-mails and paperwork. But all the words blurred together, and his mind raced in circles, and no matter how hard he tried, he couldn't stop checking Twitter, bracing himself for all the different ways the news could leak in 140 characters or less.

Eventually, he gave up. He left his phone in his car and came here—the dark, empty sanctuary of his church. Desperate for a sliver of peace, but finding none. Every time he closed his eyes, he saw Vivian, beckoning him in the same way she did in his dreams when he could never reach her. The longing. The despair. The anger and the guilt. All of it expanded inside of him now, impossible to escape.

He rubbed his eyes with the heels of his palms. His knuckles throbbed. He had yet to ice them, despite Mom's concern. Despite Autumn's—the woman whose head he had bitten off, no matter how much he denied Reese's accusation.

Autumn walked into a storm, completely innocent of anything but showing up on time, and he'd snarled like a rabid dog. He hadn't even bothered to introduce himself to the camera guy who'd been standing inside his living room. He'd been downright rude.

Maybe that's what was going on. The verse from Matthew unfolding in real life—the one about leaving your offering at the altar in order to reconcile first with your brother. Autumn deserved an apology, and he needed to end this horrible day having made at least one right decision.

Paul headed out into the balmy night.

It was humid and the air smelled like petrichor.

He read about the phenomenon once in some earth-science magazine. It was the name of an oil that the earth released into the air before rain begins to fall. He remembered because he'd found it so fascinating at the time. The smell of impending rain was a scientific fact due to something called petrichor.

Thankfully, he reached Autumn's apartment before any rain actually fell. And just as he arrived, somebody else was leaving. He slipped inside, rode the elevator up to the fourth floor, and knocked on her door.

A few seconds later, it swung open.

Instead of a short, auburn-haired woman on the other side, he found himself facing a big, burly man with grizzly bear arms, a can of Goose Island 312 in his hand.

Paul stepped back, his attention darting to the apartment number on the front of her door. "I'm sorry, I must have the wrong—"

"You here for Autumn?"

"Yes." Uncertainty drew out the word.

The large man called for her down the hall, then opened the door wider. "Wanna come in?"

"That's all right."

Autumn appeared under his arm, holding a

running shoe in one hand. As soon as she saw him, she stopped moving. "What are you doing here?"

"I just wanted to . . . um." Paul didn't typically stammer. And he wasn't too prideful to apologize with an audience. But he felt so on display. How did he know Autumn wasn't just venting to her boyfriend about what a jerk this guy Paul Elliott was?

"Who is it?" another voice called.

A female voice.

And then the voice appeared. It was a young woman—the same height and build as Autumn but with brown hair instead of red.

Autumn quickly shoved her foot into her sneaker. "I was just on my way out. We can talk outside."

Before the wide-eyed woman or the uncommonly large man could ask any more questions, she stepped out into the hallway and closed the door in their faces.

Outside, a strong breeze blew, tussling his hair. "I'm sorry for coming by unannounced. I didn't mean to interrupt your night."

"You didn't interrupt anything." Autumn crouched down to adjust the tie on her running shoes. When she straightened, her cheeks were flushed, her eyes wide. Probably from his jarring arrival. "I was looking for an excuse to get out of there. My sister and her new fiancé can be pretty revolting."

Ah. So the big burly man was Autumn's future brother-in-law. "Do they live with you?"

"Claire does. Not Trent. He has his own place, but they keep forgetting about it." She glanced up at her apartment window, the flush in her cheeks growing more pronounced. "Do you want to walk? My sister's probably watching us right now."

"Sure."

They started moving as inky clouds rolled across the sky, making the dark expanse above even darker. A gust of warm wind pushed at Paul's back as an awkward tension settled between them. Did she feel it too? Or was it just him? "I wanted to apologize about earlier. For how rude I was to you and your friend."

"Oh."

"Reese said I bit your head off."

"It's all right."

"No, it's not," he said. "I'm sorry for treating you that way, and for canceling at the last second."

They turned a corner and kept walking. Cars drove past, but the sidewalks were empty. Whatever was brewing on the radar must have chased everyone inside.

"How's your hand?" she asked.

Paul shook it out, then curled it into a fist. In high school he'd had a girlfriend who left a hickey on his neck. He'd been mortified to face his mother, just as he'd be mortified to face his family tomorrow, with bruises on his knuckles. "Not too bad."

He waited for her to ask more questions. Like, what had caused him to hit a man at a sporting goods store? It was the typical question a person would ask, only Autumn didn't.

He jammed his hands into his pockets. "How are things going at Redeemer?"

"Okay. Everyone's really nice."

"Mitch only hires the nice ones."

"As soon as I get my feet under me, we can start working on the campaign."

"Oh. Right." His response came with a stilted pause.

"Mitch let me book the church for the tribute. This woman named Ina May Huett suggested having a reception so all of us could watch the video together." Even through the dark, he could see her cheeks turning increasingly red, as though she found each word more embarrassing than the one before. "You should mark your calendar for Friday, June twenty-third."

"I'll make sure to do that."

"Where are your kids?" she blurted, as though eager to change the subject.

"At my mom's." Paul rubbed the back of his neck. "Tomorrow's Mother's Day and somehow she's doing *me* a favor."

They walked quietly for a block or two.

Paul was trying to figure out a way to release her, to tell her it was okay to start her evening jog. She didn't need to keep walking with him.

But then she said, "That must be hard."

"What?"

"Mother's Day."

Paul thought about the deformed clay pot he'd pulled from Tate's backpack yesterday afternoon. His classroom Mother's Day project. Mrs. Cranswick hadn't even written him a note in warning. "Thankfully, they have a pretty fantastic grandmother to celebrate."

Autumn smiled, and although it was sad, it eased some of the tension between them.

"Unfortunately, that same grandmother has a birthday two weeks later, and I never know what to get her. Gift-giving has never been my area of expertise."

"That's not true," she said.

He quirked his eyebrow—a polite nonverbal, *How would you know?*

"You got me those Tootsie Pops."

"That wasn't much of a gift."

"It was to me."

Something warm nuzzled up against Paul's heart. The way a cat might brush up against its owner's leg. It was a nice, nonguilty feeling. One that had him looking away. "There's only so many homemade photo calendars you can give a person, you know?"

"We used to make those for my Grandma Ally. A photo calendar every year for her birthday. Paintings on Christmas."

"Paintings?"

"Every year, on the Friday after Thanksgiving, my mom would cover the basement with tarp, get out three blank canvases, open up some new paint, and tell us to have fun." A faraway smile spread across her face. "My grandmother would exchange them out every year, taking down the old ones, putting up the news ones."

"That sounds like a fun tradition."

"It was."

They'd come upon a park. The swings swung back and forth in the breeze like little ghost children were sitting on them, pumping their little ghost legs. There was a gazebo and a basketball court with a basketball abandoned and alone beneath one of the hoops. Paul was struck with an idea. An impulsive, slightly crazy idea.

"You need to relax and have some fun."

He scooped the ball up, pleasantly surprised by its firmness, and gave it a couple of bounces, checking to see if it was as inflated as it looked.

Autumn stopped, looking at him with a fair amount of circumspection.

"You any good?" he asked.

"I played in high school," she said, the dubious sound of her voice throwing her answer into question, like she wasn't certain that she really had played any such thing in her youth.

"Wanna play?"

"Basketball?"

He gave the ball a few more dribbles. "Winner can buy the loser ice cream."

"Doesn't the loser usually buy?"

"Well, if you really want to buy me ice cream . . ."

Her mouth went slack, like instead of playfully baiting her into a game of one-on-one, he'd transfigured himself into a warthog. She looked over her shoulder, as though checking for witnesses.

"You said you were looking for an excuse to get away from your revolting sister and her fiancé."

Her attention flicked up to the cloud-laden sky. "I think it's going to rain."

Paul dribbled a little quicker. A little lower to the ground. Passing the ball smoothly from one hand to the other. "You sound scared."

"I'm not scared."

He chuckled, then picked up his dribble and spun the ball on the tip of his finger.

The smell of petrichor was more potent now, and the clouds looked ready to unzip, and the spontaneity of this particular moment felt refreshingly good. Back in the sanctuary, he'd been depressed with his own pathetic-ness. His mother had given him permission to let loose, have some fun, and Paul had ended up in the office. He used to know how to have fun. He just hadn't bothered with it in such a long time.

She swiped the ball off his finger and walked to the top of the three. "Shoot for possession?"

"You can go ahead and have it."

She bounce-passed the ball. "Check."

He bounce-passed it back, sizing her up. She was tiny, which put her at a distinct disadvantage. He decided he would give her the first basket just as Autumn faked right, crossed over, and drove past him for an easy layup. The ball clinked through the metal chains. She caught it on the way down and flipped him the ball. "One, zip."

"A lefty, huh?"

"Maybe."

Smiling, he dribbled to the arc and bounced her the ball. "Check."

She sent a sharp pass back to his chest.

"You sure you shouldn't guard me a little closer?"

"You're past the three."

"I've got a pretty sweet shot."

She rolled her eyes. "I'll take my chances."

Without looking away from her face, he sent the ball sailing toward the hoop. It swished through the chain-link net. He kept his arm up in the air, wrist cocked. "It's like riding a bike."

A dimple in her right cheek flashed.

"Two. One. Your ball," he said.

This time, he bent low, ready to stop the drive. The gentleman in him let her score her layup. The man in him demanded he not lose to a girl. Especially one this small.

She dribbled a few steps closer, her face screwed up in concentration, then drove, but he was right there with her. She picked up her dribble and pivoted.

Paul towered over her, so close he could see a sharp white scar by her left temple. Autumn was stuck, and breathless.

"Now what are you gonna do?"

A low rumble of thunder rolled across the sky, followed by a distant flicker of lightning. Paul looked up. Autumn took her shot. The ball hit the backboard and fell through the hoop. She laughed. "That's what I'm gonna do."

A raindrop fell on his nose. Another on his ear.

The drops turned into sprinkles that pattered against the blacktop. Another rumble of thunder. Another flicker of lightning. He looked at Autumn, who cocked her head, as if waiting for him to call it.

But if she wasn't, then neither was he.

He checked the ball, raindrops wetting his hair as she stepped closer, her knees bent. "You're not gonna give me the shot?" he asked.

"I'm a quick learner," she said.

Paul made like he was going to drive, and she was right. She was quick and she was touching him. It was a distracting feeling, as he wasn't used to being touched by a woman. He pulled back, keeping his dribble. He tried to drive. She stopped him. He crossed over. Faked. Pulled up. Shot the jumper.

The ball clanked off the rim.

With a laugh, Autumn snagged it and dribbled to

the three. He chased after her just as she sent the ball sailing. It sank through the net and the sky let loose. Sheets of rain fell from the clouds.

Autumn threw her arms into the air. "Four to two!"

Paul went after the ball. When he dribbled, it splashed and slurped against the pavement, throwing more drops into the air. The game turned wild. Goofy. They ran around the court. Guarding. Teasing. Gently pushing and shoving. Autumn couldn't miss. She was impressively on fire.

"This is crazy!" he shouted through the downpour, his face and hair and clothes and shoes soaked straight through.

She drove past him, her feet splashing against the puddles.

And somehow, in the midst of the fun, in the midst of the rain, Autumn won. Ten to eight. She threw her head back, her face tilted toward the crying sky, and let out a whoop, then hopped around in a victory dance, laughing.

Paul had lost, but somehow he was laughing too. And he was happy. Deep-down happy. The kind of blessed relief he'd longed for in the sanctuary.

He knew it was a feeling that wouldn't last. Feelings never did.

Maybe that's what made this kind so exquisitely good.

Its very fleetingness had him squeezing the moment for all it was worth, relishing every drop.

Twenty-Nine

Paul and Autumn walked inside Cameron's like an explosion of motion and noise. She was already laughing at something he'd said, and as soon as his wet shoe hit the white linoleum, he slipped. She caught his elbow. The door knocked into his back. He said something funny and she burst into laughter all over again.

A teenager stood behind the long counter, staring at them as if they were drunk.

They probably looked that way, stumbling inside with their waterlogged shoes and their big goofy grins.

Autumn let go of Paul's arm and swallowed her laugh, trying to appear less . . . inebriated. Even so, the light, giddy feeling remained—so unfamiliar it felt like a foreign object. Something to be examined with squinty-eyed suspicion and ready tweezers. Something as odd and strangely delightful as the *squish-squish-squish* of her running shoes as she walked up to the long glass display.

Paul joined her.

Cameron's was a small eatery in Lakeview that served ice cream and Philly cheesesteak. The place had sun-yellow walls and small ceramic tables barely big enough for two. The baby-faced girl behind the counter grabbed a nearby ice cream scooper and held it aloft like a startled gunslinger. One caught napping on the job.

A shiver wrapped its way up Autumn's spine, but it wasn't the nervous kind. The sudden clash of cold air against her damp skin left her with a serious case of goose bumps. She hugged herself, rubbing her hands up and down her arms. "I'll take a hot fudge sundae, with extra hot fudge, please."

"And I'll take two scoops of Blue Moon." Paul removed his wallet from his back pocket.

"What are you doing?"

"Ordering my ice cream."

"I'm not talking about your strange order."

"Blue Moon isn't strange."

"It's pastel blue."

"Have you ever tried it?"

Autumn waved her hand in the air; then she shot a dramatic, pointed look at his wallet. The thing that had elicited her question in the first place. It was as wet as his jeans. "I won, remember?"

"I think it's permanently scarred into my brain."

"Then why are you getting out your money?"

"I made that deal assuming *I'd* win."

"How very sexist of you."

"It had much more to do with your height than your gender." He gave her a cursory look up and down. "Also, what are you planning on paying with?"

Autumn had no comeback.

She'd left her purse at her apartment. She never imagined she would need it. Being here, in Cameron's, with Paul Elliott seemed surreal. She held up her pointer finger. "Fine, but I'm paying you back."

"If it helps you sleep at night." Paul set a wet ten-dollar bill on the counter. And for the first time since their lives intersected, Autumn noticed that the furrow between his brows was gone. Completely smoothed away.

"I used to think the same thing, by the way," he said.

"About what?"

"Blue Moon ice cream. But Reese and Tate are always ordering it, so one day I tried it and it was so good I didn't even notice it was pastel."

Autumn wrinkled her nose.

"It tastes like Froot Loops."

"Excuse me." The girl behind the counter had finally found her voice. The poor thing had been standing there, her attention volleying back and forth, back and forth, like a pendulum. Currently, it had paused on Autumn. "Aren't you that woman? The one who survived the explosion?"

And just like that, the foreign object was tweezed away.

"Yeah," she mumbled.

"Wow. You're like a superhero or something."

The statement startled her so decidedly from

the moment, the girl might as well have shoved Autumn's face in the container of cookies and cream. It reminded her of the time her best friend, Paige Stoltz, got her heart broken by Christopher Fry, who was a total jerk but also really cute and flirtatious and horrendous at math. He also happened to live next door. So when he came over two days after the breakup asking for help with algebra, all devil-may-care and charming, Autumn couldn't say no. She had no way of knowing that Paige would stop by an hour later and catch them laughing together on the couch.

Autumn's remorse had been instantaneous.

Just like it was now.

What would Reese say? How would she react if she could see Autumn flirting with her father when she was supposed to be helping Reese remember her mother?

The teenage girl, who was obtuse when it came to picking up on social cues, scooped up their order and prattled on about Tragedy on the Tracks. How her uncle worked for the CTA and how for a little while they all worried he'd been on the train because he lost his cell phone and nobody could get through to him.

By the time she handed them their ice cream with a cheery smile and told them to enjoy, Autumn felt like someone had pumped her stomach full of rocks.

"Do you want to go sit?" Paul asked.

"Sure."

He gestured to a table in the corner by the window, then grabbed a handful of napkins before taking a seat. The weather had mostly cleared, but leftover raindrops ambled down the glass, splitting and joining back together in a variety of paths.

Autumn jabbed her spoon into the fudge.

"So," Paul tried. "Your sister Claire. Is she younger or older?"

Autumn looked at him rather dryly. "You're very nice."

"Why do you say that?"

"She's five years younger."

"Really?"

"She's twenty-six. I'm thirty-one."

Paul made a noise, this puffy sort of hum, then took a bite of his Blue Moon. "Do you have any other siblings?"

"An older brother named Chad. He's married to Jane, and they have three adorable children. Calliope is four. Talulah is two. And Isaac is newly arrived."

Usually, Autumn relished the look on people's faces when she said her nieces' names. Tonight, she bulldozed her way through them, careful to keep all traces of flirtation or anything that could be mistaken as flirtation out of her voice.

"Isaac doesn't really fit, does it?"

"They call him Ike."

"Ah." Paul scraped another bite onto his spoon. "Your parents?"

"What about them?"

"I don't know. Are you close?"

"My mom and I were very close, but she passed away."

He blushed. "Oh, right. I'm sorry. Reese mentioned that at—" His blush deepened. "I'm sorry about your mother."

Autumn shrugged. "It was a long time ago."

She hated herself for saying it. She always did, and yet she kept on saying it. To make whoever was offering the condolences feel less awkward, she guessed. Only all it ever did was make her feel worse. Like enough time could erase a person. Rule them insignificant.

"Mother's Day must be hard for you too, then."

His acknowledgment touched her. They shared a look that had Autumn quickly dropping her gaze. "What about your parents? You seem close with your mom. What about your dad?"

"He's not a part of my life."

"Oh."

He shrugged like it didn't matter.

"He's still living?"

"Somewhere in Nashville, I think. That's what was on the return address of the last birthday card he sent, anyway. He walked out when I was ten."

Autumn frowned. Losing a parent at that age was hard enough. Knowing they left of their own volition? That had to be something else altogether. "Your mom never remarried?"

Paul shook his head. "Your dad?"

"He sure did." She dug her spoon into thick chocolate fudge and scooped the warmth into her mouth. When she looked up from the mixture of white and dark brown, Paul was studying her. For a split second, she was positive she'd gotten fudge on her chin, and wiped at it hurriedly. "What?"

"I sense a tone."

His observation had Autumn remembering that he was a certified psychologist—a male version of Jeannie True, which meant he would pick up on certain cues, like voice intonation.

"Don't worry," he said. "I'm not going to psychoanalyze you."

Autumn heaved a sigh. If Claire were here, listening to what she was about to say, she'd give the most exaggerated, long-suffering eye roll. "It's not so much that my dad remarried. It's how fast he remarried."

"How fast did he remarry?"

"Ten months after my mother died."

Paul let out a low whistle.

See, she wanted to tell her sister. Most normal people understood how incredibly fast and insensitive that was. *Yes,* Claire would say. *And most normal people would have built a bridge and gotten over it by now.*

"She died in a car accident when I was eleven."

The confession popped out without any forethought. It just came, straight out of the blue, like Paul's ice cream. And with it, a mortifying lump in her throat. She shoved another bite of hot fudge sundae into her mouth, but it was too late. The words were out, and Paul was staring in this strong, steady way that left her feeling balanced and unbalanced, all at the same time.

"I'm sorry," he finally said.

"It wasn't *your* fault."

"It wasn't yours either."

A therapeutically appropriate response, but not an informed one. She resumed her sundae swirling, her gut churning. The fudge had melted most of the ice cream into a thick, creamy soup. "She was driving to my first gymnastics meet. I didn't even really like gymnastics that much. But my best friend at the time was obsessed with it, so I kept whining and whining until I got my way and then . . ."

She closed her mouth, not wanting to continue.

"Autumn?" Paul's eyes were filled with compassion. "We worship a big God."

She looked down into her melted ice cream.

"The fate of your mother didn't rest on the shoulders of an eleven-year-old girl who just wanted to compete in her first gymnastics meet."

It was a kind sentiment.

But he didn't know the truth—not the whole of it.

Nobody knew that but Autumn and her father.

person led them around the school without touching. Mrs. Hayes was very adamant that we couldn't physically direct our partner. We had to tell each other what to do, and we weren't allowed to stand around. We had to move. Everyone was pretty excited because we got to leave the classroom.

Mia and I were partners, and she went first. I tied this bluish-green scarf around her eyes and waved my hands around to make sure she couldn't see, and then I made her walk around doing the funniest things. I kept telling her to step over objects or walk around things that weren't really there. I had her walk up and down the same hallway three times.

When her time was up, I made her guess where we were before she took the blindfold off. She thought we were by the cafeteria, but really, we were in the stairwell next to our classroom. It made us laugh.

Then it was my turn.

Mia tied the scarf around my head, and as soon as she told me to take three giant steps forward, my heart started beating so fast, I thought I was going to pass out. I got so sweaty and shaky I had to sit down on the stairs.

I couldn't handle not seeing anything. I had to take the blindfold off, and Mia had to go get Mrs. Hayes, and she sent me to the nurse, who took my temperature and wanted to know if I was diabetic, but I'm not. I think I'm scotomaphobic.

Has anything like that ever happened to you?

From,

Reese Rosamund Elliott

P.S. My mom got Tate a piñata for his sixth birthday party. She stuffed it full of Fun Dip, which is one of Tate's favorites. I wonder if I would have freaked out at his party if Mom would have blindfolded me.

Thirty-One

A Yorkshire terrier yipped at Mr. Collins's feet as he answered the door. He was an older, male replica of his daughter—Chloe, the artist. A college student at the University of Chicago, who had been in the process of going from gallery to gallery in hopes that at least one of them would show her work.

Scooping the barking dog up into his arms, Mr.

Collins welcomed them inside, his attention lingering on Autumn longer than Seth. He stared at her painfully. Almost accusatorially. As if he understood the full scope of the situation in a way Ina May Huett and Anna Montgomery hadn't.

She touched her scar—the feathery one along her jaw. She wiped at it like it was food on her face and found herself wishing she were horribly disfigured. Or paralyzed from the neck down. Something tragic that would take the sting off Mr. Collins's grief. Because his Chloe—at least—didn't have to suffer.

But instead she stood inside his house, healthy and whole. Perfectly intact.

"My wife will be downstairs shortly," he said, his voice gruff. "Kelsey should be home any minute."

Kelsey was Chloe's younger sister.

The girls were five years apart, like Autumn and Claire.

Mr. Collins led Seth into the dining room, where he could set up the camera equipment. Autumn slipped off her shoes, taking in the small, tidy townhouse, particularly struck by a framed piece of art hung on one of the walls.

Bright colors. Fluid strokes. The piece drew her closer—near enough to see the small signature in the bottom right corner. Autumn couldn't look away. Not even when Mr. Collins stepped up beside her.

"Your daughter painted this," she said.

He nodded.

It was stunning. A work of art reminiscent of the greats—Monet, Cézanne. It oozed with untapped potential. "She was very talented."

Mr. Collins nodded again.

"Have you ever thought about showing it in a gallery?"

"We would, if an art gallery wanted it."

An idea that had begun forming ever since Autumn beheld Daniel Montgomery's wall of business awards took on firmer edges. What if they created their own gallery? A Tragedy on the Tracks gallery. They could show Chloe's art in the lobby of Redeemer the night of the tribute. Along with Vivian's photography. And anything else family members wanted to share.

"I remember her," Autumn said.

He looked at her then, some of his gruffness melting away as the small dog licked frantically at his arm. "You do?"

"I saw her a couple times on the train."

Mr. Collins turned into a hungry pauper. A father who had only memories left to hold and would do anything for more to add to his collection.

"This one time, one of the passengers wanted to see what was in her portfolio." He'd been a smarmy-looking man, much too old to flirt with a girl Chloe's age, but Autumn left that part out. "He kept raving about her work. He kept going on and on about it, until Chloe jokingly said that he was welcome to buy it."

Mr. Collins waited, like there should be something more. But that was it. She didn't have anything else to give. She had handed him a pebble, when he'd been hoping for a diamond.

The front door swung open.

In walked Kelsey, taking Autumn's breath away.

Seventeen. Lover of music. A girl who dreamed of attending Juilliard and had played a heart-rending solo during the funeral. And also, Chloe's doppelgänger. She looked so much like her sister, they could have been identical twins.

"Sorry I'm late." She held a violin case, and her cheeks were rosy, as though she'd just been running. "I missed the train and had to wait for the next one."

The train.

Kelsey Collins rode the train.

She set her violin on the floor beside the welcome mat and took the wiggling, overexcited dog from her father's hands. "Where's Mom?"

"I'll go get her," Mr. Collins said.

He went upstairs, leaving Kelsey and Autumn alone.

Kelsey let the dog give her several kisses on the lips.

Autumn watched in fascination, trying to wrap her mind around Kelsey—a clone of Chloe—

riding the train back and forth from violin lessons. "How do you do it?"

"Excuse me?"

Autumn inched closer, hungry for an answer. So much so, her heart beat faster inside her chest. If she saw this girl on the L, she would most definitely think she was seeing a ghost. She would think it was Chloe, back from the dead, tempting fate. "How do you ride the train?"

Kelsey looked at her oddly and set the dog on the floor. "I don't know. I just do."

"But how? After what happened, *how?*"

"I couldn't at first," Kelsey said slowly, taking a small step back, away from Autumn's intensity. "But I kept trying. And then one day . . . I don't know. I was able to do it."

Autumn stared, unblinking.

Until Mr. Collins returned. He was pale, and his wife wasn't with him. "She said we can go ahead without her. She's not feeling very well tonight."

Autumn wasn't fooled.

It was obvious from the look Mr. Collins and Kelsey exchanged.

Mrs. Collins wasn't unwell. She was broken, irrevocably fractured. And something as paltry as a tribute was not going to fix it.

A week and a half into her new job and Autumn was beginning to live two very distinct lives. The one after work, wherein she met with the objects of her obsession. Visiting homes. Interviewing family members. Poring over her notes. Bringing ghosts back to life. Somehow this world was more real to her than the other life she lived during the day at Redeemer.

There she behaved like a well-adjusted member of society. Someone who went to work and accomplished tasks and interacted with people like a normal person. She was starting to get a handle on the names of her coworkers, the church's social media accounts, and currently this—her first big project.

One that included Paul Elliott.

A man who existed in both of these lives.

She hadn't seen him in almost a week. It was disquieting now, sitting in a small conference room with him and Mitch, all professional as they went over plans for the campaign. As if their odd night in the rain never happened.

It felt a little like they were secret friends. But they weren't really friends—secret or otherwise. They were . . . acquaintances. Strange acquaintances who had shared a moment. One Autumn replayed often, but especially now. Outwardly, she familiarized herself with the campaign's purposes. Inwardly, she kept second-guessing the information she had divulged about her mother. Maybe that was it. She had shared something intimate, and she felt exposed.

After addressing the goals for the campaign,

they went over the ways in which Paul could leverage his platform—which had been steadily growing, thanks to the success of his book—in order to better accomplish those goals. They drew up a list of the things he had time for and the things he didn't, as well as action points for the various churches involved.

When they were finished, Mitch expressed his excitement and congratulated Autumn on a job well done, then shook Paul's hand and excused himself for another meeting just as a text came through on Autumn's phone. It was from Seth. He wanted an address for tonight's interview—their third one this week.

"Reese has been asking about you," Paul said.

Autumn looked up from her phone. "She has?"

"She wants to know when she can help again."

"Oh. If she's available, I'd love her help next Wednesday." They were scheduled to meet with Mary Welling, a divorced mother of two who lost her father in the explosion. Her oldest daughter was Tate's age.

"That should work," he said.

"We should get yours rescheduled too."

Something dark clouded his expression. "Yeah. I'll have to check my calendar."

Her phone dinged again.

She turned it to silent and slipped it inside her purse, unsure what to say next. "Do you know what you're going to get your mom for her birthday yet?"

Paul groaned.

It was a friendly sound—one that broke apart their stilted decorum and placed them back on the basketball court.

"Not a clue," he said.

"What are you doing tomorrow morning?"

He cocked his head. "Why?"

"Because I have an idea. I think your mom will love it."

Thirty-Two

"Who is Paul Elliott?"

Dad's question had Autumn turning around, away from the window. The blinds swung back and forth, chopping apart the sunlight. Growing up, she and Chad always had to close them on Saturday mornings. The sun had the most obnoxious way of shining directly at the television screen, completely obscuring their favorite cartoon characters—Tommy and Chuckie, Phil and Lil, and that horrid Angelica, who wasn't actually angelic at all.

Leanne was gone, off running last-minute errands for Dad's surprise retirement party, which meant it was just her and Dad, who stood there in the living room holding the remote control.

Autumn didn't understand how it was possible. How could a name that carried so much significance fall off her father's radar? And what was she supposed to tell him?

"He's, um, he's participating in the tribute."

Understanding dawned slowly. She could see it sliding into place. It came in the form of severed eye contact, his mouth drawing into a straight line. The Elliotts weren't just another family who had lost a loved one on that horrible day. Her father might not have immediately remembered the name. But it was still there, lurking in unpleasant memories—wrapped up in despair and relief.

Dad scratched the top of his head. It was mostly bald. What hair he had remaining was buzzed short with a pair of clippers. "He's bringing his kids?"

"It's not a big deal. I'm helping him with something, and we need the basement to do it. We aren't going to be in your way."

Autumn wondered if he'd press for details. Ask more questions. Like why. Why had she invited Paul Elliott and his children over for such a random activity? Why did she feel compelled to help them?

Claire would ask.

So would Leanne.

Probably even Chad.

But Dad just sat down on the recliner and turned on ESPN. "So, how many people are going to be invited to this shindig tonight?"

"What?"

"Your sister and Leanne are many things." He quirked his eyebrow at her knowingly. Disapprovingly. "Discreet isn't one of them."

Autumn held up her hands. "Don't look at me. I told them you wouldn't want a party. But you know how Claire is. Once she gets an idea in her head . . ."

"She doesn't let it go."

"Not easily, anyway."

Dad heaved a long, heavy sigh, then picked up a small bottle of Tums from the end table and rattled a couple of tablets onto his palm. For as long as Autumn could remember, he'd suffered from acid reflux. "What am I supposed to do with myself?"

"Act surprised?"

"I don't mean at the party. I mean after." He leaned back in his chair, something like regret shining in his eyes. "I don't know, Autumn. I spent so much of my life being a police officer. Now I'm supposed to turn in my badge and fill my time with golf?"

Autumn squirmed.

She and Dad didn't wade into deep waters. They stayed in the shallow end, where things were comfortable and safe. When Autumn woke up from her coma and Dad came in to see her for the first time, he joked that she'd missed the opening game of the season. The White Sox had won. Chris Sale had pitched a solid game. Now here he was, creeping toward the deep end when Paul was due to arrive any minute with Reese and Tate.

"I don't know, Dad. Enjoy life, I guess."

Her father harrumphed.

She wasn't sure what it meant. Did he object to enjoying life? Or did he think his life was perfectly enjoyable as a working man?

Autumn wiped her palms along her ratty jeans and looked back out the window. Paul had just pulled up to the curb. Her heart gave a funny leap at the sight of Tate hopping out from the backseat. And then she smiled, because Tate was wearing a Cubs shirt that said World Series Champs. She hadn't told Paul what they were doing. But last night she'd sent him a text. He might want to dress the kids in clothes he wouldn't mind trashing when they were done.

Paul had dressed Tate in a Cubs shirt.

Autumn opened the door, letting in the morning air just as Tate bounded inside, not bothering to wait for an invitation.

"My dad says you have a surprise for us!" His body brimmed with unspent energy. So much, someone might think the kid had a giant cup of coffee for breakfast.

"I do," she said.

"He said he doesn't know what it is, but he made us wear these shirts. My grandma gave them to us last Christmas. Not my grandma-

grandma, but my Grandma Regina. She's my mom's mom. Dad said it would be funny."

"Well, Officer Tate, your dad's right. It *is* funny."

Reese and Paul stepped in behind him.

They were wearing the same shirt as Tate, just different sizes.

Paul caught Autumn's eye and shot her a quick, almost imperceptible wink.

"Cubs fans, huh?" Dad asked, standing from his recliner. "I'm not sure I should let you inside my house." And yet he stuck out his hand and shook Paul's.

"I assure you, sir, we are no such thing."

"No way. We love the White Sox and only the White Sox," Tate said. "My Pop used to be a groundskeeper at Comiskey Park."

"Is that right?"

Tate nodded up at Autumn's father, his hazel eyes round with awe. "Are you Miss Manning's dad?"

He gave the kid an amused smile, unused to being met in such a manner. Balding men in their sixties didn't typically inspire awe among seven-year-olds. They didn't typically inspire awe among any-year-olds. "I am her father."

"Wow!"

Dad chuckled, then turned to Autumn, obviously perplexed.

"Officer Tate, I'd like you to officially meet my dad, Officer Tom."

Tate puffed out his chest and gave Autumn's father an enthusiastic handshake. "I'm going to be a police officer when I grow up."

"Are you?"

"Yep. You don't have to be good at spelling to be a police officer. You just have to be brave."

"Bravery should definitely be a requirement."

Autumn was too anxious to stand around making small talk. She interjected, quickly introducing her father to Reese, then hurried Paul and his children down the stairs to the unfinished basement, where she'd already covered the cold, hard floor with tarp.

As soon as Paul caught sight of the two blank canvases propped against the cement wall, several opened cans of paint, and a couple of paintbrushes, his face flooded with understanding.

"Your mom's birthday gift," Autumn said, her stomach dancing with nerves. She brandished two handkerchiefs from her back pocket and handed the purple one to Reese, the red one to Tate.

"I don't get it," Reese said.

"Your dad wasn't sure what to get your grandmother for her birthday. This is something my mom used to do with me and my brother and sister for my grandma when we were your age." She glanced at Paul.

She had hoped he would smile, and he did. What she hadn't expected was the sheen in his eye, like he was indelibly touched by Autumn's gesture. Like nobody had ever paid him such a kindness before.

"What are we supposed to do?" Tate asked.

"Well, you paint. However you want. The canvas is yours." She took Tate's handkerchief and tied it around his head. Then she helped Reese with hers.

Both kids stood off to the side, unsure.

"I'm not a very good artist," Reese finally said.

"That's the great thing about this kind of art. No artistic talent is required." To prove her point, Autumn dipped a paintbrush into the yellow paint and gave it a fling, like her mother had taught her as a girl. Yellow drops splattered the canvas and the wall behind. One that was already dried over with similar splattered patterns, each one a fond, messy memory.

Autumn handed Tate the paintbrush.

He stared down at it as though she'd just handed him Willy Wonka's golden ticket. "I can do that down here?"

"It's been done lots of times before," she said. "The bigger mess you make, the better the painting will be."

Tate spun around to face his dad. It was obvious he needed his confirmation for such a crazy thing. Paul was the boss, after all. When Paul lifted his shoulder in consent, Tate didn't need to be told twice.

He dunked his paintbrush into the green and gave it a good whip. A glob of paint splattered against the yellow. Tate clutched his side and laughed maniacally. Like a kookaburra. It was such a contagious sound, Autumn laughed too. So did Paul.

Tate went for more, grabbing some blue this time.

Reese stared at him, and then, very tentatively, she picked up an unused paintbrush, dipped it into a can of purple, and gave it such an uncertain flick, the paint barely left the brush, let alone hit her canvas.

Autumn folded her arms. She longed for Reese to forget—for just a moment—that people died and darkness was real and tributes were necessary. She longed for Reese to laugh and dance like her little brother.

"You really have to fling it," she said.

Reese tried again, with only slightly better results.

"Here." Autumn picked up a spare brush from the ground. "Like this."

She modeled again, with red paint. Only this time, she made a point to really exaggerate her movement.

Reese watched intently, her brow furrowed like her father. Then she dipped her paint into more purple and tried again.

"Excellent!" Autumn cheered. "See how cool it looks?"

And it did.

Droplets of bright purple dribbled across white

canvas in a curved, swirling path. She encouraged Reese to do it again. And again. And again. With each whip of the brush, Reese's inhibitions melted away. Her movements grew more confident. More self-assured. Free. The canvas gained color. Red mixed with purple mixed with a golden beige.

Meanwhile, Tate's canvas barely had any white space left at all.

He dunked his brush so deep into the black, the entire thing was covered in paint, and when he wound back to hurl it at his artwork, a giant glob flew off and hit Reese in the face.

She shrieked.

Tate stopped.

A silent, uncertain second stretched between them, like the moment right after a coin flip, when the whole thing could go either way. Before Reese could land on indignation, before anything might be ruined by angry accusations between two siblings, Autumn sent a spray of red at Tate.

It splattered the side of his face.

All four of them looked at each other, wide-eyed and frozen.

Then Tate let loose another one of his cackles and exacted his revenge. He sent more black paint flying, this time at Autumn. And Autumn slung paint at Reese. And Reese shrieked again, this time in delight, and aimed at her father, who until this point, was nothing but an innocent bystander.

Chaos erupted.

Paint flew in every direction. It was a rainbow of wet, flying color that sprayed the two canvases, sprayed the tarp covering the floor, sprayed the cement walls all around. They laughed and they slipped and they shrieked and they slid, making a giant, glorious mess.

Autumn had paint in her hair and paint running down her back. Tate had thrown down his paintbrush and was now scooping up the stuff with his hands and smearing it on whomever he could get to. Reese was laughing and Paul was laughing and Autumn was laughing.

All of them were laughing.

So hard that tears streamed down their paint-streaked faces.

Thirty-Three

Everyone sang out a gusty "Surprise!" as soon as Dad and Leanne walked inside the house. Dad would not be winning an Oscar anytime soon, but nobody seemed to care that his shock was clearly an act. Guests descended on him with hand-shakes and back pats and hearty congratulations for years of faithful service.

All of it was very much deserved.

While Autumn's father might not have been the most hands-on dad in the world, he certainly had been a loyal, hardworking, dedicated police officer, and the force would miss him.

Autumn stood off to the side near the food with her stepcousin Veronica, who had greeted her with such verve that one would have thought Autumn had spent the past year doing dangerous missionary work in Pakistan instead of hiding in her apartment. Veronica had driven over from Rockford for the occasion. She was three years younger than Autumn and very talkative. For the past ten minutes, Autumn had nodded at appropriate intervals while Veronica went on and on about her boyfriend and whether or not they were moving in the right direction.

Autumn didn't mind. She felt strangely light. Like nothing could possibly annoy her, not even her stepmother.

"He's a brilliant drummer," Veronica went on.

Autumn nodded, glad for an excuse to avoid socializing with a bunch of people she hardly knew. Officers and office workers from the force—some with significant others, some alone. Leanne's coworkers. Several acquaintances from Christ the King Presbyterian. Dad's partner, Nick, who was years away from retirement, his wife, Violet, and their two identical boys, both of whom were Cal's age. Anytime anybody greeted them, they growled like jaguars.

Cal stood by her mother's side, stoic and disdainful, like she was above such nonsense, while Jane bounced a fussy Ike in her arms and Lulu played with the jaguar-boys. She and the twin boys had an entire conversation of nothing but growls, and now the three of them were doing somersaults on the floor. Well, the boys were doing somersaults. Lulu was putting her head on the floor and tumbling sideways while Leanne's parents and Aunt Kathy clapped.

Kathy was Dad's only sister.

She'd driven down from Milwaukee with her dog, George, a springer spaniel who was currently romping around out back.

"Is that blood?" Veronica asked, peering at Autumn's ear.

"What?" Autumn rubbed at the spot, suddenly self-conscious.

Veronica looked closer. "No, it's not blood. It looks like . . . like paint."

"Hey, you two." This from Jane.

She and Chad had moved to the food. Jane patted Ike's bottom while he mewled like a cat. This was what he did, no matter how much he was bounced or patted, nursed, burped, or rocked. The kid cried more in his first two weeks of life than Cal and Lulu combined.

Veronica was properly distracted. She forgot all about the red paint behind Autumn's ear and her drummer-boyfriend and began cooing over the baby. "He looks just like his daddy."

"Doesn't he?" Jane said.

"Poor kid," Chad muttered, picking up a plate and loading it with tacos and guacamole. The entire house smelled like Cinco de Mayo.

Laughing, Veronica took Ike's little fist and gave it a wave. "I want a dozen babies just like you after I get married. Yes, I do! Yes, I do!" She stopped her baby-talking. "He's so adorable, I could eat him right up."

"I could eat this food right up," Jane said. "Chad, honey, don't get me any beans. Ikey will never sleep tonight if I eat them. But I'll take some of that rice. Lots of it. And another taco." She turned to Veronica. "This kid wants to nurse constantly, which leaves me absolutely famished. The weight's just falling right off. It wasn't like this with Cal and Lulu. I really struggled after them."

No, she didn't.

Jane had gained twenty pounds each with both girls and was back in pre-baby work-out clothes one month later.

She knew because Leanne could never get over it.

"With this kid, I'm turning into one of those annoying women who can eat whatever they want. If I weren't so sleep-deprived, it would be magical. Autumn, you sure look happy today."

Autumn stopped moving, taken aback by Jane's sudden conversational pivot. She'd been trying to rub off the dried paint behind her ear.

"Yeah," Chad said, putting an extra scoop of rice on his wife's plate. "What are you so smiley about?"

She covered her smile and blushed, like she'd been caught doing something inappropriate for parties.

"You're glowing!" Jane's tone turned accusatory. And delighted.

"I'm happy for Dad," she lied.

All three of them looked at her as though she had enchilada sauce on her face. Or maybe speckles of dried paint. She'd taken a thirty-minute shower, and she still hadn't gotten it all.

"Aren't I allowed to be happy for dad?"

"Of course you are. It's just . . ." Jane was probably thinking about the brochures and the intervention and Jeannie True. Then she glanced across the room at Seth, like Autumn's happiness might have something to do with him. "It's just nice to see, that's all."

Before Autumn could respond with a self-conscious thank-you, a loud *thunk* stopped the conversation. Lulu had run straight into a wall while chasing one of the jaguar-boys. Jane startled, then quickly passed Ike to Chad and hurried over to console her middle child, whose face was screwed up in the kind of dramatic cry that was so intense, it produced no actual sound. At least not for several seconds. Not until Jane patted her back and little Lulu found her breath.

Then the wail rushed out so piercingly, everybody at the party stopped to make sure she was all right.

She was.

Lulu was always all right.

Chad stood there holding a distraught Ike and a very large plate of food. Autumn took her nephew off his hands. In the past, she'd always been able to soothe her nieces. Jane had joked that Autumn was a baby whisperer. But Ike refused to be soothed, no matter how much she cooed at him. By the time Lulu was settled and checked over, he was the one wailing. Jane came to his rescue. Autumn grabbed a small plate of food and slipped outside, farther away from the noise.

George, the springer spaniel, joined her by the stoop, sniffing her plate while Ike's crying melded with the boisterous conversation filtering outside.

She sat down and patted George's head, and then she fed him a chip.

"I saw that."

She twisted around.

Seth stood on the other side of the screen door holding a plate of chips and salsa, a kind smile on his face. Last night he'd asked Autumn if it was okay that he come to the party. Claire had given him an invitation. She assured him it was. Seth had always gotten along so well with her dad.

The hinges groaned as he pushed open the door. It whacked shut behind him as he sat beside her. "Now that your dad's retired, he'll be able to spray some WD-40 on all the things that squeak."

"And after that, he will fix everything that leaks. And after that, he will probably drive Leanne crazy."

Seth laughed.

George prodded her arm with his wet nose, tail wagging, eyes pleading for another chip. Autumn tossed one out into the grass, and the dog went hunting as a warm breeze rustled the leaves on the bushes.

"You seem to be in a good mood," he said, giving her a nudge with his elbow.

Her mind rewound to the morning and the bewildered look on Dad's face when he handed her towels as she stood on the top of the basement stairs, covered in paint. She hadn't laughed that hard in such a long time. And it felt good— helping the Elliotts. "I am."

"You wear it well."

Warmth crept across her cheeks. A swell of fondness rose inside her. She had the strongest urge to rest her head on Seth's shoulder. The interviews were taking so much of his time, and he wasn't being compensated. And she didn't deserve his help. Not even remotely.

He took a bite of his chip.

She took a bite of her enchilada.

George came over to beg for more scraps.

"We should go to dinner sometime."

"What?"

"We should go to dinner sometime," he repeated.

"Sure." The answer popped out, completely reactionary.

Seth asked her to dinner, and she said yes. That was how it had always been. For two years before the explosion.

"I promise I don't have any expectations," he said.

"I know."

"Then why do you look like a deer in the head-lights?"

"You just caught me off guard."

Seth smiled at her. His face was sun-kissed, as if he'd spent the day outside. "Do you want to change your answer?"

She looked at him—this man who had always been so steady and strong. Maybe it was the lightness still left over from this morning's laughter. Or maybe it was old feelings stirring back to life. All she knew was that right then, with George sniffing around the grass, sharing a meal with Seth sounded oddly comforting, like putting on her favorite sweatshirt on the first day of fall.

"You're going on a date with Seth?"

Claire asked the question the second she stepped inside Autumn's apartment. She'd stayed late after the party to help clean. Autumn had planned to, but the guests lingered and Leanne had assured her it was okay; she could go home.

Now she sat up straighter, a puzzle piece in hand. Before the door unlocked and opened, she'd been hunched over the coffee table, trying to complete her latest purchase—*Mona Lisa* in jigsaw.

Claire set her purse on the small table by the door. She was also holding a large plate of leftovers. Tacos and enchiladas, and guacamole that would be brown by tomorrow. She looked at Autumn with raised eyebrows, waiting for an answer.

"He asked me to go to dinner sometime."

"And you said yes?"

"It's just dinner."

Claire dipped her chin and looked at her like she was being purposefully dense. "It can't be *just dinner*. Not with Seth."

"He told me he doesn't have any expectations."

"And you believe that?" She slipped off her shoes and didn't bother to put them in the closet. This was starting to get under Autumn's skin. She liked a tidy apartment. Was it really that hard to put your shoes where they belonged? To put your dishes in the sink after you used them? To put your socks in a laundry basket?

"Why can't we go to dinner as friends?"

"Because Seth doesn't want to be your friend."

"Did he tell you that?"

Claire walked into the kitchen and put the leftovers into the refrigerator. "Why do you think he's helping you with the tribute?"

"Because he's a nice guy?"

"C'mon, Autumn. You owe him some honesty."

"Maybe I don't know what's honest!" She didn't. When it came to Seth, her feelings were so confusing that she didn't know how to tease them apart. When he proposed, she'd said yes because she'd always planned on saying yes. But for some reason, she struggled with feelings of resentment. Then she broke up with him, and she missed him. She missed him for months afterward, and now he was back, and a part of her thought it was nice.

Autumn shrank back against the couch and closed her eyes.

"Do you still have feelings for him?"

"Of course I still have *feelings* for him. We were together for two years."

Claire sat down on the couch beside her. She pulled up her knees and crossed her legs. "He's a good guy, Autumn. He doesn't deserve to have his heart yanked around."

"I know."

Seth's goodness made this whole thing that much more confusing.

Thirty-Four

Tuesday, May 30, 2017

> God works in mysterious ways.
> —Mrs. Fayeville's go-to answer
> whenever Tommy Bennett asked
> a question in Sunday school

Tommy Bennett asked a lot of questions.

We were only eight, which isn't much older than Tate is now. I would think most eight-year-olds—especially eight-year-olds whose parents faithfully attend church every Sunday—would not antagonize their Sunday school teacher with such theologically perplexing inquiries. Childlike faith and all that.

Not so with Tommy Bennett.

I swear, his sole objective in that class was making Mrs. Fayeville squirm. You could always see the dread in her eyes whenever he raised his hand.

One Sunday, while she was teaching us a song that put all sixty-six books of the Bible to a catchy tune, Tommy's hand shot into the air. We'd reached the part where we sang, "Es-ther, Job, Psalms, Pro-verbs" and Tommy had a question. It was about the book of Job.

Specifically, how could God let such a bad thing happen to a man who hadn't done anything wrong?

Mrs. Fayeville went a little pale.

She paused from the song and opened up the Bible and read the very last chapter out loud, then clapped her hands in front of her large chest and said, "See? Job learned his lesson and God gave him more children and livestock. It all turned out all right in the end."

Tommy said, "Tell that to the children and the goats that are dead."

I remember sitting there, cross-legged on an itchy rug in the shape of Noah's ark, thinking, *Tommy's right. What about those dead children and goats? Didn't God care about them?*

Last I heard, Tommy's a pastor in Houston.

So maybe Mrs. Fayeville gets the last laugh.

I don't know, Maud.

Today I had an interview with Jordan Brokaw.

He lives in a seedy apartment complex in Englewood. His particular studio was shabby but clean, with a rickety crib pushed off to one side. The room smelled like cigarettes. Not the overbearing scent of a current smoker, but the stubborn, vague scent of an ex-smoker. Jordan sat on a sagging couch with his hair neatly trimmed, tattoos running up and down both arms, and a one-and-a-half-year-old girl named Linaya on his lap.

Reese wasn't there.

I haven't seen her since we painted pictures for her grandmother. She was supposed to help with an interview last week, but she got sick. According to Mitch, a nasty flu virus was making its rounds through the Elliott household. It traveled from Reese to Tate to Paul, back to poor Reese again.

It worked out okay. I'm not sure Paul would have wanted her going to that part of town. I'm not sure Jordan would have handed his daughter over to Reese if she'd been there.

He cried when he talked about his girlfriend and his son. Angela and Vincent. She had been twenty-two. The boy had just turned four.

According to Jordan, he'd been a deadbeat father who dropped out of high school and made money selling drugs, then promptly spent every cent of that money on the drugs that he sold. He was high when his daughter was born. And he was high that awful day, when Angela and Vincent died and Autumn didn't.

Thankfully, Jordan said through his tears, Linaya wasn't with her mom.

She'd been spending the night with her grandparents.

According to Jordan, burying his son and the mother of his children had been the biggest wake-up call of his life. He got clean. He got Jesus. He got his GED. And recently, the judge gave him joint custody of Linaya. He shares her with Angela's parents. They're the ones who helped him get clean and introduced him to Jesus. They expect him to make something of his life.

For his daughter, and for theirs.

According to Jordan, Angela and Vincent saved his life.

If not for them, he'd be behind bars right now.

Or dead in a gutter.

He owes them everything, he said, mopping at his eyes.

Indeed.

God works in mysterious ways.

"Mia doesn't even like baseball," Tate said.

"Yes, she does."

"No, she doesn't. I asked her one time, and she said it was boring."

Reese glared at her brother like he was the world's biggest pest. "I'm older than you, which means I get first dibs."

"That's not fair. I can't control when I was born."

"Yes, actually, you can."

Tate looked wary.

"I made sure I was born in 2005, the same year that YouTube was created."

"Nu-uh."

She gave Tate a bored, superior look. "Do you even know how babies are born?"

"Reese, that's enough." Paul fanned the four tickets in his hand like playing cards. Pop shared season tickets with two other retired grounds-keepers. A thank-you for their hard work over the years. They were good seats too. Right behind home plate. In years past, Pop took Paul and the kids. Now, Pop's health was too poor to sit through an entire game, and Mom refused to leave Pop alone for such a long period of time.

He called Mitch to see if he could go, but Mitch's oldest had a soccer tournament. There were some other friends Paul could invite, but none that he particularly wanted to. Which meant they had a fourth, unused ticked, over which the kids were arguing.

Tate wanted to invite his school friend Owen.

Reese wanted to invite Mia.

"We can rock-paper-scissors for it."

"No way," Reese scoffed.

"Why not?"

"You cheat at rock-paper-scissors."

"I do not!"

Tate's vehement objection was fair, as he absolutely did not cheat at rock-paper-scissors. He always won, but he didn't cheat. Paul knew because he observed him. A lot actually. It didn't seem possible that Tate could always win a game that was essentially a game of chance, but somehow he did.

"What about Autumn?" The suggestion came out before he could censor it, but even if he could, he didn't think he would.

He hadn't seen her since the paint war broke out in Mr. Manning's basement. Paul had been so sure the paintings would be wrecked. But once they were removed from the mess, they looked so much different. Abstract and colorful. His mother's birthday had been this past Sunday. She had adored them.

He and Autumn had exchanged a few short e-mails about the marriage campaign, but he'd been so consumed with the Great Flu-pocalypse of 2017, he hadn't been able to do much of anything. He was too busy keeping his head above water and Lysol-spraying every surface of his house. Now, finally, everyone was on the mend. To celebrate, they were going to enjoy a baseball game this weekend. He didn't want his children fighting the whole time. And as strange as it may be, he enjoyed Autumn's company.

"Really?" Reese asked.

Paul shrugged. "She likes the White Sox."

Reese looked eagerly at her brother, who seemed to be weighing the idea.

Autumn Manning, or his buddy Owen.

Owen liked lightsabers and Nerf guns, but neither of those things would be an option at the baseball stadium. Autumn let him roll around in paint and called him Officer Tate. It seemed this last bit won out in the end.

Paul pulled up her name in his contacts and prayed she would say yes.

Thirty-Five

A heat wave had rolled into the Midwest, turning the tail end of Chicago's spring into an erratic guest with severe mood swings. Yesterday had been a pleasant seventy-five degrees. Today, the temperature reached for ninety. Leaving Autumn, Seth, and Reese crammed into a tiny oven-of-an-apartment with a faulty air conditioner, interviewing Sandra Reid, whose five-year-old son was an absolute terror, only instead of correcting him, she kept sighing heavily at Reese, who was doing her best to keep him corralled and entertained.

On top of that, Sandra wouldn't stop glaring.

She glared when Autumn shook her hand. She glared when Seth set up the equipment. She glared when she went through pictures on her laptop, and she glared as she talked about her sister, Ashley, who had been riding the train that day.

Sandra went on and on—about how Ashley had

Autumn said. "Reese really wanted me to come. I wasn't going to tell her no. Not when she's struggling. Not when she's still grieving her mother."

"So . . . you're wanting to fill that void?"

He might as well have slapped her.

How could Seth say such a thing? If anybody should understand why that particular accusation would hurt so deeply, it was him. Autumn wasn't Leanne. Nor would she ever be Leanne. "I would never try to replace Reese's mother."

"I shouldn't have said that." Seth sighed. "I'm sorry, Autumn. This is just weird. And I just don't want to see you get hurt."

"Get hurt by who?"

"This Paul guy."

Before she could express her incredulity, the waiter came and poured their wine.

Seth nodded his thanks, then set his elbows on the table and leaned forward. "He seems like a royal jerk."

She bristled. "He's not a jerk."

"He was incredibly rude to you, Autumn. And to me."

"He was having a bad day."

"Does he make a habit of punching people on bad days?"

She started to sputter. Seth had it all wrong. He was mutilating Paul's character because of one unfortunate encounter. Paul was a grieving widower and an amazing father and a pretty decent basketball player. He wasn't a jerk, royal or otherwise. Seth was just jealous. And for nothing. "You promised me that there weren't going to be any expectations."

"You promised me forever."

What was left of her appetite vanished.

She didn't have the energy for this.

Not tonight. Especially not after that interview.

Shaking her head, she scooted her chair back and walked to the door.

Seth reached her just as she was stepping outside onto Michigan Avenue. "Wait, Autumn. I'm sorry."

"That was not fair."

"I know. I shouldn't have said that. It's just . . ." He ran his hand down his face. "I'm worried about you."

Several people glanced in their direction. Autumn was positive one person's eyes flickered with recognition. "Well, join the club. Jane's president. Claire's the treasurer. I'm pretty sure both of them will let you in."

"Autumn."

"What?"

"Do you really think these interviews are helping? Are they doing what you thought they would do? Because tonight didn't feel like closure."

Autumn shook her head.

"And a baseball game with the Elliotts?"

"Seth."

"Hear me out, okay? What happened was a huge ordeal. For you. For him. I'm not denying that. I can't imagine how awful it must have been, thinking his wife was alive, and then realizing she wasn't, but you were. I can see how confusing it would be. I can see how feelings might get mixed up."

"Nobody's feelings are getting mixed up." Seth was talking like she was purposefully trying to trade lives with Vivian. They were just going to a baseball game.

"It was traumatic. I understand that. But Autumn, what I don't understand is why we came to an end. I don't understand why we broke up." He stood there, looking at her pleadingly. Like they were on Mars and she was in possession of the last tank of oxygen. "I still love you."

"Seth."

"If you said you wanted to get back together right now, I would. I'd walk down the aisle tomorrow."

A hard knot tied itself in the back of her throat.

"Help me understand. What happened? How did we go from in love, ready to spend our lives together, to this?"

All of her anger whooshed away.

How well she understood the frustration of not

understanding. She was desperate for answers too. But she didn't have any. At least none that made sense. When she woke up in that hospital room, her emotions had been so out of sorts. The doctors assured her this was normal. They would level out. But time had done nothing but add more confusion. Seth wanted an explanation, but she didn't have an explanation to give him. "I don't know. I'm sorry, but I just don't know."

He deflated like an old party balloon.

And there was nothing she could do.

The woman they pulled out of the rubble wasn't the same woman who boarded the train. And Tragedy on the Tracks wasn't just some *huge ordeal*. It was life-changing. The old Autumn—the woman Seth had fallen in love with—died alongside everyone else.

Thirty-Six

Despite every lick of sense inside her, Autumn showed up. Every time she picked up her phone to call Paul with some lame excuse as to why she couldn't go, she would think about Tate's kookaburra laugh as he flung paint at his sister or the excited way Reese called out her grandmother's car window, "See you tomorrow for the game!"

So she showed up in her White Sox T-shirt and

her White Sox baseball hat, determined to prove Seth wrong. Nobody was getting anybody mixed up. Nobody was trying to replace Vivian.

Besides, the seats were behind home plate. Her father would skin her alive if she said no.

When she climbed out of her car and her heart lifted at the sight of the Elliott children waiting for her on the front stoop, she told herself this was normal. Reese and Tate were really cute kids. Anybody's heart would lift. They were also wearing White Sox shirts and White Sox baseball hats, and when Paul came outside, so was he.

The four of them were matching.

Paul smiled, like he found this amusing. "Who's ready for some baseball?"

"I am!" Tate pumped his fist into the air while jumping up from his spot, then raced out the front gate.

"Perfect weather for an evening game," Paul said.

"Sure is," Autumn said back, her tone off. Too high, maybe? She was nervous, so she couldn't tell.

Tate raced ahead of them, tearing a path down the sidewalk. Autumn stopped. It took a moment for her brain to catch on. Tate and the family were walking down the sidewalk. Toward Diversey.

Toward the train stop.

Idiotic realization struck. How could she not

have considered this? It was a White Sox game. Of course they would be taking the transit system. They would get on the red line on Diversey Parkway and ride it south all the way to 35th. It made no sense to drive.

"Are you okay?" Paul asked.

"I, um . . ." Autumn forced herself to swallow. To take a breath and relax.

Tate—finally realizing that his family wasn't following him—stopped and backpedaled. Literally. He ran backward as though someone hit Rewind. "What's the matter?"

Autumn scrambled for some logical reason as to why they should all cram into her rattletrap of a car and endure Chicago traffic when they could take a nice stroll to the stop and hop on the L. "I forgot my Ventra card."

"That's okay," Tate said, taking her hand. "Dad has money. He can pay for your ticket. They aren't very expensive."

He tried tugging her along, but Autumn's feet had glued themselves to the cement. And something like understanding flooded Paul's eyes. Of course he would understand. He dealt in fear for a living. Fear was probably the main reason why a guy like Paul Elliott had such job security.

"You haven't ridden since . . . ?"

She gave her head a sharp shake.

No. She hadn't.

Embarrassment came like an aftershock.

Sudden, hot embarrassment. It had been fourteen months. Autumn lived in a city where the transit system was woven into the everyday fabric of life. Chicagoans didn't avoid the transit system. They used it.

But she didn't.

She not only avoided it, she avoided it to her detriment. Paying for gas and astronomical insurance premiums when she didn't have the money to pay for either. Crawling through traffic any time she needed to get anywhere. The endless search for a parking space. And all for what? Did she really think Benjamin Havel was lurking in the shadows, waiting to plant another bomb?

Autumn gave her head a small shake and told herself it was time to stop being ridiculous. Thousands, if not millions, of people rode the train every day. Before the Big Bad Awful thing happened, she'd ridden it herself hundreds, if not thousands, of times.

"We can drive," Paul said.

"No. It's fine." Autumn forced one foot to step in front of the other. She could do this. She *would* do this.

"Autumn, this isn't necessary. We can take my car."

It *was* necessary actually. After last night's horrible date with Seth, wherein she found herself in the exact same position she'd been in months and months ago when she gave him the ring back, the train felt very necessary. She took another step. And then another. She kept stepping until it didn't feel so forced or mechanical. She imagined how proud Jeannie would be. She had an appointment scheduled for Monday late afternoon. She was going to sit in that leather chair and tell her all about it. The moment she conquered her fear and got back on the train and survived.

Yet again.

Autumn rattled the thought away.

Tate skipped ahead of them, waving his hat in the air, his blond curls bouncing in the sunlight. Reese and Paul kept shooting nervous glances at Autumn, like she'd just announced—with a greenish face—that she didn't feel so well.

Paul insisted a couple more times that they should drive. Nobody minded. It was not a big deal.

But Autumn had turned adamant. She was going to overcome this. She was going to take back this part of her life.

She purchased her ticket with shaking fingers. The machine spit out her pass. She pressed it against the red scanner and pushed through the turnstile. All of it was so horribly familiar. The white noise echoing from the elevated train tracks. The faint smell of urine as they walked up the cement steps.

How bizarre that she had done this fourteen

"We didn't go through what you went through."

No. They'd gone through worse. They lost loved ones. Autumn, on the other hand, hadn't known any of those people. At least not then. Back then, they'd been nothing but strangers. She looked up from her hands.

Reese and Tate stood off to the side, shuffling their feet uncertainly.

Her shame grew. They didn't need this. They didn't need her ruining their day. She should have never accepted Paul's invitation. But he stood above her, outlined by the evening sun—a paragon of patience.

"I'm sorry," she said.

"You don't have to apologize."

"Yes, I do. This was supposed to be fun."

"And it will be. As soon as we get to the game. Thankfully, there are a lot of ways to get there besides a train." He offered her his hand.

Autumn blew out a long breath, and then she took it.

Paul Elliott pulled her to her feet.

And with the motion came a flash of memory. Swirling snow. Shooting pain. This same man reaching out his hand. All of it came, so startlingly clear, Autumn lost her breath all over again. "Has this . . . has this happened before?"

His eyebrows pulled together. "Has what happened before?"

"This." Autumn cupped her forehead, fighting a

bout of lightheadedness. "You, helping me up. On that day."

"You don't remember?"

Every drop of warmth drained from her cheeks. She didn't remember anything. She had zero recollection at all. Until this memory slid into place. One that had been lost for fourteen months. One that involved—of all people—Paul Elliott. "You helped me up off the ground? But why?"

He scratched the back of his head. "We ran into each other, and you fell."

"When?"

"On the platform, right before . . ."

Autumn shook her head, dumbfounded. She had finally found someone who knew something of those mysterious two hours. Paul Elliott!

"You were running up the steps and I was . . . I was turning around."

"I was in a hurry?"

"It seemed like it."

"Did I say anything? Did we talk? Do you remember any details?" The questions tumbled out, one after the other. She asked them desperately, anxiously, greedily, like she was a starving woman and every detail, a morsel of food.

"Not really. You had a box. I helped you up—"

"I had a box?"

"Yeah."

"What kind of box?"

"Just a regular box. Cardboard. Not very big."

"Did you see what was in it?"

"There was a picture frame that broke when it fell." Paul seemed to think back, but then he shrugged apologetically. "I'm sorry. That's all I remember."

Thirty-Seven

People crowded around the stadium, enjoying the sun and what was left of the day's heat. Autumn stared at her phone, anxious for a reply from her sister. She tried calling her first, but Claire hadn't answered. So she sent a text from the back of a taxicab on the long ride over.

Do you know why I would have had a box on that day?

So far the message was delivered, but not read.

They shuffled toward the front gate, Autumn's mind straining with the effort to recall. But no matter how hard she tried, she couldn't remember anything else. She was stuck with a lone puzzle piece in the midst of two unaccounted-for hours.

Tate grabbed his father's hand. "There's nothing like baseball on a beautiful day."

Paul laughed.

It was a funny thing for a seven-year-old to say.

Then Tate grabbed Autumn's hand too. And Reese's attention could be felt like a hot ray of sun on Autumn's back.

Her phone buzzed.

What day?

She slipped her hand from Tate's and quickly typed back a reply. **Tragedy on the Tracks. I was carrying a box.**

You remember?

I had a memory.

"No phones in the stadium!" Tate announced. "Right, Dad?"

Autumn looked up from her screen.

"You aren't allowed to be on your phone during a baseball game. That's an Elliott family rule. Pop says it's Zack religious."

"That's sacrilegious," Reese muttered with a long-suffering eye roll.

Paul handed the tickets to a round man sitting on a stool in front of one of the turnstiles.

Autumn's phone buzzed again.

No idea y u had a box. Sorry.

Releasing a frustrated breath, she slipped the phone inside her purse and followed Paul and his kids to the nearest concession stand. Paul bought nachos, a hot dog, some cotton candy, a bag of peanuts, and three bottles of water before turning to Autumn. "What'll it be? Popcorn? Candy? Bacon on a stick?"

"I'm not hungry, thanks."

"You don't want anything? Not even a box of Cracker Jacks?"

"Dad ordered ribs in a helmet last year," Tate

chimed. "He said he paid for it with my college tuition."

"It did cost a small fortune."

Last year?

They'd gone to a baseball game last year—mere months after Vivian died?

She peeked at Reese, who had barely said more than a few words all evening. She looked moody and taciturn, the same way Autumn had felt last night.

"You really don't want anything?" Paul asked.

"I already ate."

He shrugged, then turned to the person behind the stand and dug a couple twenties from his wallet. "Could you throw in another water?"

The woman took the money and scooted the goodies over the counter.

Paul handed the nachos to Reese, a water to Autumn.

"I can pay for this," she said.

"It's not a big deal."

"But I still owe you for the ice cream."

Reese's attention snapped up from her nachos.

Tate snatched his hot dog and ran to the condiment table, looking gleefully at the giant dispenser of mustard in the same way most boys his age would look at a tub full of candy. Paul gathered the waters and the peanuts and the bag of cotton candy while Tate started drenching his hot dog.

"That's disgusting," Reese said.

"Mustard isn't disgusting. It's my favorite food."

"Mustard isn't a food, and if you're not careful, it'll stain your teeth green."

Tate stopped his squirting. "Mustard's yellow, not green."

"Good job with your colors," she said sarcastically. "But it has enzymes that interact with the enamel on your teeth. If you have too much, it turns them highlighter green."

Tate stared at his sister. "I don't believe you."

She shrugged, like it didn't matter. She had no skin in the game.

Paul rubbed the top of Tate's hat. "She's teasing you, buddy. I won't be able to breathe through my nose until you finish that thing, but I promise, your teeth will not turn green."

On their way to their seats, they passed in front of a booth filled with overinflated White Sox merchandise, the kind that always caught Autumn's eye as a kid. She would beg for some sort of knickknack, but Dad rarely acquiesced, because why did anyone need a twenty-dollar key chain, let alone a kid too young to drive?

"Can I get a baseball hat?" Tate asked.

"You already have one."

"For my birthday?"

"Your birthday isn't until July."

Tate set his hot dog on the table and started

rifling through the baseball cards. "I promise I won't ask for anything else."

Reese scoffed, like she knew better, then picked up a foam finger. "I've always wanted one of these."

Autumn stepped beside her. "You mean you don't have one?"

Reese shook her head.

Paul plucked it from his daughter's hand. "We don't need props to cheer."

"Foam fingers are not props. They are a vital staple in the baseball industry." Autumn dug inside her purse and aimed her voice at the frowning man behind the booth, who was currently eyeing Tate as he touched everything in sight. "I'll take two foam fingers, please."

"I can get it," Paul said, reaching for his wallet.

Autumn shook her head. No way. He was not going to buy these foam fingers. Sure, it would cost an arm and a leg, but she had a good-paying job now. And a roommate. This was the benefit of enduring Claire. And she really wanted to give something to Reese. She really wanted to make the girl happy.

"Letting you pay goes against everything my grandfather taught me."

"Tell your grandfather this is the twenty-first century. Besides, you're not going to have any money left for foam fingers once Tate is through."

He had a small bat tucked under his arm, a

baseball mitt in one hand, a White Sox coffee mug in the other.

"Tate!" Paul barked. "Put that stuff down."

Tate started whining.

Autumn quickly paid for the fingers and handed one to Reese.

Ten minutes later, they filed into their seats, right behind home plate. The field stretched in front of them, meticulously groomed. The dirt finely raked, the pitching mound perfectly sculpted, the grass carefully mowed, forming a pattern of light-green and dark-green stripes that stretched to the fence. The lights were already on, even though dusk was a couple of hours away.

Autumn inhaled deeply through her nostrils. She loved baseball. She missed baseball. And last year had been quite the season. Maybe not for her team, but definitely for Chicago. Yet all of it had passed her by. History in the making. A century-old curse, broken. A city still reeling from the aftershock of tragedy, desperately eager for something good to celebrate. Even her family— White Sox fans, all of them—pounced on the opportunity to smile and slap high-fives. When the Cubs won that final game of the World Series, her city united—not under the banner of grief— but under the banner of baseball. And all the while, Autumn lay awake in bed, listening to the muffled cheers outside her window, removed from it all.

Tate sat down beside her.

Reese sat beside Tate, holding the foam finger in her lap, like she wasn't sure what to do with it now that she finally had one. She looked pale and wore the pinched expression of a person lost in thought. The same feeling that overcame Autumn in the basement of her dad's house overcame her again. She was determined to see Reese smile.

"It's fun if you wave it around," Autumn said, putting hers on and waving it in the air. She cupped the side of her mouth and let out a whoop.

"Can I try?" Tate asked.

Autumn handed it over.

Unsurprisingly, Tate was a natural. He whooped and hollered—so exuberantly in fact, he almost knocked into the woman in front of him. Paul apologized, then told Tate to settle down as everybody came to their feet for the national anthem. Autumn took off her hat and put it over her heart. So did Paul and Reese and Tate. The four of them must have looked like an all-American upper-middle-class family.

When the song ended, everyone cheered.

And Paul did something sneaky.

He slipped past his children and took the seat beside her, scooting Tate and Reese down one. He set his elbow on their shared armrest and held out the bag of nuts. "Want one?"

"No, thank you." She shifted away—from the

bag and his arm—her attention lingering on Reese, who was picking at her nachos.

The game started with the crack of a bat.

A long fly to center field. Jackson swiped it out of the air. Tate jumped out of his seat, tipping what was left of his hot dog over on the ground, his foam finger flapping like a streamer in a windstorm.

Autumn spent the first inning twirling her Claddagh ring and picking at her cuticles. But then Cabrera hit a home run in the second, and she got caught up in the game. At the top of the fourth, Tate had to use the restroom. Paul handed his peanuts to Autumn and excused themselves, leaving her and Reese alone.

They caught each other's eye.

"When did you and my dad get ice cream?" Reese asked.

Autumn's cheeks turned hot.

She felt like an imposter. An intruder. Seth was right. She had taken her obsession too far.

"We, um, we grabbed some a few weeks ago."

"When?"

The same day her father punched a man in the face. Autumn scratched her ear. "I think you and Tate were spending the night at your grandmother's house."

She couldn't bring herself to look at Reese.

She didn't want to face her disapproval.

So instead, she stared fixedly at the baseball game until the boys returned.

Paul held a giant-sized Coca-Cola. "What did we miss?"

"Sale hit Morales with a pitch, and Morales charged the mound. The ump just got things back under control."

"Funny."

Autumn handed him his peanuts.

Instead of taking them, he dug inside the bag. The only thing separating their hands was a flimsy plastic wrapper.

She wanted to ask him more about the memory. Their run-in on the platform. But he had shared everything he could, and it was obvious hE wasn't comfortable talking about that day. It was obvious he wanted to forget what she was so desperate to remember.

She kept running the sparse facts through her mind: She left work at five. She'd been complaining of a headache. She disappeared for two hours. And now, there was a box. A box with a picture frame. Her fingers twitched over her purse. She wanted to call Seth. And if he didn't know anything, maybe her old assistant Charlene would.

"I'm glad you could come today," Paul said.

Autumn's cheeks turned warm.

Two seats down, Reese pulled off a small tuft of cotton candy and tucked it into her mouth.

"You made it sound like Reese really wanted me to come."

"She did." Paul leaned closer and dropped his voice. "She's been a bear all day. I wasn't sure if it had anything to do with the interview last night."

The interview had been horrible, but Reese didn't hear most of it. She was too busy trying to keep the five-year-old from trashing the over-heated apartment. And afterward, she hadn't seemed bothered at all. On the contrary. She'd been so excited about tonight's game.

"I don't think so," Autumn said. "She had her hands full with a little boy who was very . . . energetic."

"Sounds like Tate."

"This kid would make Tate resemble a sloth."

"Wow."

Autumn peeked at Reese again. "We should probably get Vivian's interview rescheduled."

Paul cracked open another peanut.

"I also wanted to ask about Vivian's family."

"What about them?"

"I wasn't sure if they'd want to participate."

Something in Paul's expression closed off. Like blinds snapping shut. "I doubt either of her parents will be flying to Chicago for the tribute."

The crowd erupted into wild applause.

Autumn looked around, like she'd missed a grand slam. But it was only the kiss cam. The big center field screen landed on a young couple, framing them in a heart. The boy grinned and really went for it. It was kind of obscene.

The crowd roared in approval.

Tate covered his face with his hat so he didn't have to see.

Autumn's cheeks went from warm to burning.

She didn't want to watch people kissing right now. Not when she was sitting so close to Paul. She dug around inside the bag of peanuts just as Reese let out a squeal.

A man behind them clapped Paul on the shoulder, his words slurring, like he'd had one too many beers. "Better kiss your wife, mate!"

To her absolute horror, the jumbotron had zoomed in on her and Paul. Of all the people in the stadium, her and Paul. She watched with everyone else as her cheeks mottled with red and Paul's eyes widened.

She wrapped her fingers beneath the armrests and pressed back into her seat, her heart pounding so ferociously, she swore the entire world could hear. Any second, the crowd would let out a collective gasp, because they would recognize her; and then they would recognize him. Autumn Manning, miracle survivor. Paul Elliott, the Marriage Doctor who lost his wife.

She could see the headlines:

Miracle Survivor's New Happy Ending?

Paul rubbed a spot behind his ear. And before she could protest, his lips found her cheek and her stomach squeezed into the size of a raisin.

The crowd was unimpressed.

Autumn thought she would combust into flame, like a phoenix. Paul would blink and just like that, she'd be gone. A pile of ash on the sticky stadium floor.

"Better kiss your wife, mate."

The camera panned away, in search of a less reserved couple. One who might give the crowd something more entertaining than a chaste kiss on the cheek.

Thirty-Eight

On the taxi ride home, Tate fell asleep on Autumn's shoulder. Reese crossed her arms and stared out the window, her expression grim off the glass's reflection. Autumn would have given anything to crawl inside Reese's thoughts—to know what it was that had her withdrawing so completely. Was it Tate's hand-holding outside the ballpark? Did it begin with Autumn's freak-out on the platform? It couldn't have been Paul's kiss on the big screen, although that probably hadn't helped.

She wanted Reese to know that despite how things might have appeared this evening, Autumn was on her side. She wasn't trying to replace anyone. "Did I tell you about the idea I had for Redeemer's lobby?"

Reese turned her head. Her face was extra pale in the moonlight.

"I thought it might be a good idea to create a gallery the night of the tribute. We could display your mother's photography. Hang pictures of her and the others. I'd love to collect as many as we can. The more, the better."

Reese gave an almost imperceptible nod as the taxi driver pulled up behind Autumn's car.

She reached inside her purse to pay, but Paul was sitting up front and beat her to it. Even though the cost was on *her* shoulders, she was too distracted to argue. Too in need of fresh air. She hitched her purse over her shoulder and climbed outside into the cool night.

"Dad, I need the keys," Reese said from inside.

They were the first words she'd spoken since the kiss cam.

"Tate, move! Get out of the way." There was a hysterical edge to her voice—one Autumn had never heard before.

Tate crawled out from the backseat, his eyes blurry with sleep.

Reese nearly hurdled him, and then, without a word, she ran to the house, unlocked the front door, and disappeared inside.

Paul stepped out from the taxi. "Reese?"

The cab drove away.

He exchanged a brief, worried look with Autumn, then jogged up the walkway after his daughter, leaving Tate half-asleep on the lawn, swaying on his feet to the chirping of crickets. Autumn stood there for a moment, unsure what to do. Then she took Tate by his shoulders and walked him in, guiding him safely to the couch, where he curled up on his side.

"Reese?" Paul stood outside the main-level bathroom, knocking gently on the door.

"I'm fine!" she yelled from the other side.

He dragged his hand down his face. Stumped. Exasperated.

"Do you think she's sick?" Autumn asked.

"She can't be sick. Not again."

The lock clicked.

Paul stepped back.

Reese poked her head out from the door, her cheeks splotched with red, her attention zipping from Autumn to her father.

"Reese, baby, what's going on?"

"I, um . . ." She looked down at the floor, then shut herself back inside.

Water ran from the faucet.

A toilet flushed.

Autumn peered at the thin strip of light, something very slowly clicking into place. It got closer and closer and closer and then *click,* just as Reese slipped out into the hallway.

"I'm going to bed," she mumbled. And with that, she walked past them both and hurried up the stairs.

Paul stared after her, utterly confused. "I have no idea what's going on."

Autumn pointed toward the staircase. "I think I might."

"You do?"

She shifted uncomfortably, searching for the best, most painless way to clue him in. "You don't have any feminine hygiene products, do you?"

Paul blinked—startled—like a parent who suddenly realizes he can no longer get away with spelling out words in front of his child. "You think?"

"She's at that age."

"I don't have anything." Paul shook his head, horrified. "She's twelve. How can I not have anything?"

"It's okay. I'll go get some stuff in my car." She left him there to process the news. She quickly fetched some items from her glove box. When she came back in, Paul hadn't moved.

Neither had Tate.

She didn't want to overstep her bounds. She just knew that when she was that age, she would have rather died than talk to her dad about her menstrual cycle. And the thought of handing the items over and wishing Paul good luck didn't sit right. "Do you mind if I go and check on her?"

"Not at all." His words came doused in gratitude.

Autumn offered him a comforting smile, then walked up the stairs and knocked on Reese's open door.

"What?" she said, more than a little sharply. But then she turned over in bed and saw that it wasn't her father. She pushed herself up into sitting. "Oh. Sorry."

Autumn stepped inside, and set the items on Reese's nightstand. "I wasn't sure if you needed these."

"Thank you," she said quietly.

It should have been Vivian.

Vivian was meant to be here for this moment. In this room, handing her daughter these things. But Vivian wasn't. And Autumn was. And a girl shouldn't have to go through something like this alone. Autumn took a tentative seat on the edge of Reese's bed. "Do you have any questions or anything?"

Reese fiddled with the comforter. "How old were you when you got yours?"

"Fourteen."

"Really?"

"I was the last one of all my friends." Autumn smiled. "I watched this really awful Lifetime movie when I was ten, about a girl born without a uterus. She faked her own pregnancy and kidnapped a baby."

"That is awful."

"I spent all of eighth grade panicked that was going to be me."

When her period had finally come, she had melted with relief, and she hadn't told a soul. Not her dad. Not nine-year-old Claire. And definitely not Leanne.

Paul lifted Tate into his arms, taken aback by the weight of him. The length of him. This happened whenever he picked Tate up, which wasn't often anymore—this sense of alarm, like something monumental was passing him by, too slippery to grab hold of.

He carried him up to his room. He pulled off his shoes, peeled off his sweaty T-shirt and his athletic shorts, then tucked him under the covers in his Batman underwear and kissed his forehead.

Autumn's and Reese's voices trickled into the room—faint and muffled.

Paul turned off Tate's light, let loose a "here it goes" breath, and crossed the hallway.

The sight undid him. He drank in the scene like a parched man in the desert—Autumn sitting on the edge of his daughter's bed, murmuring words he couldn't hear. Words from a young woman to a young girl taking her first tentative steps into womanhood.

The two of them laughed.

Paul's heart squeezed.

There were moments when Reese still seemed so young and innocent, but even more moments like the one he experienced with Tate as he carried him up the stairs, only instead of her weight or height catching him off guard, it was her . . . apartness. There were more and more pieces of his daughter that were becoming a mystery to him. It filled Paul with the same sense of alarm that it had with Tate. The same sense that if he didn't grab something quick, this monumentally important thing would slip away.

The floorboards creaked beneath his feet.

Autumn saw him in the doorway and stood so quickly, one would think he'd caught her handing Reese a cigarette instead of comfort. She said good-bye to his daughter, then gave him a very weak smile as she skirted past him in the door-way.

"She'll be fine until tomorrow," Autumn said. "I should go."

He had no right to ask her to stick around.

No reason to either.

But Paul had just watched her stroke hair from his daughter's forehead. He had no idea why, but he wanted her to stay. He cast around for an excuse. "I have some pictures of Vivian in my office. Bottom drawer of my desk. They'd be great for the gallery you were talking about earlier."

"It's getting pretty late."

"I know." The streetlight shone in through Reese's window, illuminating Autumn's face. He could see the faint white scarring along the right side of her chin. "It won't take long. I promise."

Thirty-Nine

Autumn ran her hand over Paul's clean, uncluttered desk. At Redeemer, hers was slowly turning into the hive of activity it had been at Fishburn & Crandal. Paul's wasn't like that at all. Everything was neat and in its place.

There were two framed photographs. One was of a young Reese, cradling a bundled baby in her lap. Even then, infant Tate had a head full of thick, blond curls. The other one reminded her of the quote Mitch shared in last week's staff meeting. *"Trying to figure out God is like trying to catch a fish in the Pacific Ocean with an inch of dental floss."* The picture was of Paul and an older man with silver hair. Both of them were wearing fishing vests with poles slung over their shoulders.

Autumn brushed her finger across the top of the frame, her attention catching on a guitar pick. It was mixed in with a container of paper clips attached to a desk lamp. She fished it out and closed it in her palm.

There were no framed photographs of Vivian.

Those had been put away. She wondered when he did it. And why. Did they cause too much pain, seeing them every day? Or was he simply trying to move past the woman who'd given him thirteen years of marriage and two beautiful children?

Autumn opened the bottom desk drawer.

A notebook rested on top, its cover turned back.

She lifted it up to search underneath, but two slanted words at the top of the page caught her eye.

How Long

A poem?

She turned the guitar pick over in her fingers.

No, this wasn't a poem. It was a song.

Autumn couldn't resist. She found herself bent over the notebook, reading the evocative lyrics, swept up in the emotions they stirred. Loneliness and pain and grief, edged with the kind of beauty that pierced a person's soul.

"You stayed."

She yelped and dropped the notebook on the desk.

"Whoa," he said, holding up his hands. "I didn't mean to scare you."

A laugh escaped into the air, one so deranged, it left heat pooling in her ears. "I scare easily."

"I'll have to remember that."

Autumn scratched her elbow, her heart beating erratically.

"I feel like I owe you a gigantic thank-you."

She waved him off.

"No, really. I'm glad Reese had someone here when it . . . when it happened." He cringed. "I just made her period sound like something from a horror film, didn't I?"

"A little."

"Well, I'm glad you were here. She never would have told me."

Autumn shifted, hating herself for snooping. Why did she have to read anything? And why did the notebook have to fall open like that? So incriminating. Visible proof that she'd been reading things not meant for her.

"Did you find them?" he asked.

"Find what?"

"The pictures."

"Oh. No, I didn't."

He came around the desk to the opened bottom drawer. With the notebook removed, they were right there. A picture of him and Vivian on a white sandy beach rested on top. Her face was tilted toward the sun. Whoever took the photo had captured her in the middle of a laugh.

"That was in the Dominican Republic," Paul said. "On our honeymoon."

"She's beautiful."

He nodded. "We met my senior year in college. We both worked as baristas at this place called Coffee Art. She didn't actually need the job, since her dad was paying her way, but she was bored, and she wanted something to do, so Coffee Art was it." Something sad and unreachable flickered across his face. "Five months later, we were engaged."

"That's fast."

"I was captivated."

Her heart squeezed.

Coffee Art sweethearts.

A whirlwind romance.

She wished Seth were there with his camera, capturing the story.

"My mom used to call her Vivacious Vivian."

"She looks vivacious," Autumn said, looking down at the picture. She could practically hear his wife's laughter.

Paul shuffled the honeymoon photo to the back of the small stack. The one beneath was crinkled in the corners, with a small tear on the left side. Vivian wasn't in it at all, but a much younger Tate, holding up a turtle. Unlike the one before it, this picture made Paul smile. "Tank the Turtle. Man. That feels like a lifetime ago."

"How old is he?"

"Three, I think. Maybe four." Paul rubbed his thumb over Tate's baby-toothed grin, then looked up, his attention sliding to her hand. "Are you going to play something?"

"What?"

Paul nodded at the guitar pick.

"Oh, sorry. I forgot I was holding this." She put it back where she found it. "It's a good thing you noticed. I probably would have accidentally taken it. I do that all the time with pens. I have five from Redeemer already at home. Not that I'm stealing pens. I promise I'm going to return them."

"Don't worry. I won't tell Mitch."

The heat in her ears moved into her cheeks.

"This isn't even mine," he said, taking the pick and turning it over in his hand. "It belonged to my dad. He left it on the coffee table the day he walked out. I keep it as a reminder." He shook his head. "Pretty morbid, huh?"

Autumn shrugged. It wasn't more morbid than the obituaries she kept in her closet. "He's your dad. Of course you want to remember him."

"I don't want to remember him; I want to remember to never *be* like him."

"You couldn't be."

The words seemed to inflict a wound. Bring out insecurities he shouldn't have. She didn't see how he could—not regarding fatherhood. He would never leave his kids. He was the kind of father who rolled up his sleeves. Who pushed back and dug in and held tight.

"Reese and Tate have a really amazing dad. You know that, right?"

Her words were simple and entirely un-profound. Yet the furrow between his brows softened. He tossed the guitar pick on the desk, and that's when he saw it. The notebook. Opened, like a little tattletale. He looked up at her, his pupils slowly expanding. "Did you read that?"

She wanted to lie.

She wanted to say no, she hadn't read anything. But it was obvious she had. How else had the notebook gotten there? "I didn't mean to. It was open. The title caught my eye."

He set his hands over the words, like they were something to be ashamed of.

She didn't understand why. Grief wasn't a shameful thing. "Did you write it?"

He nodded.

"I think it's beautiful."

"No, it's not."

"Yes, it is."

He shook his head.

She leaned closer. "They're the words of a man dealing with the death of his wife."

He looked her square in the eye. His were the color of spring leaves in shadow, and as tumultuous as a raging sea. "I wrote them before."

Before?

"What do you mean?"

Paul didn't get the chance to answer.

Her phone started blaring "A Pocket Full of Sunshine," so loud and startling she jumped all over again. She answered with a sharp hello—like a woman harassed. It was completely reactionary. A jab of the button to make the song stop.

"What's wrong with you?" Claire asked on the other end.

Paul took a step back, shoving his fingers into his hair.

"Nothing." Autumn swallowed—an attempt to make the tone of her voice more normal sounding. But it was hard with Paul's eyes so fresh in her mind. And the words of that song. He wrote them before?

"I'm over at Trent's," Claire said.

Paul turned around and closed the notebook.

Autumn captured her bottom lip between her teeth.

"Seth stopped by a little bit ago. I said something to him about the box and he acted weird."

The box.

She had momentarily forgotten about the box.

"Hold on a second." She placed her hand over the receiving end of her phone. "Hey, Paul, I should probably—"

"It's fine. I'll see you later."

"Oh." She was going to say she should probably take the call. She wasn't going to say she should probably leave.

"I shouldn't have kept you this late." Paul turned around and handed her the honeymoon picture. "If I find any more, I'll make sure to get them to you."

"All right." She kept waiting for him to look at her, but he wouldn't meet her eye. He was busying himself with a manila file on his desk like it was suddenly the most important thing.

Startled, she thanked him for the baseball game and let herself out into the night.

Crickets chirped.

Drapes swayed in a window next door. Autumn thought she caught sight of an old woman, watching.

"Are you still with Paul?" Claire asked.

"I'm just leaving."

"Late game."

"Yeah." Autumn dug her keys from her purse. "What do you mean Seth acted weird?"

"I don't know. He was really quiet."

If Seth was quiet, it was probably because of the terribleness that was last night. "Was this before or after you mentioned the box?"

"After. He wanted to know what you said."

Autumn unlocked her car and eased inside. "Said about what?"

"The box."

"What did you tell him?"

"Nothing, really. I told him that you texted me about a box and I didn't know anything."

She started her car. The dashboard read twenty after eleven. Seth had always been a night owl. She doubted that had changed over the past nine months.

Forty

Seth didn't look surprised to see her. There was no wide-eyed shock. No *What are you doing here?* Just a strained "Hey" and some stress around his eyes as he opened the door and invited her in.

It was bizarre, being here after all this time.

His living area was unchanged.

He had the same couch and the same black leather Corbusier chairs. The same stainless steel standing lamp. The same weathered chest covered with magazines and a video game controller. Seth hurriedly gathered the mess—grabbing a few magazines off the couch—and stacked them neatly on the chest.

"Why did I have a box?"

He slowly straightened, his face slightly pink.

Claire was right. He knew something.

"The day of the explosion, I was carrying a box with me onto the train. Why?"

Seth rubbed the top of his head.

She cocked hers.

"We broke up," he finally said.

"That day?"

"Yes."

The words were so shocking, they bounced right off her. She made him repeat himself, and when he said the same thing, she stood there trying to acclimate to this new truth. It was like he'd just informed her that what she saw as blue, everybody else saw as green. She stood there, trying her hardest to imagine a shamrock-colored sky and a blue-moon-colored field. "That's what happened after I left work," she said, more to herself than to him.

He nodded.

Autumn couldn't believe it.

Seth had lied to her.

When she woke up, she'd been so desperate to put the pieces together. She asked everyone what she might have been doing during those mysterious two hours. And all this time, Seth had handed her the wrong piece. He told her he didn't know anything. But that wasn't the truth. She'd been here, in this apartment. Packing up her things. Putting them in a box.

"Who broke up with who?"

His pink face turned red.

It was all the answer she needed. Autumn closed her eyes. Maybe, if she shut out her sight, she'd have more mental space to process what he was saying.

"We were fighting a lot."

"Over Melanie Holloway?"

He didn't object.

"Were you breaking up with me for her?"

"No." But this time, she could tell. She could see that he was lying again.

Autumn laughed a high-pitched, disbelieving laugh and crossed her arms. "I need you to explain everything."

And so he did.

He sat down on the edge of a chair with his elbows on his knees and told her that they he'd had a business dinner with Melanie Holloway scheduled for Monday night. Autumn wasn't happy about it, and they got into a gigantic fight that Sunday. The next day, Seth broke up with her. Over the phone, no less. After work, she came to get her things, they fought some more, and then she left.

"Then why did you propose to me in the hospital?"

"Because I knew breaking up was a mistake," he said. "It was the biggest mistake of my life. I don't even think I meant it. As soon as I heard about the explosion, I realized how much I loved you. I realized that I couldn't live without you. It was the worst twenty-four hours of my life, Autumn. I begged God for another chance, and then we got a call that you were alive. I was determined to win you back. To make things right. But when you woke up, you didn't remember anything. I don't know, it just . . . it felt like God was giving us a fresh start."

Autumn's mind spun.

Around and around and around until she had to sit down.

When she woke up, she had been so aggravated with him. She struggled through bouts of resentment that didn't make any sense. Every time she looked at Seth, she felt angry. The doctor assured her it was normal. Her emotions would be as disoriented as her memories. But that wasn't true. Her emotions were remembering what her brain couldn't.

Seth had broken up with her.

"Don't you think," she said, pushing the words through her teeth, "that if *God* had gone to so much trouble to give us a second chance, He would have liked you to be honest?"

"I'm sorry." Seth bowed his head, his shoulders sagging. "I was afraid of losing you."

And so he had.

He lost her.

And all this time, she'd felt horrible about it. All this time, he'd let her believe she was just a touch crazy.

Lulu wailed from beneath the dinner table.

Chad and Jane ignored her.

This was what they did now. Lulu's temper tantrums had increased exponentially since the arrival of Ike. Jane said she was protesting her position as the middle child, something Autumn could sympathize with. It wasn't an easy transition for anyone, especially not for a child as doted on as Lulu.

team? She knew she packed it. She wouldn't have forgotten.

Dad had told her not to worry about it. Her teammates wouldn't care. But she cared. Autumn became that dog with a bone. Apparently she had a problem with that, even back then. Gnaw, gnaw, gnaw. Chew, chew, chew. Until her dad grew visibly aggravated. *"Autumn, forget about the bow. We'll find it when we get home."*

But she couldn't forget. She was already so nervous. Her stomach was in the tightest knot it had ever been in. And for whatever reason, her eleven-year-old self pinned the source of all that anxiety on her stupid hair. She started freaking out. And so, while Dad grew red in the face and stiff in the shoulders, Mom sighed and said, *"Oh, Tom, it's fine. I'll just run home and get it."*

"You're going to miss her first event," Dad said.

"It's not like it's going to be her last." And then Mom turned to Autumn and cupped her chin. *"Have fun. Do your best."*

Autumn never saw her mother again.

Not alive, anyway.

And it most certainly had been her last gymnastics meet.

In all the chaos surrounding the accident, the *why* got lost. Why was her mother on the road to begin with?

Autumn kept waiting for the other shoe to drop. For someone to finally put two and two together.

To straighten from the huddle of grief and say, "Wait a minute. Why wasn't she already *at* the gymnastics meet?"

Everyone would turn to her, and she would have to answer the question.

But nobody asked.

She supposed it got buried in all that tragedy and grief. Everybody was so busy coming around them in their sad little state, helping Dad arrange the funeral and feed his children and pay the bills, that nobody stopped to ask about the actual details.

"I'm sorry about Mom," Autumn said.

"Why would you apologize to me about your mother?"

"Because it was my fault."

"How do you figure that?"

"The hair bow."

Dad looked confused, like he'd forgotten all about that hair bow, but that was impossible. He couldn't have forgotten. He scratched his chin. "Let me get this straight. You think your mom died because you forgot your hair bow?"

"She was driving because of me. She was driving because I forgot it."

He shook his head. "I'm not the most religious man, Autumn. But I do believe in God. And the last I checked, He's the one in charge."

Forty-One

Jeannie True lifted her eyebrows at Autumn's vehement statement. She had emphasized all four syllables, since all four syllables were profoundly significant.

He lied to me.

Autumn wanted Jeannie to understand why this was such a big deal. She wanted her to understand so she would stop raising her eyebrows in that annoyingly placid way and start looking a little indignant on her behalf.

"When I woke up, I was upset with Seth. I was hurt and angry whenever I looked at him."

"That must have been confusing."

"It was! I felt horrible. Seth cried and begged me not to give up on us when I broke up with him, when he was the one who gave up on us first." Autumn stopped short of banging her fist against the leather arm of the sofa chair.

Jeannie didn't look indignant at all. She looked calm and logical and mildly unimpressed. "Did you tell Seth how you were feeling?"

"The other night?"

"When you woke up from the coma. Did Seth know you were experiencing these confusing feelings toward him?"

"Well." Autumn looked down at her hands in her

lap and thumbed the Claddagh ring, the crown facing away from her heart, because her heart wasn't taken. She'd felt so dreadful when she turned it around. And a small part of her had relished that dread. She deserved it. She deserved to feel dreadful, just like she deserved to wear this imposter ring while her mother's hid somewhere in a heap of ash. "I thought they'd go away and we'd be fine."

"Do you think he would have explained if you'd told him how you were feeling?"

No. He wouldn't have.

He would have let her go on believing that she was poor, confused, surviving Autumn—out of sorts and illogical, thanks to a nasty bump on the head. But then, it was Seth. Seth wasn't a liar. At least not typically. That was probably why the whole thing came as such a shock. And he'd lied so egregiously.

Jeannie sat behind her desk, fingers steepled, looking at Autumn until she started to feel as twitchy as the spastic betta fish. "Do you wish you hadn't broken up with him?"

"No."

"Then why are you so upset?"

"Because he lied. And I felt so guilty. I didn't need any extra guilt. Not when it wasn't my fault."

"But the explosion," Jeannie said. "Benjamin Havel's bomb that took the lives of twenty-two people. That was your fault?"

338

Autumn sat on the bench, watching the trains come and go. People filed on and off them. They had places to go and people to see and things to accomplish. She sat there with her phone powered off, replaying Jeannie's words and Sandra Reid's words and her father's words. Over and over again —on a loop, like the trains.

"Last I checked, He's the one in charge."

So what did that mean?

God took Mom's life? He was the one who made Autumn forget her hair bow? If that was true, why would He let something like that happen? If Autumn's mother was destined to die that day, why did God involve Autumn at all? And if Autumn wasn't destined to die in Tragedy on the Tracks, then why did she have to be on that train?

Her thoughts wandered to Reese, and then Paul, and the song he'd written and the honeymoon picture he kept tucked away in his bottom desk drawer and the other one he kept on his desk— with the old man and the fishing gear. *"Trying to figure out God is like trying to catch a fish in the Pacific Ocean with an inch of dental floss."*

Futile.

And frustrating.

A Mexican woman sat on the bench beside her. She gave Autumn a friendly smile and a nod, then spoke fast-paced Spanish into her phone. The platform was slowly filling up again. Autumn found herself searching for Kelsey Collins.

"How do you do it? How do you ride the train?"

A railcar approached from the distance.

People shuffled forward.

The Spanish-speaking woman dug something out of her purse and stood.

Autumn stood with her, her heart pounding in her ears.

False guilt.

False fear.

The train slowly squealed to a stop.

Autumn's body didn't feel like her own.

She thought about Kelsey Collins, trying to get on the train that first time. And then again, and again, until finally it worked.

This was how a person moved on. This was how you put one foot in front of the other. With a deep, terrified breath, she lunged on board and grabbed for the nearest bar, her hands slippery with sweat as the door closed behind her.

A static-filled voice announced their next stop.

The train released its breaks and lurched forward.

Autumn's panic lurched with it.

Her knees shook.

Her head spun.

She tried inhaling, but it didn't work. Again and again, her heart beating faster and faster. She needed out. She couldn't breathe. There wasn't any oxygen. She was going to suffocate.

Release.

She wasn't sure where the word came from, but it worked. Autumn pushed all the air from her lungs, along with Sandra's question and Seth's lie and Benjamin Havel's bomb and her forgotten hair bow.

Release.

Everything confusing. *Out.*

Everything lovely. *In.*

All of her fears. *Out.*

All that was true. *In.*

She focused on Tate's goofy laugh and Reese's stories and basketball in the rain and Sunday night dinners with her family. She focused on breathing and the rattle of the train car. The gentle sway as it rolled through a curve. The scent of perfume and gum and cigarette smoke.

The train stopped.

Passengers filed past her.

Autumn gripped the pole tighter, every muscle frozen as she kept her eyes closed. People were probably staring, but she didn't care. The doors slid shut again. The static-filled voice returned. Autumn kept breathing, like a woman in labor. She gathered all the panic into a knotted, tangled mass and released it. With every exhale, she pictured flinging it away, like the paint on Reese's brush. Tentative at first. Then with more authority. Again and again, until it couldn't control her. Until it couldn't undo her. And when she was

341

positive that she was not going to die—her heart would not explode—she forced herself to open her eyes.

She took in the calm, bored faces of fellow passengers and the apartments sliding past the windows.

The rail car rounded a bend.

A burst of evening sun shone through the glass, painting everything a brilliant gold. Nearby, a baby girl somewhere around Lilian Grace Montgomery's age winced and buried her face in her mother's shoulder.

"Every day felt dark. And then one day . . . I don't know. I guess some light showed up again."

Autumn rode that same train until night fell. She rode it all around the city until her muscles were loose, and her breathing, even.

Sunday, December 25, 2016

Dear Autumn,

My brother is seven, and he still believes in Santa Claus, even though I've told him loads of times that Santa isn't real. My dad says he wants to believe and I should leave him alone. But it's kind of disturbing when he's so willing to ignore the evidence staring him in the face. A few weeks ago, we went to a parade, and there were two guys dressed up as Santa, ten minutes apart. I know Tate saw them, and I know he had questions, but he never asked anything.

I learned the truth when I was five.

Mia told me that parents always hid presents in their bedroom, so that year, I went snooping, and I found a zebra puppet in my parent's closet. The kind with the strings. It's called a marionette. I felt really, really guilty. My stomach hurt for days! My dad says I've been blessed with a sensitive conscience, but I'm not sure it's a blessing.

On Christmas morning, I opened a gift from "Santa," and it was the zebra puppet! That's when I knew the whole thing was a sham. But I couldn't tell anybody. I had to pretend I still believed, because I didn't want my parents to know I snuck into their room. I remember Mom saying, "Oh Reese, look how adorable he is! Santa's elves really outdid themselves, didn't they?" And I remember thinking, "You're lying to me right now."

I thought that would be my worst Christmas ever. The Christmas my mom lied and I found out Santa wasn't real.

I was wrong.

Today has been the worst. Grandma and Pop and Dad keep smiling extra, extra big. They keep pretending nothing is wrong. It's like they think I've forgotten Mom's dead, and they don't want to remind me. It's like they think I'm as clueless as Tate, which is kind of insulting, because my brother is really clueless.

Anyway, I hope your Christmas was okay. Or maybe you're Jewish. I don't think you are, but just in case, Happy Hanukkah. Did you spend the day with that guy, Seth? Are you two married yet? I Googled you, but nothing new came up. Just a bunch of old articles from Tragedy on the Tracks.

From,
Reese Rosamund Elliott

P.S. If you're not married yet, I'd love to come to the wedding!

Forty-Two

To: elliottpaul@gmail.com
From: a.manning@redeemerchicago.com
Date: Thu, June 8, 2017 9:17 a.m.
Subject: contact info

Hi Paul,

I forgot to get Vivian's parents' contact information from you. Could you send it my way? We should probably also get that interview set up. June 23 is almost here.

Take care,
Autumn

To: a.manning@redeemerchicago.com
From: margohornsby@gmail.com
Date: Fri, June 9, 2017 10:52 a.m.
Subject: FW: contact info

Dear Autumn,

My name is Margo Hornsby. I'm Paul's office assistant. Below you will find the contact information you requested . . .

Blessings,
Margo

To: elliottpaul@gmail.com
From: R.Bell12@yahoo.com
Date: Fri, June 9, 2017 3:46 p.m.
Subject: the tribute

Paul,

What is this about a tribute? I haven't heard a thing about it until now, when I opened an e-mail from Autumn Manning. Imagine my surprise seeing her name in my inbox. Apparently, this woman is holding some sort of reception at your church in two weeks. She invited me to send her footage of me talking about Vivian, but I don't know the first thing about how to do that. I got the impression that you've known about it for some time.

If so, I don't understand why you haven't called me. I really wish I would have known about this sooner. I'm Vivian's mother. I have a right to know about these things. Of course I want to go. I just hope I can make it work on such short notice.

Yours,
Regina

Forty-Three

"You took the bus?" Chad's voice registered surprise. He'd been standing outside Portillo's and saw Autumn step off with several other passengers.

"Is that weird?"

"I didn't think you used public transportation anymore."

She hitched her purse strap over her shoulder and shrugged him off. Funny how indiscreet her oddities had become. Especially when she thought she'd done a good job hiding them. But if Chad knew she'd been avoiding the transit system, then she definitely hadn't hidden anything.

"Claire's already inside," Chad said, opening the front door. "What are the odds this thing she wants to talk to us about isn't really a thing?"

"It'd better be a thing."

Because at the moment, Autumn had a million other things she could be doing. She stepped inside to the hustle and bustle of Portillo's at lunch hour. It smelled like a ballpark, which reminded her of the Elliotts.

Inside, Claire was wearing flip-flops, running shorts, and a black graphic tank that said "Beach Hair Don't Care." Appropriately, her hair— the roots needing dyed if she wanted them to match the rest of her brown locks—was pulled up into a very short, windblown ponytail. This was Summertime Claire, who didn't bother with makeup and didn't have to teach a passel of kids every day.

They stood in line and ordered their food and found a table by the window upstairs. Autumn unwrapped her italian beef. It was too much for a quick midweek lunch, but she found it impossible to go to Portillo's and *not* get the italian beef.

"You had something you wanted to talk about?" Autumn prompted.

"Not really," Claire said, dumping fries onto her tray. "I just wanted to have lunch with my sibs."

"Claire!"

"What? We never get together anymore."

Autumn caught Chad's eye.

He looked more amused than disgruntled.

"Why did you tell us you had something you needed to talk to us about?" She'd made it sound so important. So classified. For a minute, Autumn had wondered if Claire was pregnant. Or terminally ill. Or second-guessing the wedding.

"Because I knew it was the only way I could get the three of us together."

Autumn closed her eyes.

She was insanely busy right now. She had no idea how Redeemer had survived for one day without a communications consultant, let alone several weeks. Keeping tabs on the marriage campaign itself was a full-time job. The conference in July was nearly sold out. Pastor Mitch had met with his fellowship of pastors and decided to invite people to participate via satellite. Many churches across the area were picking up Paul's book and using it as a study for their small groups.

On top of that, there was the tribute, already just a week and a half away.

The memorial commission board had jumped in to offer their assistance. A few women had volunteered to take over the lobby, hanging various displays. The board director's son was the owner of a local catering company and would gladly provide the food for free. And Autumn had only two interviews left: Ina May Huett on Friday, and Paul Elliott, which still wasn't scheduled. She hadn't seen Paul or Reese since the White Sox game. When she reached out to him via e-mail, he forwarded her to his assistant, Margo. She wasn't sure if he was really that busy or if he was purposefully avoiding her. Vivian's mother, Regina, seemed willing to participate. She even sent some footage via e-mail, but when Autumn tried opening it, she received an error message.

All of it tied her stomach into a knot.

The whole reason for the tribute was Vivian. They couldn't leave her out of it.

"Claire, we see each other every single day," Autumn said.

"I know. But you're always on the run." She dunked a fry into mustard and popped it into her mouth. Autumn caught herself wondering what Paul would say about Claire's condiment of choice when it came to french fries. "You've turned into a workaholic."

"You are unbelievable."

"What?"

"A couple months ago, you were on my back because I wasn't doing anything. Now you're complaining because I'm doing too much?"

"I wasn't on your back because you weren't doing anything. I was on your back because you were obsessing. You've gone from obsessing to avoiding."

Autumn could feel her cheeks turning warm.

Sometimes her sister got something right on the nose, and she did it in such a casual way, like she didn't know she'd gotten anything right at all.

"I'm busy with work and the tribute. That doesn't make me a workaholic."

Chad swallowed a bite of his chili dog. "How are things going with Seth?"

Guilt came at the mention of Seth's name. It was phantom guilt, like pain in a limb that had been severed. She'd told Claire all about the box and their confrontation. Apparently, after Autumn's psychotic dinnertime monologue, Claire filled the rest of the family in.

"It's been fine," Autumn said.

Chad looked at her skeptically. "He's still helping with the tribute?"

"Yes." And she refused to feel bad about it. The way she saw it, Seth owed her. "Can we please change the subject?"

"Yes," Claire said. "Let's talk about Father's Day, and what we're gonna do for Dad."

"We're having a cookout at the house." Like they did every year.

"That's not very special. We should do something special."

Autumn's mind wandered to Reese and Tate. Were they planning something special for Paul? Were they out for summer break yet? The schools around Chicago got out at different times, some quite late in the month. What did he do when his kids were out of school?

Chad took a drink of his Coke. "Jane's having the kids make some sort of handprint art project for him."

"That's not fair," Claire protested.

"What's not fair?"

"You have cute kids. They make your gift-giving easy."

"That's *all* they make easy." It was true. Chad looked like a president after his first four-year term, with more gray stubble than red. Little mewling Ike had pushed him over the edge. "Jane's started acupuncture. It's supposed to help her milk production."

Claire caught Autumn's eye.

They both tried really hard not to laugh.

"Make fun all you want, but if it helps my wife, I'm all for it. This transition from two to three is no joke."

"Trent's sister says it's like going from man-to-man defense to zone."

"Man-to-man defense is a lot more tiring than zone," Autumn said. "So that's not really a good analogy."

Claire rolled her eyes.

Autumn thought about basketball in the rain.

"At least Ike can't move yet," Claire said.

"It'd be nice if he slept," Chad said.

Sleep.

It was something Autumn had been getting more of lately. More and more often, she was sleeping through the 3:00 a.m. hour. The first time it happened—after she conquered her fear and got back on the train—she'd been shocked. So much so, she was positive Claire had messed with her bedside clock.

"He'll sleep after a few more rounds of acupuncture," Claire said.

Chad threw a fry at her.

Autumn took a bite of her italian beef, struck by the scene unfolding in front of her. This father of three living in the city, deep in the trenches of newborn baby-dom, having lunch with his two sisters. Chad was so normal. It so easily could have been him on the train. He could have died in the explosion, leaving Cal and Lulu without a father. Hungry baby Ike wouldn't even exist, and Jane Manning wouldn't be doing acupuncture. At least not for milk production. She'd be a physically fit widowed mother of two, making Father's Day projects for their grandfather.

Autumn looked at her sister.

It could have been Claire. Instead of planning her wedding, she'd be dead, and Trent would remember with sad fondness the girlfriend who might have been more. They hadn't been very serious when the train explosion happened. He would have moved on by now.

She looked around the second story of Portillo's. All the people eating their food, conversing. Going about their day. It could have been any one of them.

They finished their meal.

Chad ate the other half of Autumn's italian beef.

They dumped the garbage from their trays, and Autumn took a Tootsie Pop from her purse. One of the Tootsie Pops from the bag Paul had tossed at her the day of her second interview.

"Those make me think of Mom."

The words belonged to Claire.

And they came as a surprise.

Sometimes Autumn wondered if Claire remembered Mom at all.

Chad smiled. "Me too."

The three of them looked at one another and said almost simultaneously, "Shots."

A warm feeling stole through Autumn's body.

They remembered.

Every time her siblings saw Tootsie Pops, they would remember.

She quickly dug inside her purse as they walked down the stairs and pulled out the final two. She gave the brown one to Claire. The blue one to Chad.

He pulled off the wrapper and searched for the American Indian and the star. "You used to freak out so badly that an extra nurse had to come in to hold you down."

"I did not," Autumn said.

"Yes, you did."

"Mom always explained on the car ride why I needed to get a shot. 'It's medicine. Very important medicine.' Like an explanation was going to make it hurt less." Claire twirled her Tootsie Pop by its white stem. "Funny. It never worked that way."

The three of them stepped outside, to the traffic and noise.

Claire was right.

Mom did try to explain. Every time. But it never helped. A shot was a shot, and it hurt no matter which way you spun it.

What helped was crawling into Mom's lap

"Yeah."

"You know what, though? I'll be seeing him soon. And just between you and me," Ina May leaned in, like her long-deceased mother-in-law was standing over her shoulder with a ready ear, "the miracle was never my favorite part of the story, anyway."

"What's your favorite part?"

"When Jesus wept."

Autumn tilted her head. She found it odd, thinking about a weeping Jesus.

"I think it might be my favorite verse in the whole Bible."

"That was Chad's favorite."

"Who?"

"My brother. Chad. 'Jesus wept' was his favorite verse too."

Ina May gave her a quick, firm nod, like she wholly approved of her brother Chad's choice in Bible verses. She probably wouldn't if she knew Chad only liked it for its brevity. He hated having weekly memory verses for the religious ed classes they used to take on Wednesday nights. "Jesus wept" was quite an easy one to remember, and thus, Chad's favorite.

Autumn wanted to ask why it was Ina May's, but the cuckoo clock on the wall released its mechanical bird, which swiveled its head about.

It was already eight, and Seth was getting antsy to leave.

Forty-Five

Tiny blades of grass kicked up from the mower and sprayed Paul's calves like itchy pieces of hair. The sun reached down from the sky and pressed hot fingers against the sides of his face. He squinted against the brightness and pushed the mower faster.

Distraction.

That was the name of the game.

Work himself to exhaustion so his brain would think of nothing but water and food and a good night of sleep.

He wiped at the beads of sweat trickling down his temple. Heat and humidity tangled together in the late afternoon air, but he kept going like a man on a mission. He'd spent the day at his mom's, first pulling weeds out of her flower beds, then cleaning out the shed, then hanging shelves in the garage, and now mowing the lawn.

He missed this—manual labor.

A yard to take care of.

Living in the city meant he hardly had any lawn at all. He and his neighbors were all squished together on same-sized, too-small lots that cost a fortune. Maybe it was time to move. Officially start over. It wasn't like he'd ever wanted to live in the city to begin with. That had been Vivian.

Her father bought them the house. An actual house. Something Paul hadn't been comfortable with, but Vivian had fallen in love.

Then she died, and he stayed because it was the only home his children knew, and they were settled in a good school with good friends. Adding unnecessary change to the situation didn't seem wise. But maybe they were ready now. Maybe they could put their house up for sale and move to the suburbs, where life would be easier and far from bad memories.

Sweat trickled down the nape of his neck. His shirt stuck to his back.

A dog barked one yard over.

Paul dragged his arm across his face, picturing the scene. A nice house, a well-kept lawn, a dog for the kids to take care of. Grilling hamburgers out back with Reese and Tate.

Maybe Autumn would join them.

The intrusive thought made his stomach clench.

He still couldn't believe she'd read his song, and that he'd gotten so close to telling her the truth. If her sister hadn't called, he probably would have. He didn't trust that he still wouldn't, and once it came tumbling out, it would be impossible to take back. Every time she saw him, she would know what he couldn't escape:

Paul Elliott, Marriage Doctor extraordinaire, was a fraud.

A hypocrite.

A giant phony.

A man who prayed for a way out and got it in the form of a dead wife.

Paul shook his head and pushed the mower faster.

Tomorrow was Father's Day. They'd all go to church, and afterward, Mom would make Pop's favorite—pot roast and potatoes. They'd sit outside and play chess while Reese read a book or wrote a story and Tate organized a water-balloon fight with all the neighborhood kids.

On Monday, he'd go back to work and deal with the phone calls and e-mails he had yet to return to his agent, who was thrilled about the marriage campaign. He would have to respond to Autumn's e-mail. He couldn't keep avoiding her. He would have to do the interview. Then on Thursday, he'd pick up Regina from the airport, something he didn't think he'd have to do ever again since her hatred for O'Hare seemed to outweigh her love for her grandchildren.

It did not outweigh, however, her need to go to this reception. Appearances meant everything to a woman like Regina.

The tribute would end.

The marriage campaign would come and go.

And he and Autumn would be nothing more than casual acquaintances who made small talk on occasion in Redeemer's lobby.

The entire thing really depressed him.

Paul turned the mower to make a diagonal path toward the house and spotted his mother, out on the patio, waving frantically in his direction.

He released the mower's handle.

The engine went dead.

The dog barked.

And Mom yelled. She yelled for Paul to hurry. To come quickly.

"It's Pop!" she said. "Something's wrong with Pop."

Paul's heart lurched as he sprinted inside, where the kitchen faucet ran. He turned the water off.

Mom picked up the phone to dial 911. "He's in the bathroom. I can't get him out. He's blocking the door."

Paul ran to the main-level bedroom, the one that used to be Mom's but was now Pop's because he couldn't use the stairs. The bathroom door was slightly ajar, light spilling out from the small crack. Sure enough, when he pushed the door to open it wider, something blocked the way.

"Pop, are you okay in there?"

A muffled sound came from the other side. It was like Pop had been gagged. Like he wanted to talk, but he couldn't.

Behind him, Mom spoke into the receiver. "It's my father. He's eighty-five. He collapsed in the bathroom. I think he's having a stroke."

Paul didn't know what to do.

Should he try to push the door harder? How

could he be sure he wouldn't injure Pop further? But how could he be sure Pop wasn't dying right now, all alone on the other side of this door?

He knocked. "Pop? Pop, can you hear me?"

More muffled, unintelligible sound.

"Yes," Mom said, her fingers near her mouth. "Yes, he seems to be conscious. He's making sounds, but we can't understand them."

"Ask if we should try to open the door," Paul said.

Mom parroted his question. "My son wants to know if we should try to get inside the bathroom."

An interminable pause.

A panic-soaked pause.

If the bathroom had a window, he'd sprint outside and crawl through. But the bathroom didn't have a window.

Paul peered through the small crack and could see nothing but the walker and one of Pop's legs. He got down on all fours and pressed his face against the carpet to peer underneath. Was that blood? Was Pop bleeding?

"What are we supposed to do?" he asked.

"She says not to open the door. Not if he's blocking it. An ambulance is on the way."

"Did you hear that, Pop?" Paul called, his voice trembling. "Help is on the way. It's going to be okay. You're going to be okay."

That was all Paul could do.

During that torturous wait, while Mom spoke

364

with the 911 operator and Pop lay helpless on the floor, Paul repeated those words over and over. He got down on his knees, praying they were true.

Then the wail came.

And Paul could see it unfolding.

The ambulance speeding down the street, sirens blaring. The curiosity that would fill Reese and Tate as they watched, and then the fear and panic that would strike when the ambulance pulled into their grandmother's driveway.

He wanted to get up and run to them. Shield them from more trauma.

But he couldn't. He had to stay. He had to wait until the paramedics arrived with the stretcher.

And then he rushed outside, where the neighbors had begun to gather. Reese and Tate tore down the street from three houses down, their eyes wild. Paul met them on the sidewalk. They crashed into him, tears tumbling down their faces.

Tears of relief for Reese, because she thought something had happened to her dad. Tears of sadness for Tate, because he sure loved his Pop.

Paul rubbed their backs and clutched them tighter and told them the same thing he'd told his grandfather.

"It's going to be okay. It's going to be okay."

Over and over and over again.

Forty-Six

Familiar voices wove their way into the kitchen as Paul paced. Inigo Montoya and Buttercup's sweet Westley, duking it out in a sword fight. Reese and Tate were sitting in the living room, watching the only movie they could ever agree on—*The Princess Bride*.

Mom had called minutes ago, as soon as she spoke with a doctor. Pop had a stroke, and they were trying to get him stabilized. Paul was break-through-a-brick-wall desperate to get to them. To be there for his mom. To speak with the doctors himself. But the person he'd usually take his children to in an emergency was the one having the emergency.

He felt so utterly helpless here.

He picked up the phone and dialed Margo again. Mitch and Lisa were in Saint Louis for Father's Day weekend, and Mrs. Ryan was up north at her father-in-law's cabin with her husband and the three girls. Margo's line rang once more, then shuffled him to voice mail.

Paul released a frustrated growl.

He could handle it most days—this single parenting. It was stressful, sure. But doable. Then something like this happened, exposing the reality of the situation. He wasn't in control at all. He was balancing on the edge of manageability and disarray. He didn't really have a handle on anything.

Paul peeked into the living room.

Reese and Tate sat side by side on the couch. Tate's hand rested on Reese's knee. Tate would like to rest his hand on Reese's knee anytime they watched a movie. Or rest his head on her shoulder. He was an affectionate, touchy kid. The kind who would crawl into Paul's bed in the morning and ask to cuddle. And on most days, Reese refused to tolerate it.

Stop touching me, Tate.

Stop leaning on me, Tate.

Get away from me, Tate.

Not now.

Now, Tate was happily resting his hand on her leg, watching as Westley tossed his sword from his left hand to his right in a clever little plot twist, and Reese didn't seem to mind it at all.

"Hey, guys, how do you feel about going to Mrs. Green's house?"

"What?" Reese cried. "Why?"

"I need to get to the hospital to be with Grandma and help with Pop."

"I don't want to go to Mrs. Green's!" Tate said. "She's old and she smells like pee."

Paul ran his hand down his face. Tate enjoyed Mrs. Green. She was a little strict, but she had a whole closet full of board games and little army men. She was reliable and familiar and almost always home. "Tate, she isn't old. And she doesn't smell like pee."

"She kind of does," Reese muttered. "I don't understand why we can't go to the hospital with you."

Paul shook his head. He would not be taking his children to the hospital. Tate would be a hyperactive nightmare. And he didn't have any guarantee that this would end well. He had no idea how severe Pop's stroke had been. Which was why it was so vital that he get to the hospital now. An illogical wave of panic gripped him. It was as if Pop's life depended on Paul's presence.

"I'm old enough to watch Tate. I do it all the time."

Yeah. After school for an hour or two. And at least once that he knew of, she had left Tate by himself. He wasn't going to leave them alone after a day like today. He hardly felt right about leaving them at all, but his mother needed him more right now. He needed to be with Pop more right now. "I don't know how late I'm going to be at the hospital."

"Why don't you call Autumn?"

"What?"

"She can come over and hang out with us," Reese said.

Tate perked. "Yeah! I like Autumn."

He could not call Autumn right now. On a Saturday evening? To watch his kids?

Tate clasped his hands together beneath his chin. "Please, Dad. Can you please call Autumn and tell her to come over?"

His pent-up breath sailed away. Did he have any other choice? His kids were upset. He hated leaving them, and they didn't want to be with Delilah Green. They wanted to be at home, with Autumn. A woman who called his son Officer Tate. A woman who sat on the edge of Reese's bed and talked to her about womanly things. A woman who made his daughter laugh again.

"She's probably busy."

"You can at least try," Reese urged.

And so he did.

He picked up his phone, found her in his contact list, and pressed Call, half-hoping she wouldn't answer.

But she did.

She answered on the first ring.

"Hello?"

"Autumn? It's Paul."

"Hi."

He scratched the side of his head. "I'm sure you're busy right now, but I'm kind of in a bind."

"What's wrong?"

"My grandfather." Tate stared up at him with anxious eyes. Much too familiar eyes. "He's sick in the hospital."

"Oh my goodness. Is he all right?"

"I'm not sure. I need to get there to be with my mom, but I don't want to bring the kids to the hospital, and I'm not comfortable leaving them alone. Turns out, this late on a Saturday night isn't the best time to find a babysitter. Reese and Tate wanted me to call you, to check if you might be available." He took a deep breath. To keep going. To take her off the hook. To talk her out of his own request.

But she jumped in before he could say anything more. "Of course. I'll be right over."

"Please?"

Autumn wasn't sure Reese's suggestion was a good one. Their great-grandfather was in the hospital. Paul had whispered the rudimentary details when she arrived, tension creasing the corners of his eyes, tightening the muscles in his jaw, furrowing the space between his eyebrows.

Reese and Tate seemed mostly oblivious, and in relatively good spirits. Paul must have hidden the gravity of the situation from them. They hugged her when she arrived. They popped popcorn and finished watching *The Princess Bride*. Autumn sat in between them on the couch. Tate snuggled up against her, making a glorious mess with the popcorn.

It wasn't until they were cleaning it up that Reese got the idea.

"I'm not sure now is a good time."

"But the reception is this Friday."

Yes, it was.

And Paul still hadn't responded to her e-mails.

"We don't have any camera equipment," Autumn said.

"I have a camera in my room. I got it last year for my birthday. It came with a tripod and every-thing. Please, Autumn? My dad said we could do the interview. He said you wouldn't mind."

Paul said that? Then why hadn't he mentioned anything about interviewing his kids when she arrived? He hadn't given her permission. But he'd also been distracted, and visibly distraught, moving from room to room in search of his keys. And then, when he found them, he thanked her emphatically. Kissed his children. Told them to behave. And for a split second, she swore he'd almost kissed her too.

Not a *kiss*-kiss. But another peck on the cheek. An afterthought between good friends—or an old married couple.

Her heart had done an odd sort of flip.

But the kiss hadn't come, and he was off. Out the back door, hurrying to his car while Tate rummaged through the pantry for popcorn.

"Your dad really said that?"

Reese nodded decisively. "Yes. That's one of the reasons he called you. My mom *has* to be in the tribute. She's the reason I had the idea to begin with. And my grandmother Regina is coming all the way from North Carolina to watch it. If Mom's not in it, she'll be upset." The more Reese talked, the more wound up she became. Her chest rose and fell with each word, tears forming in her eyes.

Autumn held up her hands. "Okay, okay. We can do it."

Reese smiled—a broad, enthusiastic smile—looking, for the first time that Autumn could remember, exactly like her brother.

Forty-Seven

Autumn hovered her finger over the Record button, unsure if this was wise. But Reese was so determined, and Tate didn't seem bothered. And the tribute was less than a week away. If they didn't do this now, it seemed unlikely that Vivian would be in the video, and that couldn't happen.

"Are you sure you want to do this tonight?"

Reese nodded, subdued but resolute.

Wrangling her nerves into submission, Autumn pressed the button and took a seat in the armchair.

"What are we supposed to say?" Tate asked.

"You get to say whatever you want."

"Am I going to be on television?"

"You'll be on one of the big screens at Redeemer," Autumn said.

"Really?"

"And on YouTube," she added, her attention sliding to Reese.

The small red record light seemed to have rattled the girl's resoluteness.

Tate pointed to a small, white scar on his forehead. "I did an American Ninja Warrior dive off the couch and almost bled to death."

"Wow," Autumn said, biting back a smile. "I'm glad you didn't."

"Yeah. I had to get my head stitched together though."

"You know, when I said you could talk about whatever you want, I should have been more specific. Do you know why we're doing this right now?" Autumn's stomach fluttered with the question.

Tate shrugged.

"We're doing this video to remember your mom. I was hoping we could talk about her."

"Oh." Tate scratched his head. "I don't really remember my mom."

Autumn's heart sank.

He didn't remember? Already? Fifteen months and all the memories had been wiped away? But what about the first six years of his life? Every diaper change. Every late-night feeding. Every tear kissed dry. All the rocking and the cuddling and the dressing and the feeding and the playing. Wasn't it enough that Vivian was dead? Did time really have to scrub the moments away too?

Maybe, like Claire and the Tootsie Pops, Tate needed something to jiggle a memory into place.

"She got you a piñata for your sixth birthday. Do you remember that?" Autumn asked.

Tate scrunched his face, probably wondering how she knew such a thing.

"If I'm remembering it correctly, she filled it with Fun Dip," Autumn said, shooting Reese a wink.

Reese's cheeks tinged with pink. Bolstered by the prompt, she pulled back her shoulders and sat a little straighter. "She baked us a birthday cake every year too. On the eve of our birthday. And then she let us eat a piece for breakfast."

It was a sweet tradition. The kind memories were made for.

"It was the only time she let us eat junk food in the morning," Reese said. "All the other days, she made Tate and me a homemade bowl of oatmeal."

Tate scrunched his face again. "She did?"

"Don't you remember?" Reese turned her attention to the camera. "Our mom loved to read. We used to talk about books all the time."

"*Mrs. Frisby and the Rats of NIMH.*" That was Vivian's favorite. Reese had told her so in one of the letters.

Reese nodded. "She kept every drawing Tate and I made for her in a box under the bed."

"Can I see them?"

"I don't know where they went."

"Oh."

"And sometimes, she would lay with me at night. Dad wanted me to go to sleep at nine, but we'd stay up until midnight talking and laughing. She had the best laugh."

Of course she did.

She was Vivacious Vivian.

Autumn could hear the sound, even though she'd never actually heard it. But she had seen it—in the photograph from Paul and Vivian's honeymoon—and it looked contagious, like Tate's cackle, only probably more refined. It looked unhindered and free.

"She was the best mother," Reese said.

The floor squeaked behind them.

Autumn twisted around in the chair.

Paul stood in the kitchen entryway, his hair disheveled. His eyes wide as they swiveled from his kids to the camera.

How long had he been standing there? Autumn hadn't heard him come in.

"Mom loved Oz Park," Reese said, gathering Autumn's attention again. Something hard—almost defiant—glinted in her eyes. "We always went there together. She would push me on the swings, even though I was getting too big to be pushed. Sometimes we watched the sunset. And every Christmas, we'd decorate homemade ginger-bread houses."

Autumn thought about Santa Claus and the

marionette and five-year-old Reese, trapped with the truth. Did she tell Vivian about it later? Did they laugh about it together? How a zebra puppet foiled the great Christmas secret?

"She made our Halloween costumes every year. This one time, she made me look like a real-live jack-in-the-box."

Tate whipped his head around. "She did?"

"Don't you remember?" Reese asked. "She made you a Woody costume, from *Toy Story*."

"Reese."

It was Paul who said the name. The single syllable vibrated with something so dark and ominous, Autumn couldn't help but turn around. His presence charged the room, like electricity before a lightning strike. His grief. His disapproval. It was clear—he didn't want to hear Reese talking about these memories. He didn't want to be reminded of all he'd lost. In fact, he was staring at his daughter like she was purposefully trying to hurt him.

"Mom and Dad really loved each other," Reese said, her voice beginning to shake. "She packed his lunches for work. Dad bought her flowers every Sunday after church. Her favorites were daisies. They cuddled when they watched TV."

The rushed monologue touched raw, tender places.

"They were always kissing and holding hands and—"

"That's enough." The words cut through the air like a whip.

Reese pressed her lips together, her strikingly blue eyes glittering with moisture. A single tear gathered and tumbled down her cheek. She swiped at it and lifted her chin. "No, it's not."

"It's time for bed."

"I'm not done."

"Yes, you are."

Confusion coiled like a snake.

What was going on? Why had Paul's grief turned so angry, so accusatory? And how could he not see how much his daughter needed this? How potentially healing this could be for her? He was a therapist, for crying out loud. Shouldn't he know? "Paul, I know it's been a very difficult day, but—"

"You don't know anything!"

Autumn shrank away from the outburst.

Silence fell.

A startling silence.

A breathless silence.

An uncertain, deafening silence.

He pointed to the stairs. "I said, *it's time for bed.*"

Reese didn't argue.

She didn't look at Autumn.

She grabbed the video camera, ran up the steps, and slammed her bedroom door.

Autumn winced.

Paul shoved his fingers into his hair, then stalked away.

Tate sat on the couch, stunned.

She'd never seen him sit so still before.

Her own emotions bubbled and popped. Heat and shock and indignation, smeared through with guilt and compassion. For all she knew, his grandfather had passed away. For all she knew, he'd been coming home to break the news to his children, only to find them dredging up bittersweet memories of their dead mother.

Autumn stood up and walked after him. Through the kitchen and out the back door, where nighttime wrapped her in a blanket of humidity and the sweet scent of azaleas. Paul stood so still on the deck, moonlight spilling down his back, outlining every tense muscle. He gripped the railing like gravity no longer existed and if he let go, he'd fall into space.

A breeze fluttered a lock of hair that tickled Autumn's cheek. "Paul?"

He flinched at the sound of her voice.

She took a tentative step closer. "How's your grandfather?"

Nothing.

She took another step. "Paul?"

He spun around, his knuckles as white as the moon. "What were you thinking—interviewing them *tonight?*"

"Reese said—"

"She watched her grandfather get carried away on a stretcher. She watched an ambulance tear down the street and pull into her grandmother's driveway. She thought something bad had happened to *me*."

Her throat grew tight. Nobody told her that. Nobody mentioned that Reese and Tate had witnessed the stroke. If she'd known, she would have been more discerning. She would have said no when Reese popped up from the couch to get her video camera. "I—I didn't know. I'm sorry. It's just, Reese made it sound like you wanted us to do it. And she wants her mother to be in the tribute. She wants to remember—"

"Remember what?"

His voice echoed off the trees.

The crickets paused from their chirping.

Paul's chest heaved. "What exactly does she want to remember? That her mother was never around? That while other moms were tucking their kids in at night, Vivian made a point to stay at work past Reese's bedtime? At least she said she was at work. It was her favorite excuse anyway."

His words stole Autumn's breath away. Snatched it, straight from her lungs.

"Should she remember that Vivian didn't go to a single one of Tate's tee-ball games or any of Reese's piano recitals? Is that what you want to put in your stupid tribute? Is that what you want to know? That everything Reese wrote in those letters were lies?"

"Paul, I—"

"*I'm* the one who filled Tate's piñata with Fun Dip. *I'm* the one who taught my children how to ride their bikes. Vivian didn't make gingerbread houses. She didn't make Halloween costumes. Is that what you want Reese to remember?

"That her mother had her first affair when she was three? That there are nights I lie awake, terrified somebody will put two and two together and figure out there's a pretty good shot Tate's not my biological son? That some stranger could show up and take him away? Is that what you want me to say in front of the camera? That she was leaving me? That she was leaving *them?*"

He jerked his hand toward the house.

Toward his children.

Autumn could feel her eyes widening.

Widening and widening and widening.

"She said she was suffocating. She wanted out. And you know what? So did I." Paul repossessed the railing, his back muscles quivering with pent-up emotion. "I begged God for relief. Then the train exploded and Vivian died."

Paul, on the platform.

The song in the notebook.

All of Reese's letters.

"Do you think a person can alter their memories?"

"When I saw you in that hospital bed, I was relieved. God forgive me, I was *relieved.*" His voice cracked. Agony dragged at his shoulders. An entire world of it. A ravishing, insatiable guilt with the power to consume everything in its path. "I prayed for a way out, and He delivered."

Autumn stepped up to the railing and set her hand next to Paul's. "God isn't cruel."

He closed his eyes. But it was too late. A tear escaped and spilled down his cheek.

It was a tear that split a seam in Autumn's heart.

This man had shown her a piece of his soul. A jagged, ugly, honest piece that was raw and bleeding and unlovely. A piece of his soul that matched a piece of hers. "You didn't pray your wife dead." Autumn placed her hand over his. "And even if you did, I don't think that's a prayer God would answer."

Another tear spilled. Paul wiped his forearm across his face. Then he turned up his palm and laced his fingers with hers. He looked up from their interlocked hands, his eyes a storm-tossed sea. "Autumn, I'm—"

The back door opened.

They stepped apart.

Tate came outside with his blond, curly hair. Paul's hair wasn't blond or curly. Vivian's hair hadn't been blond or curly either.

"Dad?" he said, his voice small like a mouse. "Will you come lay with me?"

Forty-Eight

Saturday, June 17, 2017

> Bad things happen all the time,
> all over the world. And we believe in
> God's goodness. We believe He is good.
> We say He is good. Until the bad things turn
> personal. That's when we start to question.
> —Grandma Ally, the Sunday after 9/11,
> on our way home from church

When I was twelve, Chad had a neighbor friend named Tony who brought over the movie *Scream*. I wasn't supposed to watch it. Chad wasn't even supposed to watch it. If Leanne or my dad found out either of us were watching it, we would have been grounded for the rest of the summer. Not only was it rated R, it was a horror flick. At that point in my life, the closest I'd gotten to one of those was *Jurassic Park*. I'd been nine, and it gave me nightmares for weeks. There are only so many times you can wake your parents up in the middle of the night before they outlaw anything remotely frightening.

Tony had three older brothers, and his mother swore like a trucker, so she wasn't too concerned about R-rated movies.

One day, when Leanne was at the zoo with Claire, Tony brought *Scream* over, and I threatened to tell if they didn't let me watch it with them. So the three of us crept down into the unfinished, paint-splattered basement and watched it on a box-set television with rabbit-ear antennas.

Funnily enough, it didn't give me nightmares.

It did, however, blow my mind.

I had been so sure I knew who the psychopathic, mask-wearing murderer was. I announced my prediction halfway through and had been absolutely confident in my assertion.

Until the big reveal came, and I was all wrong. I didn't have things figured out after all.

The twist changed everything. Everything.

Vivian wasn't a devoted wife. She was an adulteress.

Vivian wasn't a doting mother. She was negligent.

And God isn't cruel.

You should have heard me, Maud.

I said it with so much conviction.

"I'll be there first thing tomorrow," Paul said.

"Honey, no. There's nothing you can do here. Sleep in. Enjoy your kids. Go to church. It's your day tomorrow."

"Ma, Pop's in the hospital."

"And there's absolutely nothing you can do to help him."

The muscles in his back knotted. "You shouldn't be alone."

"Do you really think I'd be alone with Pastor Reynolds heading up congregational care? He and Lucille are here now. Tomorrow morning, three ladies from my Tuesday morning Bible study are coming to keep me company."

Pastor Reynolds retired from his senior pastor position ten years ago, and instead of moving to a warm beach in Florida, he took over a fledging ministry with his wife and made it into something great. When a member of that church so much as stubbed a toe, a chili dinner would be waiting on the doorstep, courtesy of Pastor Reynolds.

His mother would be well taken care of.

Still, Paul didn't like being absent.

"If you want to come over, come over later in the day. After you've had some rest. Everything is going to be okay here."

Everything was going to be okay.

It was the same thing he told his children.

But they didn't know that.

The doctors seemed optimistic. His collapse in the bathroom worked to their advantage. If Pop had remained sitting on the couch, watching TV while Mom washed dishes, it could have been another hour before anybody realized anything was wrong, and when it came to a stroke, time was of the essence. Even so, they wouldn't know the extent of Pop's brain damage until the seventy-two-hour mark.

He and Mom said their "I love yous." Then he tossed his phone on his desk and scrubbed his face with his palm. It was scratchy with stubble. The kind of stubble eight-year-old Reese used to run away from with a shriek anytime he tried to give her *cheekies*—her made-up word for an affectionate, slightly aggressive cheek nuzzle.

His chest tightened. And in the silence, he could hear the faint, haunting echo of Vivian's laughter. Her voice calling him to bed.

He wasn't sure if it was memory or dreams.

Paul squeezed his eyes shut.

He hadn't stepped foot inside a hospital since the day he found Autumn Manning in intensive care. The smell of antiseptic. The sterile white room. Beeping monitors. Seeing his grandfather lying there in the bed. All of it triggered every possible emotion.

And then he came home, and he saw Reese lying to the camera.

When he first sat down here in his office, reading the letters that same girl had written, he'd been alarmed. But not concerned. He understood what she was doing.

Kids did it all the time.

He'd done it himself, in the early years after his father's abandonment.

Reese wanted to remember her mother in a better light. It was harmless, really. Much better than reality, anyway. But this—tonight—was extreme. Hearing her lies out loud as he stood there and watched rattled him to the core.

He needed to talk to her.

But when he went upstairs with Tate, her door had been locked. It was against the rules. His children weren't allowed to lock their doors. But he didn't have the energy to fight that battle, so he went into Tate's bedroom and cuddled with his son until his breathing turned heavy and slow. Afterward, his knock on Reese's door was met with a sharp, "Leave me alone."

Now the base of his skull throbbed, and exhaustion pressed in on all sides.

It had been an impossibly long day.

Paul ran his hand down his face, pulling his chin long, staring at his dusty black guitar case propped against the wall. His father had taught him how to play when he was Tate's age, and although Paul didn't want to be anything like him, it was a hobby he couldn't kick. He rolled his chair closer, and somehow the guitar ended up in his lap. He strummed the chords mindlessly.

"How Long"

It was a song he wrote before. A song that had

nothing to do with grieving his wife and everything to do with enduring her.

How long?

The unknowing answer: not much longer.

And tonight, he had confessed the whole ugly truth to Autumn.

His secret was out.

"God isn't cruel."

"You didn't pray your wife dead."

Paul knew that in his head. He even knew it in his heart. He didn't really believe God had snuffed Vivian out of existence because of a desperate prayer from a desperate man. And relief wasn't the only thing he had felt. But it was one of the things. And he hated himself for it.

He strummed the chords a little faster.

God wasn't cruel. He was a God who didn't leave Paul alone and fatherless as a boy. He gave him a man like Pop. And the most amazing mother. A woman who didn't doubt God's goodness, not even when her husband walked out the door.

He was a good, good Father.

One who loved Paul, in all his ugly imperfection. One who had loved Vivian, in all of hers.

He stopped strumming. His office went quiet. Conviction pierced him straight through.

Jesus had died for His bride; Paul had tolerated his.

Not always. The shift had been subtle. A slow

fade. The beginnings of which could be traced back to that first affair, when parenthood had turned his vivacious wife despondent. And then, suddenly, when Reese was three, she came back to life again.

Only it wasn't Paul who brought her back.

Her confession had turned him inside out. Her infidelity, her rejection. It hadn't been a sting. It had been a stab. A gapping, mortal wound. His wife had given herself to another man. And then she cried and begged for forgiveness. She promised it wouldn't happen again. Paul stayed, because that was what husbands and fathers were supposed to do. And he was a therapist now. Like the paramedics who came for Pop, Paul had the training and tools to fix what Vivian had broken. How could he possibly get his practice off the ground if he started with a failed marriage? More than that, he loved her. So he dived in, headfirst, doing everything he knew to repair the damage.

But then it happened again when Tate was two. And a piece of his heart went hard. It wasn't as ready to believe in Vivian's apologies. Should this happen again, Paul would make sure it didn't hurt so profoundly.

Self-preservation.

The third time, Vivian wanted to get help. *"I don't know what's wrong with me, Paul. Maybe we should see a therapist."*

Paul had laughed. He *was* a therapist. A highly

respected one in his field by then. And his heart had slowly turned to stone. She couldn't hurt that anymore. It was his pride at stake now. His livelihood. His wife had taken too much already. She wouldn't turn him into a failure when he was finding so much success.

Then it happened the fourth time.

"Do you even love me, Paul?" she'd asked, after he confronted her about the text messages. *"Do you really think we have anything worth saving?"*

He'd looked straight into her eyes and gave her his hard-hearted answer. *"I made vows before God."*

No "I love you."

No assurance that their marriage was worth saving.

He was prepared to lay down his career and his ministry on behalf of those vows. The ultimate martyr for his thorn of a wife.

Paul set the guitar aside.

He began to resent her because she shone a bright light on his impotence. The helplessness that he hated. To fix her. To fix them. To fix himself. So he endured Vivian. And he resented Vivian.

While God loved him.

And loved her.

Paul slid out of his chair, onto his knees on his office floor before a God who had never treated him like a thorn. Paul laid his dark, ugly heart bare. The awful prayers he had prayed. The awful relief he had felt. The part he played in it all, because he had played a part. In repentance, in humility, he confessed himself raw.

Then he wiped his eyes and thanked God for His mercy. His patience. His love and goodness and grace and . . .

Truth. The word burst forth—an obnoxious, unwelcome visitor.

Tell Reese the truth.

Taken aback, Paul shook his head—annoyed that such an intrusion would push its way into a moment like this one. This was hallowed ground. This was a holy, God-soaked intersection. Random, silly thoughts were not welcome. A good, good Father wouldn't ask Paul to unload his burdens on a twelve-year-old. She was a kid. He was the adult.

It was his job to protect her.

The truth will set you free.

Disturbed, Paul batted the irritating whisper away and went upstairs to check on Reese.

Forty-Nine

Autumn ran like somebody was chasing her. Her lungs burned. A sharp stitch stabbed her side. Her muscles cried out in protest. So did her sister. The girl who ran cross-country in college.

The girl who ran the Chicago Marathon in three hours, twenty-six minutes.

"I thought . . . you said . . . a jog."

Sweat trickled down Autumn's back. Early-morning sun shone against her shoulders, already creeping past warm. Today would be a beautiful day. Families across the city would celebrate the fathers in their lives with grilled hamburgers and cold beer and Frisbee at the park, sunscreen and bug spray. After church, she would pick up hot dog buns and potato salad, because that had been her assignment from Leanne for today's cookout. She would also pick up a Father's Day card. Something generic. Something she would sign and he would throw away, because Dad wasn't sentimental. Her mother hadn't been either.

They hadn't kept her drawings as a kid. Sometimes she'd find them in the garbage and pull them out with righteous indignation. How could they do such a thing?

Mom and Dad would look properly contrite,

and then Mom would say, "Honey, we can't keep everything you bring home from school. If we did, the house would be overrun with paper."

Autumn would huff, and then she'd hang her soggy, food-splattered masterpiece on the refrigerator, where it would stay until she was no longer paying attention.

Reese had said her mother kept all her drawings and Tate's drawings in a box under her bed. But Reese had lied. She had lied about the drawings. She had lied about the piñata and the Fun Dip and the bike rides. The Vivian Autumn thought she knew—the Vivian Autumn had built up in her mind—wasn't the real Vivian at all.

The real Vivian was a cheater.

Paul had felt relief.

Reese had lied in her letters.

Autumn ran faster.

Until Claire grabbed Autumn's arm and jerked them both to a halt. She bent over her knees, huffing and puffing. "Who . . . in the world . . . are you running from?"

Autumn clasped her side, like she might be able to press the sharpness away. But it stabbed every time she sucked in a breath.

Sparkles of sunlight rippled along the surface of the lake.

She heard a firm "Passing" as a couple whizzed past on a pair of bikes.

Autumn jumped.

Claire squinted at her. "Are you going to tell me what's going on?"

Vivian was a cheater.

Paul had felt relief.

Reese had lied in her letters.

And Claire wouldn't let her run.

Her attention zipped down the length of the lakefront, where another biker approached from the distance, closing in on a woman walking her dog.

"If I tell you something," she finally said, "you cannot breathe a word of it to anyone."

Claire's eyes widened.

"Do you understand?"

"Of course."

"Not a word." Autumn held up her pointer finger. "Not even to Trent."

"I promise. Now what's going on?"

"I went to Paul's last night."

"Again?"

"*Again?* Claire, it's been two weeks since the baseball game."

Claire held up her hands.

Autumn sighed. "His grandfather had a stroke."

"That's awful."

"He needed someone to watch his kids."

"So he called you? *You're* his go-to?"

"If you keep interrupting, I'm not going to tell you anything."

Claire mimicked zipping her lips and throwing away the key.

Autumn pulled her off to the side, onto the grass so bikers could zoom past without having to announce themselves. They resumed their jog, this time, at a slower pace. They passed the dog walker, and by the time Autumn was through unloading everything, they were a block away from home.

"I can't believe it." Claire shook her head. "The Marriage Doctor was on the brink of divorce."

"You can't tell anyone."

"I thought we already established that."

"No funny comments under your breath. No innuendos. No vague references. Nothing."

"I know. Chill."

"I don't even know how his grandfather is doing. I don't even know if he's alive. I asked, but Paul never answered. And then Tate came out, and I had to leave with all that between us. I have no idea when we'll see each other again."

"Something tells me it won't be long."

They had just turned down the walkway leading to the entrance of her apartment complex. Paul stood up from the front stoop. His hair was a mess.

Autumn's heart took off. *Thud-thud-thud,* like she was sprinting again.

"Hey," he said, his attention sliding from Claire to Autumn.

"Hi," she said back.

Anticipation radiated off her sister in waves,

making Autumn cringe. She wanted to step in front of Paul and shield him from Claire's blatant curiosity.

He rubbed the back of his neck. "Could we talk?"

"Of course."

"I'll just be upstairs." Claire took the key from Autumn, her eyes wide with knowing, then disappeared inside with a not-so-casual glance over her shoulder. In two minutes' time, she'd be peeking out the kitchen window.

It seemed terribly obvious that she knew something.

But Paul didn't comment.

"How's your grandfather?" she blurted, eager to know. "I've been thinking about him all night."

Lie.

She'd been thinking about Paul all night.

He rubbed his forehead. "He's stable. The doctors will know more in a day or two."

"It's good that he's stable."

"Yeah."

"Happy Father's Day," she said lamely.

"Thanks."

"I hope your kids spoil you," she said, even more lamely.

"Reese isn't exactly talking to me."

"Oh."

"Listen, Autumn. I need you to understand that what I told you last night . . ." He glanced toward her apartment window, as if he, too, knew that

Claire would be spying. He leaned closer and lowered his voice. "I've never told that to anyone. Not my mom. Not my grandfather. Not Mitch."

"Paul."

"I mean, I don't even know if it's true. About Tate. Vivian never said anything. And it's not like it matters to me. Tate is my son, regardless of DNA."

"Paul."

"It's just, if someone found this out. If Tate found out. I'm not sure—"

"Paul?"

He looked at her, the feathered lines in the corners of his eyes impossibly deep. She wanted to smooth her thumbs over them. Press away the stress he carried.

"I won't tell anyone." Except she already had. She told Claire, whom she'd have to swear to secrecy again. She would threaten to kick her out of the apartment if she breathed a word of it to anyone. She would do what it took to keep Paul's secret safe. Because he had trusted that secret to her. Nobody else but her.

"And the footage?" Paul rubbed his forehead again. "I don't want the things Reese said on there uploaded to YouTube or broadcast on Redeemer's big screen."

"I won't use it. I didn't even take the camera with me."

Paul deflated with visible relief. All the tension

he'd been carrying in his shoulders melted away. "Thank you."

"Of course."

There was a brief pause, wherein she wondered where this left him. Vivian couldn't be the only one not in the tribute. But how was she supposed to ask Paul for an interview now, knowing what she knew?

"It's called fantastical thinking," he said.

"What?"

"What Reese is doing. I did a bit of it when I was a kid. She wants to remember Vivian as better than she was."

Autumn glanced over her shoulder. Besides a bird hopping along the grass, the apartment complex's front lawn was empty. "Do you think Reese knew about—?"

"No." His quick, decisive answer left no room for pushback. "She's just trying to compensate for having a mom who wasn't . . . involved. I think it's one of the reasons she attached herself to you."

"Me?"

He looked up at her apartment window.

The curtains swung back and forth.

"Can we sit?" he asked.

"Yeah. Sure."

They sat down on the stoop leading to the front door, out of sight from Claire's window-watching.

"You care about her, Autumn. You see her. You validate her opinions and her ideas. You made her laugh. You helped her a couple weeks ago. It's meant the world to Reese. And it's meant the world to me."

His words made her dizzy.

Paul wound his hand around the back of his neck. "You probably think I'm the world's biggest hypocrite."

"Why?"

"The marriage campaign?"

"What about it?"

"I shouldn't have agreed to do it. My marriage—"

"You stayed, Paul. You stayed when ninety-nine percent of the population wouldn't have."

"I should have gotten help. That's what a good husband would have done. He would have gotten help."

"Maybe it wouldn't have mattered."

"Maybe it would have."

And there was the rub. They would never know. Not Paul. Not Autumn. Because Paul hadn't gotten help, and now Vivian was dead, and time marched forward, never backward. Of all the thousands of paths a person could take in life, at the end of the day, they traveled only one.

Paul set his elbows on his knees and sighed. "I want you to know that Vivian wasn't a monster. And I'm not a saint."

"I didn't think you were."

"Good." He smiled a self-deprecating smile.

"Do you regret telling me?"

He shook his head and leaned a little closer.

It was like the *Scream* movie. The discovery that Vivian hadn't been the greatest mom. That she hadn't been a very good wife. It altered things. Unbuckled whatever strap she'd wound around her emotions—her feelings for this particular man and his particular kids. It was hard to care about being faithful to Vivian when she hadn't been faithful to Paul.

He reached for her hand, slid his fingers down her palm until they were interlocked with hers. "I like you," he said. "Quite a lot."

Something light and fluttery took flight.

How odd this all was. Paul Elliott, sitting outside her apartment, telling her these things. So close she could see the thinnest rim of gold circling his pupils. He had the most amazingly colored eyes.

"And since I'm being honest, I should probably also tell you that it scares me to death."

"Me too."

She was falling for a man who was bound to have trust issues. Vivian had cheated on him. She had lied to him since Reese was three. A thing like that would leak into any relationship, no matter how strong the connection. It would be inevitable.

On top of that, there was the media to contend with.

A relationship between them would be too juicy to leave alone.

And yet Autumn was impossibly drawn. She was a broken woman falling for a broken man who had a broken past and two beautiful, broken children.

"So where does that leave us?" he asked.

"I have no idea."

The door swung open behind them.

Paul let go of her hand.

Autumn twisted around.

Claire stood there, wild in the eyes. "They caught him."

"What?" Autumn asked.

"The police caught Benjamin Havel. They found him in Utah. It's all over the news."

Fifty

Tuesday, June 20, 2017

My only regret is that more people didn't die.
—Benjamin Havel

This is what he said.

When an FBI detective named Morris Wilson took Havel into custody and a reporter captured the incident on camera, these were Havel's heartless words.

His only regret is that more people didn't die.

What is there to say in light of that?

Autumn buzzed Seth inside and paced her kitchen while Trent and Claire watched television in the living room.

The tribute was finished. And Vivian wasn't in it.

Autumn wasn't sure what to do about that, so she blocked it out and focused on other things. Like how her ex-fiancé, Seth Ryker, had condensed all that raw footage into sixty minutes of remembrance. She vacillated between worry and triumph. Sixty minutes was a long time. Would attention spans last that long? But then she would remember how talented Seth was with video and the stories people had shared, and her heart would start pounding in anticipation.

Perhaps sixty minutes wasn't enough.

Thanks to Benjamin Havel and his cruel words, the whole thing had been shoved into the limelight. Tragedy on the Tracks was back on the news. Not just in Chicago, but all over the nation. And along with it, the tribute. Reporters were calling. The mayor wanted to say a few words at the reception. Mitch had expressed concern that Redeemer might not be big enough for all the attendees, an issue Autumn never would have imagined when she first booked the sanctuary in April. Penny—the big-boned woman who loved canary yellow—suggested they set up a live video feed so they could stream the event online. Her son was tech savvy and would take care of the details, so he got together with the commission board, who said they would gladly host the feed on the memorial website.

In all the fuss and all the rush, Autumn hadn't seen Paul.

According to Mitch, he was busy helping his mother pick out an assisted living home for his grandfather.

"I like you. Quite a lot."

How many times had she replayed those words over the last few days?

She needed to talk to someone about her confusing emotions, but Jeannie True wasn't available after hours, and Autumn had too much going on at work to slip away. There was Claire, but Autumn was already nervous about how much her sister knew. She made a habit of telling Claire, at least three times a day, not to breathe a word. Claire got so fed up with the reminders, the two of them had erupted into an argument. It was such a loud one that Roland knocked on their door, shirtless as usual, to make sure everything was okay.

What Autumn needed was a friend.

She used to have them before. She and one of her coworkers—Kendall—used to go out for happy hour after work on Thursdays. Maybe she would give Kendall a call once the tribute was over.

Seth knocked on her door.

Autumn flung it open.

He stood on the other side, brandishing a flash drive.

Her stomach turned a somersault.

Five minutes later, they had settled on the couch with Autumn's computer opened on her lap. Claire and Trent stood behind them, ready and waiting. With a deep, nerve-riddled breath, Autumn clicked the touch pad and watched what Seth had done.

It was breathtakingly beautiful.

She sat there, straight backed, hand pressed against her chest, taking in every word, every captured moment. The best of their lives.

Until the one came that shouldn't have been there.

Couldn't have been there.

She reeled back against the cushion.

Reese was on the screen.

Talking about her mother.

The footage she'd assured Paul wouldn't be there was somehow very much there.

"How did you get this?"

"What do you mean?" Seth asked, his attention still on the screen.

Her fingers turned to ice. This couldn't be happening. She was dreaming. Or this was a joke. Claire had told Seth Paul's secret, and they were playing a very nasty, cruel joke. "How did you get this footage of Reese?"

"She sent it to me."

"Who did?"

"Reese."

"How did Reese send you this?"

"I don't know. I thought you gave her my e-mail address."

The room began to spin.

Claire caught Autumn's eye.

"I never gave Reese your e-mail address," Autumn said.

"Then she must have gotten it off my website." Seth pushed Pause, freezing Reese's face on the screen. "Is something wrong?"

Autumn opened her mouth, but no words came. What was she supposed to say? How could she explain to Seth that they needed to remove it right away?

"I think Paul was worried about it," Claire said.

Autumn whipped her head around and glared at her sister.

"Why?" Seth and Trent asked the question at the same time.

"It's nothing," Autumn blurted. "It's fine. It's just . . ."

"You don't like how it turned out?"

"No, I love how it turned out." But even to her own ears, her tone came out wrong. Pitchy and high. Like an out-of-tune warbler. "I just don't think Paul wants Reese in the video."

"Why not? It's a really great interview."

"It doesn't really matter why not. He's the father, and he doesn't want it in there."

Seth wasn't buying it.

"Then why did you do the interview to begin with?" he asked.

She wasn't sure what to say to that.

"Autumn, I spent a lot of time on this."

"I know. And I'm grateful."

Seth shook his head. He was visibly frustrated. Autumn couldn't blame him. He *had* spent a lot of time on this. And he wasn't being compensated. Given the circumstances, you could say he was being the opposite of compensated. "Look, if Paul doesn't want Reese in the tribute, then you can have Paul call me, and I'll take it out."

Autumn started to panic.

But what was there to do? She couldn't explain the situation to Seth.

That was not an option.

She would have to get ahold of Paul. And so, as soon as Seth stormed away, fed up with the whole thing, she excused herself from the apartment and found somewhere private to call him.

"*Pick up.* Please, please *pick up.*"

But her call went to voice mail.

Autumn hung up, then called him again.

And again.

And again.

Fifty-One

"I'll take a chocolate almond croissant, two sticky buns, and . . ." Even though Regina was still sleeping and would probably continue to sleep long after his children finished their sticky buns, he needed to order her something. She had a radar for these kinds of things. She would find the Floriole bag in the garbage or spot a smear of glaze on Tate's cheek, and then she'd know. She would know that he went to the bakery and didn't bother to get her anything. Of course, whatever he got her would be all wrong. She'd complain. She'd throw his selection away or hand it off to Tate, who would be thrilled.

There was absolutely no winning with a woman like Regina.

He perused the display case for whatever looked the most fattening. Not out of spite, but real concern. He didn't think it possible, but there was even less of her now than there had been before. When he saw her waiting for him outside O'Hare, his first thought had been anorexia.

"What's the filling in that one?" he asked.

"The gateau basque?"

"Sure."

The woman smiled. "Pastry cream."

"That has a lot of calories, right?"

"It's definitely not light."

"Perfect. I'll take one of those."

Floriole was a bakery a short walk away from home. He'd gone many times throughout the years with his children. They loved the sticky buns, and Paul let them enjoy one every year on the back deck on the first day of summer break.

Today was the first day.

Tate was thrilled.

Paul was stressed.

He paid for his order, then stepped out into the sun. It was only seven thirty in the morning, and he was already exhausted. This week had been so filled with unpleasant things, it was almost as if it were being deliberately cruel. Reporters kept calling, wanting to know if he would give a statement regarding Benjamin Havel's arrest. People on social media were going crazy.

Reese kept telling him about this tweet or that tweet as if Paul wanted to know.

He had too much on his plate to concern himself with Benjamin Havel.

Work, for one. Preparations for the marriage campaign. Searching for an assisted living home for Pop, who was recovering a little more every day. The end-of-the-school rush, which included Reese's big current events project. Gathering Vivian's best photographs to display at Redeemer for tonight's tribute. And now, Regina, her presence in his home giving him flashbacks of life after Vivian died, when she'd stayed for an entire week, floating about the house in her night-gown, upsetting his children with her random outbursts of grief.

Paul needed more coffee.

He needed a quiet moment alone with his children before he squeezed in a few appointments for the day. He needed to speak with Reese about tonight. There would be pictures of Vivian in the tribute, and her photography would hang in the lobby. But her interview would not be a part of it. Autumn had given him her word.

Autumn.

The one beacon of light in all of this mess.

But he couldn't think about her now.

So he'd shoved all of his emotions—all of his feelings about her—into a box that he'd open later, once this crazy season had passed. It would even itself out, eventually. The tribute would pass, and Regina would go home, and they'd get Pop settled, and the marriage campaign would come and go. Life wouldn't always feel like he was drinking from a fire hose. For now, though, he had to focus on one task at a time or he would go insane.

His current checklist item: eat breakfast with his children.

Paul pulled his phone from his back pocket.

He had forgotten that he'd turned it off after Regina sent her fourth text message yesterday. Something about Tate needing a haircut. The problem was, Tate didn't want a haircut. The text before that had been about a mildew smell in the basement. The one before that had been about Reese and an attitude adjustment. And the one before that had been about needing healthier food options in the pantry.

Paul couldn't handle it.

He was already stressed, so off his phone went.

Out of sight, out of mind.

After work, he'd helped Mom move Pop's things into his new home, where he would move next week. They pacified themselves by saying things like "just for now" and "this is temporary" and "when he's stronger." But Paul knew the statistics. At Pop's age, especially after a stroke, the chances of him coming home were slim. Age and fragility had won another hard-fought battle.

The whole thing had been so draining that Paul had fallen into bed without remembering his phone at all. With the bag of goodies in hand, he turned it on now and headed for home. No sooner had he turned a corner when it *buzz-buzz-buzzed* to life. One alert after another.

Text messages and voice mails.

His annoyance was instantaneous.

Especially when the first text message on his screen was from Regina. **Call me, please.**

She sent it this morning.

Below it was a cryptic, slightly alarming text from Mitch, also sent this morning. **We will get this straightened out.**

And below that, one from Autumn, sent last night. Call me ASAP.

Get what straightened out?

Confused, Paul checked his missed calls. There was one from Regina that came right before she sent her text. Two from Mitch, who never called this early. And seven—*seven!*—from Autumn, all of which came yesterday.

Before he could listen to any of the voice mails, his phone buzzed.

Regina.

Irritated, Paul pressed the phone to his ear and said a curt hello.

"Finally!"

Good morning to you too.

"A reporter just knocked on the door."

He bit back a growl. Already? Before eight in the morning? Wasn't Havel's arrest old news by now? "They just want a statement about Havel. Don't answer it."

"Too late. I already answered it. In my night-gown. And do you know what she wanted to know?"

No, but Regina was bound to tell him.

"She wanted to know if I had anything to say about your *divorce.*"

"What?"

"That was *my* response."

Paul stopped and shook his head, as if doing so might change Regina's words. Rattle some sense

410

into what she was saying. But it didn't work. A reporter was at his door, wanting to know about a divorce?

"I told her of course there wasn't any divorce, but she said she received an anonymous tip that Vivian was leaving you the day of the . . . the day of the *you know what*. Why would she say such a thing? What's going on? Last night *that woman* came over and now a reporter? Oh, for heaven's sake, she's knocking again!"

"What woman?"

"That woman—Autumn Manning."

"She came over last night? When? Why didn't you tell me?"

"I tried telling you, but your phone was off. And I needed to go to sleep. It was a very long day. I left you a note on the counter."

Paul shut his eyes, trying to make sense out of what was happening. "Regina, listen to me. Don't let Reese or Tate near the door."

"Where are you?"

"On my way home."

She started talking again, in a somewhat shrill, demanding voice.

Paul didn't listen.

His thoughts raced.

Mitch's text. We'll get this straightened out.

Autumn's phone calls.

Seven in a row.

Her unexpected visit.

A reporter on his front lawn, wanting to know about a divorce.

He hung up on his mother-in-law and ran home. He circled around back to avoid the reporter and came inside forty-two seconds later, huffing and puffing. Regina glided into the kitchen, dressed for the day, her bony face a mask of alarm.

"Reese isn't in her bedroom."

"What?"

"I just went upstairs to check on her, and she isn't there."

A knock sounded on the door.

"Oh, for heaven's sake! I told her I would speak to her after I freshened up, and she will not stop knocking."

Paul hurried through the kitchen.

Tate sat on the couch watching cartoons, his face covered with Pop-Tarts crumbs.

"Reese!" Paul called up the stairs.

"I told you, she isn't up there."

Paul ignored Regina and called again.

No answer.

Another knock on the door.

Regina flung it open, and shrieked at the reporter to go away.

Paul raced up the stairs, two at a time.

Reese's room was empty.

Her covers were rumpled, with an iPad on her pillow.

She wasn't allowed to have the iPad in her

room. Paul was very firm about that rule. But here it was. "How did this get in here?"

"She asked if she could play some game called Snapchat."

"When?"

"Last night while you were gone. I was too tired to argue with her."

Paul picked it up and touched the screen.

A Twitter feed appeared.

Reese had searched his name, and it was currently scrolling with speculation and half truths. Phrases like "hidden affairs," "what a fake," and "physical abuse" jumped out at him.

Paul's stomach turned to rot.

Mitch's text. We'll get this straightened out.

Autumn's text. Call me ASAP.

Regina stood in the doorway. "Paul, please tell me what's going on."

Fifty-Two

The second Autumn's screen lit up, she snagged it off her nightstand. She answered so quickly, it didn't have a chance to make a sound. "Paul, thank goodness."

"Is Reese with you?"

She pulled her chin back at the sharp greeting. "Reese?"

"My daughter. Reese. Is she with you?"

"No." And yet, Autumn caught herself looking about her bedroom, like maybe Reese was there, hiding under the bed, and she just hadn't noticed. "Why? What's going on?"

"Did you tell someone?"

"What?"

"About Vivian. Did you tell someone?"

No!

How could he even ask such a thing?

Those were the words she wanted to shout. A loud, definitive, *Absolutely not!*

But that would be a lie.

"A reporter just knocked on my door wanting to know about a divorce."

"What?"

"It's all over the Internet."

A dull buzzing gathered in her ears. No. Claire wouldn't. Autumn had been so clear. So irritatingly, overwhelmingly adamant. So much so that they got into an argument. "Paul, I'm—"

"I have to go."

And before she could say anything more, the line went dead.

Autumn stood there in her bedroom, paralyzed. Frozen. Numb.

She opened her laptop and Googled Paul Elliott. She clicked a link that brought her to Twitter. She caught snatches of words. Whole conversations among strangers, out there for the entire world to see.

Looks like the Marriage Doctor is a fake.

They all are in the end.

I read his book. It was drivel.

Why do you think she was leaving him?

Isn't it obvious? He couldn't keep it in his pants.

If my man looked that good, I wouldn't be leaving.

I heard there are speculations of abuse.

He assaulted my cousin inside a sporting goods store a couple of months ago.

He was probably in cahoots with Havel.

Autumn reared back from the vitriol, as if the words had bitten her. These people were tossing around speculation as though it were fact. As though they had the corner market in truth when their truth couldn't be more wrong.

They didn't know Paul.

They didn't know anything.

Tears built in her eyes. Awful, stinging tears.

How had this happened?

And how would Paul ever forgive her?

When Autumn was a girl, her mom used to read her and Chad and Claire the story of Chicken Little.

Autumn would laugh at silly Henny Penny's antics, but her mother would get very stern about the moral. *"Disaster is disaster, Autumn. We do not get hysterical about things that aren't disastrous. We are not Henny Penny."*

Mom didn't like drama.

She was not a fan of theatrics.

If something crazy happened in society or politics, she would shrug her shoulders while everyone else fell into panic mode. In the days after she died, whenever Grandma Ally would get particularly fulsome in her grief, Autumn would think, *Mom wouldn't like that, Grandma. You're being a Henny Penny.* And then she would go into her room and cry.

If her mother were there now, she would probably say something like, "This isn't the end of the world, Autumn. The sky isn't falling."

Maybe she was right.

Maybe none of this would matter in five years.

At the moment, though, as Autumn paced inside her bedroom, it felt pretty awful.

Seth was boarding a plane to Puerto Rico for his cousin's wedding. Reese was still in the tribute footage.

And Paul was being eviscerated on social media.

All because of Claire.

How *could* she?

How could she tell anyone about Paul and Vivian when Autumn told her, multiple times, not to tell anyone? Just thinking about it made her face so hot, it felt like she was standing in front of a bonfire. The level of betrayal she felt right now was probably the same level of betrayal Paul felt when the reporter knocked on his door. The only difference was, Claire was Autumn's sister, so of course Autumn would forgive her. They would eventually get over this and move on. Autumn and Paul, on the other hand? She wasn't his sister. She wasn't his girlfriend. When it came down to it, she wasn't his anything.

There was no reason for him to get over this.

With shaking hands, she opened the editing software on her computer. She wasn't familiar with it. Her stomach churned as she stared at the screen, her finger poised above the touch pad.

She was about to mess with the video.

But what other choice did she have?

In three hours, Redeemer would be packed with reporters and journalists and so many people Autumn knew. Not just in her head. Not through snippets on Facebook. But really knew. Ina May Huett, Anna Montgomery, Mr. Collins and his daughter Kelsey, Jordan Brokaw and Linaya, and every other person she interviewed over the past two and a half months.

All of them would file into the sanctuary after looking at the displays in the lobby, and they would expect sixty minutes of video about the victims of Tragedy on the Tracks. A tribute to celebrate the lives of their loved ones. A tribute that was supposed to bring closure.

But Autumn couldn't show it. Not like it was. Not when she promised Paul it wouldn't be there. Not when she already broke his trust by telling her loudmouth sister his secret. Drawing in a shaking breath, she clicked and dragged over Reese, then pressed Delete. She dug her fingers into her clammy palms and hit the Replay button, hoping it was that simple.

The movement of Ina May's lips no longer matched the sound. Autumn's heart thudded.

She tried to fix it, but every time she clicked on something, she made it worse.

Autumn stared wide-eyed at the screen. She had ruined the video. She couldn't show it.

And she couldn't show the original on Seth's jump drive. Not with Reese in the footage.

What was worse—she couldn't explain to anyone why.

Fifty-Three

Lord, help.

Paul hit his knees in the middle of Lincoln Park. The sun was beginning to droop in the sky, making its inevitable descent toward the horizon, and still, no sign of Reese. Her absence put everything into sharp perspective.

He didn't care what anyone was saying online.

He didn't care that his agent kept calling.

He didn't care that he could lose every single one of his clients.

All that mattered was finding his daughter.

She had been missing all day. *All day*. He called the police. He filed a report. But they couldn't put out an Amber Alert because there was no sign of an abduction.

"Has she run away before?" the officer had asked.

Paul had to say yes.

He had to explain about the time she ran away to Autumn Manning's apartment.

He hated the way the officer had nodded knowingly.

Like Reese was a typical runaway.

Like she would probably show up soon enough.

This is Chicago, he wanted to scream. *This is a dangerous, crowded city, and my little girl is out there alone!*

His mother was searching.

Regina was searching.

Mitch was searching.

Mrs. Ryan was searching.

They called all of Reese's friends. They'd gone to all of Reese's favorite spots. They scoured Lakefront Trail. They went to the White Sox stadium. They alerted the CTA. They combed the neighborhood, and now he was combing the expansive park along the lakefront, and still no sign. And the farther the sun traveled that familiar arc across the sky, the more his desperate heart raged.

It was half past five.

She'd been gone for ten hours.

Ten hours.

He couldn't think. He could barely breathe. He wanted to crawl out of his skin.

Awful, terrible thoughts flew at him. A spiral of what-ifs that spun and spun and spun. What if they didn't find her? What if someone had her? What if Reese went missing forever and he never saw her again? He should have listened when he felt the urge to tell her the truth. Maybe if he'd listened, she wouldn't have been so shocked by the awfulness on Twitter. Maybe she wouldn't have run away.

Please, Lord. Please give me another chance.

The plea welled from the deepest part of his soul.

He pressed his face to the ground, feeling like Jesus in Gethsemane. Sweating blood. Begging God for a different cup. And in the middle of his sweating, the sound of laughter—a little girl's high-pitched giggle—floated to him on a breeze. It sounded so similar to Reese when she was younger that he sat up, bits of grass sticking to his forehead.

A chubby-legged, brown-haired toddler ran toward the steps leading to the Lincoln statue. A woman with the same color hair scooped the girl up into her arms before she could get there and spun her in a circle. Something Vivian had never done. She didn't fill piñatas with Fun Dip for Tate,

420

and she didn't watch sunsets at Oz Park with Reese.

His thoughts jerked to a halt.

Oz Park.

Reese told Autumn that Vivian pushed her on the swings at Oz Park.

Please God. Please let her be there.

Paul squeezed his eyes shut, praying that what he was seeing wasn't a hopeful figment of his imagination. Looked again. Beyond the playground, past the kids swinging and climbing and chasing and the parents supervising and scolding and cajoling, a skinny girl sat on the edge of the Dorothy statue.

A pair of unlaced Converse All Stars sat at the statue's base. Bare feet dangled above them. Dark, bushy hair cascaded down her back. Her shoulders were slouched and blessedly familiar.

It was Reese.

Thank You, Jesus, it was Reese.

Paul released a desperate breath. One he'd been holding all day, his throat tightening as he quickly shot off a group text with trembling hands.

She's okay. I found her.

He strode forward through the chaotic mass of children, his knees like wax. If she saw him approaching, he couldn't tell. She didn't wave. She didn't smile. She didn't acknowledge him at all. She just sat there, as still as Dorothy and Toto, her face aimed at the western horizon, a trail of dry tears smudging her cheeks.

His phone started to buzz.

A Praise Jesus from Mom. A Thank You, God from Mitch. A Where in the world has she been? from Regina. Paul turned off his phone, tucked it away, and hoisted himself up to sit beside his little girl, overcome with the urge to pull her onto his lap. Protect her from a broken world, where parents left and marriages failed and children paid the price.

"Reese?"

She curled her toes and dragged her arm across her face.

"Reese, look at me."

She did.

Reluctantly.

Her chin wobbling.

"Why didn't Mom love me?"

The question tore him in two. It rent him right down the middle. It was the same one he'd asked about his dad when he was a boy. The question he swore his children would never have to ask. And yet here she was. Asking it. He might have protected her from his broken marriage, but he hadn't been able to protect her from an indifferent mother. No matter how much Paul compensated, that wasn't something he could hide.

"She did love you, Reese."

She shook her head, tears pooling over her

lashes and tumbling down her blotchy cheeks, chasing each other in a race to her chin. "Why didn't she love me like moms are supposed to love their daughters?"

Paul wanted to press back. He wanted to insist that Vivian had loved Reese very much—in her own way. But then, what would that teach his daughter about love? Instead, he wrapped his arm around her and pulled her close. "I don't know."

He hated the answer.

He hated it so much.

But what else was there to say? Even if he understood all the intricacies of why, what possible explanation could erase the pain? What else was there to do but hold her tight while she buried her face in his shoulder and wept?

"I'm so sorry, baby," he whispered. "I'm so, so sorry."

Her thin body shook.

Paul rubbed circles into her back and breathed deeply through his nostrils and prayed that a father's love would be enough. He prayed that God would help him comfort his daughter.

"I'm sorry too," she said, her words muffled in his shirt. "I shouldn't have told anyone."

"Told anyone what?"

Reese hiccupped and rubbed her eyes. "I kept trying to alter my memories, but it wasn't working and I was mad. I was mad at her for leaving, and I was mad at you because you never talked about it."

His stomach turned cold.

Mad at her for leaving?

"I didn't want to pretend anymore."

"Reese, what are you talking about?"

"I e-mailed the reporter who came to my school. I told her the truth, and now everybody knows. It's all over Twitter."

Her words swirled around him.

He was Dorothy. Reese's confession, the debris-ridden tornado.

He had it all wrong.

Reese knew. Somehow, someway, his daughter knew that Vivian was leaving. She hadn't learned the truth this morning on a Twitter feed; she'd lived with the truth for months. Possibly even *years*. She was the anonymous tip. Not Autumn. Not one of Vivian's old friends. Not the man he had punched in the sporting goods store. But Reese. This whole time he thought he was protecting his daughter, shielding her from the truth—when really he had forced her to carry it on her own. In silence. All by herself.

"I'm sorry, Dad. I'm so sorry everybody knows our secret."

Our secret.

If ever any words could punch him in the gut and steal his breath, it was those. "Listen to me, kid. It *never* should have been your secret to begin with."

Fifty-Four

Gum. There, among the silver and copper coins sparkling beneath the water, was a small gob of pink gum.

In five short days, it would be three months since the fountain's inauguration. Three months. And already, there was gum at the bottom.

Autumn stared hard at its design—the intricately sculpted steel bird emerging from the ashes. A phoenix taking flight. The commission board loved the symbolism. Rebirth. Renewal. A reminder to the city that while tragedy happened, it didn't win.

She ran her hand along the plaque. Traced her finger along the inscribed words.

Tragedy on the Tracks, March 28, 2016
Twenty-Two Lives Lost

One life spared.

The tribute was meant to be her phoenix. A search for closure, sure. But more importantly, something that gave her survival purpose. An offering of healing in the midst of so much unnecessary pain.

For a fleeting moment, Seth had captured it.

And then she ruined it.

Right now, all those people were sitting in the sanctuary, waiting for a miracle survivor who wasn't going to show. Her attention lifted from the plaque. A woman was staring at her. Autumn quickly looked away, wishing she was wearing her White Sox hat so she could pull her brim lower. She was positive the woman would come over. Tap her shoulder. "Hey, aren't you the lady who survived? Aren't you supposed to be at that big church for the tribute everybody's talking about?"

She braced herself for the moment.

But when she snuck a peek, the woman wasn't any closer than before, and she was no longer staring. Autumn had landed herself in the same place she'd been in months ago. Borderline agoraphobic, paranoid everyone recognized her.

Only now, she couldn't hide in her apartment.

Claire would eventually show up, and Autumn would attack. She'd turn feral at the sight of her blabbermouth sister. She'd tear out a clump of her bottle-brown hair. She'd say things she'd regret. And poor Grandma Ally would have to watch from heaven, distraught that her two lovelies were at it again.

It was best to stay away.

Her phone buzzed.

It had been buzzing for the past thirty minutes.

The first one was from Leanne. We're here! Full house already.

The second, from Chad. U here? Jane wants to talk to you about something.

The third followed before Autumn had a chance to read the second. Only a suggestion! Won't take long.

The one that came in now was from her sister. It was the third one she'd sent in twenty minutes. Every time Claire's name popped up on her screen, the feral thing inside would start clawing about for an escape.

Penny had sent one too. Are you okay? We're worried.

A part of her kept waiting—hoping—that Paul would text. But nothing came from him. He wouldn't care where she was. He was probably glad she was gone. Her absence probably took some of the spotlight's glare off him and all those horrible things people were saying.

It was the least she could do.

Autumn sat down on the fountain's ledge. She scuffed her shoe over a name neatly etched in the brick. Vincent Poole. Most people wouldn't know that he'd been four years old. Most people wouldn't know that he loved airplanes or went to speech therapy twice a week or called his baby sister Linny-Lin. To most people, Vincent Poole would be nothing more than a faded name engraved in red brick.

Another text came.

Where r u????

Autumn shut her sister off while old familiar feelings stirred inside.

Guilt. Shame. Anxiety.

Why?

Why did Paul's grandfather have to have a stroke? If he'd never had the stroke, Paul wouldn't have called her to watch his kids, and if he never called her to watch his kids that night, Autumn never would have agreed to interview Reese. If Autumn wouldn't have interviewed Reese, Reese never would have sent anything to Seth. Paul never would have told her the truth about Vivian, and in turn, Autumn never would have told Claire.

Paul's secret would be safe.

Their relationship would be intact.

The tribute, ready to share.

She'd be at Redeemer right now, standing backstage with the mayor, eager to show the poignantly beautiful video Seth had put together.

Instead, she was here, rubbing her shoe along Vincent Poole's brick, asking God the one question she couldn't escape and He wouldn't answer.

Why?

"Excuse me, miss?"

Autumn looked up from Vincent's name, her muscles tense.

A greasy-haired man with greasy clothes was tapping a cigarette free from a pack of Marlboros. "Do you have a lighter on you?"

He didn't recognize her at all.

Paul walked toward the front doors of Redeemer with his heart in his stomach. It was the last place he wanted to be. After such a hellish day, he wanted to lock himself inside his house and watch a movie with his children. But Regina had called shortly after she sent her reply to his group text, her voice swollen with irritation.

"I didn't travel all this way for nothing. And I certainly don't want to go by myself."

She marched ahead of him now, her heels *click-click-click*ing against pavement in a brisk staccato.

Paul hurried ahead of her so he could get the door.

He thought the lobby would be empty by now. He'd been counting on it—this assumption that he could slip into the back while the lights were low and take a seat without drawing attention.

But the lobby wasn't empty.

People shuffled about.

Some gathered in tightly knit circles, talking in hushed tones.

Others wandered aimlessly from one display to the next, like they weren't sure what else to do. There were paintings and awards and picture collages. A man with a shiny bald head and a business suit scratched his chin and studied Vivian's photographs like a critic at an art gallery.

There was a charge in the air. An unidentifiable

hum. As though something unexpected were occurring.

He caught two women staring. They quickly looked away. But they weren't the only ones gawking.

A wave of heat rolled up his neck. The strange current in the air was probably due to him. Paul Elliott, giant phony, potential abuser, had just walked inside Redeemer.

"Reese!" The relieved cry belonged to his mother, who had just stepped out of the ladies' room.

She hurried over and wrapped his daughter in a hug.

Regina pursed her lips. She thought Reese had run away for attention and that gushing over her now would only encourage her to do it again.

Mom, apparently, did not agree.

She carried on with her affection while telling Paul, over Reese's head, that Tate was having a lot of fun playing with Mitch's boys, who were almost as hopeless as Tate when it came to sitting still for any length of time. Paul had called Tate as soon as he and Reese finished their conversation next to Dorothy and Toto. He figured his son would be worried, like he'd been the first time Reese had gone missing. This had been much more serious than before. Reese had been missing for so much longer. But Tate barely stayed on the line long enough for Paul to get the words out that his sister was fine. When Lisa picked up the phone, much more attentive than his son, he could hear all the boys making machine gun and lightsaber noises in the background.

"Oh, this day," Mom said, giving Reese another hug. "It was almost the death of me."

She didn't know the half of it.

Paul's mother didn't get on the Internet. Other than the occasional birthday present ordered online, she didn't have need for the World Wide Web. When it came to her phone, she preferred using it for actual conversation. Reese tried to show her Facebook once, but Mom thought it was the silliest invention since the pet rock. *"Why in the world would anybody care about what I'm doing?"*

Then she saw a picture of food—some Paleo meal one of her neighbors had posted—and that pretty much sealed the deal on her opinion.

Unless someone had told his mother—and he doubted, in all the chaos of looking for Reese that anybody had—she wouldn't know about Vivian leaving or the rumors spreading and splitting and growing like cancer cells.

The two women were staring again.

So was the bald man who'd been studying Vivian's photographs.

Regina looked at her watch. It was a Kate Spade, something Paul knew only because she'd told him so on the drive from O'Hare yesterday morning. "Shouldn't things be underway by now?"

"Yes," Mom said. "But I heard in the ladies' room that Autumn isn't here yet."

The news gave Paul a jolt. He pulled his attention away from the gawkers.

"Isn't she the woman who organized the event?" Regina asked.

"Yes. Nobody seems to know if there's going to be a video."

Reese looked up at Paul with wide, worried eyes. "Do you think it's because of my interview?"

He set his hands on her shoulders. "She didn't include it, Reese."

"She didn't?"

"She never picked up the footage."

"But I sent it to her friend, Seth."

Paul received another jolt.

Reese had sent her interview to Seth?

"Paul," Mom touched his arm, "what's going on?"

"Let me see what I can find out."

He excused himself and found Mitch on the other end of the lobby welcoming a small crew of caterers.

"Mitch."

He turned around. He looked the same way now as he'd looked when they went out for lunch at Lou Malnati's a couple of months ago, right after he dismissed Bill Meadows from the elder board.

"Where's Reese?" Mitch asked.

"With my mom."

"Man, what a scare."

"This has probably been the worst day of my life." As soon as he said it, another wave of heat rolled up his neck. His wife's death should probably be the worst day of his life.

"Well, this has probably been the craziest day of mine."

"My mom said Autumn isn't here?"

"She's not coming."

"What?"

"I don't know. She sent me a text a half hour ago, apologizing. She said she couldn't make it. Something's wrong with the video, I guess. I have no idea. All I know is that this isn't my gig. I'm not supposed to be in charge. I'm not even supposed to be working right now. But since I'm here, I'm the default decision maker."

"Sir, do you have a place for the dessert?" The question belonged to a young man with acne and floppy hair.

"Someone's getting a table."

The kid nodded.

Mitch ran his hand down his face. "First, Reese goes missing. Then Autumn doesn't show. And these rumors? Paul, I have no idea how they started, but we will get this cleared up."

Paul's attention slid to the floppy-haired kid.

He didn't seem to be eavesdropping.

"Not all of them are rumors."

Mitch's eyes widened, then narrowed. It was a narrowing followed by a slow-moving smile that turned up his face. The kind of awkward grin a person put on whenever they were pretty sure, but not entirely positive, that their leg was being pulled.

"Vivian was leaving. It's why she was on the train."

Mitch's smile melted away. He blinked, dumbstruck.

Once realization settled in, once he processed what Paul had told him, there would be hurt. A sense of betrayal. A secret of such magnitude wasn't meant to exist between friends like them. Paul owed him an apology, but before he could deliver it, one of the worship art directors, along with an intern, came down the hall carrying a long table.

"Does this work?"

And then Penny appeared, wearing yellow capris.

As soon as she saw Paul, she gave his arm a squeeze. "I'm so glad to hear Reese is okay. I was praying all day long."

"Thank you."

"The mayor's looking for you," she said to Mitch. "He wants to get started."

"Started with what? We don't have a video."

Fifty-Five

For as long as Autumn could remember, Dad had hidden a house key beneath the squat, odd-looking garden gnome sitting in the dirt at one corner of the house. She had no idea who bought that garden gnome. It had always been there, like it came with the house purchase. But surely, whoever lived there before her family would have taken their garden gnomes with them, which meant her mom probably bought it, a weird thought for adult Autumn to think.

Was her mother the type of woman who purchased ugly garden gnomes?

As a kid, she hated having to dig that key out, since it wasn't the only thing living under the heavy stone. There were creepy-crawly things—spiders and worms and pill bugs. If she ever locked herself out, she'd rather wait on the front stoop until Leanne or Dad came home.

Today, that wasn't an option.

Dad and Leanne were at Redeemer with everyone else, and she was here, because she needed somewhere to go that was private and wasn't her own apartment. She didn't want greasy-haired people asking for lighters, nor did she want glances—even though innocent—from a stranger exacerbating her paranoia.

So she rode the train here. She had renewed her Ventra card the week before and carried it on her now. A single silver lining from all that had transpired. Autumn Manning was working through her fear of public transportation.

She dug the key out from its hiding place, then let herself inside the house. The door hinges creaked as she stepped inside. It was odd, standing there in the empty silence. She couldn't remember the last time she'd been there alone. Whenever she came, her family was around, filling the tiny space, separating it somehow from the home she took her first steps in. The home she said her first words in. The home she fought with her siblings in. The home she lost her mother in.

This little living room had welcomed so many people after Mom died. Family and friends and acquaintances jammed themselves inside, circling around Dad and Grandma Ally and three motherless ducklings, like more people meant less pain. Back then, Leanne had been an acquaintance from church. A nice lady with smooth hands who rubbed Autumn's arm and brought over Tater Tots casserole.

What would have become of Leanne had Autumn never forgotten that hair bow?

"We worship a big God."

"He isn't cruel."

Paul's words.

Autumn's words.

They twisted around the memories, turning them into oddly shaped, mysterious things. Like a face you thought you recognized, but upon closer inspection, didn't.

Without turning on any lights, Autumn crept into the basement, each rickety stair groaning in protest. She pulled the chain on the hanging light, and a soft white glow cast itself against the paint-splattered wall.

Laughter echoed in the room.

Mom's and Claire's and Chad's now joined with Paul's and Reese's and Tate's. It was as though the sounds had been baked in.

She ran her fingers along a trail of black droplets.

It never seemed like the end product would be anything worth saving, let alone hanging. The process was so wild and out of control and messy —flinging paint at the wall, getting it all over one another. And yet somehow, when the canvases dried, they always turned out so beautifully.

A sound broke through the quiet.

Autumn froze.

It was the front door opening.

There was a moment or two of stillness, and then?

Floorboards creaked overhead.

Somebody had just walked inside the house.

Not two sets of footsteps, like Dad and Leanne.

But a solitary intruder.

All Autumn could think, in her frozen state, was that she didn't lock the door behind her and now someone was inside.

Creeping around upstairs.

With painstaking slowness, she grabbed a nearby broom. She crept toward the stairs, then climbed one at a time, stopping and wincing whenever the wood squeaked. When she reached the top, all was deathly still.

Autumn placed her fingertips against the door and eased it open.

Dad was standing on the other side.

He hollered.

She screamed.

They both jumped apart.

It was lucky she didn't fall backward down the stairs.

Miracle Survivor Breaks Neck, Tumbles to Death

Dad clamped his hand over his chest. "You nearly gave me a heart attack!"

"I'm sorry! I thought you were at Redeemer."

"*Someone* didn't show, and I had to leave." He gave his chest a few pats with his fist, like he was trying to cough a tickle out of his throat or drum up a belch. A telltale sign that he was suffering through a bout of heartburn.

"Where's Leanne?"

"She's still there." Dad's attention moved to the broom in her hand.

Autumn propped it against the wall.

"What were you doing down there—sweeping?"

"No."

He went into the kitchen and grabbed a bottle of Tums off the top of the refrigerator. He poured a few into his palm and popped them in his mouth.

The kitchen filled with the sound of crunching.

When he finished, he filled a glass with water and took a drink. "Why aren't you at Redeemer showing this video you've been working on?"

"I ruined it."

Dad took another drink. "Why would you do that?"

Autumn hesitated. She made a mess of things by telling Claire. But what did it matter at this point? The damage had been done already. The world knew. She took a deep breath and let it all come spilling out. The truth about Vivian Elliott and her feelings for Paul and his children. Claire blabbing and all the awful things being said on the Internet. Reese e-mailing the footage to Seth, and Autumn's attempt at fixing it.

When she was done, so was the water in Dad's glass.

"You've had a rough go," he finally said.

"Yeah."

"Sounds like this Paul fellow's had a rough go too."

Autumn nodded, waiting for more.

But it wasn't in Dad's nature to offer more.

"I told Paul that God isn't cruel."

"That's good."

"You don't think He is?" Her question came out desperate. She was starving for feedback. Encouragement. Wisdom. Something to take her off the craggy, shifting ground she was currently standing on.

Dad looked at her. When it came to questions of theology, he'd never been verbose. To him, faith was a private matter. He went to church on Sundays. He sent his children to religious ed classes on Wednesdays. He treated people with common decency. He worked hard, and he provided for his family. He did not typically discuss his thoughts on God with his children. Unless, of course, one of those children had a mental breakdown at dinner that left everyone stunned.

"I mean, after Mom died," Autumn said. "Did that thought ever occur to you?"

Dad scratched his chin. "You know what I've learned about God?"

Autumn leaned in.

Eager.

Curious.

Filled with anticipation.

"Circumstances don't dictate who He is."

She waited for more. An elaboration. An

explanation. Something more filling for her ravenous, hungry heart.

But Dad just filled up his water glass again and said, "You should probably call your sister. Everyone's worried."

And then his phone rang.

He pulled it out of his pocket and said hello. He covered the talking end with his palm and mouthed the words, *It's Leanne.*

Autumn stood there, listening to his side of the conversation.

"A little better." He gave his chest a couple more fist-pats. "She's here."

There was an exclamation on the other end.

Nothing decipherable.

Just excitement.

Leanne was relieved that Autumn was okay.

"I was pretty surprised myself . . . Yeah, she's fine . . . Uh-huh . . . Yep . . . Okay . . . The *what?* . . . All right. Will do . . . You too."

Dad slipped his phone back into his pocket. "That was Leanne."

"I gathered."

"She says we need to turn on the computer and watch some living video something or other?"

Living video something or other? "You mean the live video stream?"

"That's it."

"Of the tribute?"

"That's what she said."

"Why would she want us to watch that?"

Dad shrugged. "I'm not sure, but she was very insistent."

Fifty-Six

As soon as Dad booted up Leanne's computer, Autumn opened Safari and found the memorial website for Tragedy on the Tracks, where the tribute was meant to stream live. The thing was, there was nothing to stream. Autumn had made sure of that.

A small circle spun on the screen while whatever they were meant to be watching loaded. Dad pulled up a chair beside her.

Finally, the circle stopped.

Anna Montgomery filled the screen. She stood behind a small podium in the center of the stage, so unexpected that Autumn leaned back in her chair. The slight woman with the shy smile was talking into the microphone about the time she ate peanut butter and jelly sandwiches with Daniel under a bridge while it rained.

Autumn touched her lips, which were smiling along with Anna's. This time as she listened, she couldn't help but think of her own rainy-day story, with Paul and basketball and laughter and ice cream. He might never talk to her again, but she would always have that memory.

The audience clapped.

Mr. Collins was up front now, talking about the time his teenage daughter came home with a pair of butterflies tattooed on the back of her neck. He'd been livid. Outraged. Chloe was grounded for two whole weeks. "But when I had a chance to settle down," Mr. Collins said, "I was secretly proud of her. Chloe was a girl who knew what she wanted, and she went after it with tenacity, no matter what anybody else had to say about it. It's something I will remember every time I see a butterfly. My tenacious Chloe, chasing her dreams."

A butterfly taking flight.

A phoenix taking flight.

Straight out of the ashes.

Caroline Winslow, the younger sister of Margaret Winslow—a forty-year-old accountant who had been working late during tax season—walked to the podium. Autumn found herself thinking, *Oh, I hope she tells the story about the water balloons and the cat.*

These were real people to her now. They weren't just family members of the dead she stalked online. They were people she would hug should she run into them on the street, because despite all her eye-rolling, she was as much of a hugger now as Claire.

Right at this moment, that behemoth-sized church was packed with people, and Autumn knew a significant chunk of them. People who were choosing to celebrate, even though the plans had gone all wrong. People who had survived, just as she had.

And she was blessed because of them.

It didn't make the hard easier. It was still there, as horrible as ever, and probably always would be, so long as men like Benjamin Havel walked the earth. Real evil existed in this world. But real good did too. Beauty that Havel could not erase. In fact, his heartless words had them holding on to it all the tighter.

Autumn was watching it unfold right now as Ina May Huett hobbled up on the stage.

What story would she tell? This woman who had been born during the Great Depression, started dating her late husband on the heels of World War II, and marched with Martin Luther King Jr.

The old woman nodded at the crowd, then adjusted the microphone. It let out a sharp squeal that had her hands jerking back. She laughed a nervous, jittery laugh.

"Excuse me," she said, her voice shaking. "I wasn't planning on coming up here today. My husband was the one who liked speaking in front of a crowd. I prefer tea with close friends. Although, at my age, I don't have many anymore."

Autumn considered herself one of them. As she

leaned closer, she knew without a shadow of a doubt that she would visit Ina May again. The woman had so many stories to tell, and Autumn couldn't wait to listen to them.

"But I felt the Lord's prompting, and I've learned that when He nudges, it's best to follow, no matter how crazy. My husband was Lazarus Huett. I believe he was the oldest on the train. We were married for sixty-five glorious years, and I have to say, I'm overwhelmed. Overwhelmed by the bravery that's represented in this room.

"It's not easy to keep going. It's not easy to get back up after life knocks you a hard one. But the people in this room have all gotten back up." She gave the podium a small, but determined bang with her fist.

Autumn sat there in the small den, wondering if the same was true for her—the miracle survivor. Had she gotten back up?

"I kept wondering, now what story could I tell about my Lazarus? After sixty-five years you accumulate a lot of them. I started to thinking, why not talk about his name? My Lazarus used to get teased for his name. I loved his name. And I hated his name."

Ina May seemed to lose herself for a moment. Not more than a second or two. Then she blinked and continued on with her story. "His mother named him after her favorite story in the Bible.

Proof that when all seems lost, our God is a God who can accomplish the impossible.

"Laz and I went through our troubles, just like any other married couple does. We both had our fair share of weaknesses and flaws. I won't say who had more."

A chuckle rippled through the crowd.

"But I feel like I need to confess that the story his mother loved started rubbing me the wrong way. You see, the Lord had gone and given me a husband crazy for kids and me a body that refused to bear them. The more my friends started having babies and the harder I prayed for my own Lazarus moment and the longer Jesus tarried, the more resentful I became."

Autumn thought about Anna Montgomery and the frozen embryo.

She pictured her in the crowd, nodding along. A woman like her would understand.

"Mary and Martha only had to wait a few days. Why was I having to wait years and years? My sadness gave way to anger. And anger, like it usually does, gave way to bitterness."

Autumn pictured the framed photograph of the chubby, drooling baby sitting on Lazarus's knee.

"Is that your grandchild?" she had asked.

"Heavens, no. The Lord didn't give us any children of our own."

It had been nothing more than a passing comment. One that came and went with little effect. Sure, there was resignation in her voice. But her tone spoke more of a person who wished they'd gotten a scoop of chocolate instead of vanilla. It definitely hadn't spoken of a person who'd passed through a long and weary battle without a victory in the end.

"Finally, my husband had enough. He said, 'Ina Honey, if you don't let this go, that beautiful heart of yours is gonna shrivel up into a tiny, ugly prune.' Hoo boy, did I tear into him a good one. I started going on about time ticking away and how all my friends' children were growing up. And how much I hated his name because where was my Lazarus moment? When was God gonna show up and perform *that* miracle? And he looked me in the eye, and he said, 'Ina May, you have your Lazarus right here. It doesn't get much better than this, baby.'"

People laughed.

So did Ina May. And then she shook her head. "God never gave me children."

The crowd went silent.

"That was a hurt I had to learn to live with. But you know what I've come to love about that Lazarus story?" The old woman paused, like she expected someone to answer from the audience.

Autumn answered from her chair in a choked, barely-there whisper. "Jesus wept."

"What's that?" Dad asked.

She shook her head, not wanting to miss a single one of Ina's words.

"Before Jesus performed His big fancy miracle, He met those two sisters in the middle of their pain, and He wept alongside 'em."

Breath knotted in Autumn's throat. Tears gathered in her eyes.

God isn't cruel.

Because the cruel didn't weep with the hurting.

"That's our God." Ina May gave her finger a wag. "We worship a God who might not give us the miracle, but He will always give us the comfort. And that, my friends, is the God I see here, alive and active in this sanctuary today." She gave the podium one more enthusiastic pound, then hobbled off the stage.

There was a moment of silence.

Autumn sat in the chair, stunned.

She didn't understand how it worked. She didn't understand why people starved to death and children ended up in orphanages while barren women longed for babies. She didn't understand why a cigarette break could save one person's life while driving home to get your daughter's hair bow could snatch another's. She would never understand why *those* people. Why *that* train. Why *her.*

But maybe she'd been asking the wrong question.

Maybe comfort wasn't to be found in the *why.*

Maybe comfort was to be found in the *who.*

A God who wept.

There was a lull on the stage, as though the sanctuary needed a moment to breathe in Ina May's words. And then, Jordan Brokaw, ex-drug addict and dealer, walked up to the podium. Seemingly bolstered by Ina's profession of faith, he took the microphone, and he began to share his testimony.

His was a story Autumn had struggled with.

Did God have to kill a mother and her little boy to save a young man? Of course not. God didn't need tragedy to accomplish His work. And Benjamin Havel wasn't a marionette on a string, like Reese's zebra puppet. He was a broken man with free will who caused real pain. But God refused to let that pain remain meaningless. Because God was good. It was a goodness she'd seen with her own eyes.

Maybe it was time to stop trying to make the puzzle pieces fit.

Maybe it was time to let go of the why and remember the Who.

"The thief comes to steal and kill and destroy," Jordan said. "But Jesus came that we might have life, and have it to the full."

Like a phoenix, Autumn had been pulled from the rubble. Only instead of rising from the ashes, she had curled into a ball on top of them.

The entire nation had celebrated her survival.

And for the past year, that's all Autumn had been doing.

Surviving.

Until a twelve-year-old girl named Reese Elliott showed up on her doorstep and interrupted everything.

Fifty-Seven

Paul held the armrests of his seat like he was watching a horror film and at any second, the crazy person with the chain saw would jump out from the shadows. It was a grip that didn't loosen. Not when the mayor said his words. Not when Mitch stood up front and made a suggestion. Not when the first brave soul walked onto the stage to share a memory.

Now a young man stood up front. A young man with a big story.

"The thief comes to steal and kill and destroy," he said. "But Jesus came that we might have life, and have it to the full."

Many had spoken before the young man, and through it all, Paul's grip on the armrests remained steadfast. Through it all, his heart pounded inside his chest. He kept telling himself he didn't need to go up there, even when the old woman named Ina May Huett started talking about God's nudges. This wasn't a nudge. His heart was pounding for nothing.

Jordan finished.

Everyone clapped.

Reese turned to Paul. "I want to go up."

"On the stage?"

"Yes."

His heart beat harder.

"Please, Dad? I know what I'm going to say, and I promise it's not a lie."

"Honey . . ."

"Will you come up with me?"

Paul wanted to tell her no. He wanted to stay in the shadows and keep his daughter there with him, away from the gossip and speculation. He wanted to protect her. It was his job to protect her. And yet he'd tried that already—his way—and Reese had suffered.

She wanted to go, and he couldn't send her alone.

Paul forced himself to let go of the armrests.

Together they stood from their seats, and they filed past Regina's knees, and they made their way up to the front while the entire sanctuary fell silent. So silent, Paul was sure everyone would be able to hear his pounding heart.

The truth will set you free.

The words budged into the front of his mind, wholly unwelcome. He was walking up front for Reese. She would say what she wanted to say, and they would sit back down. He certainly wouldn't be exposing himself in front of a jam-packed sanctuary, especially not with Regina and his mother among the crowd. He dragged his sweaty palms down his jeans, telling himself the words meant nothing.

When they stepped on stage, a soft *click-click* broke through the quiet, confirming his fear. People were taking pictures. Any second, this would be all over social media. His daughter would join the fray of awfulness being spewed on Twitter.

The truth will set you free.

Paul closed his eyes. His brave daughter, on the other hand, stepped up to the podium and adjusted the microphone. "Hi. My name is Reese Elliott. My mother was Vivian Elliott."

Somebody in the audience coughed.

There were a few more clicks.

Reese took a shaky breath. "She wasn't a very good mom."

Whispers rippled down the aisle. Paul shifted his weight from one foot to the other, unsure where Reese was going.

"But she was really good at her job, and she bought me nice clothes. I don't remember her laughing a lot, but when she did, my dad said that if sparkles had a sound, that's what they'd sound like. My mom's laugh."

Had he really said that? Was Reese telling another lie?

But no, he had said it.

A long time ago. Reese couldn't have been older than five.

It was before the second affair.

Afterward, Vivian had stopped laughing. Or maybe she hadn't. Maybe Paul had just stopped listening.

"She bought me the book *Are You My Mother?* by P. D. Eastman. I don't remember her ever reading it to me, but my dad did." Reese caught his eye and gave him a shy smile. "He read it to me every night for a whole year when I was five, and he would make the funniest voices."

He smiled back.

Whenever he got to the part where the big thing said, "Snort!" he would say it with such loud ridiculousness, Reese would erupt into hysterical giggles. It didn't matter that he did the same routine night after night—his snort growing progressively louder and wilder—she laughed and laughed just the same.

Sparkles, like Vivian.

"I didn't have the best mom," Reese said into the microphone. "But I have a really, really great dad. And he loves me a lot."

Paul blinked, and wiped discreetly at his eyes.

Everyone was staring at him.

He could feel their attention like the hot sun.

He tried to swallow, but his mouth had gone dry. And his heart continued to hammer. He looked at the podium, then out into the sanctuary, the faces imperceptible in the dim lighting. If he wanted, he could step up to the microphone and publicly dismiss the rumors. He could tell everyone that none of them were true. Or he could take Reese's hand and together, they could return to their seats.

But his daughter was looking at him, her eyes glittering.

The truth will set you free.

He ignored the nudge once before.

And he had begged the Lord for a second chance.

With his pulse racing, Paul stepped up to the microphone. Unlike Mrs. Huett, he was used to speaking to large crowds. But all those times, the crowd had been *for* him. He was the expert, and they, the eager sponges.

This was a little different.

"I'm Paul, Reese's father." He cleared away the shakiness from his voice and set his hands on either side of the podium. "A lot of things are being said right now on social media. If you don't mind, I'd like to take a quick moment to share the truth about me and my late wife."

Fifty-Eight

Wednesday, June 28, 2017

> The two most important days of
> your life are the day you are born
> and the day you find out why.
> —Mark Twain

I'm a long-time fan of Tom Sawyer and Huckleberry Finn. And for that, I will always be grateful to Mark Twain. But I have to say, I think he got this one wrong.

A person could find out why, and do nothing about it.

A person could find out why, and die on a train the next day.

It's an insatiable question—why. The kind you can ask and ask and ask and ask without ever getting your fill. Like my niece Lulu, with one why leading to the next why that leads to the next that leads to the next.

Take this recent conversation as an example, between her and Chad:

"We can't forget to pick up bread at the store."

"Why?"

"Because we're almost out."

"Why?"

"Because we eat a lot of bread."

"Why?"

"Because our family likes toast."

"Why?"

And around and around and around it goes; where it will stop, nobody knows.

It's been five days since I ruined the video and Paul made his big confession online. A confession that left me admiring him even more. Somehow he managed to speak the truth with decorum. He wasn't explicit, and he remained respectful of his late wife.

Vivian Elliott, a woman I don't know. A woman I will never know.

For the past five days, it's all anybody's been able to talk about. The Marriage Doctor's failed marriage has been such a big deal, everybody seems to have forgotten the fact that I never showed up with the video. It helped that the impromptu tribute—wherein guests were invited up on stage to share whatever memories or hopes they wanted to share—went so well.

Still, I apologized to Mitch.

Several times.

With much contrition.

He said it was okay. He said that Paul told him about the mix-up, which means Reese must have told her father she sent the video to

Seth, and her father must have put the pieces together regarding my absence.

I asked Mitch yesterday how Paul is doing, in light of everything.

"All right. Laying low."

It was a vague answer.

I think Mitch is still pretty shaken over everything.

On Monday, Paul resigned from the marriage campaign.

Mitch and the elders and the fellowship of pastors had an emergency meeting. They'd been prepared to put the whole thing on pause. Do another regroup. When out of nowhere, someone contacted them about an up-and-coming Christian speaker with a passion for marriage. His name is Laurence Brown, and he's based out of Seattle. Since he's relatively new to the scene and trying his hardest to make a name for himself, he was affordable, and also eager.

Now, instead of e-mailing Paul with questions or thoughts or suggestions, I e-mail Laurence. He always replies promptly, enthusiastically, and I find myself wondering, *Does he have any secrets of his own?*

It's funny how life turns out.

There are so many twists and turns, it's impossible to guess where one decision will lead.

Claire and I had our big fight.

I didn't pull her hair, but I did get close. So close, in fact, that Leanne had to jump in between us. She yelled. I don't know if Leanne has ever yelled. For a second, she reminded me of my Grandma Ally. For a second, I thought, *Maybe we'll find a way to make this relationship work after all.*

Anyway, Claire swears she didn't tell anyone, not even Trent, who confirmed it. So there's really no reason for me to be angry with my sister. The information about Vivian must have leaked another way.

You have no idea how badly I've wanted to call Paul with this news. But the truth is, I did tell Claire. I blabbed his secret to my sister without his permission, and then when he told me not to tell a soul, I didn't bother to tell him that, whoops, I already had.

I miss him.

A lot.

So I've been keeping myself busy.

There's plenty to do.

Claire's wedding checklist lengthens every day.

Tonight I visited Ina May for some evening tea. We're going to make it a monthly thing.

Tomorrow I'm having lunch with Anna Montgomery. As it turns out, she's been looking for a church, and she loved the reception at Redeemer so much that she wants to make it her home. It helps that they have such an excellent children's program, the reason Jane and Chad have started to attend as well.

Seth is back from Puerto Rico, and now that he understands why I was being so weird about the sudden appearance of Reese on the screen, he's working on taking her out so I can upload the tribute to YouTube and the memorial website as originally planned.

I went to lunch with Kendall on Sunday. We picked up where we left off, like the weird prolonged stretch of zero contact never happened. It was natural and fun, and we laughed a lot.

On Monday, I slipped away from work for my last appointment with Jeannie True.

I don't think I need it anymore. I haven't visited the cemeteries since that day back in early April when Reese showed up at my apartment. I don't stalk anybody online either. I added one last newspaper clipping to my binder—an article about the tribute—and I put it away, in the storage unit in my basement. I don't have time to obsess over the dead anymore. Not when my life is so full of the living.

Somehow I am learning to put one foot in front of the other.

Jeannie said she'd hold on to my file, in case something happened and we needed to resume.

Until then, I have you, Maud.

The cheapest therapy around.

Friday, June 30, 2017

Dear Autumn,

I'm really sorry for lying in the letters that I sent you, and in the video you took of me for the tribute. I think I might be the reason why you didn't show up. I didn't mean to ruin it. I was just trying to alter my memories, like in that book <u>Freak the Mighty</u>. Anyway, it didn't work.

But the tribute ended up being really cool. Did you watch it online?

You should have heard Grandma Regina afterward. She was furious with me for saying my mom wasn't a very good mom, and even more furious with my dad, for never telling her that he and Mom were having problems, and also for telling everyone in that church and online about it. He had to drive her to the airport the next day. I don't think I'll be seeing her again anytime soon.

It's finally summer break. My current events project went really well.

Tate's been super annoying. He no longer wants to be a police officer. He wants to be a detective. He's obsessed with Sherlock Holmes. Grandma bought him one of those magnifying glasses. He keeps looking at me through it and calling me his "dear Watson."

I've been writing a lot. I included a new story, in case you wanted to read it. I miss you. Maybe you can come over for dinner again sometime.

Love,
Reese Rosamund Elliott

P.S. Anna Montgomery is paying me to help with her kids on Monday and Wednesday afternoons this summer! It's called a mother's helper. She already set it up with my dad and everything. She thinks I'll be really good at it.

Fifty-Nine

Autumn sat on the edge of her bed and laced up her shoes for a late-evening run. Trent and Claire laughed about something in the living room, cuddling again. Autumn had a hard time stomaching it. Hence the running shoes.

The apartment buzzer rang.

"I'll get it!" Claire called down the hall.

Autumn double-knotted her laces and slipped on the Fitbit she ordered as a celebratory gift for herself after uploading the tribute to YouTube.

It already had over fifty thousand views.

Indistinct voices filtered down the hallway.

Followed by Claire's singsong call, "Autumn, it's for you!"

She stepped out of her room and stopped dead.

It was Paul.

He was standing just inside the door, looking hopelessly uncomfortable.

"Hi," she said, a little breathlessly.

"Hi," he said back.

Paul.

She couldn't believe it. He was standing in her apartment, doing odd things to the ache inside her chest. His presence somehow lessened and intensified it at the same time.

His attention dipped to her running shoes. "Do you have a minute?"

"Of course."

And before Claire could say a word, Autumn slipped out and closed the door.

They stood in the hallway.

He opened his mouth, like he was going to start talking right there.

"Hold that thought," Autumn said, hitching her thumb at the door. "They're probably looking out the peephole right now."

462

Paul nodded, then followed her down the stairs, out into the balmy evening.

His hair was a mess. The corners of his eyes, pinched. Somehow it only added to his appeal. Tall, dark, and tortured. And also handsome. He gestured down the street, and the two of them began to walk.

"How are you doing?" Autumn asked.

"I'm okay. Reese seems to be doing really well."

"She wrote to me the other day."

"She did?"

"Is that okay?"

"Yeah," he said. "That's fine."

"She wasn't lying about anything. Unless Tate doesn't actually want to be a detective."

"No, that's very true."

"I guess that means I can't call him Officer Tate anymore. I'll have to change it to Detective Tate." She blushed as soon as she said it, because when would she be around Tate to call him anything?

But Paul smiled at his shoes and said, "He'll love that."

It planted the tiniest mustard seed of hope in her heart.

"How's your grandfather?" she asked.

"He's settled in his new home. It's nice. His recovery's slow, but he's making some progress."

"And your mom? How's she doing with it all?"

"Heroic. Strong."

"And you?"

He blew out a long, heavy sigh. "It's been hard, seeing him deteriorate so quickly. But that's age for you." Paul scratched the top of his head. "How are you doing?"

"I'm good."

"You look good," he said.

More warmth crept into her cheeks.

And then they spoke at the same time.

"Autumn, I—"

"Paul, I'm—"

They laughed a little nervously.

Paul told her to go ahead.

"I'm really sorry for telling my sister."

"It's okay."

"No, it's not. I told her before you came over that morning. I should have told you I told her, but I felt so bad about it. I know it's probably not worth much, but she swears she never told anyone."

"It was Reese."

"What?"

Paul ran his hand around the back of his neck. "Not that this is any excuse, but one of the reasons I was so short with you on the phone that day was because Reese had gone missing."

Missing?

But of course.

The first words Paul had spoken to her. *"Is Reese with you?"* Only, in light of everything that followed, his question had been pushed right out of her head.

"For ten hours."

"Ten *hours?*"

Paul nodded. "She e-mailed my deep dark secret to a reporter who visited her class for that current events project she was working on."

"Wow."

"Yeah. Turns out, she knew about Vivian the whole time. My secret became her secret, and I had no idea she was holding it." He shook his head, like he should have known. "It's good that it happened. It's good that the truth came out."

"But what about . . . ?"

"Tate?"

"Yeah," Autumn said.

"Nobody's said anything. I don't think they will. Now that I'm not holding the burden anymore, it doesn't seem as likely. If that makes any sense."

It did.

They turned a corner and continued walking.

"Surprisingly, work's been fine. My clients still want me as a therapist. Margo's actually received more calls than usual. She has the fun task of trying to figure out who actually needs help and who's just curious to meet the infamous Marriage Doctor." He wagged his eyebrows when he said it, and lowered his voice in a mocking tone.

It came as a relief—hearing him joke.

"What about speaking? Is that a thing of the past?"

"I don't know. Maybe someday. If anybody will want me. It's all out there in the open now. In God's hands. We'll see what He does with it."

Autumn pictured a phoenix, rising from the ashes.

"I've missed you," Paul said.

Her muscles went weak, because oh, how she'd missed him too. Like crazy, she'd missed him. "Likewise," she said.

He caught her eye. The intensity of his gaze had that light, fluttery thing in Autumn's chest returning. "My kids have missed you too."

"Likewise," she said again.

Paul smiled. It was a smile that transformed his entire face. He had dimples like parentheses. And crinkles in the corners of his eyes. "Reese wants to know what you're doing for the Fourth of July."

"Watching fireworks, like the rest of America."

"Well, if you want to watch them with us, we have a pretty decent view from our rooftop."

The light, fluttery thing grew lighter, and more fluttery.

Fireworks with the Elliott family. Who would have ever imagined?

"That'd be nice."

Paul nodded and looked around. They had ended up in a familiar park, with the gazebo and the playground and the basketball court. And there, sitting all by itself beneath one of the hoops, like a wink from God, was the ball.

"It's still here." He scooped it up and gave it a firm bounce. "And it's not flat." His smile widened into a grin. "What do you say, Manning? Up for a rematch?"

Autumn glanced up at the night sky, impossibly awake. Rejuvenated by a rush of adrenaline. Or maybe it wasn't adrenaline. Maybe it was something more powerful. A grand adventure, at the very beginning.

The moon shone overhead, and a couple of faint stars. They were hard to make out in the city, but they were there just the same. "What are we playing for?"

"Oh, I don't know. Ice cream? Winner buys?"

"You haven't learned your lesson, huh?"

"Oh, I learned my lesson." He dribbled the ball closer. Paul Elliott smelled uncommonly good—fresh linen and clean soap and the vaguest scent of cologne. Like he'd put some on early this morning and it had mostly worn off. "I won't be making the same mistake twice."

Autumn set her hand on her hip. "What mistake is that?"

"Underestimating you." He handed her the ball. "Ladies first."

She bounced it back, her grin giddy and uncontainable.

She didn't know what the future held. She didn't know if the path before her would be mostly straight or filled with twists and turns. She didn't know how long it would intersect with Paul Elliott's.

She knew what she wanted.

She knew what she hoped for.

She knew what she thought was best.

But more important than that? She knew God was good, and right now, Paul was standing in front of her, crouching down, a playful glint in his eyes.

This was going to be fun.

A Conversation with Katie Ganshert

What served as the inspiration for *Life After*? Have any of the events or characters in the book grown out of your real-life experiences?
Thankfully, no. It started with a news article. I'd just finished writing *A Broken Kind of Beautiful*, which meant I was on the hunt for a new idea. And here was this true story I found somewhere on the Internet of this horrendous plane crash nobody could have survived. Except somebody did. A small boy with hardly a scratch. I remember staring at his picture and the decimated plane, a story slowly taking shape in my mind.

I sat down and I wrote it—this book about a sole survivor, only instead of a plane crashing, it was a train exploding. When I finished, I quickly realized it was in need of a massive overhaul, one I didn't have the energy for at the time. So I tucked it away and wrote *The Art of Losing Yourself*. And then the Gifting trilogy. All the while, the train story (as I used to call it) languished on my hard drive. For five years. And then one day it was time to take it out and dust it off. Timing, I guess, is everything.

Wrestling with the problem of evil is a key theme of *Life After:* why terrible things happen to some people and do not touch others, and the lasting effects of those events. As you wrote, did your perspective on the problem of evil change?

My perspective didn't change so much as shift. This was a challenging topic to tackle—the fallout of evil and its seemingly inequitable distribution. How could I explore this reality in a hopeful, satisfying way on the pages of a novel?

I wrestled for a long while, and then I remembered a conversation I had with a friend on Facebook. We were talking about suffering and the story of Lazarus, and how God's timing is mysterious but purposeful. Because Jesus delayed in coming to the aid of his sick friend, He was able to show Himself as something more than Healer. He was able to show Himself as someone who could raise the dead back to life. And while we were pondering this, my friend said, "Before that, though, Mary and Martha got to experience Him as their comfort." When Mary and Martha came to Jesus full of grief and confusion, He didn't reprimand them. He saw these two hurting women, and He wept with them, knowing full well what He was about to do. It's an incredibly short, incredibly powerful verse: "Jesus wept."

We will never understand the complexities of why. It would have been impossible for me to answer that in any satisfying way by the end of *Life After*. But maybe if we focused instead on *who,* the *why* would grow strangely dim. That's the journey I went on as the author and the journey I took Autumn Manning on as well.

Life After is a hard book to categorize. It starts out with a dramatic event, there are mysteries to uncover, there are moments of levity, and it has a unique female protagonist. What kind of novel did you set out to write, and how did it change?

I'm not sure the original draft would be recognized by readers, so drastically did this novel change along the way! But I'm really pleased with the way it turned out. I set out to write a contemporary romance novel in a different city. There were several scenes leading up to the tragic event as opposed to its happening right off, and the bulk of the story took place weeks after the explosion.

During revisions it became clear that this premise lent itself to something deeper, more haunting. We made several big changes, like setting the story a year after the explosion. We changed some characters completely, and we took what was previously exposed and tucked it away, creating more mystery.

Chicago plays a strong role in this novel. Why did you decide to set the story in that city?

I knew I needed a big city with a train. I landed on Chicago because I've been there multiple times, and since I'm only a three-hour drive away, I knew this would make for much easier research. Plus, my cousin Melissa lives in the area. She not only spent a day driving me around so I could establish a vibrant, believable setting; she also answered a lot of random text messages as I went along.

Although Autumn is not able to easily accept the normalcy of her rowdy family, they provide a stabilizing factor for her. What serves as the inspiration for the Mannings?

My family is pretty rowdy. Both of my parents have nine siblings. Yes, nine. I have more than forty first cousins. Several of the siblings on my mom's side live locally, and we attempt to have a monthly dinner at my aunt Peggy's house, which is always a boisterous affair. The Glynn crew doesn't do quiet, so there's plenty of inspiration to draw from. ;-)

But as far as Autumn's family, the characters weren't fashioned after anyone in particular. We have the older, steady brother with a wife and three little children. The younger, free-spirited sister and her fiancé. The stalwart father who loves big but isn't big on words. Like many families, there's loss there too and the challenge that comes when someone new is grafted in. I like to think of the Mannings as everyone's family.

What do you hope the reader will leave *Life After* with?
A newfound sense of wonder that God is a God who weeps with the hurting.

Describe a normal writing day for you. What kind of routines do you count on?
I usually start my morning with coffee, a doughnut (I'm addicted), and my Bible. Some mornings I need to get the kids ready and off to school or, for our daughter who has special needs, off to various therapy appointments. Other mornings, my husband takes over so I can stay in my pajamas, open up my laptop, and dig in. I don't have the focus I once had, so it's hard to jump in and out of a story. It's a sad fact, but even a short interruption can harm the day's productivity. So the best mornings are the ones where I turn off my Internet, turn off my phone, and completely immerse myself. Between kids arriving home from school, I also have a window to catch up on related tasks (e-mails, newsletters, mail outs, social media). When I'm on deadline, I sometimes have to work in the evenings or on the weekends, but the older I get, the more I appreciate the time that should be reserved for family, friends, and sanity.

What authors inspire and influence you?
Liane Moriarty is a new favorite of mine. Her ability to write such real, vibrant characters with

so much honesty and wit inspires me as a writer. I've always been a big fan of Francine Rivers, who has paved the way for exploring hard things. She writes such grippingly flawed characters and has long inspired me to do the same. And of course, there's J. K. Rowling. I recently went to Harry Potter World in Orlando with my son, and I was just blown over by the fact that all of it—the entire world and its accompanying fandom—came about because she got this idea and was brave enough to sit down and write it.

Can you give us a hint about what you are working on next?
I can tell you it's different from anything I've attempted so far. I was inspired by a podcast on *This American Life* called "The Problem We All Live With." I want this to be a story that explores the tricky nature of perception, and forgiveness, in all its varied forms. Ultimately I want it to answer this question: What does it mean to be human? It's going to stretch me as a writer like I've never been stretched, and I feel a huge responsibility to do well.

Here's the opening quote by Claudia Rankine: "The world is wrong. You can't put the past behind you. It's buried in you; it's turned your flesh into its own cupboard."

Acknowledgments

Rewriting this book was an intensive project. The story went through several large transformations, and apart from the following people, it wouldn't be what it is now. Thank you . . .

Erica Vetsch, for organizing a writing retreat for the two of us in Galena all those years ago, wherein we drank way too much Diet Coke and I polished off a big chunk of the train story in its original form. I couldn't have done it without your support and encouragement.

Melissa Sanko, my amazing cousin, for driving me around Chicago and answering all my incredibly random questions. You brought the city to life. Any errors or inconsistencies in the setting are 100 percent my own. Heaven knows you did your part in helping me get it right.

Courtney Walsh, for brainstorming with me when I was in the throes of massive revisions. What did we do before Voxer? Anytime I hit a snag in the plot (which was pretty much daily), you helped me find an authentic, believable way out.

Jeannie Campbell, my very first critique partner and long-distance friend, for helping me wrap my head around every scene that included a therapy session.

Rachelle Gardner, for always being in my corner. For talking me off ledges. For believing in my voice and helping me believe in it too. You are truly amazing.

Shannon Marchese. What is there to say? You have the most impressive gift of seeing what's not yet but could be. You're more than an editor; you're a coach. And I'm a better writer because of you.

Lissa Halls Johnson and Laura Wright, for all your hard work and attention to detail.

Mark Ford, for an absolutely exquisite cover.

The whole team at WaterBrook, for all the things you do—big and small—to get my words into the hands of readers.

The Ganshert Gang, for being the absolute best street team around.

My husband. You do laundry. You cook dinner. You get the kids off to school and you take Salima to speech therapy. You even load the dishwasher (even though you don't load it the right way). You rub the knots of stress from my shoulders, and you are so quick to ask, "How can I help? How can I get you some more time?" You are my favorite person in the whole wide world. I hit the jackpot when I married you.

And always, the One who weeps with those

who weep. On this side of eternity, there are so many unanswered whys, but all of it fades away in light of who. Every word, every story, every character and idea comes from You. May all of it be for Your glory.

About the Author

Award-winning author KATIE GANSHERT graduated from the University of Wisconsin in Madison with a degree in education and worked as a fifth-grade teacher for several years before staying home to write full time. She was born and raised in the Midwest, where she lives with her family. When she's not busy penning novels or spending time with her people, she enjoys drinking coffee with friends, reading great literature, and eating copious amounts of dark chocolate.

You can learn more about Katie and her books at
katie@katieganshert.com
www.katieganshert.com
Twitter: @KatieGanshert
Facebook:
www.facebook.com/AuthorKatieGanshert
Pinterest: http://pinterest.com/katieganshert

Center Point Large Print
600 Brooks Road / PO Box 1
Thorndike, ME 04986-0001 USA

(207) 568-3717

US & Canada:
1 800 929-9108
www.centerpointlargeprint.com